PRAISE FOR KRIS

"It's hard to even find words to describe the experience of reading *A Sparrow in Terezin* . . . and that's exactly what it was: an experience—moving, powerful, poignant. Kristy Cambron's sophomore novel is gorgeous and heartrending, a World War II story packed with romance, bravery and sacrifice, interwoven with a modern-day thread. She has a permanent place on my must-read shelf."

—MELISSA TAGG, AUTHOR OF *FROM THE START* AND *HERE TO STAY*

"Cambron is a marvelous new star in historical romance. *A Sparrow in Terezin* has it all: suspense, romance, World War II history, and a dual story line that doesn't let the reader catch her breath. Highly recommended!"

—COLLEEN COBLE, *USA TODAY* BESTSELLING
AUTHOR OF THE *HOPE BEACH* SERIES

"Once again author Kristy Cambron weaves an amazing tapestry of past and present in her sophomore novel, *A Sparrow in Terezin*. In this beautifully written journey of faith, Sera and Kája are two women separated by time and circumstance, yet each must find the courage to trust and recapture love through God's healing grace. Cambron's detail to history shines as readers are transported seamlessly from the warm, sandy beaches of San Francisco's coast to the frightening ambience of World War II Europe. I found her depiction of conditions at the Nazi concentration camp at Terezin to be well-researched and hauntingly accurate. *A Sparrow in Terezin* is a captivating story not to be missed!"

—KATE BRESLIN, AUTHOR OF *FOR SUCH A TIME*

"In *A Sparrow in Terezin* Kristy Cambron's poignant prose reminds us of the 15,000 children sent to Terezin Concentration Camp during World War II—fewer than 100 of those children survived. Cambron writes more than novels woven with both contemporary and historical story lines—although she does that with poignancy and realism. What Cambron has mastered is writing novels that are a testament to the past . . . to a time of both unfathomable loss and courageous sacrifice that we should honor in our hearts and minds."

—BETH K. VOGT, AUTHOR OF *SOMEBODY LIKE YOU*, SELECTED
AS ONE OF *PUBLISHER'S WEEKLY'S* 2014 BEST BOOKS

"A *Sparrow in Terezin* shines a light on a rare and precious beauty amidst the ashes of the Holocaust. Woven of equally compelling contemporary and historical threads, the story presents a fresh and haunting look at a part of World War II history I hadn't been aware of—the children of Terezin. Main characters Sera and Kája captured my heart and made me care, keeping me up nights to see them through. A beautiful follow-up to Cambron's debut!"

—LORI BENTON, AUTHOR OF *BURNING SKY*, *THE PURSUIT OF TAMSEN LITTLEJOHN*, AND *THE WOOD'S EDGE*

"Compelling, haunting, and impossible to put down, Kristy Cambron's second novel in her Hidden Masterpiece Series is as intriguing and beautifully written as *The Butterfly and the Violin*. Two stories in two time periods, skillfully woven, began with the unexpected and kept me turning pages to the very end . . . Highly recommended."

—CATHY GOHLKE, CHRISTY AWARD-WINNING AUTHOR OF *SAVING AMELIE* AND *BAND OF SISTERS*, FOR *A SPARROW IN TEREZIN*

"Kristy Cambron has created a beautiful story of parallel journeys: one during World War II, the other during modern day . . . This is a story that will embrace readers who love a mix of modern and historic, romance with emotion, beauty with an awareness that God sees every sparrow."

—CARA PUTMAN, AWARD-WINNING AUTHOR OF *SHADOWED BY GRACE* AND *WHERE TREETOPS GLISTEN*, FOR *A SPARROW IN TEREZIN*

"Alternating points of view skillfully blend contemporary and historical fiction in this debut novel that is almost impossible to put down."

—*RT BOOK REVIEWS*, 4 1/2 STARS TOP PICK! FOR *THE BUTTERFLY AND THE VIOLIN*

"In her historical series debut, Cambron expertly weaves together multiple plotlines, time lines, and perspectives to produce a poignant tale of the power of love and faith in difficult circumstances. Those interested in stories of survival and the Holocaust, such as Eli Wiesel's *Night*, will want to read."

—*LIBRARY JOURNAL*, STARRED REVIEW FOR *THE BUTTERFLY AND THE VIOLIN*

". . . debut novelist Cambron vividly recounts interwoven sagas of heartache and recovery through courage, love, art, and faith."

—*PUBLISHERS WEEKLY* FOR *THE BUTTERFLY AND THE VIOLIN*

"... emotionally engaging and very hard to put down."

—CBA Retailers + Resources for *The Butterfly and the Violin*

"Cambron's debut novel is rife with history, faith, and hope. It will entrance readers with its poignant characters, intriguing plot, and unpredictable love story."

—Suzanne Woods Fisher, bestselling, award-winning author of the Lancaster County Secrets, for *The Butterfly and the Violin*

"Fresh. Fascinating. Unforgettable. *The Butterfly and the Violin* is a masterpiece of a debut. From stunning cover to satisfying conclusion, this poignant novel marks Kristy Cambron as an author to watch."

—Laura Frantz, Christy Award finalist and author of *Love's Reckoning*

"*The Butterfly and the Violin* held me captive from first note to final moment. Just like the beautiful violin Adele plays, Cambron lyrically weaves words and emotions, carries you through a simultaneously heartbreaking and uplifting story, and leaves you yearning for more. Absolutely spellbinding!"

—Katherine Reay, author of *Dear Mr. Knightley*

"*The Butterfly and the Violin* is a powerful debut novel that weaves together a touching contemporary story with dramatic events in World War II. A compelling plot and an intriguing cast of characters illustrate that even in the darkest times, when evil seems impossible to overcome, hope can be found through trusting God and using our gifts as an act of worship. Readers of historical fiction will be captivated by this inspiring novel!"

—Carrie Turansky, award-winning author of *The Governess of Highland Hall* and *The Daughter of Highland Hall*

A
SPARROW
i n
TEREZIN

ALSO BY KRISTY CAMBRON

The Butterfly and the Violin

A
SPARROW
in
TEREZIN

A HIDDEN MASTERPIECE NOVEL

BOOK TWO

KRISTY CAMBRON

THOMAS NELSON
Since 1798

NASHVILLE   MEXICO CITY   RIO DE JANEIRO

Published in Nashville, Tennessee, by Thomas Nelson. Thomas Nelson is a registered trademark of HarperCollins Christian Publishing, Inc.

Published in association with Hartline Literary Agency, Pittsburgh, PA 15235.

Thomas Nelson titles may be purchased in bulk for educational, business, fund-raising, or sales promotional use. For information, please e-mail SpecialMarkets@ ThomasNelson.com.

Scripture quotations are taken from the King James Version and the HOLY BIBLE: NEW INTERNATIONAL VERSION®. © 1973, 1978, 1984 by Biblica, Inc.® Used by permission. All rights reserved worldwide.

Publisher's Note: This novel is a work of fiction. Names, characters, places, and incidents are either products of the author's imagination or used fictitiously. All characters are fictional, and any similarity to people living or dead is purely coincidental.

Library of Congress Cataloging-in-Publication Data

Cambron, Kristy.
    A sparrow in Terezin / Kristy Cambron.
        pages ; cm. -- (A hidden masterpiece novel ; 2)
    Summary: "Two women, one in the present day and one in 1942, each hope for a brighter future. But they'll both have to battle through their darkest days to reach it. Today. With the grand opening of her new gallery and a fairytale wedding months away, Sera James appears to have a charmed life. But in an instant, the prospect of a devastating legal battle surrounding her fiance? threatens to tear her dreams apart. Sera and William rush to marry and are thrust into a world of doubt and fear as they defend charges that could separate them for life. June 1942. After surviving the Blitz bombings that left many Londoners with shattered lives, Kaja Makovsky prayed for the war to end so she could return home to Prague. But despite the horrors of war, the gifted journalist never expected to see a headline screaming the extermination of Jews in work camps. Half-Jewish with her family in danger, Kaja has no choice but to risk everything to get her family out of Prague. But with the clutches of evil all around, her escape plan crumbles into deportation, and Kaja finds herself in a new reality as the art teacher to the children of Terezin. Bound by a story of hope and the survival of one little girl, both Sera and Kaja will fight to protect all they hold dear"-- Provided by publisher.
    ISBN 978-1-4016-9061-8 (softcover)
    I. Title.
PS3603.A4468S68 2015
813'.6--dc23   2014040983

Printed in the United States of America
15 16 17 18 19 20 RRD 6 5 4 3 2 1

For my mom.
And for Becky Monds—my forever friend.

"Be strong and courageous. Do not be afraid; do not be discouraged, for the Lord your God will be with you wherever you go."

—Joshua 1:9 NIV

CHAPTER ONE

—

July, Present Day
Sausalito, California

The last thing a bride needs to fret over on her wedding day is whether the ceremony will take place.

It was an unproductive thought in the midst of trying to manage pre-wedding jitters. Nevertheless, the familiar doubt continued to plague her heart, and Sera James, still caught up in the shadow of an uncertain future, all but gave in to it.

She ran her fingertips over the string of pearls at her nape and stared out the first-floor bedroom window of the Hanovers' California seaside estate. She scanned the horizon, taking in the beauty of the setting sun as it created flashes of diamonds across the bay, wondering if William had the same doubts. Would he be out there waiting on their beach?

A gentle knock drew her attention to the bedroom door.

She turned and found the familiar face of her friend Penny, who offered a hushed greeting from the hall. She presented a serene, pink-glossed smile.

"Sera? It's time," Penny said, her voice whisper soft, and stepped into the oversized bedroom. Her strawberry blond hair hung in soft waves and danced about her shoulders as if tossed by the playfulness of the sea breeze outside. "Everyone's waiting."

Sera nodded. She dropped the pearls back down to graze her neck and rested her hands at her sides.

So he is waiting . . . for me.

She dotted the corners of her eyes to catch the birth of soft tears.

God—William's not backing out. Even though our future's so uncertain.

Sera took a deep breath, hoping it would infuse her with courage.

With one last look in the antique floor mirror, she gave a final adjustment to the sweep train on her vintage column gown and asked, "Well, am I ready?"

Her hair was loosely tucked in a French chignon, with elegant, retro-inspired waves that shined like liquid chocolate against the thin, diamond-studded headband donning her crown. The silhouette was accentuated by simple pearl drops that dangled from her ears and the nipping of an intricate lace overlay in a deep V along her collarbone. She wore a pop of classic red on her lips.

"I'm overwhelmed, my dear friend." Penny grinned, eyes twinkling. The jade color of her tea-length chiffon gown shimmered when she angled past the antique four-poster bed that expanded out into the center of the room. "You are stunning. And I look at art masterpieces all day."

She winked on the last words.

"And I see our Sophie's loan made it here, safe and sound."

Sera reached up and placed a hand over the elegant pearls resting over her collarbone, thinking of their friend. "Yes. Sophie hated that she couldn't be here, but sent these pearls as the 'something borrowed.' She said every girl needs to wear pearls on her wedding day."

Penny nodded. "There's wisdom in that, I'd say."

"Yes, there is." Sera instinctively smiled.

Sophie Haurbech-Mason was the sweet old friend who had been a major factor in bringing both Sera and William to their wedding day. They'd tracked and found Sophie, the owner of a painting, who turned out to be a Holocaust victim who'd been saved as a little girl by the painting's subject. In many ways, it was the connection Sophie had to that painting that began Sera's own journey—to find love and to finally trust again.

But here she was, poised to walk down the aisle, and all of a sudden she wished Sophie was there to coach her through the moment. The pearls, lovely as they were, felt more like a lifeline than just a piece of vintage finery.

"I feel like I'm forgetting something," Sera said as fluttering once again threatened to overtake her stomach. She dropped a hand to her waist, trying to calm the butterflies that had made a home there.

"You haven't forgotten anything," Penny offered, and looked pointedly to the floor where Sera's toes peeked out from beneath the gown. "Except you're barefoot. Here. Let me help you through all this."

Sera knew the last thing they needed was a bride to fall flat on her face. She hooked her fingers through the straps of the heels on the bed and took Penny's arm. She picked up the delicate lace train and took careful, tiptoed steps.

Penny maneuvered them through the odds and ends that painted the bedroom in a sea of tissue paper, using the toe of her shoe to kick a white box out of the way in true Penny fashion.

"How does he look?" Sera dared to ask.

Penny scoffed. "I sure hope you're referring to the groom. Because if you're talking about his gorgeous younger brother, I'd say Paul Hanover is about as insufferable as ever. Spruced up for a wedding or not—there's little to admire of him except for that smile."

"Yes. I did mean the groom." Sera stopped by the door and allowed Penny to stabilize her as she stepped into her peep-toe heels.

"William looks fine. Taking a few deep breaths here and there. I'd wager he's not half as nervous as you. But then again, maybe your soon-to-be husband is just better at hiding his emotions." Penny paused, then tipped her shoulders in a light shrug. "Most men are."

"And what did you say about Paul? Are you two at it again?"

"Fighting like cats and dogs? Whatever. I can't stand him, even if he is something of a looker. We just can't seem to agree on anything." She stood tall and held Sera's arms wide, to take a grand look at her. "But enough of that. I can manage to put up with him for one night. Right now I want to marvel at you."

Sera took a calming breath and instinctively bit her lower lip over the slight fluttering feeling that continued twirling about in her midsection. She ran a hand down the vintage pin-tucked satin at her waist and brushed her palm along the side of the skirt.

"You think he'll like it?"

Penny nodded. "Yes. But he's not marrying a dress. He's marrying you," she said, and squeezed Sera's palms before letting go. "And you"—Penny paused to hand her a nosegay of bright-red peonies from the hammered glass vase on the nightstand—"are beautiful. And you're not losing me, you know. At least that's what I tell myself, that we're not really losing the friendship. We'll still have it, despite the distance."

"I know."

"So, do I need to give the old speech? About how you're not really losing an assistant"—Penny shook her head over the glaze of tears that showed in her eyes and smiled—"but gaining a husband?"

"No jokes, please." Sera laughed, emotion hitching in her throat. "Not now. I'm not sure I can take them from you."

Penny nodded and tilted her head in a light manner. "Good old Manhattan will just be an airplane ride away. You'll find me there anytime you need me. After, that is, we get every last piece in your gallery shipped out here." She smiled and wiped at a tear that was threatening to trail down her cheek. "But truly—I hope all of California knows what a gem they're getting."

"And I know the one I'm losing. How am I going to walk into the gallery every day without you by my side? You're my best friend," Sera added, tearing up herself. "I feel like I'm being cut down the middle."

"Oh no—don't you do that." Penny began fanning her face with her hand. "Think of raccoon eyes in the photos you'll have for the rest of your life unless you stop it this instant! We still have weeks of work ahead of us to get the gallery moved to the West Coast. We can cry all we want then, okay?"

She nudged Sera a bit with an arm around the shoulder.

"One last hug," she said, enveloping her in the sweetness of a friend's embrace. "Now, off we go."

Penny winked and led them down the hall.

Sera followed behind her friend, past the office where she'd sat more than a year before, waiting for the head of the Hanover clan to greet her about a potential commission. The commission to find a painting of a Holocaust-era violinist—Adele Von Bron— and the unfolding of the story that would eventually bring them together.

They passed the great room, with its wall of windows and sweeping views of the water, its cozy fireplace and whisper-soft lighting, where she and William had sat on so many quiet evenings, talking and dreaming about their future together. It's where he'd knelt down on one knee, with tears in his eyes, and asked her to be his wife.

The estate house had seemed magical then. And inviting. And so full of promise for their future. That was until the week before, until they'd received the terrible phone call that set everything in motion to move the wedding up by more than six months.

"Are you sure he looked okay?" Sera laid a light touch on Penny's elbow to pause their march toward the back door. "I mean, he doesn't look like he wants to change his mind about all this?"

Penny tilted her chin down and glared at Sera as though through a pair of bifocals.

"Why would he dream of changing his mind? He followed you to Paris so you wouldn't have to go alone. You've been engaged for months. And you love him. You told me yourself—he's the love of your life. I'm quite sure he feels the same about you."

"But we decided to go ahead with the wedding now on such short notice. We haven't even packed everything up yet. Think of all the crates that still have to be shipped here from New York. The gallery is still under renovations and is months away from opening. And Will's just going back to school. Think of his life, and my work, and our families . . ."

"You're about to walk down the aisle and you want to talk about crates and school schedules?"

Sera felt a blush tinge her cheeks under her friend's motherly stare.

"No. Not exactly."

"Then what has you playing the role of the jittery bride? It's not like you."

Sera wished she could tell her what was going on behind the scenes. But the truth was too difficult. Best to state the obvious and leave the rest out.

"I'm not thinking about old ghosts, if that's what's underneath that intense glare of yours. Nerves about being left at the altar were put to rest quite a long time ago."

"Good." It took Penny no less than a split second to chime in. "Because the altar won't be empty this time. And your former fiancé has no place in your vows today."

"Of course not," Sera agreed. "But it still doesn't change

the fact that we don't know what's going to happen tomorrow. Everything is so uncertain. After all, I could walk out there and—"

"Marry the man you love."

Sera stared back at the openness in her friend's eyes, saw the understanding, and finally exhaled the breath she hadn't realized she'd been holding.

"That's it?"

"That's it." Penny nodded. "You love him. Say 'I do.' Pledge your heart to him and for one day at least"—her shoulders rose on a dainty shrug, as if the answer were just that simple—"forget the rest."

Was it that easy to forget the uncertainty?

Twilight greeted them as they stepped through the French doors at the back of the house.

Sera followed her maid of honor along the smoothed cobblestone path that was etched through the garden. It looked enchanting, having been softened by the flickering of tea-light candles that lined the path all the way to the edge of the sand.

"Wait," she called out to Penny, who halted in her steps and turned round.

"What's the matter?"

Sera shook her head. "Nothing, I just—" On a last-second whim, she stooped and slipped her feet out of the classic white peep-toes. "I need to leave something behind."

It felt right to lose the heels, as if she were choosing to hold nothing back. Sera was walking toward her future. It was waiting—*he* was waiting, out on the beach, for her. The shedding of one last barrier between them made her feel all the more free. She wanted to have the option to run if she chose.

Sera tossed her heels up on the cobblestone path and after nodding Penny on, took her first barefoot step down in the sand.

The last of the evening's sun washed down over the beach.

A salty sea breeze caressed her cheeks as the beauty of the kaleidoscope sky and lively bay waters created a backdrop behind them.

The bay looked like it did all those months ago when she'd first come to California; it toiled, deep blue and uncaged, stirring in chaos along the edge of the estate. It mirrored the circumstances in which she'd come into the Hanovers' lives, they having been thrust into a legal battle to win back their estate and she, unknowingly at the time, about to fall in love with the eldest son when they first walked together through the sand.

William stood before her, in a gray linen suit and white oxford unbuttoned at the collar. His stance was relaxed. And he looked sincerely happy, with a wide grin that melted over his features the instant he locked eyes with hers.

Sera had to remind herself not to run all the way.

She took each step slowly, remembering what it had cost for them to reach this moment together. She saw the faces of his family beaming around them: his mother, ever smiling and supportive. His younger sister, Macie, was there with her husband, Eric. Penny had turned to stand opposite William's younger brother, Paul, the free-spirited musician with the quick wit and wicked-good looks. Sera bit her lip over a suppressed smile at the thought of Penny's insides tying in knots at having to put up with the best man.

And then her gaze turned back to William.

He waited patiently, with his hands clasped in front of him. The sea wind toyed with his hair, leaving it the way she loved it: just a touch windblown across his forehead. And she smiled with sheer contentment, maybe for the first time, as her soon-to-be husband reached out for her hand.

He cradled her fingertips in his as if they were made of the most precious porcelain and escorted her up to the small altar on the sand. It was fashioned out of a simple white garden archway that was softened by a bower of brilliant summer peonies and banners of draped white fabric that flowed in the breeze.

She handed her bouquet to Penny, then turned to William as she joyfully laced her fingers with the warmth of his.

He looked down at the hem of the gown she'd lifted in her walk through the sand and tilted his head.

"No shoes?"

"Uh," she whispered back, feeling her shoulders tilt up in a shrug. "I guess I felt like leaving something behind."

He winked at her. "You're stunning."

Sera's eyes misted.

"So are you," she whispered before thinking, then felt the light tinge of a blush when he laughed at her automatic reply.

"Well, that's a first for me, I'd say."

Sera's heart felt free on that beach.

As she held William's hands in her own, and as they exchanged rings, pledging to love and honor him all the days of her life, Sera finally understood what it meant to find lasting love. William was an honorable man of God—the best she'd ever known—and now they would belong to each other.

The service was short, just the way they'd wanted it.

The minister called the group into prayer, and Sera lowered her head to rest on William's shoulder. The words prayed over them were lovely. They were binding and spoke of such promise for the blessings of the future. They almost made her believe what Penny had told her in the house: just marry him.

That's it.

The rest would just have to work itself out.

The prayer ended and on a spontaneous smile that burst forth from both of their lips, they were pronounced husband and wife.

William gathered her up in his arms with a grin of contentment and kissed his bride. Sera closed her eyes and leaned into him, winding her arms around his neck as he leaned in to whisper a tender "I love you" against her ear.

"William Hanover?"

The voice broke into the bliss of their lovely sunset beach.

Sera's eyes popped open.

William's body stiffened in her arms for only a moment, then he placed a single kiss at the base of her neck and drew away. He took a step in front of her, as if to shield her from a threat. She drew up close behind him and threaded her fingers tight with his.

"Evening Carter," William said, nodding to the older gentleman.

Sera had met him a few times over the last year. He was an acquaintance of the family, but she knew better than to think his presence on their beach was simply to offer his congratulations.

He nodded back, the gesture laden with quiet emotion.

"Good of you to come. Our families have been friends for a long time, so of course you're welcome to stay and celebrate with us." William tilted his head to a long table set up not far from where they stood with vases of elegant blooms and tiny candles flickering light through the fallen dusk. "We've only just been married."

Carter shook his head. "I wish that was all I was here for, but there won't be time for dinner."

William raised his eyebrows and asked, "Now?"

"I'm afraid so. They're waiting up at the house." Carter inclined his head toward the glow of lights shining from the back windows of the estate house. There was activity: a car with blacked-out windows and a pair of men walking around, indicating that Carter had walked to the beach unaccompanied as a courtesy.

He then gave a respectful tip of his head in greeting.

"Evening, Sera."

She didn't nod back. Instead, she leaned in closer to William's back and answered with a reluctant, "Hello, Carter."

No, God . . . please. Sera tried to remember to breathe.

This can't be happening. Not now.

Her heart thudded beneath the lace overlay at her chest.

Paul stepped forward and blurted out, "What's going on?" His customary bravado was evident in the stance he took in front of the newly married couple.

"Stand down, Paul."

William shot his younger brother a look that suggested he not argue.

The younger Hanover didn't seem inclined to listen to the authority in William's patriarchal tone. Instead, Paul crossed his arms over his chest and planted his feet deeper in the sand. He gave the unwanted guest a steely glare.

"Someone should tell him he's trespassing on private property."

William shook his head. "Now's not the time to go into this, Paul."

Surprisingly, Penny took a step forward too, as if she was drawing a line for which side she'd chosen to fight. She looked every bit a member of the Hanover clan with bouquets planted at each hip and a scowl on her face, standing shoulder to shoulder with the younger Hanover brother in the sand.

"Uh," Paul muttered under his breath and shook his head. "He can't take you anywhere."

"I think the fact that he's here right now"—William paused, then looked up to the house before continuing—"would suggest he can."

The matter-of-fact edge to his tone gave every indication that he was in complete control. Sera had no idea how he managed it; she could have melted right there in the sand.

Paul notched his chin higher in the air.

"Then he'll have to go through me."

Macie stepped forward and draped her arm over their mother's shoulders as she questioned, "William, what on earth is going on here?"

"It's all right," he started, raising a hand to steady them. He turned to his younger brother and whispered in a voice only the three of them could hear, "Paul, you can't know how much I appreciate your loyalty. I won't forget it. But right now I must ask you to think of the family." William tilted his head toward the group edging up behind them. "And please step back."

Sera's heart nearly broke when she turned to find Macie comforting their mother. Mrs. Hanover had bowed her head and continued to dab a tissue to her eyes. Those faces that had beamed with such unabashed happiness only moments before now looked on in stunned disbelief.

William stepped up and placed a hand on his brother's shoulder. "It's not your fight—not this time."

Paul eyed him for a moment, considering. "I don't care what's happening—I'm on your side."

"I know that. And when I need it, I can be certain you'll have my back. But right now it's out of your hands, little brother."

After a brief pause, the younger Hanover eased his stance, though he certainly didn't look happy about it. He nodded slightly, then took Penny's elbow in his hand and gently pulled her with him as he retreated back in the sand. He stood off to the side of the bride and groom but kept his rebellious air fully intact.

William nodded to Carter then before turning to Sera.

He gently unlaced his fingers from hers, then brushed a hand over the apple of her cheek. She tried to meet his hand, but her fingertips were shaking too badly to grab hold. He turned her palm and pecked a gentle kiss to her fingers.

"I had doubts," Sera admitted, biting her bottom lip over the vulnerability of saying the very thoughts out loud. "Before I ever stepped into the sand, I worried that you wouldn't be here. Not because you wouldn't want to but because of the uncertainty ahead of us. Whether we should have gone ahead with the wedding. But you did come, didn't you? You waited for me on our beach."

"I fell in love with you on our beach," he whispered over the sound of seagulls pitching and soaring off somewhere behind them. "From the first day. Remember that? When I was hiring you to find a lost painting?"

She gave an embattled nod, pushing back tears.

"And I found you as well. So no, Sera, nothing could have kept me away. Not even this. I'm just sorry you only got to wear that beautiful dress for an hour."

Sera shook her head in defiance, never breaking the connection of his eyes to hers, though they stung with hot tears.

"It's not your fault," she said, then added a firm, "I trust you."

William looked back at her, he, too, keeping the connection with her eyes, though a rush of wind blew in around them. It almost felt as if their dreams were scattering with it.

"Will," she whispered, leaning into him. "I trust you."

He didn't answer her.

Instead, he scanned the side of her face and brushed a lock of hair away from her temple, its softness having danced about in the breeze that kicked up off the water. He calmed the tendril by gently hooking it behind her ear.

"Let me go?"

He'd whispered the question, though it held such strength that she felt she couldn't refuse. Not now, when everything they'd hoped for was being turned on end.

"Can you do that, love?"

Sera nodded, though she dreaded hearing what was to come. He gave a final squeeze to her hand before letting go. She forced her eyes to close when he walked away from her side, heard the *chink* of metal to metal before her heart officially sank, knowing that their world had come crashing down.

Sera turned and collapsed into Penny's waiting arms. The

bridal flowers were quickly discarded in the sand at their feet. She cried, uncaring about the raccoon eyes now, realizing that what they'd been dreading was their new reality.

"William Hanover," Carter said with feeling in his voice. "You're under arrest."

CHAPTER TWO

March 15, 1939
Prague

enacing clouds painted the sky over the Charles Bridge.
Daylight was weak and unable to cut its usual path through low-hanging clouds that had forced an eerie blanket of snow over the city. Kája noticed the lack of light as they walked along the Vltava River and how the old town square was shrouded in a pitiful gray.

Good, she thought. *How could we leave if the sun were shining?*

It was March and yet there was no promise of spring.

No flowers adorned shop window boxes. Stoves still burned throughout the day, warming Prague's citizens as during the worst chill of winter. It should have been gray on a day like this. Any other color would have convinced Kája she was dreaming. That the lovely old streets weren't full of motorcars and scores of soldiers with loaded guns. The Czech people couldn't be standing in the cold, some sobbing out clouds of frozen breath and others watching in stunned disbelief as a regime moved in to infect their city with red swastikas. She had to trick herself into believing that the snow mounded on the street corners was because the children had been at play and piled it into forts, not because it had been cleared so the Nazi army could move through unobstructed.

She sniffed against the bitter cold. A punishing rush of air burned her nostrils.

"Kája?"

Her attention was pulled from the activity in the streets back to Hannah, her older sister, who had come from behind and hooked an arm around her elbow.

"Come. We must hurry," she chastened, pulling her along.

Hannah's voice was tinged with alarm. Though her whisper was audibly soft, an unmistakable firmness chided in Kája's ear. The hand that tightened round her elbow was fused with caution, and Hannah's lovely golden eyes that had so often smiled back at her were, on this day, quite void of anything but fear. They stared back now with a layer of rebuke at her distraction.

"You ought not look back."

"I'm sorry. Yes," Kája said with a nod, and pulled the funnel collar of her evergreen wool coat up tighter round her neck. "I am coming."

It took courage to divert her eyes from the flurry of activity around them, but still Kája obeyed.

It was the first time in years they'd stepped out on the streets without the Star of David sewn on their garments. They'd never been so bold before; surely they'd be spotted. Found out. Detained and then—

Kája's gloved hands shook, for the realization of what they were trying to do had become overwhelming. If they were caught without the proper identification on their person, the penalty would be severe. She tried not to think on it, even as they continued their weave through the crowd. She was grateful for the thickness of her auburn hair; the chignon at her nape kept the chill of the wind from sneaking down the full length of her neck. To greet that, too, would have only added to her trembling.

She lowered her head against the wind and followed with quickened steps behind Hannah's husband, Jakob. He cut a path for them, walking along at a steady pace. Not so quick, though, that anyone would notice. He looked up now and then and would check over his shoulder, watching the army as it moved in. He'd even paused more than once and whispered that they were to stand still for a few moments and offer a Nazi salute to the caravan of motorcars as they roared by. There they'd stood in a fog, the three of them caught up in the mire of their own minds, arms extended in cold salute to the Nazis as a mass of people lined the streets.

Jakob walked along now with clear purpose and strong steps to match. The train depot was miles away and he was clearly intent upon them reaching it, in spite of the German forces nipping at their heels.

"Jakob?" Hannah whispered and rushed up to his side. "Can we not hire a car? The walk to the depot is too far and with the snow . . ." She coughed lightly, trying to catch her breath as he continued walking. She shivered and drew her shoulders in closer to him. "Please."

He shook his head, keeping his eyes focused on the city streets out in front of them.

"A car would never make it through this. The streets are clogged with the military. And they're checking every vehicle. We've got a better chance on foot."

"We'll never make it."

"We must. Your parents will be waiting at the depot"—he paused, stealing a glance back at Kája—"to meet us for the train."

Kája watched as Hannah reached out with a gloved hand and tugged at the sleeve of his coat. It was a latent plea, but enough that he halted and stared back at her.

"The walk is too far and—"

"I swore to your father that I'd see his daughters safely to the depot. I'll not falter in keeping my word. Blast the snow and the crowds. Blast Hitler's army even; we're going."

The crowd near them pulsed as a hail of snowballs tore through the air and dusted the front of a tank with tiny dots of snow. The flurry of aggression startled Kája and she blinked back at the sight of it. It was like a sneeze against the charge of an angry rhinoceros. How could they think the snow would do anything but anger the beast? The convoy was undeterred and the action served only to agitate the crowd further. Several women cried out. Young men pelted the passing army with snow as several soldiers began to break form and move toward them.

Kája's first instinct was to step back, which she did, and almost turned her ankle off the side of the icy curb. She righted herself and clutched the small traveling bag she carried closer to her chest, looking at the nervous activity that continued to press in around them. While the German citizens saluted a welcome to their countrymen, the Czech people were becoming increasingly unhinged. Rush to the depot or not, the three of them couldn't stand still when at any moment the marching soldiers could be poised to suppress the crowd with any means necessary.

"Here! Hannah," Kája said, and tugged her sister back by the elbow. "Over here."

Jakob followed until they were tucked in the small alley between a butcher's shop and an old apothecary with ancient-looking floor to ceiling windows. The shades were pulled down tight and the front door, made of old polished wood and delicately etched glass, looked as though it had been hastily boarded up from the inside. A Closed sign had been taped up in the window, though one side had come loose and the paper curled back out of view. It was a world boarded up against the coming storm.

Loud pops erupted in the distance—several of them in rapid succession, at which their little group froze in unison and exchanged glances. Jakob was tall, enough so that he could survey the horizon of the crowd over their heads. He squinted past the activity in the street, his attention drawn to the sight of something far off. Concern marred his brow.

"Jakob." Hannah leaned into his side, nails digging into the sleeve of his coat. "What was that?"

Kája answered before she could stop herself. "Gunfire?"

He shook his head.

"No. The tanks. Or a backfiring engine, I'm sure."

Hannah's eyebrows raised, accentuating doe eyes. They appeared misty. From fear, perhaps? Kája slid a hand into hers and squeezed her palm.

Hannah erupted into nervous tears.

"Jakob—this is madness! Don't you see? We cannot make it!"

"Do I need to tell you again what is happening here?" He lowered his head so the brim of his hat tipped her forehead. "Or can you look around and see for yourself?"

"But if we wait, surely we can—"

"Wait for what?" He shook his head. "We have no time. If you and your sister wish to get out of here, we must go—*now*. The visas I have may not even get us out today, but certainly not tomorrow. It is rumored that the chancellor himself is coming; security will be like we've never seen before. No one will get out then. You can pass for members of my family only so long before someone gives us all away. The daughters of one of Prague's well-known physicians would be spotted easily. The Nazis won't allow you to slip through their fingertips. They're grasping for you."

"But if the chancellor comes, then surely he will bring order with him. I have heard that the worst the Nazis will do is make us all register. And shop at certain times of day. We'll wear the stars on our clothing as they ask. What is so bad in that?"

"Hannah." Kája shook her head. "I don't think they *ask* for anything."

It was foolish to think the Nazis were merely an enemy.

Kája knew better. She thought of the Jewish shops that had

been burned all over Europe the previous November. About windows smashed in the streets and Jews who, as a result of the *Kristallnacht* programs, had gone missing in the night, never to be heard from again.

Were those missing men, women, and children registered too?

"No, Kája. Listen. We are Christians, you and I, from our mother's family. Surely they'll see that in us. We have documentation and can prove our ancestry. And our parents mean no harm to the Third Reich. They are quiet people." Hannah waved her gloved hand out over the crowd. "They're not like those who would challenge the Germans. They cannot be the tiniest threat."

"There is no challenge in a handful of snow and that is all these people have. And though you may be Christians, the Nazis would consider you half Jewish because of your father's heritage," Jakob whispered, though the harshness of his words cut into the air with a force of fog. "They will register you and your sister, yes. Along with your father. They will dictate when you shop for any scraps of food that are left behind. You will wear your star and because of that they will spot you easily. Then eventually they will take you away from me, my Hannah, and kill you."

Like her sister, Kája was stunned to silence.

The two women stared back, frozen, even as the passing convoy caused an eerie tremor to shake the ground beneath their feet and the crowd moved along in a dazed ebb and flow around them.

"Kill us?" Kája breathed out the question, sure she'd been mistaken in hearing the words of prediction come out of her brother-in-law's mouth. *"Why?* What have we done to them?"

"Yes. How do you know this?" Hannah's voice was a shaky mumble at best.

"It doesn't matter how," he whispered. "It is the truth of it that is important, the truth of what will come."

"It matters to me." Kája took a step toward him. "After the changes in legislation, Father told me that it would be best if we left for a while. Just for the ease of things. So our studies would not be disrupted. He expected that we'd be gone a few months at most. When he suggested . . . I never thought . . . I never wanted to leave Prague like this. Not with our friends and neighbors in such danger. And Father's own sister. Our cousins. How could he think of leaving them all here?"

Jakob's forehead creased with what she judged as regret. "We cannot help them now. We must help ourselves."

"Then we're not just going to stay with family in Palestine, are we? You believe we'll be gone longer than a few months. That war really is coming."

When Jakob didn't answer, Kája exchanged glances with her sister.

Hannah swallowed hard.

Kája didn't need sunlight to see the truth; knowing shades had already drifted across her sister's face.

"We're never coming home, are we?"

Hannah's face shifted as if she were finally giving up trying to hide something, with the blast of engines and the cadence of soldiers' footfalls tromping in the street behind them. War was no longer *coming*—it was *here*. Staring them in the face. It was bleeding evil, trickling in the streets like vessels carrying death to the heart of Prague. Pushing them away from the only life they'd ever known.

"You knew?" Kája dared look back at her sister now and exhaled in a frozen cloud of pent-up breath. "Both of you, and you said nothing to me?"

Hannah looked positively sick; the color in her cheeks had sunken to an even more vacant shade of gray than before. She looked away, peering down at her snow-dirtied spectator heels, then bit her bottom lip and closed her eyes on an embattled nod.

Kája stepped back, as if she'd been smacked across the face.

She wasn't a child. In fact, at twenty-one, she was anything but. She'd heard the same reports. Had listened as her father read newspaper articles about what was happening to the Jews once the Nazis had annexed the Sudetenland the year before. Shops had been raided—though there was always proper justification cited. Businesses had been burned. Jews had gone missing. And no one asked questions. No one stood out against the Nazis who marched before them now, for fear that their family would be next. Some terrified souls had even done the worst—committed suicide as a means to self-select out of the impending terror they were certain the Nazis would bring.

All of this Kája hadn't been shielded from. But never had it crossed her mind that their flight would mean they'd never come back. Not when Prague was wounded. Not when so many would be left behind.

Jakob stepped forward, compassion in the softness of his eyes, and addressed her directly.

"Kája, we meant only to shield you until we'd boarded the train. Your sister knew if we spoke of it, you'd not leave with us today. Your father knew this as well. He made us swear to only tell you after we'd all gone."

"I cannot," she mouthed, even as her head began emphatic shaking on its own. "We can't leave like this. Our friends . . . What about our aunt? And cousins? They're still at home. Just two blocks away from our front door. They haven't any idea we're leaving them."

"We must." Hannah's voice cut in with a harsh whisper. "Jakob is right. I shouldn't have stopped us, but I was scared and unprepared for all this. It sounded easier last night when we talked of the route to the depot. But this? It feels like we're staring at the edge of hell somehow."

Kája gazed out at the scores of people beyond the alley. The marching continued, the eerie sound creeping up under her skin in a chill that pricked goose bumps down the length of her spine.

"Kája, I should have told you. *We* should have. But Father made us promise to get out, no matter what. And that is why we must go. Jakob has a plan." Hannah looked up at her husband, her face wet and now streaked with half-frozen tears. "Haven't you?"

He reached up with a finger exposed from the cut-out tips of his gloves and dusted it across Hannah's cheek. "Yes. We'll go to the depot and we'll board a train. No matter what, I swear it. And then we'll worry about tomorrow, yes?"

Hannah gave a nod with seemingly renewed strength. She dropped her hands from Kája's shoulders but continued the steady stare.

"Kája? Are you ready?"

Kája nodded along with her sister, though it was the last thing she wanted to do.

Worry about tomorrow? How could she? Kája's heart felt like it was bleeding along with her beloved city. Here. Today. Where they hid in the alley and any hope had frozen in the snow at their feet. War meant everything. It could steal away today as well as tomorrow. It could take their beautiful city, and the souls in it, to hell and back without batting an eyelash.

Kája breathed out a prayer for them as they left the shelter of the alley and cut into the biting wind yet again. She trailed behind Jakob, murmuring soft words, not really knowing what to say to God but trying nonetheless.

Was he there? Did he see?

God . . . is any of this really happening?

The snow fell around them. Engines continued to roar. And they moved through the streets, pace quickened but not so much that anyone would notice a pair of Jews without their telling stars, heading for the train depot and the prayer of a life beyond.

It wasn't until she spotted her father on the platform that Kája felt like she could finally breathe again.

She saw him and their mother, he short in stature but so noble in presence, with his gold-rimmed glasses and steady shoulders weaving his way through the crowd. Her mother was walking behind quite closely, eyeing the crowd with a certain air of numbness painted over her features. Her father's eyes lit up when he spotted them; her mother's misted with relief in connecting to the sight of her daughters appearing through the cloud of steam.

Jakob shook his head slightly, stopping her father's advance toward them. His eyes darted over his left shoulder and then back again. Kája followed their path and noticed that a group of soldiers, armed and with icy cold voices, were arbitrarily ordering passersby to surrender their visas for inspection. They looked rough and unfeeling. Their faces were void. Their eyes looked without soul as they detained person after random person.

Kája shivered and pulled her coat in closer round her neck.

Jakob tilted his chin toward a small alcove behind a row of metal stairs. It was shrouded in darkness and the group, following her brother-in-law's silent instruction, immediately edged toward it. The moment her parents joined them in the alcove, Kája dropped her bag to the ground and fell into the warmth of her father's arms.

She cried, having no idea when bravery had left and tears took its place until she was sobbing against the scratchy wool star on the front of his coat. Her mother, always sweet and apologetic for pain of which she had no responsibility, ran the gentlest graze of a hand down the side of Kája's head. She smiled, a forced, mostly flat turn of the lips, and with the elegance Kája had always seen in her, valiantly fought back tears of her own.

"There, there. My young Kája," her father soothed, speaking her childhood pet name as if it were honey on his tongue. "We are all here. This is good. You see? God is watching out for us."

"My girls. Hannah. Kateřina." Izabel Makovský whispered the words and pulled prayer hands up to her lips. They were trembling, much like Kája's had been out in the streets. "And, Jakob. How can we thank you for bringing our girls here safely?"

He pulled an arm around Hannah's shoulders and inclined his head in a quick nod.

"No thanks is required," he offered, then pulled Hannah in closer. "But I confess that I prayed with every step. And we have still to board a train out from here. And another after that."

"I'm sorry," Kája whispered, suddenly noticing how overcome with emotion everyone was, and began wiping at the front of her father's coat. She stepped back, dabbing at the wetness under her eyes. "I hadn't expected any of this. Not to cry now, when we're all here. I'm just so glad to see you." Kája reached for her mother's hand and she grasped it, gratefully squeezing her fingers. "Both of you."

"My dear Kateřina, how does one ever expect"—her mother paused, eyes checking the soldiers on the platform, her bottom lip trembling ever so slightly—"something like *this?*"

"I don't know, *Matka*. Prague is no longer our own, is it?"

Her mother looked refined, as always, in the brave nod she returned.

This woman of stature in Prague's social circles wore her breeding well, even as she stood in the dim, cobwebbed corner of the train station. She wore a dark mink coat, with gloves the color of a robin's egg and a black hat with ostrich feathers that tipped down over her right eye. Pearl studs peeked out from her ears. Though frosted with gray at the temples, her hair was the deep auburn of her daughters'. It, too, was pulled back, lovely and proper-like with rows of silky waves, just as she'd always worn it. She was a picture of perfection in the midst of their crumbling reality.

Kája guessed that her mother had dressed up for the journey, even worn her best clothes. But why? Finery for what was ahead didn't make sense. She looked at her parents, barely listening to what was being said as her father whispered with Jakob, noticing only the etched image of them standing there in the darkness of the momentary hideaway. They looked steady, beautiful even, against the invading soberness of Nazi green all around.

The vision of her parents felt like home somehow, no matter where they were.

"There is a train car, the one second to the last of the line that has no soldiers checking over the visas. Do you see it?" her father asked Jakob, even as he stole glances over his shoulder.

"Yes." Jakob nodded.

Kája peered over her father's shoulder and noticed that it was indeed true. There was a single entrance at a single car with steps somehow unimpeded by Nazi uniforms. There was no way to be sure the same would be found inside but, despite the risk, the path to the train appeared clear for the moment.

They would have little time.

"If your visas have made it through the line of checks into the depot, then you're only steps away. But you must hurry," he cautioned, and held out his hand to shake Jakob's. His son-in-law swallowed hard and clasped her father's palm in both of his. In a voice laden with emotion, her father faltered, coughing over the last words: "I give them to you."

Hannah edged around Kája and embraced her mother, crying urgent tears.

Jakob nodded and whispered, "*Shalom,*" before gently pulling his wife away. "We must go." He leaned in and pecked a kiss to his mother-in-law's cheek. "*Matka. Shalom.* God be with you."

"What is this?" Kája watched with her heart constricting

in her chest. She recognized anguish. It was all over her mother's face. It poured out of Hannah's tears. And her father, steady though he always was—he, too, had hands that shook and glasses that couldn't disguise the tears that had formed behind them.

Instinct was something Kája sorely wished she lacked at the moment. It spoke to her now, whispering words of dread, weaving tales about what would happen to the parents who—it was evident—would be left behind.

"Kateřina dear, you must go." Izabel stopped abruptly and pulled at the fingertips of her gloves, shedding them in mere seconds. She placed them in her pockets. On a pause, as if to remember the moment, Izabel took her youngest daughter's cheeks in her bare hands and stared back in her eyes. "We shall catch the next train. Yes?"

She nodded, no doubt hoping her daughter would believe her. Kája's bravery was fleeting and no matter how much she longed to, she found she could not return the gesture.

Her will was firm. "No. We will not leave you."

"I will stay with your father until it is time to board our train. But your train is ready to go now. And you must be on it. We will meet again soon, my sweet."

Instead of agreeing, Kája shook her head. She pressed her gloved hands over her mother's, loving the touch of warm, gentle hands against her exposed skin. They felt so alive and in the moment, Kája didn't want that connection to end.

"Matka . . . I am a Jew as well. Can we not all stay together and catch the next train?" Kája found it easy to beg. It seemed unfathomable that this could be the last moment their family would all be together. She pulled her mother's hands down, not wanting to accept it, then tugged her mother's arm up against her side with firm intention.

"No. You must go now." Izabel closed her eyes, pain taking over every distinguished line on her face. "I will watch over your father and our home until you return. I will even watch over your studio and your beloved books so they'll be ready for the next time you should want to read them. Everything will be just as it once was."

"I don't care about a paint studio or books right now!"

"But you will, Kája. You will care. And your life must go on until we meet again. Do you understand?" She reached in her pocket and retrieved what felt like a handful of stones when pressed against Kája's palm. "Take them. Your grandmother's pearls. I have their mates—both of them," she breathed out, referring to the pearl studs in her ears. The earrings were lovely, with the tiny star sapphire that winked out from the top of the setting. They were unique to be sure, and familiar, as Kája always pictured her mother wearing them for special occasions. "And I promise to return them to you soon."

Izabel coughed over a sob, then pulled her hands away and left them up in the air as a sad shield between them. She turned away, looking off into the space of dirty brick and dust in the corner.

"Hurry now, or you'll be late for the start of your classes."

Kája looked from her father back to her mother again, suddenly confused. "But I'm not going to school today, *Matka*. You know where we are going—"

Izabel cleared her throat over the words.

"Yes. Yes, of course." She shook her head, obviously overcome. "Jakob? Please go. I can't . . ."

"Yes." Her brother-in-law immediately stepped forward and picked up Kája's traveling bag. He then took her by the arm and whispered, "Kája? We must go. Now. There is no more time."

"No!" Kája grasped for the fur-trimmed lapels of her mother's coat as Jakob and Hannah tugged her toward the light of the train platform.

Kája wanted to stay in the shelter of the stairwell with her parents. To see that they were properly looked after and that there was indeed a train they would board. That the hope of tomorrow wouldn't die with that final image of them.

She didn't think of tomorrow again until she'd been ushered onto the train and fell into the coldness of the first seat she saw. Kája's coat absorbed the physical chill, yet her heart found no warmth.

Jakob sat across from them, silent but alert.

Hannah occupied the space next to her, seemingly trying to breathe, though Jakob would look up from time to time and offer an encouraging nod. Still, she sat with her back poker straight and her eyes flitting about as she looked at the people walking outside their closed compartment, holding her breath with every shadow that passed by.

Condensation snaked down the glass window that over-looked the sad world of Prague beyond. She pressed her gloved hand to it, smearing the tears. The journey should have plagued Kája with fear. It might have, even moments before. But now, as their exodus began, she found nothing but numbness inside.

The tiniest seed of resolve sprouted in Kája's heart when the wheels screeched and the train groaned forward, spreading the drops of water in lonely trails down the glass. She kept her hand fused to it, as if it were the last connection to her parents. They were out there—somewhere. She pictured them standing on the other side of the window, dressed so beautifully, waving a sad good-bye to the departing train. But the vision fizzled, fading away in the cloud of steam behind them, along with the rest of Prague and a sea of Nazi uniforms.

Lord—my journey back to Prague begins now.

CHAPTER THREE

The early-morning sun tipped up over the horizon in a spray of delicate yellows and golds, its light casting a haze of shadows against the voids between the downtown buildings.

Sera sat in the driver's seat of William's Jeep, chewing on her thumbnail as she stared at the back doors to the municipal building. She kept willing them to open and release her husband back to her side.

From the moment William had been led away from their sunset beach with handcuffs behind his back, Sera had flown into action. Immediately following the painful sight of William's head ducked under the door of a police car, she'd charged through the front doors of the estate house and into his downstairs office. She'd maneuvered the train of her wedding gown out of the way so she could sit in the chair behind the massive desk and pulled open a drawer to begin rummaging through.

"Sera." Penny had appeared and hovered in the office doorway. "Are you all right?"

"Of course I'm not all right," she offered, her tone distracted.

She'd found the list of business contacts William had left in the desk drawer and began thumbing through them with her manicured nails. The sound of muffled crying floated in from the foyer. Sera tried to ignore it—picturing his mother in tears would only make things worse.

Sera slammed one desk drawer and yanked open another.

Penny looked out into the hall, then turned back and clicked the door closed behind her. She dropped her tone to a whisper.

"Sera, what in heaven's name is going on? His family is out there, confused, shocked. If you know something about this, please go out there and tell them what it is."

Sera froze, sensing the weight of what had just happened finally bearing down upon her. She closed her eyes against the fear, against the disappointment in having the best moment of her life turn into the worst in a matter of seconds.

"Sera?" Penny's voice echoed against the stillness of the room.

Sera hadn't noticed how hushed everything was until a kiss of wind brushed the office windows, signaling that their sunset beach was still alive outside. It was empty now; their reception meal would go uneaten and the flickering tabletop candles had likely all been snuffed out. William was gone. He was gone and she was sitting in a wedding gown, alone.

Sera opened her eyes and took a deep breath.

"He told me he'd leave it right here." She began rifling through the drawer again, only glancing up when Penny remained quiet. Sera found her standing with arms folded over her middle, stoic almost, eyeing the scene.

"Leave what? What are you looking for?" Her words were whispered into the silence between them. Softly. Without reproach. And Sera found that because of the softness in them, she couldn't turn her away.

"I'm looking for Lincoln Stahlworth's number. I should have put it in my cell phone. I suppose I didn't want to believe I'd really need it. What was I thinking?" she chided herself, and continued rummaging through the pens and odds and ends all the way to the back of the drawer. "I have to call his lawyer. William gave me instructions on what to do if this happened."

"If this happened? Sera, your husband was just arrested—*at your wedding!* And forgive me, but you don't seem the least bit surprised." Penny edged toward the desk. "So do you want to tell me what's going on? Or at least go out there and give his family some sort of explanation? Anything would do to calm them down, because they're beside themselves. Paul's so angry he's ready to go tear down the jail with his two hands, and I think the last thing we all need right now is two Hanovers behind bars."

Penny looked incredulous.

It pained Sera to see that look in her friend's eyes, like she was hurt that Sera hadn't confided in her. That William's family was in shock. That, yes, Sera knew exactly what was going on; both she and William did. They'd had mere days to process the possibility, as soon as his lawyer's office had called with the news that there was an investigation into the Hanover company finances.

"Sera? You've never kept anything from me before—especially not something as big as this."

Sera exhaled and rested her elbow on the desktop, cradling her forehead with her palm. She peeked out from the side of her hand to find Penny, just a few steps away, watching her with the desk in between them.

What else was left but to tell the truth?

"The Hanover Corporation—and William in particular—is being investigated for fraud."

Penny drew in a breath and took a step closer. "What kind of fraud?"

"When William gave back the money from the family inheritance last year, part of the assets were missing. An investigation was already underway, though we didn't know the full extent of it then. We do now."

"What assets?" Penny asked, and fell into a chair opposite the desk.

"Do you remember when you found William through the art auction website?"

Penny nodded. "Of course I do. It was in a photo of a vase the Hanovers had put up for sale that we first saw their painting of Adele, and we made the connection. I remember William was liquidating his grandfather's assets. Selling some of the family heirlooms and such. But that's not out of the ordinary, is it? Families do it all the time."

"But that's just it." Sera paused and looked up at her friend. "The art wasn't his to sell."

Penny creased her brow, asking, "I don't understand. He was acting on behalf of the family. He was executor of his grandfather's will, right?"

"He was. And yes—he did liquidate much of the estate because his father wasn't in the picture. William's grandfather was an avid art buyer and over the years had amassed quite a collection. Picassos. A Renoir. Even an early Manet. But more than three years ago, the artwork was signed over to the Hanover Corporation as collateral for a very large loan."

"How much money are we talking about, Sera?"

Penny bit her bottom lip, waiting for an answer.

A pent-up breath escaped her lungs. Sera exhaled, long and low. Somehow, saying the words out loud made them even scarier. She feared saying them would somehow make them true to those whom she trusted most. If Penny couldn't be convinced of William's innocence, who would?

"Somewhere in the range of twelve million dollars."

Penny's eyebrows arched up with the truth. No doubt she was trying to figure out the same thing Sera had—why twelve million dollars would matter to a family who had more than ten times that.

"But that's a leaf blowing in the breeze to the Hanovers, right? Forgive me for saying it, but your husband's family has money coming out of their ears."

"Had. William didn't take the inheritance, remember?"

"But the family still has quite a bit of it. So why would he need a few million when he gave up more than 100 million?"

Penny was right, of course.

The Hanovers seemed the picture of American prosperity. They owned a lavish beachside estate. A vineyard outside Napa. They owned a private jet for the company, which the family had for their own use. They owned a Park Avenue apartment and still had a rather large townhouse in London's South Kensington neighborhood. All in all, they had more than one leaf blowing on a breeze; they owned a tree of them. So it begged the question— why the loan?

"Well, that question doesn't matter to the authorities. They say someone behind the scenes transferred ownership of the art collection to the Hanover Corporation almost four years ago. When William turned around and sold the art last year, he didn't know that it was no longer his to sell. Officially, it belonged to his investors. The price for the transaction was twelve million dollars and it was buried in the company books. Somehow they've traced the money back to William. His signature is on the loan and then on each bill of sale for the art."

"Which means?"

Sera looked up, knowing the truth would show all over her face. It did no good to hide it. Penny could see straight through her without trying.

"Which means that my husband could be in some serious trouble."

Penny rushed around to the back side of the desk, just in time for Sera to crumble in her arms. Penny cradled her hand at the back of Sera's head, whispering soothing words as she cried.

"How long have you known about this?"

"Only a few days," Sera mumbled, hiccupping slightly.

"And this is why you moved the wedding up?"

Sera nodded.

"You silly girl," Penny whispered on a sigh, and pecked a kiss at her temple. "Why didn't you tell me that's why you were so quick to jump into this? And here I thought you two just loved each other so much that you couldn't stand to be apart anymore."

"We can't stand to be apart. That's *why* I married him. Whatever happens, I won't wait around on the sidelines. If I'm his wife, I can walk through this with him. It's as simple as that."

"Sera." Penny's doubt seeped through in the tone of one word. "Are you sure he—"

"I know what you're thinking, Penn. But he didn't do this." Sera's heart sank with the flicker of doubt in Penny's voice.

"You're positive?"

Sera pounded her fist on the desk. "He told me he's innocent and I believe him. You don't know him like I do."

"Are you sure you know him?"

"Penn, we've been engaged for months. We've spent time together over the last year, holidays, flying from coast to coast just to be a part of each other's lives. He's been in the gallery a hundred times. It's not like we rushed into this. We may have made the decision to move the wedding up but that doesn't mean it was blind. I know who he is and he'd never lie to me."

"I never said he'd lie to you." Penny paused, as if fighting to choose her words oh so carefully. "I just have to think that in order to hand down an indictment for the things you're talking about— wouldn't the feds need to have some pretty strong evidence?"

Sera pulled back from Penny's arms and stared back at her, to find the loving support she'd expected to see was only half there. The rest of what she saw was pure speculation. Doubt had rushed over Penny's features like a wave.

It hurt to realize the truth.

"You think he did this?"

Penny shook her head immediately. "I didn't say that."

"Then what are you saying?"

"Sera, you're my friend. I love you dearly. I only want what's best for—"

"Don't say you want what's best for me!" Sera pushed back the desk chair and sprang to her feet, leaving Penny kneeling at its side.

"It *is* what I want—always."

"And I want to be with him. I *need* to fight for him, even in something like this. It could get much worse, I know. But I trust him. That's why I married him. Not because we were afraid of an arrest or even because I wanted to be at his side through it all. I married Will because I love him. And with love, trust is given without question. I'm his wife; I owe him that at least."

Her friend's will looked solid. She was loving in her doubt; that much was evident. But it meant that convincing others of her husband's innocence wasn't going to be an easy task. If her closest friend had doubts, who wouldn't?

Penny rose up and tilted her head toward the door.

"And what should I tell them? They're waiting on the other side of that door and I think they're going to demand some sort of explanation when I walk through it. Right now you're the only one who can give it to them."

Sera notched her chin in a show of solidarity. She stood tall with squared shoulders and a poker-straight stance.

"You tell them that I'm getting on the phone with William's lawyers and that we'll have him back home by morning. I don't care if I have to make calls all night and wake up half the city in the process—he's coming home. And after that, all of the Hanovers will take this thing one step at a time."

Penny hesitated only a moment. She opened her mouth as if she wanted to say something but thought better of it and instead nodded, then turned toward the door.

"And, Penn?"

Her friend turned on her heel and quietly said, "Yeah, Sera."

"Tell them he's innocent. They'll want to know that."

It hurt now to recollect the doubt that was so quick to overtake Penny's features. She'd looked sorry, almost sad that Sera had made a mistake in marrying William. But she didn't think of it that way. Sera had doubted once, when they'd found the painting that was the key to his family's inheritance. Her heart hurt now to admit that she'd doubted him before and she'd been wrong. So wrong. She couldn't do that to him a second time.

Sera pushed the memories away.

No. We can't focus on the worst-case scenario.

Her thoughts had been laced with prayers, all night even, as she made phone calls and waited to hear confirmation that he'd be released. But the call never came. One night stretched into two. Then three. And while William's lawyers fought to get him released on bail, his family was pulled into a bond hearing.

Sera had been forced to watch as her husband was led into court the next Monday morning, shackled and in an orange prison uniform, to answer the charges brought against him. It was like a dream, as if she were living someone else's life. And she'd held her breath for the longest of moments after the innocent plea was entered, waiting to hear whether the judge would rule Will would come home.

And so she waited now, with every muscle tensed, when the back doors moved. They parted in the center and finally opened. The tension eased ever so slightly on a sigh of relief. William's tall form emerged in a wrinkled suit, his oxford unbuttoned at the collar and the jacket swung over his shoulder.

The instant she saw him trotting down the concrete steps, Sera burst from the vehicle and ran up to meet him. He dropped his suit jacket to the ground as she jumped up and threw her arms around his neck. Sera couldn't care less if someone did catch a glimpse of their reunion; it was enough just to know she could hold him.

William looked down at her jeans, Converse sneakers, and white cotton tee and whispered, "The last time I saw you, you were in a beautiful dress."

Sera shrugged. "Who needs a wedding dress at the courthouse except a bride?" She lifted up on her toes to plant a welcome kiss on his lips. "Me? I'm already happily married."

"Happily?" he chided, and looked around them. "Here?"

She joined him in looking around at the buildings, still partially hidden by early-morning shadows. "Well, I admit I'd have thought of a dozen more charming places to spend a honeymoon. But at least here I'm not alone."

They looked at each other then.

It was a quiet, breezy morning. And though making light of the circumstances didn't seem the best thing, they'd hastened to reach each other so quickly that now, in the midst of the stillness, they didn't exactly know what to do except stand together, embracing, without the necessity of words.

"You're not alone, Sera. And you never will be again—not if I can help it."

"I know, Will." She ran a hand over the collar of his shirt, absently trying to press some of the wrinkles out. He caught her hand, cradling it in his own.

"Sera." He closed his eyes for a moment and inclined his head toward hers, meeting her forehead with his. "You have no idea how sorry I am."

"You don't have to be," she countered, shaking her head against his. "It wasn't your fault. We knew this could happen. Your lawyers had already warned us that an indictment could be handed down. I just wish I'd gone to law school instead of spending so much of my college years trekking around museums. Maybe then I'd have a clue as to what they're talking about with these charges."

"But you should have had better for your wedding," he added. "For your life. You don't deserve any of this."

A SPARROW in TEREZIN

Sera cupped her hands on the sides of his cheeks and looked him in the eyes. They were dark blue and cloudy. Ashamed maybe, but full of vulnerability nonetheless. She felt compassion that the events of the last few days had knocked him to his knees. It was there, in his eyes, in the concern melted over his features.

"And you don't deserve it either. We'll fight this, okay?"

William nodded, albeit reluctantly, then stooped to pick up his jacket from the ground. Sera took it from him, brushed off the fabric and swung it over one arm, then laced her fingers with his.

"Lincoln called me with an update right after the bond hearing to let me know when you'd be released. He's been working on the case personally since you were brought in. I don't even think he's slept."

William raised his eyebrows. "Old Stahlworth called you himself?"

"Even in the middle of the night when he's had to."

"You wouldn't think a partner would keep such hours."

"He said you're his most important client."

A mocking chuckle escaped his lips. "That's because his most important client is almost always the one who finds himself in the most trouble. And I think the temperature of the water under my feet is set to boil at present."

"I was so relieved the bail hearing went in our favor, especially after they read over the list of charges. I wondered if he was having doubts that it would go our way."

William shook his head. "Not a chance. Lincoln Stahlworth is worth his weight in gold. He's one of the only men I've ever met who could outwit both my father and my grandfather. If there's a challenge out there to be met, I assure you—he's first in line to conquer it. He's assured me we have a good case."

"At least he's on our side and you're coming home because of it." Sera leaned into him, laying her head on his shoulder as they walked back to the car. "So what comes next?"

"Let's forget it for now." Will looked at the golden signs of dawn that peeked through the early-morning clouds. "Let's have one morning together where we don't have to think about this. I'd like to get a good, strong cup of coffee and blot the last few days from my memory if I can."

"Are you sure? We have to start planning your defense."

He shook his head. "Not today. Not on the first day we're together as husband and wife." He lifted her hand still laced with his and kissed the inside of her wrist. "The charges will keep. I assure you—this mess will still be here tomorrow, and the day after that until we're back in court."

"But you're innocent. I can't believe anyone would suspect you of something like this. How can they possibly think to pin this on you?"

"I should have gotten out of this company long ago," he mumbled, raking his hand through his hair. "And I have a sinking feeling that your husband may have been a rather trusting fool when he stepped into the shoes of the former CEO."

She stopped and stared back in his eyes. "I don't understand."

"There's only one man on the planet who can make heads or tails of this," he offered on a frustrated sigh. "He may be estranged from the family, but the lawyers are going to insist that I speak with my father."

CHAPTER FOUR

April 15, 1940
The Daily Telegraph
Fleet Street, London

I'm looking for a . . ." A gentleman entered the room, glanced down at a scrap of paper in his hand, and looked back at the few ladies sitting in the waiting area. "Miss Kateřina Makovský?"

Kája looked up, summoned from the copy of *Vogue* magazine she'd been mindlessly leafing through for the last hour. She raised her hand.

"Yes, I'm here."

The man was tall, with blue eyes that smiled in greeting when he spotted her from across the room. He shoved the scrap of paper in his pocket and nodded.

"Good. We found you."

He was more casually dressed than she expected for an office environment; no tie, unbuttoned gray pin-striped vest, and white shirt sleeves rolled up on his forearms. His hair was even mussed a bit, having curled around the ears instead of being parted and combed back like she was used to seeing on the men of London.

Kája stole a look down at her prim navy suit, wondering if that and the pearls she'd worn would have her sorely overdressed for her first day on the job. But if she'd be out of place, he didn't seem to notice. She dropped the magazine on the chair opposite her and stood, then did a quick sweep to press the wrinkles out of her navy skirt as she crossed the room. She stopped in front of him, accepting the hand he extended in greeting.

"Not waiting too long, I hope?"

"No, sir. Not at all."

He inclined his head toward the newsroom and held the door wide so she could step through.

"Follow me then."

Kája did and found a stark contrast to the quiet waiting area she'd been sitting in for the last hour. The other side of the door boasted a flurry of activity. Typewriter keys hummed. Phones rang incessantly, over one another. People passed by every which way—gentlemen in suits, ladies in dresses—all chattering on and seemingly without notice that a new employee had been brought into their midst. It was business as usual—a chaotic busy they all seemed quite used to.

He ushered her through the crowded hall, talking loudly over the noise.

"I'm Liam Marshall—one of the reporters assigned to the war beat, whom you'll be supporting."

Kája followed along behind him, taking in the bustle of the scene as they walked.

"I admit I'm not the usual candidate for an office tour guide, but we find ourselves down several secretaries at the moment, so there you have it. It was either I show you about or make you wait another hour or so. I know it's stuffy in that waiting room—at least they open the windows on pleasant days like this, right?"

"It was quite all right, sir. Thank you."

Mr. Marshall ducked past a young man with speed in his feet and a rather large stack of files teetering in his arms. He placed a hand out to move her to the side, then continued walking when the young man had scurried past them.

"Don't worry about the 'sir.' Liam suits me fine around here.

We don't hold many pretenses, as you can see. Everyone rolls up their sleeves when there's a newspaper to get to print. Remember that we're all in this together and you'll get along smashingly."

Kája hated to imagine what her mother would say if she were to dare address a man by his Christian name, and possibly, he by hers. It wasn't at all proper, at least not in the way she'd been brought up. Kája made a mental note to call him Mr. Marshall instead of Liam, and to try to be casual about it when doing so.

"And you come to us from where?"

"Oxford," she said, stopping short of adding her habitual "sir" at the end. It was going to take some effort to break herself of her mother's long-ingrained habit.

"I'm sorry?" he nearly shouted behind the shrill ringing of a telephone nearby. He leaned in closer.

"Oxford," she repeated, lifting up on her toes to raise her voice to his ear. "I transferred there to finish up the last year of my master's studies in English."

"Did you now? Well done." He paused, tilting his head to the side as if his interest was piqued. "Do forgive me, but that's not an Oxford accent I hear, is it?"

"No," she answered, surprised by his casual tone, and notched her chin a shade. "It's not."

"So you come to us by way of . . . ?"

"Prague, originally."

"Prague? My goodness. You are far from home. But you must have family in England?"

She shook her head. "No. I stayed with family in Palestine last summer before continuing my studies in England. I'm just here until—" She stopped herself from blurting out, "Until I can find a way back home to Prague."

Thank goodness. That could have been disastrous.

She thought it better to avoid familiarities about the fact this job may only be temporary for her. England, and *The Daily*

Telegraph with it, was simply a means to an end that would take her home. She glossed over the fact that she'd spent the last year separated from her parents, who were still back in Prague, and Hannah and Jacob, who'd managed to stay with family in Palestine.

The topic of her Jewish heritage was left out altogether.

"Well, that is . . . with things so uncertain back east, it's not easy for a writer to secure a steady position. I'd hoped to find something at home but it just wasn't possible." She cleared her throat and continued only after she felt sure she'd given a somewhat sturdy answer. It was believable, but barely. "So here I am."

"But there's a war going on *back east,* isn't there?"

She nodded. "Yes."

"And yet you find yourself here, where war looms as well."

Up to that point, he'd seemed only casually interested. But her one-word answer seemed to have stirred up something other than the anonymity she'd hoped. He nodded. And smiled, as if sated for the moment.

"We are fortunate, then, to have such an academic in our midst. No doubt you shall give the rest of the office chaps a run for their intellectual money."

"I'm not certain I wish to run against anyone, sir."

She almost winced when the formality of the final word popped out of her mouth like clockwork.

"Is that so?" A smile tipped the corners of his mouth. He didn't comment further, but he looked as though the retort had struck a nerve somewhere.

"I know I haven't quite got the knack for a British accent just yet, but I'll keep working on it."

"Fair enough," he added, and held out a hand to the hallway ahead of them. "After you, of course."

The moments that followed passed by in a whirlwind.

They breezed through the newsroom at a feverish pace. Kája's heels clicked along behind him as they wove around desks, passing by endless file cabinets and too many bustling office boys to count. He took her to a smoke-laden switchboard closet and introduced her to a bevy of ladies, most of whom seemed to show passing curiosity for a new girl until they received their next inbound call. He then took her to the mail room and for a turn past the office kitchenette (should she require a mid-day cup of tea). Their tour finally came to a stop in the back of the large newsroom, behind a sea of desks occupied by the paper's bustling reporters.

"And your desk is right here."

Liam paused long enough to clear an armful of folders and papers that had been strewn across the desk. It looked like a stack of crossword puzzles, of all things. He swept them up in his arms, used his elbow to rub at a cup ring on the oak surface and, with a smile, presented it to her.

"Sorry about that. I'd been using the empty space," he offered. "But then, here we are. Your new home at *The Daily Telegraph*."

Kája looked over the desk.

It was oversized and made of sturdy oak. There was a desk lamp, the kind with a wide brass base and double shade of green porcelain. The desk boasted drawers that appeared deep for filing and the overhead lighting was surprisingly bright. And for how the newsroom bustled with the endless cadence of typewriter keys and ringing phones in the background, it appeared a rather quiet corner of the office. It could be called charming even, with a large wall of oversized windows that allowed the sun to bathe the area from mere steps away.

Kája felt a smile press over her lips.

"It's all right, then?"

"Yes." She nodded, genuinely grateful. "*Dobře*. It's good, thank you."

In fact, it was better than good; it was near picture perfect.

"Oh, if you're wondering about a typewriter," he added, tucking the files under his arm. He turned back to her. "They've ordered one for you. It should be here straightaway. If I know Edmunton, he won't want his secretary to go without one for long."

Any smile generated by the pleasant desk dropped off her lips immediately.

Secretary.

The word burned at the writer in Kája's heart.

"I'm sorry? Did you say 'secretary'?"

"Yes." He tilted his head slightly, eyeing her with an eyebrow raised. "Is there a problem?"

"No. Not at all," she rushed out, holding up a hand in caution. With office jobs scarce, the last thing Kája wanted to do was appear ungrateful for any opportunity, even if there was a mix-up in the hiring process. She had to admit she'd felt an immediate letdown though, when she considered the likely level of pay for a secretary. "It's just—I'd interviewed for and been taken on as a copy-editor. I was told to report here today. Am I in the wrong place? On the wrong floor, perhaps?"

"Classic," Mr. Marshall mumbled, giving a hint of an apologetic smile, and shoved his hands down in his pockets. "Then they didn't tell you."

"Tell me what, exactly?"

"Not only are you in the right place, Miss Makovský, but you're looking at all we've got as far as an opening is concerned. The job is for a secretary to our rather stodgy old senior editor," he said, and inclined his head toward the glass-walled office opposite them.

A middle-aged man was shut up inside it, quietly it seemed, until he picked up a phone and yelled something to the poor soul on the other end of the line.

Kája flinched.

"I'm sorry to be the one to tell you, but that would be Herbert Edmunton. Your new boss."

She didn't move for a moment.

"I think there's been some mistake."

"Quite right." He stood tall, arms folded and files tucked against his chest, looking back at her with regret evident upon his face. He nodded agreement. "I can see how this might be distressing to you. I, for one, wouldn't blame you in the least if you saw fit to walk out that door at this very moment. You wouldn't be the first secretary to do that after one day."

Kája swallowed hard. "The last secretary quit after one day?"

"Secretaries. And it was within a week." He grimaced. "But what does it matter? We have a copy-editor from Oxford here now. And given the fact that she's already had the grand tour and her desk is cleared off and everything . . ." He pulled out the wooden swivel chair and patted the back with his palms. "Why not give it a try? What's the worst that could happen?"

Kája ran a hand over the pearls at her nape, thinking on it.

The worst?

By the looks of her new boss, she was ill prepared for such imaginings. He looked about as cuddly as a rock. Still, something told her that Mr. Marshall was right. She'd come halfway across the city that morning, from Oxford and Palestine months before, and from the stark reality of Nazi-occupied Prague before that. It seemed rather cowardly to turn around and go home now.

Kája nodded agreement.

"Thank you, Mr. Marshall." She swept the skirt under her and took the seat he offered, then inclined her head in a polite nod. "I'd be very pleased to stay."

One day. She vowed to give it a solid day of effort. Beyond that, only God knew if it could work.

"Supplies." He leaned forward and tapped a hand to the top drawer. "Paper, pencils, and file folders. You'll find a small dictionary in there, too, though I'd go down to the archive library for any real research."

Kája's heart skipped a beat. "You have a library?"

"If one could call it that." He laughed. "You'll see what I mean when you venture down to the basement. It's not as impressive as Oxford, so you'll have to temper your expectations, I'm afraid. The books are old and covered in an inch of dust, but they should suffice in a pinch. You're free to roam down there whenever you wish."

"Thank you, I'm sure." She looked down to survey the supplies in her top drawer.

"And in case you were wondering . . . you'll find your gas mask is on your bottom left."

When Kája turned back to face him, he pointed to the bottom drawer.

"I'm a bit surprised you're not carrying your own. I thought most everyone did in London."

"Well, I used to but we'd heard that the scare was over. The women in my building have all but stopped carrying them now. They keep saying that the sirens are just drills and it's ridiculous to think of wearing them in the summer when it's so hot."

"Well, just as a precaution, then, you'll find that every desk has one. We all move about the office quite regularly in the mighty pursuit of putting ink to paper every day. You can imagine. Edmunton thought it a better strategy to outfit the desks, just in case anyone forgot to bring theirs in. He may be an old killjoy, but he's an orderly one at that. Safety first, I'm afraid."

Kája opened the bottom drawer.

She stared back at the mask that was tucked there, a big-eyed, black thing with a circular vent at the mouth and adjustable straps that looked akin to snake-like appendages. She couldn't imagine wearing it. Hated the sight of it for the memories it caused to float to the surface of her heart.

It was terribly frightening that the item had become some strange part of their new normal. In the streets of London and Oxford alike, the last year had seen women and children carrying masks about as they carried a handbag or a skipping rope. She'd even seen a woman pass by with a buggy in Grosvenor Square; her baby had been wrapped in some horrible canvas contraption that looked like a beekeeper's suit. The picture of that sweet child with such innocence to what was happening in its world—it fairly turned her stomach.

He must have seen the shades of fear wash over her face because Liam cleared his throat and offered, "My apologies, miss. I didn't mean to frighten you. As you said, it's just a precaution. I'm sure we'll never have need of them."

"No." She quickly closed the drawer, not wishing to look upon the eyesore a moment longer. "No, of course not. But it is a comfort to know it's there, whether we'll have need of it or not."

The interaction between them seemed awkward then. No one liked talking of war. Of gas masks and air-raid sirens that cried out in the streets without warning. But they'd breeched the uncomfortable topic and it seemed there was little left to do but turn to work.

"Well," he sighed, and offered a respectful nod of the head. "You're all set, then?"

"Yes, thank you." She nodded, looking away almost immediately.

It was a paltry response, she knew. But she feared that if she looked at him a moment longer, every fear bubbling in her heart would somehow show upon her face. She wasn't one to give up her privacy easily.

"Good. Welcome aboard," he whispered, having leaned in at her side. "And now that you're one of us, might I offer a piece of advice?"

She was hesitant, but nodded agreement.

He studied her a bit more earnestly.

"Do you want to be a serious journalist?"

Kája took issue with the question. The fact that he had enough bravado to ask it of a complete stranger was telltale. She notched her chin higher in the air and answered, "Of course."

"Then stop Edmunton in his tracks now. Your position has seen four secretaries in the past two months."

"But I was hired as a copy-editor, remember?"

"So were they," he countered. "And they managed to tire of his demands within a week. If you can make it as a secretary longer than they, it will be much to your credit. If you're here because you want to be a serious journalist, then you must make him take you seriously."

"How?"

"Find your story. Write it. Push it under his nose. He'll only reject a secretary for so long. If it's a good story written with heart, eventually he won't be able to help himself and he'll have to publish it."

He gave her a last nod of the head and Kája watched as he walked away.

Though she disliked the blunt delivery, he was right. Mistake or not, if she wanted to be taken seriously, she'd have her work cut out for her. She'd have to prove her worth.

Kája exhaled and set out to find her bearings by inspecting the supplies in her drawers. She pulled one drawer out, scooting back with her chair, and noticed that the wheels had rolled over a sheet of paper at her feet. It left a line of roller marks across the center of the page, but she could see it was one of his cross-word puzzles that had floated down to the floor and landed in the shadow of the desk.

"Oh, Mr. Marshall," she called out after snatching it up, thinking to catch him before he'd gone. But in looking up she saw a sea of unfamiliar faces across the newsroom. He'd blended in somewhere, finding another desk to haunt with his smiles and opinions.

Well, she thought, and slid the sheet of paper into her top drawer. *This is the oddest office I've ever seen. Copy-editors are secretaries and war reporters are working on the crosswords.*

She sighed.

When would the world make sense again?

CHAPTER FIVE

May 22, 1940
The Daily Telegraph
Fleet Street, London

Kája turned the corner and stopped dead in her tracks when she saw the glow of a single lamp lit against the basement archives. A man sat at a long wooden work table in the center of the room with tall bookshelves and ancient ledgers all around him. His features were encased in the dim light of a table lamp.

It had been five weeks and they'd rarely spoken since her first day of employment, but she recognized him even from behind: Liam Marshall.

He'd leaned back in the wooden chair and stretched out his feet to rest upon the edge of the tabletop, casually reading the worn leather book in his hands. His hair was slightly mussed and his hand rested on his chin as if deep in thought. It surprised her then that he looked up at her quiet steps and without warning, connected his blue eyes with hers.

Kája faltered, almost dropped her armful of books, then recovered quickly by readjusting the bundle in her arms. He watched her with a half grin on his lips and took off his reading glasses. He set them on the desk.

She thought it polite to smile in greeting, so she did so, respectfully, and moved to continue on her way. Her heels clicked on the concrete floor as she hurried by.

"I see that you weren't deterred by my description of the library."

His question halted her at the bottom of the stairs.

Kája had expected him to ignore her. After all, she was about as prim and proper as a secretary could be—not flashy and flirty like most of the other office girls who leaned over the desks to admire his company. She thought for sure he wouldn't pay her any attention with her high-collared suit and long hair tightly coiffed. But it seemed she was wrong.

He was paying attention.

He'd asked her a question and she was fumbling in the awkward silence as seconds ticked by without her having issued a reply.

She turned and answered quickly, "It's not as bad as you make it sound. It is a library, if a rather humble one."

"*Humble* is a word for it. We don't get many visitors down here, except for during the drills, of course." He glanced up at the ceiling on the last words. "Some of the overnight chaps had to come down here last night, as a matter of fact."

"I know. We've been down here several times in the last few weeks, and I spent last night in the Anderson shelter behind my flat."

"I'm sorry. London's not given you much of a welcome, have we? We've had a few drills lately but that's all there is to it. Nothing to worry about." He snapped his book shut on a sigh. "On most days it's just a quiet spot for reading."

"I was just looking for a book myself." She tilted her chin down to the stack in her arms and started toward the stairs. "I'll be on my way since I found it."

"And a few others, I see." The wooden desk chair squeaked as he dropped his feet to the ground and stood up. He laid his book on the desk. "Edmunton send you down here?"

She turned, blurting out, "No. Not exactly," and had to step back lest she bump clean into him. He stood confidently close, only a few steps away from the bookshelf nearest her. "I was just doing some research."

He noticed the book in her free hand. "*Queen Victoria's Gardens.*" He arched an eyebrow in question.

"I like gardens." She shrugged. "Poppies. They're beautiful. And they remind me of home."

"Prague has an abundance of poppies?"

She nodded. "In some areas, yes. There are fields of them. They popped up, growing wild after the Great War. And they are a symbol to remember those who sacrificed everything, especially given what we could be facing now."

"Hmm. And here I'd thought flowers were synonymous with peace. Thank you for the education."

He stole a quick glance at her stack of books.

She turned slightly, hoping to take the bindings out of his view. He seemed to notice her attempt at hiding the titles and leaned in a step closer.

"It's just a bit of research." She looked down at the tips of her shoes, willing the warmth of her coloring cheeks to fade before she dared look up again.

He shook his head. "No—you misunderstand completely. You're not in trouble. You work here and everything in this archive is at your disposal."

"Thank you." Kája managed a faint smile, upturning her lips in the slightest show of cordiality.

"I only meant that I'd not have taken you for a fan of Dickens. Austen or Brontë, maybe. But Dickens can be so severe. Are you quite taken with the downtrodden, then?"

"No. But his books are well written and I like to think I can learn something from what he has to say. And seeing as the fiction section is small . . ." Her voice trailed off as she tilted her head over her shoulder to the bookshelves behind them.

"I hadn't thought anyone else noticed the size of it," he said. "Deplorable. Hardly any Shakespeare. One could forget we're in England by the looks of this place. Better off going to the libraries open to the public. They're all free, you know. But here is probably closer. I understand."

She answered softly, "Thank you," and moved to pass by.

"It's just . . ." It was the openness in his voice that stopped her. She turned. "Yes?"

"Well, I've seen you in the newsroom. You work hard. Keep to yourself. And you're a skilled editor on the stories Edmunton lets you touch. I'm afraid he has marginal respect for the professions of women outside this office," he noted, shaking his head. "Even less for the switchboard operators and secretaries he must employ within it, now that most of the men are going off to fight. I'm afraid he finds that this war hasn't been very kind to him in that regard and it colors how some might be treated."

"I may have noticed something to that effect." But she thought of the fact that Liam, a skilled reporter, was working on something as lackluster as crosswords. "And does he have respect for the reporters on the war beat or do they also find themselves assigned menial tasks?"

He smiled at her moxie, an unexpected hint of a grin that took her completely off guard.

"What do you mean by that?"

"Nothing," she said, and adjusted the stack of books in her arms, intent upon walking away. "I'm sorry to have disturbed you. I didn't expect to run into anyone down here at this time of the evening unless accompanied by air-raid sirens."

He stood tall and shrugged. "Well, some of us keep odd hours."

She muttered, "I've heard" before she could stop herself and immediately bit her bottom lip. Why had she said that?

His eyebrow arched again, but this time his face broke into an open smile.

"You've heard about me?"

"Yes. No," she said, shaking her head, embarrassment taking over. "Not you in particular. What I mean to say is—the war beat. I've been informed about the reporters in your section."

"Have you?" He crossed his arms over his chest. And kept smiling—*at her.* "And what tales have been spinning about us? All stories of gallantry, I hope. Enough to make our Churchill proud?"

"Nothing exactly. Just that you're in and out of the newsroom but you always send your stories in. You often report from the front lines now that we're at war. The hours you keep are a mystery sometimes—just as the locations you're sent are."

"Oh. Is that all? Men of mystery, are we? Sounds rather glamorous for a petty reporter. I'll have to demand Edmunton give me a raise for that added mystique. This could make a gentleman walk a little taller when all is said and done."

She paused. With a cautious tone to her voice, she added, "You must enjoy creating the crossword puzzles, then."

"Well, I admit it's not exactly hard-hitting journalism. But if one enjoys what he does, why question the assignment of it?"

Liam looked at her for a long second before he finally broke the connection.

He leaned over to a nearby bookshelf and scanned the titles with his index finger until he stopped, having found the one he was looking for. He pulled an encyclopedia from the shelf and gently placed it on the top of the stack she held in her arms.

"Here," he said and turned to gather his things. He swung a worn leather satchel over his shoulder and grabbed up the book he'd been reading. "If it's completing crosswords you're really interested in, you'll find that edition will serve you much better. But I warn you, Miss Makovský—Edmunton doesn't take to others nosing into his reporters' assignments, so to speak. Best watch your step."

"I didn't mean to question his assignments—"

"No. Of course not," he added, studying her a bit more intently. "And I suppose a good puzzle should pique the interest of any learned individual such as yourself. I must say that I've been curious as to why my submissions have been wandering off. Crosswords aren't usually interesting enough that secretaries would seek to edit them before they go to print. But I suppose I must concede that they are interesting to *you*."

Kája stood still, the wave of his statement having fully washed over her. She reminded herself not to be shocked. And certainly not to let her jaw drop on his comment. It was clear that he knew she was looking at his work. The only question was, did he know why?

"Please do put Friday's crossword in my desk when you're finished with it," he noted, and tipped the brim of a fedora down over his brow. She wasn't lost in the casualness of how he smiled as he walked toward the stairs, leaving her quite taken aback in his wake. "And douse the light when you leave. We're under blackout orders, you know."

CHAPTER SIX

Sera had stolen a quiet hour in her favorite spot at the estate. She'd melted into the den's cushy chair by the window, overlooking the span of bay waters beyond. She was reading, as she often did now, but found that churning thoughts had drawn her gaze from the pages in her hand to the span of blue outside.

The transition from a life of East Coast hurry to one of West Coast solace proved difficult in the whirlwind weeks following their wedding. Sera's gallery opening was still months away. And though she had weeks of work to get it up and running, all effort in that area of her life had seemed at least temporarily stalled. With the uncertainty swirling around William's forthcoming legal battles, they'd opted to forego a honeymoon and instead move into the estate house until their future was more certain.

The arched oak door creaked, breaking into her thoughts. Sera looked up to find William standing in the doorway with hands in the pockets of his jeans and a tired look upon his face.

"I thought I might find you here."

Sera closed the book she'd been reading and turned it over in her lap.

"Lately I'm always here."

She offered him the warmth of a smile.

He walked over to her side and dropped a kiss on her lips, then slid into the couch opposite her. Sera needed no further explanation. The weary lines etched in his forehead spoke on their own. William had news and by the looks of him, it couldn't be good.

He leaned forward, rested elbows to his knees, and exhaled. "We need to talk."

"Okay," Sera answered, her heart constricting from the weight of worry those words often bring. "What is it?"

"Well, I wish I could say the news is better."

The hold she had on the book in her hands got tighter. "Go on."

"I met with Lincoln this afternoon."

"Without me?" Sera untucked her legs and sat up straight. "William, I thought we were doing this together."

"We are. I promise you that. It came up at the spur of the moment and he was there, so I asked. I wanted the truth."

Sera nodded. *Choose your battles.* For whatever he was struggling to tell her, the last thing she wanted to do was argue over every meeting they had with the legal team.

"And?"

"I asked him to give me the run-down of what we're facing— with no frills." William reached out for her hand. He gave her fingertips a gentle squeeze before continuing. "The charges of felony grand theft and forgery carry three years apiece. The prosecutor's offered us a deal. It's about what we expected. Six years in a state prison."

"Six years for something you didn't do? I hope you told him we'd never consider it."

"Of course I did. To which he said it would be a minimum of ten if we go to trial and I'm convicted on all counts. That's with no priors."

Sera stared back, feeling shock course through her.

"Ten years. For a first offense?"

He cleared his throat. "It would seem so in this case. They tack on a penalty enhancement of four years if the property stolen is valued at more than three million dollars. And depending on the judge we get, he or she could recommend a more severe penalty than the prosecutor is asking for. Though Lincoln believes we can argue it down."

"How?"

"Well, if we plead guilty to the underlying charges, he could negotiate dismissal of the enhanced penalty and again, depending on the judge, we could get probation."

"I think I understand what you're telling me." The room felt like it was spinning. Sera took a steadying breath before continuing. "If you plead guilty, you could possibly avoid prison but not a record."

He nodded. "Looks that way."

The full weight of what they faced hadn't been real before that moment. It had only been a maybe—a distant possibility since the handcuffs had shackled his wrists. Now they sat, stone-faced and silent, as William recounted the severity of it all.

"But what can they possibly have against you? You only became CEO a couple of years ago."

"They say they have evidence that I took the money and sold the artwork out from under the company—all of it."

"But you didn't do it. How can they have evidence of something that didn't happen?"

"They have enough," he sighed. "Which ties back to an e-mail trail, bank accounts, signatures on legal documents."

Sera paused. A thought came to her in a flash, one that she hadn't wanted to entertain before. But now, as he faced at least a decade of their lives behind bars, it was worth the risk to hurt him by saying it.

"William. You don't think your grandfather had anything to do with this, do you?"

"I didn't want to think that but now"—he ran an agitated hand through his hair—"well, I'm just not sure."

"Is all of this happening because you gave your inheritance away? That was your grandfather's fortune but he gave you the choice, remember? He wanted you to live a different life—the one God had been leading you to. Surely the investors don't claim ownership to you. How can the company do this to you simply because you wanted something different? You didn't sign your life away when you agreed to take over as CEO."

"No. But they did own the artwork and the money that came in for it."

Sera pressed her fingertips to her temple and closed her eyes for a moment.

She tried to breathe. To pray, even. It was a battle to picture a way out of the mess they faced, but with eyes closed, the only thing she could see was the coldness of an empty seat across from her.

"Having second thoughts?"

Her eyes popped open and the first reaction flew without thinking: she furiously shook her head.

"Never."

"I know you didn't sign up for all this, Sera. To be humiliated in the public eye. To be the wife of a shamed man and a family who could be all but torn to shreds in a courtroom. Regardless of whether I claim innocence, the media will crucify us if they can."

"I know," Sera agreed, and slid out of the chair to kneel by his side.

"Are you sure you're ready for the possibility of it?"

"I am, because I don't care about all that."

She took hold of both of his hands and looked back at those eyes that were so stormy, so embattled with fear of the future. Sera leaned into him and with all the courage she could muster, said, "Listen to me—it's all going to be all right."

Sera could feel the insecurity growing in her midsection,

could sense the ache growing in her belly, even as the words of prayer melted over her heart.

I trust you, Lord. We trust you. I've always said I trust you, no matter what.

But this? This could be really bad.

"We are going to beat this, okay?" She took her hands and cupped the sides of his face. "I told you out there on our beach—remember? I love you and I *trust you.* That's it. That's all you need to know. The media has no place between us, okay? We'll keep the storm on the outside and you'll see; it will only push us closer together. We'll pray our way through this if it's all we can do. I'm on your side."

William took her hands from his face, cradling them in front of him.

"I'm not sure it's going to be that easy. I haven't spoken to my father in almost three years, except for when I called him for information on the painting of Adele. He had nothing to offer me then and I expect will have nothing for me now."

"But why? Why wouldn't he want to help his eldest son? Surely you can reach out to him. No child could be so lost to a parent." The questions bled from her heart out her mouth. Sera knew each family was different, of course. But a father leaving his son to face prison alone?

It wasn't possible.

Sera felt like she had ice water pumping through her veins. The shock of it all, the severity of the battle ahead, and the brokenness the family had sustained over the last several years—they had the power to steal away any future she and William might have dreamed of.

"There's more to it, Sera. More has happened that I just can't go into right now."

"With your father? I know you've been reluctant to share anything other than the fact that he walked away. I've come to know your family over this past year but where your father is concerned, everyone is tight-lipped. It's as if he ceased to exist."

Her eyes darted across his face, drinking in the pain, feeling the heartache her husband always tried to keep so protected. But to look back at his face now she could see every ounce of hurt he'd tried to bury. It came up fresh, bubbling to the surface.

"Just old ghosts." He shook his head. "They were buried with my grandfather and again when my father walked away from his family. I won't unearth them—not even to save my own skin. The past is water under the bridge and that's where it has to stay."

"But if talking about this will help in your defense, why can't you?"

"Let's just let the lawyers handle it. It's what we're paying them for."

"William, I don't understand. Are you asking me to back off?"

He sat before her, but in the instant Sera saw the cold curtain drop over his face, she had her answer. In the blink of an eye, he seemed miles away. It was the past hurt that he refused to share she feared now more than anything, for it had the power to destroy any future they might have.

What was so terrible that he couldn't trust her with it?

"William," she began, and paused to wipe the tears from her cheek. "You know I'm not a wait-and-see kind of girl. If there's something to be done, I do it. I'm not content to stand back in the shadows while the man I love faces spending ten years or more in prison."

"I know."

"But despite that, you're still asking me to sit here in this chair, day after day, and not get involved?"

He offered a nod.

"Yes, Sera. I am." William exhaled low and reached for her hand. His thumb rubbed the inside of her palm when he whispered, "I need you to promise me that you'll let it go. Allow the lawyers to do their job. I'm confident they can see this through."

"Well, forgive me, but I'm not. It's not their life at risk," she fired back. "It's ours. And I want to fight for it. I'm your partner, aren't I?"

"Of course you are. And I want you to know what your faith in me means; it's everything. You've never doubted, have you? You've never lost faith in me."

Sera licked her lips, tasting the saltiness of tears that had rolled down her cheek and gathered on them.

"I couldn't," she whispered through the softness of emotion pulling at her throat. "You know that."

"Yes. And your love means more to me right now than anything. The promise that you'll stand in my corner, no matter what—it's keeping me going. But if I can ask just one thing, *please* . . . let it be this."

It felt foreign for Sera to even consider his request.

The thought of stepping back, watching as he was poised to be handcuffed again—it terrified her. She pictured the tearful courtroom sobs of his mother and sister, the pain that would be in his brother's eyes as the shackles bound William's wrists and he was led away. She saw any future for a marriage fading and she was unable to stop it.

Nevertheless, Sera offered him a nod in agreement.

The choppy water splashed against the dock outside the window, mimicking the torrent of emotions in the room. Sera heard their wild rhythm only after she'd fallen into Will's arms, the necessity of any more words having finally slipped away completely.

They melted back on the sofa, besieged yet connected, Sera's heart bleeding as she buried her face in the crook of his neck. They didn't move for long moments. Didn't speak. Just listened.

What else was there to say?

Sera knew that the single nod of the head had told him what he needed to hear. He was content for the moment. But was she? A wave of guilt washed over Sera when she realized the truth; she'd never be able to stay out of it completely. Not when their life was on the line.

She'd have to convince him he needed her to help, one way or another.

CHAPTER SEVEN

July 5, 1940
The Dorchester Hotel
Park Lane, London

"Kája, my dear!"

A flash of glossy black hair signaled that Beatrix Bell, or Trixie as she preferred to be called, had plopped down in the exclusive club's half-moon booth. The switchboard operator's curls bounced against her shoulder as she raised her glass high, shouting over the band's riotous music.

"You have worked with us for three months now and finally managed to get out of the *Telegraph* office on a Friday night. Ladies, we must celebrate this momentous occasion! Tell us, Kája. What do we say again? If we want to bring luck tonight?"

Kája leaned forward in the icy silk dress she'd borrowed from one of the office girls and shouted back, "*Hodně štěstí!*"

Trixie beamed a winning smile and winked. "That's right, ladies. *Hodně štěstí!* Our sister from Prague wishes us good health and the best of luck! This is a toast all the way from Czechoslovakia, so let us not waste it. If you please!"

The gaggle of office girls tipped up their tumblers of wine and clinked the glasses together, chiming "*Hodně štěstí*" in unison.

"To prosperity." Eleanor, one of the sweeter switchboard operators who always hid behind her wire-rimmed glasses,

66

giggled when a flock of chaps walked by and tipped their hats to the girls' impromptu toast. She elbowed a blonde next to her. "For good measure, right, Mary?"

"And dancing!" Mary linked arms with her and beamed. "Yes, and an end to any wretched war!"

"Who wishes to talk of war? I so tire of it. All we've seen are blasted drills. And that's sure to be all we do have. Our boys will be coming home soon; mark my words. And what do we want them to find? Morose secretaries with ill dispositions and rationed hosiery? Or girls with a little *zip* about them?" Trixie rolled her eyes to the ceiling and nearly snorted over a laugh, then drew in close to the huddled girls. The electric blue of her dress accentuated the deep chocolate of her eyes. She leaned in and offered an exotic, drawn-out whisper. "Look around you, ladies. I ask you— what do you see?"

Like the rest of the girls, Kája looked over the scene.

It was an upscale nightclub, to be sure, one they'd not visited before, and was it ever hopping. Ladies danced and crooners crooned to the swing band music. Bedecked in gold and flashing like diamonds overhead, the club's chandeliers twinkled, seemingly brought to motion by the foot stomping of the club's revelers. Sequins danced in the light. Red lipstick highlighted joyful smiles. Uniformed gentlemen lit cigarettes for ladies. Tumblers were downed and then refilled in haste. And there they all sat, secretaries and switchboard operators, dressed in their finest, toasting the future just as sparkly as the rip-roaring London nightlife erupting around them.

"London's not at war! She can't be and look like this. Especially not on Park Lane. Why, that would be a sin."

Trixie tossed out a carefree smile. She slipped an arm over Kája's shoulders and leaned in close, tapping the side of their heads together in the process.

"London is dancing. She's glittering and oh so *alive!* Why,

I'd not be surprised to see our new prime minister himself walk through those doors and down a jigger or two. After all, this is one of the hottest clubs in all of London Towne"—she paused, eyeing them all playfully—"and I intend to dance through the middle of every air-raid siren from here to Buckingham Palace if it pleases me!"

It was fanciful. And over the top, but even Kája had to smile.

Though perhaps a bit misplaced, their ebony-haired friend's energy was intoxicating. For in the world of Trixie Bell, war was far removed from the glittering life of Park Lane. A fantasy perhaps, made only more romantic by the presence of uniformed officers and wealthy gentlemen who might ask them to dance. She, like some Londoners, held the impression that the prospect of war reaching Britain was quite unlikely. The world had already been at war once. Why ever would they need to do so again? Gas masks and rations were dark things, not amorous fodder for a posh and lively Saturday night.

"Do you not agree, Kája?" Trixie turned to her, arching an eyebrow in a playful manner.

"Yes, Kája, you've seen the other side of the world, haven't you? Won't you tell us what it's like under the Germans' rule?" Mary leaned in close, waiting most intently for an answer.

Kája bit her bottom lip on a smile, unable to hold it back. "Prague is the other side of the world now?"

"Well, as far as our world is—yes." Eleanor tapped a fingernail on the rim of her tumbler. "We hear that Hitler's even marched into Paris now. Can you imagine Nazis parading under the shadow of the Eiffel Tower? It's unfathomable. Paris is so full of romance and mystery. However could it be overrun by a foreign army? Do tell us, Kája, what you saw of it. Is the outlook of another war nearly as black as everyone says?"

The girls all looked in her direction and it seemed, for a split second anyway, as if the entire club had quieted and held its breath for her answer. The girls stared back, Eleanor through the glasses tipped on the edge of her nose and Mary, slight and flippant as she was, twirling a finger around one of the blond coils at her nape.

"I don't know that I'm the right person to judge the outlook of war. But for us, things began to change when the Germans came into the Sudentenland through annexation two years ago." When she saw at least one quizzical brow arch up and Mary's perpetually confused face staring back, Kája explained a little further. "It's in the borderlands where most of the German-speaking Czechs live."

"Mmm." Trixie nodded agreement. "Yes, and they rolled into your country with tanks and soldiers, all to cause a big fluff of nonsense. I wish they would just pack up their arrogance and go home."

She made a motion with her hand, as if to wave the lot of the German army off without care.

"No, Trixie. It's more than that." Eleanor tilted her chin to Kája. "Go on, Kája."

"Well," she began, and took a deep breath. Finding the words proved an arduous task. She'd not spoken of her last moments in Prague. Not to anyone. "I remember the sight of German troops moving into the city. It was spring. Still terribly cold in March. They rode in on motorbikes and cars, some in tanks even. The army marched in and the people all came out of their homes to watch."

"You didn't support them, did you?" Mary looked horrified by the prospect.

"No. Of course not. But we weren't sure what to expect. There were so many of us—stunned really—all lining the streets."

The blurred voices of passersby in the streets of Prague came alive again and whispered in her heart. She could envision the crowds. Could see the snowballs hurled through the air. The pungent smell of gasoline, the grinding of tank treads, and the roar of engines were suddenly all around her again. And she remembered how they fairly ran to the depot—she, her sister, and Jakob—through the biting cold. In her mind's eye the snow continued to cry down, floating in a soft haze all around them. Kája looked around now, overcome by the stark contrast between a glittering London club and the remembrance of that last cold, snowy day in Prague.

"Kája? Wake up," Trixie said, and snapped in front of her face. "Doll, you just took forty winks on us—and in the middle of a club, I might add!"

Kája shook her head and rolled her eyes, trying to play off the rise of memories.

Eleanor elbowed Trixie in the side softly, but quite deliberately.

"Look, you've gone and taken our sweet secretary here and given her a fright. She looks positively sick." She reached across Trixie and patted Kája's hand on the tabletop. "Dearest Kája. Don't worry. Trixie is our worldly one—yes. But she makes herself a trifle on occasion, when she doesn't know how to keep her yap out of it."

"I do no such thing." Trixie lit a cig and with a little added pomp, crossed her arms over her chest. "And Kája's not a switchboard chatterbox like us. She's a *writer*; writers are going to brood. Let's just leave it alone, then. War talk will edge up under anyone's skin. If she wants to fret over it, then we let her. Perhaps have a change of subject to something other than mad talk of Nazis and armies marching in the streets."

"And it couldn't be better timed," Mary whispered, and let out a low whistle as she inclined her head to the door. "Doll dizzy alert."

The rest of the girls followed Mary's lead and looked in the direction of the bustle past the dance floor. In had walked a group of dapper gentlemen in white dinner jackets, all dressed to the nines. They owned generous smiles and just the right amount of arrogance to turn heads all over the joint. They shook hands with several others in the club, uniformed servicemen and older gentlemen in suits who obviously knew the infamous boys from the war beat. And smack-dab in the center of the group was the ace reporter himself, Liam Marshall, wearing a heart-stopping smile as he greeted several comrades.

Kája had noticed Liam right off. She glanced across the club, only out of curiosity of course, making certain to look away before anyone noticed.

Rumor had it that he frequented the local pubs not far from Fleet Street's newspaper offices and kept the company of the other rough and tumble boys on the war beat. They were scrubby around the edges; smart London boys with sharp pens and even sharper wits, but often with raucous, pint-influenced judgment that pegged them as notorious even in Park Lane. But Liam seemed to enjoy tangling with the lot of them. Stepping out to a posh club hadn't seemed part of the persona surrounding him, until now.

"Well, well. The boys from the beat have decided to take a step up in the world." Trixie blew smoke out in a cloud in front of them and with a wink to the other girls, stood up. She snuffed out her cigarette in the ashtray on the tabletop. "I suppose that's my cue to grab a gent for the Jitterbug."

Eleanor smiled. "Which one?"

Trixie tipped her shoulders up into a pronounced shrug. "I've an idea which ones to set my sights on. If they can afford to buy me all the champagne I want off ration, then they get a dance. After all, they've got more to offer in the long run than overconfident newspapermen." She flipped her raven curls before trotting off into the crowd.

"She's a live wire, that one. Doesn't even wait for a gent to ask *her."* Mary smiled and borrowed a cigarette from Trixie's purse, then lit the end and took a long first drag. "But at least she knows what she wants. How many of us can say the same?"

Eleanor leaned in. "Think the boys will come over here and talk to us?"

"I'm not even sure they'll notice us," Kája offered, trying to keep the mood light and her interest marginal.

It seemed as though the boys had noticed their table. Mary's eyes moved from their place at the door back to the booth and after a brief pause, trained her view on Kája in particular. A sly smile pressed onto her lips.

"Well now. I'd say my question has been effectively answered. There is a good chance they will join us, given the way the ace reporter can't take his eyes off our molten-haired beauty from Prague."

The girls reacted.

Mary leaned in and Eleanor audibly gasped, whispering, "What? Kája?"

A wave of embarrassment flooded warmth into Kája's cheeks when Liam scanned the club and of all the monstrously awkward moments to do so, somehow locked eyes—with her. In being caught in her surveillance of him, she quickly looked away, diverting her attention to the surface of the tabletop instead, hoping to look only mildly curious.

Eleanor shook her head. "Kája, please don't consider it. That one has more dates thrown at him than the king of England. If you've got any smarts about you, you'll look the other way now."

"Who says I've considered anything?"

Mary, ever pragmatic, spoke up with a hopeful voice, saying, "Just give her a breath, Eleanor. She hasn't said anything yet." She paused. "Kája's got a head on her shoulders. She'd never be interested in him. Right, Kája?"

"Of course not. I barely know him. We pass each other in

the newsroom here and there, but he only speaks to me when he needs more paper or a replacement ribbon for his typewriter. He's gone most of the time anyway. And in case you can't tell by his rumored company, a prim secretary from Prague is not at all his type. How do you know he's not looking at one of you?"

Kája's hand was fused around the tumbler in her hand, though Mary still managed to reach over and gently pat her wrist in a motherly fashion.

"You're right, of course. We've all noticed the smile on that one," Eleanor said, rolling her eyes. "We know you're smarter than to tangle with that mess of a chap, no matter how handsome he thinks he is. He's all newspaper—always will be. He doesn't have time for any date more than once, I'm afraid. And I heard he's been called up anyway."

"Called up?" Mary asked, voice lifted on the question.

Eleanor nodded. "The RAF. He's reporting at the end of the month."

Kája didn't know why, but something about what her friends said didn't sit well with her. It was as if the man they all saw wasn't who he appeared. She couldn't say why exactly, but something wasn't right.

She glanced over at Liam again. He didn't notice her this time and continued in his jolly smiles and handshakes.

"Come on, Eleanor. Let's abdicate." Mary winked. "To test our theory? If we're all off dancing, maybe we'll see who asks our dear Kája to dance first. Then we'll know for sure."

Mary leaned forward, looking with an unveiled glare as Eleanor slid from the booth.

"It's well-meaning, you know—our worry. And since you're still new and Trixie's not here to say it, I will. Steer clear, Kája. If that one's noticed you at all, you'd be better off going back home to the Nazis. There's far less heartbreak to be found there."

Kája wasn't sure, though there was little time to care.

A couple of the boys from the beat were already threading their way through the crowd, heading for their table. Kája found that her friends, while well-meaning in their cautions, were less inclined to form a protective barrier around her than they were to see if they were correct in Liam's notice of her. They were quick to jump up, claim a gentleman nearby, and waltz off to the band's jazzy tunes.

Abandoned or not, Kája couldn't blame them.

The mood was light all around; she actually would have liked to dance, too, even if just to forget her troubles for one night. She'd borrowed an evening dress and Trixie had finger-waved her hair in a long cascade about her shoulders just for the occasion. She'd been primped and plucked like a princess that night. Why shouldn't she want to join them?

Aloof though the glances had been, Kája could feel each time Liam's eyes had settled upon the booth in which she sat. And now that she was alone, he seemed a bit freer with his liberties. He excused himself from the group of revelers and in less time than she had to think of what she'd say, he was in front of her, standing tall with hands in his pockets and a casual grin on his face.

"Why, Miss Makovský. Didn't expect to see you in a place like this."

"Good evening to you, too, Mr. Marshall." Kája lifted her voice over the lilting music, wondering exactly what he meant, but bit her tongue over the remark.

"And where have your friends gone off to?"

She pointed to the flashes of glittering dresses and easy smiles that permeated the dance floor. "I believe they're already dancing."

"Yes, I saw them leave you alone here." He nodded, though he made no move to leave. Instead, he slid into the booth without invitation. She scooted over a shade on principle.

"Do you dance?"

She looked up, fighting the inclination for her eyes to widen at his question.

She hadn't expected this. Her friends would never approve. What's more, alarm bells were ringing in her head.

Kája tilted her chin toward the dance floor. "I'm afraid I don't know this one."

His eyebrow arched up.

"It's a waltz," he noted, clearly speculative. "You mean to tell me you don't know the waltz? With your proper Prague upbringing?" He crossed his arms over his chest and looked down his nose to her. "I'd never believe it in a hundred years."

Kája's response wouldn't have been impressive, she knew. But she had little time to think on it. Without warning, the magic fizzled. Conversation faded and the band's instruments screeched to an off-key halt. The revelers on the dance floor froze, as did everyone else, then turned and looked about as soon as the searing call of air-raid sirens began blasting through the air.

The dance floor turned into a chaotic jumble of rushing bodies as men and women darted for the doors. The girls, having forgotten their reproach over Kája's budding interest in the office playboy, faded from view and were eaten up by the crowd. The overhead lights flickered, then went out altogether, leaving only the candlelight from individual tables, setting tiny dots aglow like stationary fireflies across the space.

Kája's heart was set to racing and she bolted a split second later, hoping to flee outside with the rest of the crowd.

She never made it to the door.

Liam was behind her, his hand authoritatively latched on to hers. He edged her back from the door gently, but with clear intention.

"Kája, this club is an air-raid shelter," he said, pulling her back. "It's just a drill, I assure you."

"You don't know that. How can you know it's just a drill?"

"Because we've had no reports of German activity anywhere near the Channel. If we had, all of London would already be in our shelters by now. If it were real, the street would be the worst possible place you could be during a raid."

"But my friends. Everyone is leaving . . ."

She looked around, searching the chaotic scene for a flash of Trixie's dress or Eleanor and Mary's bouncy curls in the mass of people rushing for the exits.

Liam halted and with a tenderness she hadn't expected, stared back in her eyes.

"And I'm sure that they'll be looked after. The boys on the beat are good chaps. They won't let anything happen to them, okay? I promise. They'll be fine."

He seemed sure of himself, like always. But this time, something different flickered in his eyes. There was no jesting. Instead, it had been replaced by a depth of care that Kája wouldn't have suspected he possessed. Their interactions had been few and she'd formed an opinion that didn't quite match the man before her. This man was noble. Almost fearless in a way she couldn't quite explain.

He made her want to trust him.

Liam gripped her hand, softly but surely, guiding her to the back of the club. He shrugged out of his dinner jacket and spread it upon the floor beneath a nearby table. He then helped her under the tabletop and placed one of the flickering sconces on the floor by her feet.

"Here. Stay put until they signal the all clear."

Suddenly afraid that she'd be alone in the middle of a bombing raid, Kája pulled at his sleeve. "But where are you going?"

"I have to help, in case it's real. I've been to bombing sites before and I've been trained in what to do. I won't go far," he promised. "I'll come back for you."

He whisked away in the dark then, melting into the throngs of the crowd.

Kája huddled on the floor, scared out of her mind, trembling like a wilted flower as the sirens cried. And though she knew Liam would return to ensure her safety, Kája was just as certain that she couldn't be there under that table when he got back. Not when he'd noticed her and made a point to pick her out above all others.

When the lights came on and it was announced as a drill, Kája slid out from under the table. With care, she folded Liam's dinner jacket and laid it in the booth, then slipped out into the night alone.

⎯

"You left the club."

Kája looked up from the pages of her book to find Liam standing at the foot of the archive library stairs, dinner jacket casually tossed over his shoulder and the bow tie dangling against his white tuxedo shirt. He leaned against the open door.

"It was just another drill, you know. You'll get used to them eventually."

She nodded, feeling exposed, hoping he couldn't guess she was fearful of spending another night in a bomb shelter surrounded by terrified people but still alone. Noticing a chill in the basement air, she pulled her black dinner coat closed around her shoulders.

"The sirens managed to sour the mood. The girls went home and I had work to do, so I came back here."

"On a Friday night, no less. I'm quite sure you are the most dedicated employee Edmunton has ever had. He'll be ecstatic when he hears of it."

Liam walked over to the table and tossed his jacket upon it, then pulled out a chair across from her. The wooden chair legs scraped against the floor as he sat down.

"You didn't miss much; most of the crowd thinned soon after. I'd say the more dedicated revelers found solace in an after-siren cocktail. At least the band still managed to keep a beat through it all."

With a sideways glance, Kája noticed that Liam looked up at the clock on the wall. She knew how late it was—nearly midnight, the last time she'd checked. She wasn't fooling him. It was ridiculous to be there at that hour.

She attempted to hide her work, edging a few sheets of paper up under the book she was reading.

"It's quiet as a tomb around here."

Kája nodded. "Yes, it is. I'll wager that doesn't happen often."

He was right, though some reporters moved about upstairs, watching the wire for news of the war. It still didn't change the fact that it was late and certainly not appropriate for them to be there alone—sitting inches apart.

Vulnerability wasn't a game she wanted to play with him, not now. Not ever. And certainly not after he'd set his sights on her at the club. Instead of giving Liam the upper hand, which she would surely have done had she chosen to look him in the eyes, Kája ignored his statement and centered her nose back in the research book beneath her fingertips.

"Found yourself on the receiving end of a late-breaking assignment, I see?"

Before she could stop him, Liam leaned forward and edged the corner of the papers out from under her book. She slid her hand over the top of the page seconds late.

"My crossword puzzle from yesterday's edition."

Kája shifted uncomfortably and pulled her work in closer.

"You really are interested in them, aren't you?"

He waited. She said nothing.

"What's the matter? You seemed a bit aloof back there at the club. And then I came back and you'd left without a word."

She offered a polite smile. "It wasn't my intention to appear that way."

He tapped his index finger on the tabletop, in what one might have judged as nonchalance. But she knew better. Liam wasn't one for mincing words—or for hiding feelings unless it suited him.

"And when I was sitting right next to you. Since you were alone at the table, I figured—what could it hurt to take a spin around the floor?"

"That was kind of you." Kája turned back to her book. "It's a shame the drill ruined the mood of the night."

"Is it?"

Despite the distance between them, Liam crossed the table and reached over quite carefully and placed his hand over hers. He left it there as the seconds ticked by on the clock behind them.

"Kája."

When she lowered her pencil so that it dropped down to the tabletop, he slid his hand away, just grazing her skin with his fingertips. Kája looked up, keenly aware that the warmth in his eyes would be the first thing she'd see.

She wasn't disappointed.

He might have been baiting her for evading his offer to dance. Or teasing, as was his general way about things. Regardless, the look he offered now was too open. Too sincere. And he'd never said her name in that way before, not without a "Miss Makovský" tacked on. To hear it now pricked her heart in the most unexpected way.

"As your co-worker, it would have been polite to stop by out of obligation. But as a friend, which I hope to be considered," he said, his gaze warm and unmoving, "I wanted to offer an *honest* hello. I'm sorry if I fumbled it, but I asked you to dance because I wanted to. No one made me. I'd think up a more clever explanation now if I thought it would fool you."

"You didn't fumble," Kája answered, tearing her eyes away to catch her breath.

"And that back there, the bashing around clubs—that persona troubles you. That's why you left?"

Kája shook her head. "No. Despite the fact that the other girls in the office tried to warn me off from being friends with the office playboy, I don't believe it's who you really are."

He paused, looking as though he wanted to say something, but thought against it and asked a more direct question.

"And who do you think I am?"

Kája thought about it for a moment, the risk of opening up to him. Had she still lived in Prague, she wouldn't even be sitting there with a gentleman alone. But Kája had changed in the last year. Leaving home had opened her eyes. Moving to London had widened them further. And now, because of how her view of things had changed, she wasn't frightened to confront him directly.

She closed her book and laid her hands upon it, giving him her full attention.

"Fine," she breathed out. She leaned in slightly and lowering her voice to a whisper, asked, "Are you a spy?"

Liam didn't flinch from her question. Instead, he looked to have anticipated it. He leaned in until they were eye to eye and searching her face, whispered back, "I believe the Yanks call them spooks."

"No matter what they're called—I think you are one."

"And do I look like a spy to you, Miss Makovský?"

"I hate to puff up an already arrogant peacock, but I have reason to believe that you and your typewriter may be involved with British intelligence. Working with exiled governments in London, perhaps, or carrying out operations overseas. And you're sending codes out, right here in this newspaper."

"May I?" he asked, and reached for her book.

Kája nodded agreement. He slid the book out from under her hands and lifted the sheets of paper from beneath it. Liam scanned the pages, then dropped them on the table and reclined back in his chair.

"And here I thought you were just another pretty face."

In spite of herself, Kája fought back the shadow of a smile.

"Journalists don't just happen across British intelligence codes hidden in crossword puzzles. Unless they put them there themselves."

"And secretaries don't complete crossword puzzles like this."

"This one does." She tipped her chin up in defiance.

"How long did it take you?"

"I don't know. Ten minutes, maybe. Why?" she added, staring back at his reclined form.

"No reason." He may have brushed it off, but the look on his face had changed. He seemed more intent somehow. More focused.

"You travel more than any other crossword creator I've ever heard of."

"It's war time, Kája. Every man is traveling right now, including me. I am assigned to the war beat, or have you forgotten? I'm not immune to serving my country."

"And yet you never appear in uniform. I think you don't, because you can't—being undercover."

Liam leaned forward again but this time, allowed the front legs of his chair to connect hard against the floor. Seriousness flashed in his eyes and he met her glare head-on.

Kája wasn't put off by the change of temperature in the room. In fact, the plan had worked. Her attempt to prick the edges of his temper had drawn the earnestness out of him, enough anyway that she thought he might actually tell her the truth.

"You also speak German," she said, her breath hitched on a gentle pause. "But you pretend that you don't."

"And how have you come to that conclusion?"

A soft sigh escaped her lips.

"Have you forgotten when that informant came to the *Telegraph* office last month? He was from Berlin and you greeted him. Quietly, but I heard you. They may have whisked the pair of you into a private office but I was standing by, doing Edmunton's mindless filing in the cabinets. From there, I heard all I needed to. In fact, you have a knack for languages. And codes, according to this hidden message telling anyone who deciphers it to contact the paper." She held up the crossword puzzle before him. "Why Edmunton would employ you in writing the crossword puzzles with your skills is beyond me."

"Are you accusing us of something?"

The directness in his tone was a bit out of character. It didn't hold the usual hint of a smile one would have expected from him. He was more intent now. His words carefully chosen, with the true depth of his interest just held at bay.

"Other than the fact that you're not covering your tracks very well? Not a thing. But since you're so keen on advice, here's some for you: you might want to come up with a better story if you want to fool anyone other than your grandmother about what you're doing."

"You don't know what you're talking about."

"Liam, I heard you've been called into the RAF, yet I know the quality of your eyesight. I think that's why you read down here, to stay out of sight in your glasses. That gives doubt to your pilot story altogether; they couldn't pass you as a flyer. And articles are sent to *The Telegraph* written by a mysterious journalist who remains nameless, only he is privy to quite sensitive information. Information that only His Majesty's intelligence service would know. Those articles are printed under Edmunton's name, are they not? And being his secretary, I've seen more than one piece of paper come across his desk with the name *Bletchley* on it—though he tries to keep those in his locked filing cabinet. So I think all this has to do with more than writing stories for the newspaper. In fact, you're always asking me to change the ribbon in your prized Remington, but I submit that I've never actually seen you use that typewriter. *Not once.*"

"Is that so?" Liam hesitated, but only briefly.

"Where do you go all the time? You're not writing here in this office, so you must be doing it somewhere else."

Evading her question entirely, he noted, "This office doesn't have the monopoly on typewriters."

"Regardless, all the facts point to it. You're not who you say you are, Liam Marshall. There's something going on here and I want to know what it is."

Liam looked back at her, with shoulders squared and glare direct, and did the one thing she'd have never expected: he smiled. Any shred of irritation melted away and he let loose a wide-toothed grin that melted over his face and would have stopped the heart of every other secretary in the office.

"Miss me, did you?"

"What?" Her forehead crinkled on its own.

"Admit it," he ordered, the grin happily plastered across his face. "All those times I've been gone. You missed seeing me around here."

Insufferable. The man was insufferable to no end. "I said all of that and 'You missed me' is what you took from it?"

"I think you have an overactive imagination."

"Not quite."

He held up his hands in mock surrender. "No, no. I don't judge you for it. I've known far too many journalists and their mannerisms to find fault in yours. You're a writer; all writers are afflicted with the gift of story, whether it's imagined or not."

"I haven't imagined anything." Her shoulders tipped up in a shrug and she added, "I just wondered what you're hiding, that's all."

"Why do I have to be hiding anything? War doesn't run on one of your schedules, Kája."

His barb struck a target he couldn't have known existed. Guilt and fear—the constant companions that had been shut up in the recesses of her heart—they nudged her to remember the face of war she'd already seen. The image of her parents came back, shattered by loss on the train platform. She pictured them now with darkness marring their silhouette and the Nazi regime hovering close by like a bloodthirsty overlord.

Regret latched on, dictating her thoughts.

"I know that," she whispered, the words fighting their way to the surface even as she refused to look up at him. "I found out well enough when I had to leave half of my family back in Nazi-occupied Prague."

It was the first time she'd ever spoken of it, had ever come close to speaking of who she really was to anyone in London. And now, just like her inquisition of him, part of Kája's story was out on the table.

She chanced looking up at him. Not with her head, just with her eyes. They met over the table. And instead of teasing, his eyes offered something else entirely: openness.

The sincerity was something she hadn't expected from him. She knew it was rare. To see it now was something she couldn't refuse to acknowledge. It prompted her to continue.

"I told you. I have no family here in England. Remember? That first day in the office, you asked after them. I fled to Palestine with my sister and her husband. But things are not much better there. And our parents," she admitted, swallowing hard. "They were left behind in Prague."

"Why?"

"We had no choice. Or rather, they made the choice to get their daughters out while they still could. It was our last chance. The Nazis marched in and we ran out." Auburn waves fell over her shoulder and she brushed them back, even shrugging slightly as she tried to play off the tears that were glazing her eyes. "You see . . . I'm half Jewish."

In a world such as theirs, she knew what it meant. And so did he. Concern marred his brow.

"You were running for your life." He tilted his head to the side, ever so slightly. "And that's why you're here? Because it's safer for you."

She wiped at her eyes. "I shouldn't have said anything. I'm sorry to have brought you into my troubles."

"Everyone in London has troubles." Liam opened his hands palms up and laid them on the table in front of him. "But what if I told you I was an open book? Since you've stuck your pretty little nose in further than anyone has a right to, you should know that I might have explained myself had you simply thought to *ask*."

Liam didn't say anything else for a moment. His gaze was soft and unassuming. It fluttered her heart in such a way that she wondered if he had a notion to kiss her. It wasn't unlike him to fly on the wings of the moment, no matter what was happening in the world around him.

Kája pushed back the feeling of the nervous pit growing in her midsection.

"I didn't know you well enough to do so. No one does."

"And an exchange of wits is the only way to pull civility out of me?" He leaned back, eyebrows tilted up in question. "Classic. The occupational hazards of espionage do sink deep into one's character."

"No," she answered. "I hadn't thought to trade wits. And I didn't set out to investigate behind your back. You dropped a crossword under my desk weeks ago and I should have said something then. I'm sorry. I just didn't know you."

He sighed.

"Well, I'm here. Sitting in front of you. What would you say to me now?"

"That we all have things that remain hidden. Things we're not able to reveal." She paused, choosing her words. "My father used to say that all of time is set to a clock—God's clock. We're given so much of it from sunrise to sunset each day. And it's in God's will that time continues to move. He watches over all of us, wherever we should go. He's watching over my people in Prague and the people here in London, Liam, even as we spend nights in bomb shelters. And especially when fear overrides our feeling of safety."

Kája had said his name softly, with feeling she hadn't expected, and he seemed to respond to it. Something in his face changed. And his shoulders eased—melting away the defensiveness, signaling her permission to continue.

"You're a part of that. I saw something in you tonight that I'm not sure you give others the chance to see. It wasn't about chasing adventure. You truly cared about the people in that club, didn't you? There was no way to know it was a drill and yet, you ran toward danger. You put others before yourself. And when you step out in the thick of battle and send your stories back, you're printing words that give people hope. All of us are walking around with gas masks, but it's some of the words in this paper that keep us going."

"I have no virtues even close to that measure of praise," he began. "Drills are just practice. But the news is serious enough. Talk of war and men going off to fight and die in it—that's serious business. And in my own way"—he sighed on the words—"I suppose that's how I deal with it—work. Clubs? Dancing? They're just diversions. It's tricky business, living up to others' standards when you're hiding secrets of your own. But you already know all of mine, don't you?"

"I'm not sure I do."

"Of course. Being Edmunton's secretary means you would become privy to the innermost details of his work. But I had to ensure we could trust you first." He tapped his finger against the crossword puzzle on the table. "It's a tactic for Bletchley Park, the code-breaking center for His Majesty's intelligence. A recruitment test. If anyone can complete it in twelve minutes or less, they qualify."

Kája looked down at the crossword she'd completed without knowing what weight the action had carried. She'd found patterns but only held it as a theory. Now she knew there was truth to it.

"And that's your job, then? The secret recruitment of government agents through the newspaper?"

"Partly. But not so secret anymore, except from everyone else in this office." Liam ran his fingers through his hair and smiled, as if giving up. "And by the way, I use journals."

"What?"

"I've written in journals since I was a boy. The Remington is a beautiful piece of machinery, but I have always preferred putting real pencil to paper."

"Me too." Kája returned his openness with a gentle smile. "I've even kept a journal here in London."

"So I suppose I owe you an apology for making you change so many typewriter ribbons. Edmunton thought it would prevent others from asking too many questions, so we kept up the practice as a ruse." He shared a boyish smile. "I don't think he bargained on hiring someone like you."

She felt warmth blush her cheeks at his praise. "So Edmunton is working for Bletchley Park too?"

Liam shook his head. "No, but he's allowed them to keep me here and to use the newspaper for recruiting purposes. It's why I'm given leeway, so to speak, with the hours I keep around here."

"Are any of the others boys on the beat involved?"

Liam didn't answer.

Seconds ticked by on the wall clock, accentuating the silence between them then. It was getting late. Kája wondered what he was thinking, why he stopped short of telling her more.

"May I see you home?"

His question was a surprise, but she tried not to show it.

"I have a little more work to do first," she said, offering a soft smile. She lifted the edge of her book from the table. "If that's all right. Though not on the crossword."

"That would be fine with me. I'll wait."

He stood and walked over to a bookshelf in the back. She heard his steps approach a moment later and the chair scraped the floor when he sat across from her once again.

Liam held up the book in his hands.

"I thought I'd see what the grand fuss is all about."

Kája returned his smile, offering a soft laugh to go with it. "You may not like Dickens, seeing as he's quite taken with the downtrodden."

He allowed his mouth to tip up in a casual smile as he took reading glasses from his jacket pocket and slipped them on the bridge of his nose.

"Then I suppose I'm most fortunate he's not the only one."

CHAPTER EIGHT

September 7, 1940

East End, London

Air-raid sirens screamed in the background.

"Liam? It's just a drill, right? It must be another false alarm."

Liam's grip on her shoulder was steady, fusing her back up against the brick-walled building behind them. His eyes scanned the late-afternoon sky between the downtown shops.

"I don't think so. Not this time."

"But how can you be sure?" Kája whispered, and joined him in the surveillance of the sky above them, knotting her hands as she looked up into the cascade of soft blue.

There was nothing out of the ordinary about this afternoon.

It was an unseasonably warm Saturday. The sun beat down, baking the city in a heat reminiscent of high summer. Kája had woven her hair back in a loosely braided coil at her nape and wore a light, belted sundress of black-and-white pin-dot, all to stay cool as the mercury rose.

The heat looked to be the biggest story maker of the day, at least until the sirens began to wail behind them. But it still meant next to nothing—there had been far too many false alarms over the past months to worry now. Everyone had become almost immune. There was no need to panic.

At least they thought there'd been none.

Now the people, the buildings, even the very air around them felt laden with anticipation. It was as if time had been paused somehow, as if all of London were holding its breath.

Liam shook his head, still scanning the sky.

"Something doesn't feel right."

"What doesn't feel right?"

Kája looked up with him just as a series of loud pulses boomed in the background.

Intense pressure rushed in from somewhere, almost as if the heat had managed to crawl beneath her skin and push from the inside out. She stood breathless, darting her eyes from the sky back and forth to Liam's form in front of her. Her ears popped with another release of pressure from somewhere behind them.

"Liam," she whispered, her fists knotted together. "What was that?"

There were still people hurrying along on the streets, passing them without a second glance. If it hadn't been for Liam's quick hands pulling her to the cover of the alley, she might have kept strolling along through the flower market with them. But now, in the midst of their Saturday-afternoon walk to buy flowers, everything had changed.

He had changed.

Right before her eyes, Liam had transformed into the fearless reporter she'd imagined him to be when out on assignment. She could see it in the calculating movements of his eyes, the firm set to his jaw, and the agile hold to his stance; he looked ready to spring at any threat.

It unnerved her that he was so quiet.

"Liam?"

"Shh." He gave the command with a finger to his pursed lips and an almost inaudible puff of exhaled breath. Still his eyes scanned overhead, his body blocking her from seeing much of the activity in the streets.

The sirens screamed louder then. Closer. Echoing off the brick with a shrill wail that set her heart to racing. The crying sound made Kája want to ball up her fists and cover her ears with the agony of the panic it could generate. It screeched into the bottom layer of her subconscious, echoing the fear that at any moment, great iron-bellied beasts could be ripping through the sky with bombs aimed at their heads.

They'd heard the earsplitting sirens before, many times. They'd prepared for attacks by ducking into air-raid shelters, even by clamoring under desks at *The Daily Telegraph* office one particularly scary morning. Everyone in London had prepared. Hitler had been bombing air fields and military targets for nearly two months, so the city was on edge. But even so, it just didn't seem likely that it could ever happen—not in the heart of London.

To be safe, the boys on the beat had taken to escorting the ladies home from the office, for fear that the drills would become a reality. But who'd have thought it would threaten them on a Saturday-afternoon walk to the East End flower markets?

Kája stood with her back to the bricks, barely breathing.

Liam's nearness gave her a sense of solidarity, that at the very least he'd know what to do if the worst happened. When he noticed that his hand was clenched tight around the shoulder of her dress, he looked at it, released her, and allowed the tense lines in his face to ease.

He offered the oh-so-soft caress of a look that in the moment did nothing to calm the speed of her already racing heart.

"Did I hurt you?" His tone was heavy, weighted by seriousness.

Kája met his glance and shook her head through the urgent screaming of sirens.

"No." The tension was so thick, she could barely talk. She had to fight for the one-word answer that tumbled out.

People scurried in the background, their voices feeding into a nervous hum of shouts and chatter as frightened onlookers poured out into the streets. Car horns honked, crowds gathered. The streaming voices of operators could be heard over loudspeakers, directing people to proceed to the nearest shelter. Children cried out somewhere behind them as nervous Londoners picked up their speed and suddenly began running by.

Liam asked again, louder this time, with a directness that demanded an audible answer.

"Kája? You're all right? Yes? I didn't hurt you?"

She stared back, her eyes never breaking the connection with his.

Usually his nearness would have given her strength. But with those few words, her heart now beat wildly, thumping as if it demanded to break free from the confines of her chest. It made her knees feel weak, warning her she could drop at any second.

A shuddered breath escaped her lips. "No. You didn't hurt me."

"Good."

His hand rose up and the softness of his palm met the heat of the skin at the back of her neck. He pulled her close. Fast. In a sudden kiss that she hadn't time to process. As London threatened to explode around them, with sirens alive in the background and instability drawing a curtain down over the city, Kája sank deep into the shelter of his arms.

It was the audaciousness in him that drew her. The connection she needed in that moment. For something solid and alive. She relished giving in to a longed-for kiss from him and closed her eyes. She dropped her purse and wound her arms around his neck, melting into the brick behind her back.

"Liam!" A fervent voice behind them broke their momentary connection.

He drew away, still looking in her eyes, pupils darting slightly and shoulders raising with each indrawn breath. His arms dropped to his sides and he edged back.

"Liam." A short lad in a white dirt-smudged oxford ran up. "There you are!"

Kája recognized Dory Sills, the war beat's scrappy writer nicknamed Smalls because of his short stature, even shorter fuse, and rather high-pitched voice that took to squeaking when he was riled.

Either he hadn't seen the pair in each other's arms or he chose not to comment on it. She bowed her head and ran fingertips around her lips, hoping the soft red of her lipstick wasn't mussed. She tried to remind herself that the man had probably seen many a secretary in Liam's arms and almost immediately chided herself for being so reckless as to allow him to kiss her, and she to kiss him back in return.

Smalls ignored what he may have just seen and paused, hopping about as if his shoes were on fire.

"It's happening everywhere. Coming in on the wire, it is—from the Fire Brigade. I called in to the *Telegraph* as soon as I heard. Got the scoop on it. There's minor damage all over—shops and such missing roof tiles, small craters in roadways—that sort of business. But Harford Street's had a three-story building knocked flat. They haven't reported any casualties yet but we might expect some. A church is heavily damaged in Brockley and I hear tell there's shrapnel raining down over on Brownhill Road."

The ferocity with which he tossed out updates on what was happening around the city made Smalls sound like a mouse with its tail caught in a trap. Knowing what she did about Liam's activities with British intelligence, she knew these reports had the power to change everything.

Liam's eyes narrowed. "The Luftwaffe has bombed residential areas?"

"Looks like it. Along with the industrial ones. Woolrich has just been hit pretty hard." The confirmation of bombs falling on innocent citizens sent her closer to Liam's side.

"The Royal Arsenal?"

"Aye. All but demolished."

Liam took an authoritative step toward Smalls. "And the Royal Dockyard?"

"Fire-bombed, mate." He exhaled, looking to the ground, seeming especially sorry for the last bit of news. "Along with Surrey."

"Surrey docks?" Liam hissed, frightening Kája even more. "You can't be serious."

"Look there. Timber yards on fire," Smalls said, and pulled him out to the side of the street to point over the span of red brick buildings, in the direction of the Thames. "Still going on."

Giant plumes of black smoke, choking and curling up to the tips of the powder-blue sky, marked the horizon. The tops of the buildings created a ghostly outline against the billowing cloud of black and a mountain of roaring orange and yellow, the snake-like flames licking upward in an evil trail of destruction.

"It doesn't look real, eh? But it 'tis, all of it. Burning like hell's on fire down there." Smalls motioned to a high point along the horizon. "The lumber yards were stocked. Everything's ablaze. Factories. Docks. Anything that will hold a spark's gone up. Gas lines broke and fire's gone out of control. I heard tell that even our East End rats are running from it." He started hopping again, each lifted foot taking him inches closer to the inferno. "Throwing themselves down into the water, they are. Miserable creatures drowning under oil slicks that have caught fire on the surface."

The roar of fire engines blared out then, punctuating Smalls's frenzied words.

"Well, there they go," he echoed as a fire engine roared past.

"Looks like the bells have gone down—all the fire chaps are being called out. A group of us are headed down to see if we can help, and I knew I'd find you down at the markets today so I came to fetch you straightaway."

An odd whirring beyond the pulse of activity drew Kája's attention.

She looked up and in a rush of horror saw them: giant black birds in the expanse of blue overhead. Bold flocks of hundreds it seemed, hovering above them in formation, darting through the clouds of smoke as if weaving a horrid death dance in the sky.

Kája's hand flew up to cover her mouth. "Dear God . . ." She pointed to the swarm of planes overhead. "Liam, look!"

They stared up at the sky in unison—she, with shuddering breaths of terror, and Liam, with a terse set to his jaw that made her wonder if he was breathing at all. He looked about as angry as she'd ever seen him.

The planes dropped black specks—bombs. And not just one or two. Kája's body trembled with each load that was released. Over and over, down they fell, chasing every soul in London like the pitter-patter of raindrops from the sky. And though the sight alone would have been terrifying enough, the sound of falling bombs—the odd screeches and shrill whistles that sounded almost otherworldly, and the dreadful crashes and booms that followed—fairly stopped her heart.

"Come on, Marshall." Smalls waved his hands wildly. "We've got to go. The docks, eh? The Germans have bombed sites all over the city! We've got to report on it."

"Not now. I can't just leave—"

Liam looked to Kája.

A curtain of darkness had fallen over his face; it was unmistakable. His eyes that were always so soft and open when they greeted her had turned hard. Cold. Somehow they'd grown almost as black as the smoke swirling into the sky above them.

"Go," she urged him with a gentle press of the shoulder. "I know you have to. I'll be okay."

"You hear that?" Smalls danced forward a few steps. He craned his neck toward the bustle of chaotic activity down the street. "She'll be fine. Makovský here is sturdy and smart; she can take care of herself. Come on, mate!"

Liam ignored Smalls and gazed into Kája's eyes, not breaking the connection. He shook his head and took a measured step closer to her.

"No. I'm not leaving you."

Kája pushed him back slightly, with a light touch to his upper arm.

"There must be a shelter near here. I'll be looked after. *Go.*"

He shook his head again, in a firm denial.

"Kája. It's not the reporting," he tore out, a harshness in his voice. He swept his hands through his hair, agitation evident in the action. "I need you to know that I would never leave you. Even if I have a duty beyond myself . . . you know I couldn't just abandon you here."

She nodded. "I know that. But you needn't worry about me. I understand who you are and why you have to go."

The sirens continued, this time directly behind them, with deafening cries from the crowds to punctuate the fear that had been so quick to overtake them. Children howled out in the street, the sound more terrifying than the pulse of frequent booms in the distance. A piercing whistle tore through the sky behind them—were the bombs getting closer?

God, help us.

A loud burst of energy shook the building behind them. First a loud boom, then another. And another. Kája caught a shrill scream in her throat as Liam grabbed her round the waist and knelt to cover her, dust and dirt floating down to curtain them with each fresh blast.

A pile of bricks splintered the sky not far down the street in front of them. She could hear their harsh patter as they rained down upon the pavement.

Liam looked up at Smalls then, who had taken cover by crouching against the side of the building nearest them.

"Go. I'll catch up." He waved Smalls to take off in the direction of the Thames.

"'Twas luck, mate," he shouted back, referring to the bombs that had just pounded barely a street over. "Won't be that way for long. Looks like this whole area's going to be under fire before nightfall—if the flames don't catch us first. Best to get her under cover!"

"I'll be there as soon as I can," Liam shouted to the young reporter, who didn't wait.

Smalls nodded understanding, then skipped forward on his jittery feet and ran in the direction of the smoke plumes, looking up at the sky as debris continued to fall.

Liam turned to Kája and grabbed her shoulders.

"I promise—I'll get you to safety," he shouted over the roar of the sirens in the background. "There's an ARP shelter on Columbia Road. It's not far. I know they'll take you in. You'll be safe there for the night, if need be. It's properly outfitted to care for hundreds."

Kája looked around, the full weight of the carnage nearly shocking her clean out of her shoes. Her hair had come loose in half-braided waves, with tendrils that breezed about the back of her neck. She was conscious of the gentle caress but able to focus on little else and found herself mumbling, not even sure of the words coming out of her mouth.

"I need to go home to my flat. My neighbors . . ."

"Kája, the Germans are bombing us out. Do you hear me? You might not have a flat left. And I can't take the chance of you running all over the city with bombs falling down. Do you understand me? I need to know you're safe or I can't go."

Even as her body began trembling, Kája nodded, feeling a surge of energy as she looked around. She heard cries and the whirring of fire engines somewhere in the distance, felt the pungent smoke burn the inside of her nostrils with each painfully indrawn breath.

"My neighbors. They own the building. They're good people. Kind to all of us . . . They'll be terrified."

She shook her head, willing reality to fade to the back of her mind so she could focus on what she needed to do. Columbia Road was the nearest ARP shelter? It had to be safer than those tiny Anderson shelters half buried in the ground behind their building. Perhaps if she could get back there . . . convince them to come with her to the larger shelter . . .

"No. I have to find out if they're okay."

Liam patted a hand to her cheek.

"Kája?"

Her eyes flitted about, darting from the sight of fallen buildings to the crowds running for cover as the roaring of engines filled the sky. She tried to focus—Liam was saying something, wasn't he? His eyes were searching, the side of his face now smudged with dirt.

"Did you hear me?"

"Yes," Kája answered, her mind still darting from one thought to the next. "There's a shelter on Columbia Road."

"Look at me." Liam cupped her face in his hands, forcing her eyes to make solid contact with his. "I know you want to help, but it's time to go. You can't go back to your flat now. Do you understand?"

Kája nodded, then shifted her eyes over to a bustle of activity over his shoulder. She looked up the street. A hole had swallowed a bus in a tangled mess of concrete and twisted steel, with bricks strewn and smoke rising from the crater. Men and women blackened with soot had run to the site and were digging through rubble with their bare hands.

People were crying, shouting, pulling at piles of debris that had spilled into the street before them.

Liam pulled her attention back to focus on his eyes. "We'll get you out of here. We're going someplace safe."

All Kája could think of as Liam led them along the street was that her parents had sent her away when things had begun to turn bad for the Jews in Prague. They wanted her safe and had risked everything for it. Did they know that in this moment, their daughter was smack-dab in the center of the most dangerous place in the world?

———

Kája choked when she tried to breathe.

The overpowering smoke burned her nose and tortured her lungs for attempting to take in fresh air. She tried to open her eyes but when she did, everything around her was still a haze of darkness.

"Hello?" she cried out, unsure whether anyone would be there to answer her.

Kája's ears refused to stop ringing. She pounded a fist to the side of her head, trying to jar her senses awake. The effort did little, except to emphasize that her ability to hear had been all but completely cut off. With shaking hands, she ran her fingers across her temples and down over her ears, willing them to work. Her fingers met with a hot, sticky mess that warmed the left side of her cheek and neck.

She faltered and stumbled about on her feet. She tripped over something and instinctively looked down. It was a form—still and heavy—marring her path. A person sleeping? Had a bench overturned in the night?

Kája fell back against a wall, wondering where she was.

She remembered the bombs of the afternoon before, when

they'd taken cover at the market and Liam had left her in the safety of the Columbia Road shelter. It was well known and close. He'd promised to come back for her after he'd gone to help at the docks. But hadn't that been hours ago?

A lull in the sirens had signaled the all-clear later that evening but she couldn't leave; she'd promised to stay until he came back for her. But when the sirens had started their fervent cries again two hours later, she'd been shut up in the market shelter with hundreds of other terrified strangers, all miserable as they tried to endure the sirens' wails through the night.

Kája had meant to nap only for a few moments, knowing Liam would surely come for her soon. But she'd been jarred from a heavy sleep and remembrance was slow in coming back.

Where was he now? And why was everything so blurry, the edge of her mind so scattered?

The surroundings bled into focus and finally she heard something discernable: wretched wailing. The muddled sounds in the large shelter faded back into her consciousness until she could deny the smoke and carnage no more.

Had they been hit?

Oh God . . . what is happening?

Men—grown men—cried.

There was coughing everywhere. Choking and sputtering. Kája looked around, the momentary lapse into tunnel-vision now easing her eyes into focus on the chaos of the horrific scene. The air was clouded with smoke and ash. Soot-covered figures darted before her. She glanced up and saw, with the little light there was, that the shelter lanterns still hung from the ceiling above her. Their glass hurricanes were broken and swinging from their wires. Any light they might have offered had been snuffed out.

"Over here!" She heard the sound of a man's screams and turned toward the sound. "We need a doctor!"

Those nearby shouts were followed by the sound of high-pitched police whistles. And crying. More wailing and groans. From somewhere near her, she heard a woman's sobbing cries. She turned to find her only steps away, weeping as she held a child to her chest, her arms wrapped tightly around the lifeless bundle as if every bit of her world had been shattered.

It was too much.

Kája's legs gave out and she fell back, hard, almost bouncing against the wall until her knees pounded down to the concrete floor. She choked again, unsure if she was even still breathing or if smoke had permanently charred her lungs. Her chest seared with pain as she fumbled about on all fours, grasping out in the thick air.

"Please." She didn't know what she was asking or who'd be there to help her, but she coughed out the words anyway. Her lips trembled as she tried to form words. "God . . . help me . . ."

Hands were on her then.

Firm, forcing hands. They patted her cheek and she tried to focus, but couldn't. They pushed her down to the ground, frightening her, trying to force her to lie down. She slapped back at them, for they came from faceless beings, sending her into a frenzy to get away.

"Miss? Can you hear me?" The man's voice sounded frantic, the thick cockney echoing from somewhere directly above her. "I need you to calm down now." A hand brushed over her forehead, easing her back to the hard ground. "Just lie back . . . that's it. Good. You're going to be all right now, miss."

Kája was being praised for ceasing to fight. That much she knew. But as to who spoke to her and why—nothing was clear.

"This one's hurt bad."

Are they talking about me?

No. It couldn't be.

Kája shook her head, fighting the inclination to wake up out of the momentary dream world. Another voice, a louder one, shouted, "You there! Bring that lantern over here. And be smart about it!"

Kája felt something pressing hard against her temple, causing a sting of pain to pierce the side of her jaw. She shuddered and gasped out, wishing she could scream, but her lungs refused to allow it. She fought as hard as she could, swinging fists out in the air, trying to push the intense pressure away.

Her hands were caught and lowered. Her left arm was numb and surprisingly, she could discern that it felt ice cold. An odd sense of pressure came down on it too.

"You with the lantern—over here," she heard the man yell. "Yes. That's good. Hold it right like that. So we can see her face. She's got a shrapnel wound to the head—that much I can tell. But everything else is so covered in blood and soot—"

"Golly." A man coughed. "Would you look at her arm?"

Kája heard something then—a muffled cry maybe? A voice she recognized? The whispers of men mingled in with the deafening sounds all around her. She tried to speak, to ask whose voice it was that spoke over her, but lay back in a fit of coughing.

"You know this girl?" the cockney man asked someone.

Kája could discern nothing after that, nothing certain. If someone did recognize her, they must have nodded, for she heard nothing else. Her eyes drifted closed, flitting against the muddled forms kneeling over her, and she felt herself being lulled into the welcome blackness of sleep. No use fighting. The pressure on her limbs felt all consuming, the cold creeping up her arm and pulling her away.

"Kája." She heard a steady voice take charge, felt the unexpected warmth of a hand brushing over the side of her head. "Stay with me. You hear me?"

Something patted her cheek.

"Keep your eyes open," the voice said, and then, "Look at me."

She heard the chink of metal, then the voice ordered someone, "Here. Take my belt."

A pause. More blackness inviting her to drift away, and she gave herself up to it.

"Wrap it tight around her arm before she bleeds to death."

CHAPTER NINE

"When did we get so much stuff?"

Penny tossed a book in a nearby donation box, its sound echoing off the tall ceilings of the downtown loft.

"My question would be: Why did we ship all of this junk from New York to California if we were just going to get rid of half of it?" Sera plopped down into a wing-back chair next to her friend, who was struggling to stand from a long-kneeling position. She handed her a chilled sparkling water. "Here. Let's take a break."

"You're an angel." Penny took it and fell into a nearby sofa. She ran the coolness of the bottle over her forehead before taking a drink. "But only because I think I'd pass out from another second of working in this loft. Who'd have thought that such a large space could be so stuffy?"

"And everyone says San Francisco is cool in summer. Guess we caught a rare heat wave right inside this loft," Sera answered, looking around at the mountain of crates, unpacked boxes, and tarp-covered furniture that occupied every inch of the space. "At least we can survive by opening the windows."

"If you say so, fearless leader."

"Stop that!" Sera tossed a dust cloth at her friend and laughed. "You're no longer in my employ. I'm not anybody's leader. That means you're a friend—plain and simple."

"Hmm . . . if I'm no longer in your employ, then why do I find myself in a downtown gallery unpacking about a thousand boxes of your stuff? Do all friends do that sort of thing?"

"Only the best ones." Sera grinned. "I can't thank you enough for flying back out here."

"Any chance for a new adventure is enough for me."

Sera arched any eyebrow. "Is that an homage to your decision to go back to school instead of finding another gallery position right away?"

"You could say that. Guess I'll be waitressing again while I put myself through more academic torture." Penny laughed and absentmindedly ran her hand over the softness of the baby-blue sofa beneath her. "So, since when does a modern art gallery have French-inspired nail-head sofas?"

She looked around the loft, scanning the boxes and wares that were strewn around.

"It looks like a Pottery Barn catalog up here."

"That was an impulse buy."

"Yeah? And the chair too?"

Sera ran her hand over the arm of her chair and nodded. "Yep. The chair too."

"And what about those curtains over there?"

The loft had beautiful floor-to-ceiling windows overlooking the street. They'd opened all of them and let the summer breeze flow in. It sent waves of motion through the length of the white gauze curtains, giving the space a homey feel that hadn't been there before.

Penny paused, then picked up an orange-and-white trellis pillow and hugged it in her lap. She raised an eyebrow.

Sera shrugged.

"Well, it looks so good you could actually move in here." Penny laughed, obviously making a lighthearted comment.

Sera looked away to the windows for a moment, hoping an answer might present itself.

"Wait a minute—you're not planning to move in here?" Penny's nonchalance turned to concern in the blink of an eye. She bolted upright, swinging her legs down to the floor.

"Of course not."

"Then why . . . ?"

"Penn—I just bought a few things from the furniture store. It's no big deal."

"When you have an estate house full of furniture and a husband waiting for you at home, I think it is kind of a big deal."

Sera shrugged off the comment.

"Does William know about this?"

"He's got enough on his mind."

"That's not an answer. Sera, what in heaven's name is going on?"

She hadn't wanted to mention anything. But then, Penny had a way of reading her thoughts at the most inopportune times, and in the most in-depth of ways. She could feel her friend's eyes zeroing in on her, searching her face for any inkling of what had been brewing in her heart for weeks.

"Nothing." Sera shook her head. She willed the tears not to sneak out the corners of her eyes, though they burned in protest.

"Will's got enough going on right now without adding me to the mix."

"Sweetheart." Penny set her bottle on the hardwood floor and leaned in to face her friend. "You're his wife. I think that makes you the mix."

"I just thought with the gallery opening in a couple of months I might need to spend a lot more of my time here. And if that's the case, I should have something to sit on."

Penny eyed her. "And did you buy something to sleep on too?"

Sera didn't need to answer. But then again, Sera knew whatever had been fluttering around in her heart would eventually find its way to her face. It always did.

She looked away.

"You're moving out?"

"No!" Sera shot up from the chair. Her hands needed something, anything to do. She walked over to the fireplace mantle and ran a cloth over its top, stirring a bit of long-settled dust in her haste to avoid opening up about her fears.

She could feel Penny's stare from behind her. After working together for so many years, she could tell when her friend was concerned. She got quiet and would wait; exactly what she was doing now.

"It's just . . ." Sera stopped dusting the mantle and instead ran a fingertip over a nearby framed photo. The bride and groom beamed at each other, their smiles alive and genuine. How could they have known what would happen just a few moments after they'd said 'I do'? How could they have known the ceremony would end with an arrest, their marriage shrouded with the threat of husband and wife having to be separated for much, much longer than just a wedding night?

"It's just in case." She shook her head and looked away. "You know."

"In case of what, Sera?"

"In case I need someplace to stay, all right?"

Sera could hear Penny's footsteps across the hardwood floor. And before she could stop them, her friend's arms encircled her shoulders from behind. Penny rested her chin on Sera's shoulder and whispered, "Has something happened?"

Sera raised a hand up to cover her friend's. She took hold of her fingertips and squeezed before turning around to face her.

"No."

"Then why would you think you need a back-up plan?"

"It's just that with the trial—it's got Will completely preoccupied. He's busy and—"

"He's pulling away already."

She felt reluctant in doing so, but nodded.

"Maybe."

"Maybe? How could this happen?"

"I think it's just his way of preparing for the worst. We could lose the house. I mean, it's not really my home, but I know the family would be devastated. And all of the assets are frozen pending the investigation. And if Will is sent to—" Sera choked on the words. No way she'd say them out loud. She felt the weight bearing down on her, sickening her stomach with worry.

She grasped the fireplace mantle and rested her forehead against her hand.

"We could lose everything," she said, squeezing her eyes shut on the words. "And if that happens, this loft might be the only roof we have. I bought it before the wedding, so it's only in my name. It's just in case the worst happens."

"It's okay to say you're not sure what comes next, Sera. It's okay to feel vulnerable. The man you love is facing serious prison time. Neither one of you are expected to know how to handle it. My guess is that marriage is tough on the easiest of days without adding the federal government tossing convictions around for good measure. So give yourself a break for feeling unsure, just as long as that break doesn't have you packing boxes to move in here."

Sera raised her head slightly.

Somehow the room was spinning. Between the weight of stress that continued bearing down on her and the stifling heat of the loft, she felt completely overwhelmed.

The look of concern that covered Penny's face was immediate. She creased her brow, fighting against an obvious frown as she took a step closer.

"Fine. What do you need? Want me to go to the grocery? Unpack boxes? I'm here to work. And I can stay with you as long as needed. Fall semester doesn't start up for a while, so you just say the word." She put her hands to her hips as if she were all too ready to take charge over the roughest parts of Sera's life.

Sera took a deep, steadying breath and with the most courage she could muster, whispered, "Penn, get me a garbage can. I think I'm going to be sick."

CHAPTER TEN

September 11, 1940
Kingsland Road Hospital
London

Kája battled the weight of her eyelids until they finally opened.

She'd wrestled with the heavy inclination of sleep that kept her feeling groggy and had opened and shut her eyes more than once, the brightness like an invading shock to her senses. But this time she managed to keep them cracked and turned her head to look around. The room was brick walled, with beds covered in white linens. Light streamed in from somewhere overhead. Beds lined a long, high-ceilinged hall. Windows lined the span of wall opposite her bed.

She turned, thinking to find the same sight in the opposite direction.

Instead, she saw that *he* was there.

Liam was leaning back with eyes closed in sleep, in a wooden chair that had been scooted up close to the bed. He wore the same oxford and trousers he always did—his uniform of sorts—and had hair that was resting down about his forehead. A book had been laid binding up across his chest. The reading glasses so few knew he wore looked like they'd slip off the edge of his nose at the slightest of movements.

She looked down, tracing the extension of his arm to the bed linens, to see that his hand just brushed the side of hers. That tiny connection, the touch of warmth from someone she'd come to trust, gave her enough courage to try to speak through the muddling of her senses.

Her lips felt dry and cracked, like they'd not been used for ages. She licked them and said, "The flower market."

Liam started, jarring awake so that his back straightened and his book fell to the floor with a loud *thud* that echoed off the walls. He shook his head, then settled his gaze upon her and leaned in. He continued scanning her face, as if to make sure she was the source of the voice that had awoken him.

"Kája?" He squeezed her fingertips in his. "What did you say?"

"How did Smalls know to find you at the Columbia Road Flower Market?"

A smile melted over his lips, softly upturning the corners of his mouth.

He leaned back and took the glasses from his nose, pressing them down into his shirt pocket. "And that's all you care to ask me after the fright you've issued us?" He pursed his lips and made a *tsk-tsk* sound. "Given where we find ourselves at the present moment, I'll let that line of questioning go until you've fully recovered. Then I'm going to give you heck for it."

She squinted and looked around.

"Where am I?"

"Kingsland Road. All the other hospitals were full."

What hospitals? Why would I need a hospital?

Kája tried to sit up but felt his hand upon her shoulder, ushering her back down to the pillow.

"No you don't," he ordered, albeit gently. "You'll be staying put. But I can get you some water if you need it?"

"No." A sickly swimming feeling took over her head almost immediately, causing her to lift an instinctive hand to her brow.

It was unexpected, to feel the softness of a bandage pulled taut over her left temple.

Kája looked back at Liam, scared that she was stuck in the drifting sleep and maybe he wasn't really there at all. She feared that she'd somehow been sucked into the recesses of a dream world and had yet to awaken. She immediately tried to lift her arms and looked down at her legs. She had no idea why, but she felt the need to check that all of her limbs were accounted for, despite feeling as though she'd been pulled, like Alice, through the looking glass into an unknown Wonderland.

Liam stopped her again.

"You shouldn't move that either," he said, gently resting fingertips at her wrist. Her left arm was bandaged from just below her palm to the tip of her shoulder, rendering it nearly immovable. "Not just now."

"What happened?" She'd found her words, though they sounded like painfully scratched whispers.

"Do you remember anything?"

She closed her eyes, trying to recall anything past coughing through the sooty air and the ghostly cries piercing the darkness of the shelter. Until that moment, she'd not been able to remember anything but the blackness of sleep. And then it came back in a furious flood of terror.

Her lips trembled. She brought a hand up to her mouth with her good arm and closed her eyes on the memories, feeling the power of the truth in what happened.

"Columbia Road." Kája nodded softly. "We were hit, weren't we?"

She opened her eyes and stared back at him, waiting for his denial. But it never came. Instead, he nodded, just once, and mouthed a soft, "Yes."

"You were injured. You and many others." His eyes focused on her, but they looked so tired, so embattled as he spoke to her.

"How many others?" She stared back at him, recalling the heartbreaking image of the woman holding the lifeless bundle in her arms. "Was anyone . . . killed?"

The fact that he didn't answer gave her the confirmation.

Kája ran trembling fingertips over the bandage at her brow. So others had died. The flashes, visions almost, of a soot-filled shelter . . . they were real.

"How bad was it—the bombing, I mean?"

"Well, you had a superficial wound to your left temple. Though it bled quite a lot, it's really the arm that had the doctors most worried. Shrapnel hit an artery, and by the time you were carried in, there were some scary moments to contend with. You had emergency surgery," he said, and cleared his throat. "Let's just say it was bad enough that I've been sitting here reading the same page in this book for quite a while, waiting to see those pretty eyes of yours finally decide to open and look back at me."

"My arm." It felt like a heavy, unusable mass of gauze and numb flesh. She was terrified to voice the next thought out loud. "Will I be able to . . . use it again?"

"Yes. You should make a complete recovery, though I don't think you're going to feel like typing for a while." He lowered his chin to look down on her with a stern set to his jaw. "Not until you've allowed yourself time to rest, that is. Edmunton will have to make his own tea for a while."

"Does he know?"

"Everyone knows. Mary and Eleanor were here. And I've been spelling Trixie," he said, and lifted a water glass to her lips. "Here—drink."

She did, gratefully. Her mouth felt like it was made of cotton. He must have noticed, as she took another large gulp from the tumbler. She fell back against the pillow, spent.

"Better?"

She nodded. "Much. Thank you."

It was odd to think of the girls she'd only known a short time taking shifts to sit with her at the hospital. And the fact that Liam had stayed . . . he couldn't possibly know what it meant to her. It was humbling, to say the least.

Kája looked from him to the other beds, her gaze scanning the room.

She saw beds filled with patients who must have been like her—dazed and unsure of what had happened. Women in white uniforms bustled around with trays, rolls of bandages, and clipboards tucked under their arms. There was a small group of people standing over a bed at the end of the corridor. She couldn't see much, but the lump on the mattress was only big enough to be a small child. A man's shoulders were hunched over and he cried, holding a woman who looked to have crumbled in his arms. If one had to judge the scene, it would appear they'd just lost a child.

The despair was unmistakable, both powerful and heart-wrenching. Kája's memory of her fractured family on a train platform flooded back, washing over her muddled senses. The feelings must have shown upon her face, for Liam sat up straighter, nearly rising from his chair.

"Try not to look," Liam suggested, his words soft and feeling.

"But I can't look away," she whispered. "It can't be happening, not here too."

He didn't question what she'd meant but must have assumed she spoke of Prague. He responded by edging his chair over so her view was obstructed by his shoulders. She closed her eyes, still seeing the image. No doubt the parents' tender moment would be burned upon her heart forever.

"You're not in pain, are you? I can find the doctor."

The chair creaked and she opened her eyes, seeing Liam poised to stand.

"No—please?" she asked. "I'm all right. Really. I'm just trying to remember what happened. I think I understand what you're telling me . . . the bombing last night? All these people are here from that?"

"You've been here for nearly four days, Kája, and we've been bombed in all of them."

She blinked back at him.

Had it been four days since the bombs had first fallen on their Saturday-afternoon walk? How could she have slept that long and not remembered anything? And how could the skies have rained bombs for so long?

"But that can't be." She shook her head on the words. "I remember walking through the flower market with you and . . . the sirens went off."

"Yes."

Kája bit the corner of her lip.

Thinking on the frenzied events as the first bombs fell triggered a memory of a kiss they'd shared, and she wondered if it was real or a creation of her own mind. She'd passed by him in the newsroom too many times, had walked with him through the London city streets. They'd worked together at the office, never exchanging anything more than pleasantries until one late night, a connection between them had sparked an unexpected friendship. And now, an attachment had grown in her heart. Though she'd fought hard to ignore it, Liam Marshall had found a way into the most carefully protected parts of it.

"They called an all-clear after the first bombs fell. I thought to go home but stayed on to help in the East End. And the sirens started up again and hundreds showed up. I went back because I thought that's where you'd come looking for me. And without warning, bombs started falling again in the dark."

Then a memory resurfaced. Of a familiar, embattled voice in the darkness. One she knew. One that had spoken over her with such care. Of arms that had swept up her lifeless body and somehow had carried her to safety. She remembered them around her.

"Were you . . . there?"

"Kája, we don't have to talk about this now. You should rest."

She tried to sit up straighter but fell back on the pillows again. "No—you were there, weren't you? In the shelter. I remember now. I remember hearing your voice over me. You were telling the other men what to do."

Liam looked pained, but nodded nonetheless. "Yes. I was there."

"But how ever did you find me?"

"I was on my way back to Columbia Road when the bomb hit." He leaned forward, elbows on his knees. "I got there not long after it happened. They think a bomb came right down the air shaft, exploding in a direct hit on everyone there."

"How bad was it that night?"

He looked up, eyes beset by what he must have witnessed.

"Bad enough to not mention it here, not while you and all of these other people are in hospital beds. But I can tell you that sites all over the city have been bombed. Homes. Churches. A school in Bermondsey took a direct hit the first night. And there have been fires everywhere you can imagine. Half of London is charred black."

"What about the girls from the office? You said they were here so they must be okay."

He nodded.

"All fine, though Fleet Street has taken a few hits. It's set everyone's teeth on edge, to find bombs falling around the *Telegraph*. But I looked in at your flat, along with Trixie and some of the other girls who live near you. Your building was damaged but it's still standing. They collected your things for you, as much as they could carry."

Kája nodded, sated with the fact that none of the others had been injured or worse.

"Luckily, Westminster and St. Paul's are both standing in

the heart of the city. Smoke surrounded them on all sides but the flames didn't get them. And Churchill gave a radio address today, as a matter of fact. He mentioned the 'spirit of the British nation.' Makes a chap feel a bit defiant about it all, that our greatest landmarks stood against the flames. That we're standing against Hitler together."

"Yes. I suppose . . ." Her voice trailed off.

Defiant? It was the one thing she didn't feel. She was wounded and weak, waking up to a world that had been torn to bits.

"So it's over? The RAF will protect us now that we know for certain the Luftwaffe can reach over the Channel."

Liam shook his head. "London's been bombed nearly round the clock since Saturday. There's reason to hope it'll be over soon, but we still must be prepared for the worst."

"What do you mean?" A breath escaped her lungs—one she hadn't even known she'd held. She looked around at the full beds and asked, "Is this hospital safe?"

"Kája," he said, with such care laced in his tone that she could scarcely breathe. "I think the Germans want us to believe that nowhere is safe—not with Hitler sending fire from the sky. But we're Londoners, and we'll never give in. We may be battered but we're not beaten. Not by a long shot."

"No. Of course not."

"And I hope you hear me when I say how sorry I am." He paused, then cleared his throat. "Had I known there was a chance the shelter could be hit—"

"I don't blame you—" she protested, cutting in.

Liam shook his head. "No—let me say this. I need to say it. Defiance as a whole is one thing. We Britons can pull that spirit together on our darkest day. But the view I see from inside this hospital—and by this bed in particular—is different. It's made me realize what could have been lost in the midst of what already has been."

Kája wanted to ask what he meant by that, but he continued, not giving her the chance to cut in.

"My father's dead, Kája." He looked away from her to a point outside the nearest window. "We buried him yesterday."

"What happened?"

"He worked at the Surrey docks," he answered, his tone hushed. "Long as I can remember. They were bombed that first day. I just didn't get there in time is all."

Liam said the words with such ambivalence that one might have thought him a man without emotion. But she knew better. She'd seen the fear in his eyes before he left her, had seen the passion that drove him through the smoke-filled streets to the burning banks of the Thames. And now she knew why.

"And you didn't get to say good-bye?"

Liam's hand rested on the side of the bed. She moved her fingertips until they just grazed it, drawing his attention back to her. It felt natural, almost like a sense of coming home, to have her hand brush his.

"It's not your fault," she reiterated, hoping to offer him any small glimpse of comfort. "You tried. I'm sure he knew that."

"Yes, well." He cleared his throat and moved back away from the side of the bed, his hand leaving hers cold and alone on the sheet. "There's nothing to be done about it now, is there?"

"Liam, I . . ."

She diverted her gaze to the ceiling, then closed her eyes for a few seconds, hoping to infuse herself with courage over the blast of emotion that was looming. She was angry. Angry at war and the audacity of the Nazis to take everything from them. Desperation flooded her heart; she needed to know her parents' fate. She needed to feel a lifting of that guilt for having left them behind. And now, even as she lay in a hospital bed, she felt that determination fire up in her soul again.

"I want to do something."

"You can." He nodded agreement. "You'll heal. Turn your nose up to the lot of them by getting better."

"But I want more—to fight back, maybe? You said that Churchill spoke of Britain's spirit. Well, I'm here. Now. I'm a Londoner, at least for a while anyway. And I want to be a true one. If that's standing up to Hitler's barrage, then I mean to do it too."

Liam seemed to notice her embattled will and began attempting to talk her down at once.

"Now is not the time, Kája. You need to get back on your feet first."

"Is it time for you? Tell me—will you be called from Bletchley Park to fight on the front lines?"

Liam paused, then swallowed hard and answered, "Maybe."

"Then there you have it. If you're fighting, then I want to as well. With your connections, surely you can find something for me." She inclined her head to the parents sobbing at the end of the corridor and lowered her voice. "Tell me that scene over there means something to you too."

"God in heaven, Kája. Of course it does. Do you think me a monster?"

"No, never. I just want you to understand why . . ."

"What do you intend to do, Kája? You must heal first. I cannot tell you how close you came to . . . They wheeled you into surgery, and it was only then that I realized I was standing there with your blood all over my hands."

He stopped short, clearing his throat.

"I have no wish to frighten you into submission, but you nearly died in that blast. I didn't even know your sister's name or how to contact her about your injuries. It's by God's grace I'm even talking to you right now. And with your family so far away, I feel"—he paused for a moment, as if choosing his words ever so carefully, then continued—"after what happened at Columbia Road, I feel a responsibility that you're not put in harm's way again. If there's anything I can do to prevent that, I must. So the answer to every question you're asking must be no."

Kája had heard what he said, but she felt numb, her heart broken and bleeding like the injured parts of her body. His words held depth, but not enough to make her forget the desire to do something more than just leave the hospital alive.

All she could think of now was the pain of running away. She'd left her family, left Prague behind out of fear. And still war had chased her to an ARP shelter in the heart of London. How could she run again? Something mattered in standing up to fight this time. It felt like she'd been given a second chance to make things right.

Liam sighed, a heavy-laden exhale that sounded as though it had been pent up for days. Perhaps all of London sighed at the moment. He clapped hands to his knees and lightened his features.

"There's no need to talk about all this now. Besides, there's something I've been meaning to ask you."

"Yes. What is it?" Kája answered, refusing to let her eyes produce the tears they so badly wished to. She raised her good arm up to her brow and rubbed at her aching forehead. It served as a poor distraction.

Liam reached down to retrieve the book from the floor and slid it across the top of the bedside table to her. "Have you considered taking up some new reading habits? I hate to say it about a fellow British bloke, but your Dickens isn't nearly as gripping as Shakespeare."

"Dickens?" How had he remembered that? The first time they'd met in the basement archive had been months ago. Surely it meant nothing to him? "Is that what you're reading?"

"*Little Dorrit.*" He rolled his eyes and leaned in to whisper, "But you've managed to sleep through the entire book thus far so it can't have been much good. I suggest we read *Julius Caesar* next time—much more exciting for a young journalist to find her inspiration."

The sentiment wasn't lost, even though he was trying to interject humor into the crux of a horrible situation.

"You read to me?"

Liam shifted in his chair, a bit sheepishly she would have judged, and shrugged it off.

"Yes, well. Only to pass the time until you woke up. Don't let those busy nurses fool you; it's quite boring around here, actually."

A defiant tear managed to escape and slid down her cheek.

Liam brushed it away with the knuckle of his index finger.

"Now—what was that question you asked me when you woke?" he asked, and issued one of his heart-stopping smiles.

Kája couldn't be mad at the authoritarian air in his voice.

To the outside world, he appeared as the office chatterboxes said: an ace reporter with fire nipping at his heels. But what stood out now, what surprised and even humbled her as she lay in a hospital bed, was that he revealed the man underneath.

Kája began to consider how wrong she might have been about him.

"I wondered how Smalls knew to find you at the flower market. It's not a normal place for you to venture, is it?"

"Ah, that." He sighed. Liam smiled and, pulling a poppy that had been in a bud vase by her bed, whispered, "I told him of Miss Makovský's fondness for flowers. I'd asked the other secretaries after her Saturday plans, so I knew I'd run into her there. I heard tell that Columbia Road has the prettiest poppies in all of London and I wanted her to have one."

Kája took the flower from him with her good arm and smiled softly.

"What is it?" he asked.

"I used to paint these, when I was young." She twirled the flower between her fingertips. "I had a studio. A small little corner of the world. The room overlooked the river and I could see Prague for miles. I painted our neighbors' gardens."

"That's why they remind you of home."

"Yes." She nodded. "But . . ."

Liam tilted his head to the side, eyebrow arched, and asked, "But what?"

"I'm just relieved you didn't bring chrysanthemums. In Prague, it's traditional to put them on graves."

CHAPTER ELEVEN

W̶ell, our suspicions were right, Mrs. Hanover." The doctor came into the room and set her file on the nearby counter. "Congratulations. You're nine weeks along."

They were words Sera was overjoyed—but terrified—to hear.

The bouts of nausea and lightheadedness, she'd explained away. Her life was a bower of stress at the moment. She'd expected to receive a lecture about how to manage it and encouraging her to focus on nutrition and getting enough sleep. And the exhaustion that continued plaguing her—she thought that could be explained too. It was normal to need some time to transition from the East Coast to West Coast. Of course she'd be tired.

But pregnant? *Now?*

In the midst of everything?

"Are you all right, Mrs. Hanover?"

"Yes," Sera answered, attempting to cover the near squeak her voice threatened against the word. She sat in the exam room chair and feeling dizzy all of a sudden, dropped her head between her knees. "I heard you. It's just—"

"A surprise, I'd gather."

Sera's heart fluttered. "Something like that."

A surprise?

That was an understatement. After the roller-coaster ride

they'd been on through the previous year, she wondered if anything would be mundane again. Surprises were overrated when they came prepackaged on your doorstep every day.

Sera tossed her hair over her shoulder and looked up.

"And you're sure that's what it is?"

The doctor smiled with compassion in her eyes, then glanced down at the laptop on the exam counter and began typing away.

"Yes. I am." She kept clicking away on the keyboard. "I'd like to see you back here in a month. In the meantime, I'm writing a prescription for prenatal vitamins and ordering you to get as much rest as possible."

Sera's eyes misted. She couldn't help it.

She'd imagined that someday, long in the future when the legal troubles were just a distant memory, they'd have a family. She and William would grow old together, watching from the row of rockers on the porch as their grandchildren played in the yard. They'd take their family for walks on the beach, or through the streets of Manhattan where she'd been happy for so many years.

But it had always been *someday*.

Now someday was colliding with the turmoil of their present circumstances and heaven help her, but Sera was terrified all over again.

"We can keep this quiet, can't we? From the media, I mean. After everything Will's been through over the past few months and with the court proceedings"—Sera pictured throngs of paparazzi following her to and from childbirth classes and shuddered—"I just don't want him to be hurt anymore."

"Mrs. Hanover, we'll help you in any way we can," she said, and paused to drop her hands into her lab coat pockets. She retrieved a pad of paper and pen, then scribbled on it and tore off the top sheet. "Here"—she handed the paper to Sera—"take my cell phone number. This will bypass the after-hours emergency line. You can call me day or night, for whatever you need. And I assure you this is confidential. Try not to focus on what's happening out there and instead focus on what's happening right here. Your husband won't learn of this blessing until you're ready to tell him."

Sera nodded, finding strength in the doctor's reassurance.

"One month," she said. "I want to see you back here in one month. Until then, you make sure you get some rest. And try not to worry. Okay? Everything will be fine."

Try not to worry?

Sera nodded as the doctor smiled and left the room. She even managed to take some steadying breaths as she gathered her things and left the exam room.

She kept reciting, *Everything will work out . . . Everything will work out . . .* as she marched through the waiting room and outside. It wasn't until she made it back to the parking lot and was safely in her car that she allowed herself to burst into tears.

A baby.

Sera had no idea how she would tell William he was going to be a father. The news was so out of plan. So totally unexpected. And yet, so . . . *wonderful.*

Despite the uncertainty, despite the what-ifs and the maybes swirling on all sides, Sera couldn't remember feeling happier than she did at this moment. And that was why something had to change. If she wanted her husband in their child's life, there was nothing else to do but step up and take control.

She whispered a silent prayer that when she could finally get up the courage to tell him, William would see it that way too.

———

Sera sat in the coffee shop, staring out the window at the raindrops dripping off the black-and-white awning outside.

It was an eclectic little shop, one that she and Will had enjoyed together. With dim overhead lighting and tall ceilings, it had a cozy yet modern atmosphere. There were display cases of pastries, barrels of free-trade coffee, and a long concrete counter with wooden stools spanning the wall opposite the entrance.

The gallery was hopping with renovations and contractors going in and out; there'd have been no peace there. And she wasn't ready to go home just yet. Somehow her car had driven itself to the coffee shop. There were patrons all around, some chatting and others buried in their laptops. The white noise was just right for her to collect her thoughts.

Sera spotted Penny when she breezed through the doors, shaking rain off her khaki military jacket and tossing her damp strawberry blond ponytail as she looked around.

She waved her over when their eyes met.

"So . . . your text sounded rather ominous." Penny slid into the booth seat across from her. "The words 'Meet me now' followed by the name of a coffee shop did little to calm the insane wanderings of my imagination. Good thing I hit every green light between here and the gallery."

"I know, and I'm so sorry. It couldn't be helped."

"Sounds like it. So what's up?"

Sera pushed a coffee mug over to her. "Here. Got you a mid-morning latte for the occasion."

"Occasion? Are we celebrating something, other than the fact that this rain has to end soon?"

"You could say that."

"Don't worry about it. I needed a break anyway. But you didn't get one for yourself?"

Penny took the mug and warmed her fingers around it, breathing in the rich aroma of mocha and cinnamon that spiced the air around them. Sera took a deep breath as well, but for an entirely different reason.

"No, because I've got a huge favor to ask and I suppose I'm trying to butter you up with chocolate and whipped cream." Sera took in a deep breath and just blurted it out: "Penn, I'm pregnant."

Had the table not been between them, Sera was sure Penny would have dropped coffee down her front. As it was, the oversized mug fell from her hands and landed hard on the tabletop, sloshing mocha syrup and melted whipped cream down the sides. She sailed across the booth and with a squeal that could have alerted the entire world to her unabashed glee, swept Sera up in her arms for a bear hug.

"I'm going to be an aunt!" Penn cried, happy tears misting her eyes. "Well, sort of. He or she can just call me Aunt Penny. I'll be that funny friend who takes them to the park and loads them up with gifts and sugar before I bring them home to the reality of their parents."

"That would be great." Sera laughed, smiling in spite of herself.

"So when did you find out?"

"This morning," she answered, directing her attention to the mocha spill on the table. She began absently wiping at it with the few napkins they had nearby. "Remember that appointment I had?"

"And you thought it was stress . . . I wish I could have gone with you. It would have been a bit more fun than signing for another shipment of boxes that arrived." She winked. "Though the delivery guy was kind of cute."

"Penn, you're amazing." Sera bit her bottom lip over the emotion. "You can make anything sound okay, can't you?"

"Everything *will* be okay. Your faith has brought you this far, remember? I know it's difficult, but you have to go on trusting it."

"I do. Now more than ever." Sera wove her fingers around the tips of her hair, not even realizing she was doing it until Penny calmed the nervous hand with her own. "Maybe I didn't imagine things would work out exactly like this. Well, let's be honest—I didn't expect any of this. But I still know this baby is a gift."

"So why are you crying?" She reached up and dabbed at the corners of Sera's eyes with the last clean napkin. "I hope those are happy tears I see."

"They are—yes! I'm happy. Of course." She rolled her eyes to the ceiling, trying to lighten the air.

"And what about Will? How did he react?"

Sera took in a steadying breath. It altered the air just enough that Penny's expression changed with it.

"Oh no, Sera. You haven't told him?"

"No, not yet. I only found out this morning. But I'm not sure it's the right time. He's out on bail, thank goodness. But he's got so much on his mind. This is the last thing he needs to worry about."

"Worry about? Sera, he's going to be a father. He'll want to know."

"I know that. And I'll tell him. But, Penn, I've got to do something. I'm scared. I won't let our child know its father through a series of prison visits. And that's why I called you. I need your help. I know it's terrible of me to ask after everything you've done, but I didn't know what else to do."

Penny leaned back and folded her arms across her chest.

"Okay . . . I'm waiting."

Sera nodded. "I know. That's the problem. You've already been the best friend anyone could ask for. You've come out here to help with the wedding and now the gallery opening—putting your life and everything else on hold. I don't know how to thank you, Penn. Really. I'm so grateful."

Penny smiled, one of those patented "I'm still waiting because I know you so well" smiles.

"And?"

"And I need to ask you if you'll go to London with me."

A blinking stare later, Penny's obvious question came out like a statement: "You're going to London. Now?"

"Yes. I need to figure out how to help Will win this lawsuit. I've looked at it from every angle. The lawyers assure us he has a strong defense. But that's not good enough. I told Will that it's our future, not theirs. And the bill of sale, the deposits, the transaction turning the art over to the company in the first place—everything points right back to him. Now, his grandfather's death and what happened after is from this world of years ago that I'm not a part of. For the life of me, I can't get Will to open up about it. I've even asked his mother and she tried to help, but it was always something the Hanover men took pride in, managing the business. She never got involved. And though it was hard to bring up, I asked her about Will's father, about why he left."

"What did she say?"

"Oh, Penn . . . the family is so broken. They're hurting. I saw everything I needed to in her eyes. She said he decided one day that he didn't want to be married any longer. He just walked away and she had no clue why. I believe her."

"Men." Penny huffed under her breath. She reached for the coffee mug and downed another sip, seemingly on principle.

"I don't want to open the family's wound, but the one person I think we need to talk to—William won't even consider as an option. I need to know why."

"So you're going to London to see Will's father?"

Sera nodded, knowing full well it was a less-than-ideal plan. Not only was her father-in-law estranged from her husband's tight-knit family, but she'd never met him. Never even spoken to him. It was possible he'd turn her away. Or that he'd have nothing of value to add to William's case. It was a gamble—a huge one.

"As crazy as it sounds, yes. I think that's where we might find our answer."

"And what if he won't accept you? I mean, if he walked away from his family, he might not want some daughter-in-law he's never met showing up on his doorstep asking all sorts of questions."

"I thought of that," Sera admitted.

"So what do you plan to do?"

"I received a letter from Sophie this week. She said we could stay with her in Paris if needed. It's a quick hop from Paris to London, and maybe talking to her will give us some ideas."

"So you're asking me to go to London, possibly Paris, and you thought there was the slightest chance I'd say no?"

Penny's love for all things European mirrored her own. She had to smile at how God had brought such a special friend into her life.

"Well, I have to get Will to agree to it first, but yes. If his father won't see us, then maybe Sophie can still help. After all, she knew Will's grandfather probably better than anyone."

"And she writes you letters?" Penny looked off into space and sighed, a dreamy haze covering her eyes. "How 1940s of her. She's such a child of her generation."

"No kidding. She sent me this with it."

Sera took an envelope from her purse and retrieved a folded piece of yellowing newsprint from within. She unfolded it and gently laid it flat on the table.

"There," she said, and pointed out a photograph of a lovely woman, with dark hair and eyes and a uniform hat tipped to the side of her brow. She read the headline aloud: "'*Telegraph* Journalist Missing in Prague.'"

"Kája Makovský. My goodness—she was beautiful."

Sera looked at the woman's face, smiling out from the worn image. She brushed a finger over the photograph, feeling like she knew her somehow.

"It's dated August 12, 1942."

"Yes. It's an article about how she'd gone missing during

World War II, followed by her journal entries of life during the London Blitz. The accounts she wrote are amazing."

Penny scanned the article. "So who was she? I mean, does she tie back to Will's family in some way?"

"She does, actually. Adele and Vladimir saved Sophie's life when they smuggled her out of Vienna. Well, this woman also had a hand in saving her after she was sent to a concentration camp in Prague. Will's grandfather knew them both."

"But we already knew Sophie's connection to Adele. Why would she send you an old newspaper article?"

"I think there's something here, Penn. Something to remind us what we're fighting for. Sophie told me I had to keep battling for the man I love, no matter the circumstances. And she knows what she's talking about, because she said it was this woman— her teacher—who fought for her in the same way. That no matter what, she never gave up."

"Never gave up on what?"

"Sophie says here that if it wasn't for this teacher, she'd have died in the Terezin concentration camp as a little girl."

CHAPTER TWELVE

May 7, 1941
Bethnal Green Tube Station
London

re you quite sure you want to come back to Bethnal Green? I know how close it is to Columbia Road. If you want a transfer, I can get one of the other girls to help out."

"No, I'm fine." Kája took a deep breath and readjusted the old wooden crate in her arms. "Now is as good a time as any to come back, I suppose. I can't avoid it forever."

"I know," Trixie said. "But it's been blitzy this week, and I hate seeing that look on your face."

Like the nearly one million other women who'd signed up for the Women's Volunteer Service for Civil Defense, they were office gals by day and uniformed WVS workers by night.

London had fallen into a routine of sorts, where the citizens worked during the day and made comments about the bombings being "blitzy" like it was the weather report. As soon as the sun ducked behind the horizon, they'd go into survival mode. The sirens were turned on and Londoners took to their Anderson shelters or went to sleep in the underground. They brought bags and baskets, even baby buggies loaded with whatever precious items they could carry from home. They'd settle in for the night, sleeping it out while the Luftwaffe decimated parts of the city aboveground.

Like clockwork, they'd leave again in the morning, walking around piles of brick that had fallen in the streets as they hurried to work.

"By the looks of the place, it's a good thing we're here. It's going to need all the help it can get if we're going to make this passable as a shelter for one more night. I mean, really," Trixie said, tossing curls over her shoulder. "I've got a layer of dirt on my skin just from standing here."

Kája smiled at Trixie's unfiltered comment.

"Come on." Kája laughed and led the way to the canteen. "Let's get organized. The rest of the men will be here to build the extra bunks and they're going to be hungry."

"Hungry for ration food? And tea without sugar?" Trixie shook her head. "You're right. I haven't met a man yet who would turn down food, rationed or otherwise. It's pitiful, but there you have it."

Kája dropped her crate of tea and biscuits on the canteen booth's wooden counter and looked around.

What could she say—Trixie was right. It certainly was an underground.

It was dark and not particularly clean.

They had some services, thank goodness, or it would have made their volunteer efforts near to useless. A makeshift booth had been built for serving tea, and one train car had been brought in for the canteen, where they'd be working. Another behind it was reserved for the shelter marshal and first aid station, both of which were kept busy round the clock. There were rows of bunks positioned along the wall opposite the tracks, though they were as yet unfinished. Thick canvas hammocks had been stretched out across the tracks to accommodate the overflow of people. And there were wooden slats that still had to be built above the bunks so the people could store their wares.

In a few short hours, the doors would be opened and the

empty space would be filled with Londoners of all shapes and sizes. They'd wait out the worst of the raids all packed in together, praying through the night that a stray bomb wouldn't penetrate the street above and punish those hidden beneath ground.

"See what I mean, doll? We're going to have to work our magic with this place." Trixie caught her eye and issued a skeptical glare with a tilt of the chin and an upturned eyebrow. It was so animated that Kája had to laugh.

"It's not that bad."

"Well, if we're able to brew one cup of tea down here it will be a small miracle." She pointed to a lonely corner of the tunnel, with a light that flickered overhead and water that dripped from the ceiling. "In any case, I've elected myself as chairwoman of the entertainment committee. I think that's where we'll put the turntable and the dance floor. I don't imagine anyone in their right mind would wish to sleep over there."

"I'm not sure anyone would complain at this point."

"Nevertheless, I'll go mad at our new post night after night if there's no dancing." She winked and did a twirl as she marched off. "You decide on the playlist while I fill the kettles with water."

Kája smiled after her, grateful for the added fervor Trixie brought to any situation.

In the months that had followed the first night of the bombings, Kája had found a spirited friend in Trixie Bell. Kája had been discharged from Kingsland Hospital two weeks after the Columbia Road disaster. And since her flat was not habitable, Trixie had taken her in, opening her Whitechapel flat without question. And she'd proved to be a most loyal friend, something Kája hadn't expected but was now so very grateful for.

It made the long days and sleepless nights easier to bear, knowing that Trixie was there to lighten the mood.

Kája smiled as she unpacked their crates: tea and biscuits, and galvanized watering cans that they'd found to be quite advantageous in serving tea to so many. She hadn't been focused for more than a few moments when she heard the workers tromping down the stopped escalators like stairs.

She looked up, intent upon welcoming them. But in that moment, her heart stopped on its own.

A familiar face was the first thing she saw in the crowd.

Liam's hair was casually mussed and he wore the same oxford and suit pants as always, minus the tie or jacket. He carried tools in his arms like the rest of the men and walked along the tracks to the area being fashioned with bunks. The shelter marshal was with them and began organizing the effort, pairing the men up in teams to divide the work. Liam shrugged the worn leather satchel from his shoulder and fell into line with the rest of them.

It wasn't the fact that Liam was working with the volunteers that surprised her. It was that he was there in Bethnal Green at all. The reporters on the war beat had been sent out weeks ago—to goodness knows where. Kája hadn't heard a thing from Liam, except for when he sent his stories. But to see him there right in front of her, rolling up his sleeves with the rest of the men, was the last thing she'd expected.

Trixie returned, noticing Kája's fixed glare along the tracks.

"Good, the boys are here. Now we're in for some excitement." She winked and began unpacking the rest of the crates.

Kája took hold of Trixie's elbow. "Trix, what's Liam doing here? I thought he was out on assignment."

"Oh, Liam and Smalls got back this morning," she said, casually going back to unpacking crates. "Called in on the switchboard to let Edmunton know and then they slipped into his office not long after. I'm surprised you missed them."

"Edmunton sent me to the corner shop for a supply run."

"Oh, that's right. I should have guessed why Liam would come around the switchboard closet. He must have come over when he couldn't find you. I would have said something, but I thought you knew."

"And did Liam say anything about coming here to the shelter tonight?"

"Funny enough, he did ask me about our post. He said something about wanting to be 'a real Londoner' and that's why he was going to volunteer too."

"What?" Kája whispered after hearing her own words repeated back and looked over as Liam began unpacking tools with the rest of the men.

Trixie waved her hand in the air. "I've long since stopped trying to figure that one out. In any case, he's an extra pair of hands and that we sorely need if we're going to get this place up to snuff for tonight."

"Right," Kája said, stealing one more glance over at the group of men, their hammers already flying. "Let's get tea started."

———

A knock on the train car door aroused Kája from her thoughts.

"May I come up?"

Liam stood at the steps to the first aid car, having hushed his voice to not wake the baby sleeping in her arms. She nodded and tilted her chin to the side to invite him in.

He looked around the car, seeming surprised to find a shelf above the seats lined with boxes of babies rather than supplies. There was a gurgle here and there but for the most part, the car was peaceful.

"Looks like you've got your hands full in here." He stepped up and walked in until he was by her side, looking down at the bundle she held in her arms.

"There are only four tonight," she whispered, softly patting the back of the little boy she rocked back and forth. "I've been trying to get him down for the last hour. I think I may have finally done it."

Liam cupped a hand to the back of the child's head, softly patting. "Where's his mother?"

"Asleep, poor thing." She tilted her head toward the tracks. "She's worked all day."

"And haven't you worked all day?"

He looked at her, eyes welcoming. Even after the weeks he'd been gone, it seemed as though nothing had changed. The explosion at Columbia Road had been horrible, indeed. But the one thing the memory had brought was the remembrance of his face when she had woken up in the hospital. He was a friend now, one whom she'd come to know and depend on.

The fact that he was standing here in the car spoke volumes.

"Yes," she admitted, stretching her back ever so slightly. "But the woman has three other little ones to look after and I haven't any. She needs a few hours of sleep at least, like the other mothers who have to leave at sunup and work all day. Besides, Trixie will spell me soon."

He held out his arms. "Here, let me."

"But he needs to be changed and—"

Liam took the child up in his arms and issued her a glance with mock rebuke.

"I may be a man, but I'm not completely helpless." He nodded to the train car seats behind them. "Sit. That's an order."

Kája found that she hadn't enough strength left to argue. She fell into the seat and leaned back, loving the feel of having her feet off the floor for the first time in hours.

She watched Liam as he diapered the baby and quite surprisingly, he looked like he knew what he was doing. He'd lain the child down on the seat opposite her and without instruction proceeded to change the baby in one minute flat, even remembering to powder the little bottom before he'd pinned him up.

Liam lifted the child in his arms and carried him over to her. The little boy snuggled into the crook of his neck, having dozed on through the entire changing. He sighed back into sleep as Liam settled in the seat beside her.

"I can take him."

"No, no." He shook his head. "I've got him fine. Rest your arm."

She hadn't even realized she was rubbing it. He must have seen.

Kája dropped her hand and rested it in her lap.

"I'm impressed. It seems as though you know your way around a nursery car. How did that come about?"

"Mum died when I was eight. I had three younger siblings—my two brothers and a baby sister. Dad had to work to keep us going, so you learn to diaper fast when you're a young chap running a house for the first time."

"I'm so sorry, Liam," she offered, not sure what to say.

"It was a long time ago," he whispered back.

He'd never seemed the type to complain. Kája knew he wouldn't have said a word unless she'd asked. And now, after all the months she'd known him, it was the first time he'd ever told her anything about his own family. It made the remembrance of his father's death that first day of the bombings all the heavier on her heart.

He'd lost both of his parents. She didn't want to imagine what that felt like.

"Who would have thought we'd all be sleeping on train tracks or stopped escalators? Or spending our nights in a nursery car? We do what we have to do to survive, I suppose."

Kája nodded. "How long will you be in London?"

He cleared his throat lightly. "Just for the week, I'm afraid."

"And do you know where you're going?"

Liam looked at her over the head of the sleeping little boy. His eyes connected with hers, blinking back. Offering the connection she'd so missed in the time he'd been away.

"Yes."

His one-word answer triggered a sigh she couldn't hold back. "And you can't tell me."

Liam shook his head. "Not this time, no."

"Not any time, you mean."

"But I assure you that when I can say something, you'll be the first to know."

"Will I?"

Liam dropped a hand down from the child's back and rested it palm up on the seat beside her, waiting. "I'll be gone for a while this time. But I'll write to you."

She bit the edge of her bottom lip, holding back the emotion of seeing him only in letters written on a page. She nodded, then whispered, "And I'll write back."

"Whatever happens or wherever I'm sent, I'll come back to you. I came here tonight to tell you that I want you in my life, Kája. I can't hide it anymore," he whispered, and paused with his eyes locked on hers. "What I mean is, I don't want to hide it. I want to be who I am, and that is the man who cares for you."

Kája thought about the bombing that first day and how he'd stayed by her side in the hospital. He'd not left her even when she was discharged. In fact, he'd been the one to drive her over and get her settled in at Trixie's. And he was here now. He'd come home to London for a week and his first moments upon returning had brought him to her.

Kája slid her hand in his and laid her head against his shoulder.

"Then I'm glad you're here now."

They didn't say much after that. He held the little boy as they sat in silence, listening to the sweet cadence of babies cooing in sleep around them and the far off echoing of the Germans' bombs above ground. They'd hear a blast every now and then, to which Liam would squeeze her hand as the dust fell down like flour settling in the air.

Kája held on to the moment, no longer scared of the bombs. The only thought that held her captive now was wondering how long the moment would last.

CHAPTER THIRTEEN

Cicadas burned the sounds of night into the background.

Sera awoke to their hum out the windows, forgetting for a moment where she was. It was normal to awaken because of the bustle in the Manhattan streets outside the apartment where she'd lived for the past several years. But waking up because of the gentle stillness of a summer night—it took more than a moment for her to get her bearings.

She slid her hand over the pillow beside her.

Cold.

Sera sat up straight. William was gone.

She swung her legs over the side of the bed and let them dangle while she looked around their room. The drapes were pulled open so she had a wide view of the bay. It was lovely and dark, distant lights shining from the opposite shore. The moon was full and high in the sky, creating inky shadows in the corners of the large estate bedroom. To awaken and find herself alone caused anxious prickles to form on the back of Sera's neck.

The clock on the nightstand didn't help.

2:15 a.m.

She stood and reached for the cashmere wrap from a nearby occasional chair. She pulled it over her tank top, enveloping her shoulders with its warmth. The last thing she felt comfortable doing was wandering around the vast estate home in the middle of the night, but if her gut could be relied upon at all, she had a pretty good idea where she'd find her husband.

Ever so quietly, she opened the thick-paneled oak door and stepped into the hall. It, too, looked shrouded in an eerie light, as the moon reflected off the windows overlooking the back of the estate. She walked along, sensitive to every creak and groan of the hardwood floors, and trekked down the stairs until she came to the soft glow of light shining from behind the office door.

The door was cracked open. She peered in.

William sat at the desk.

His laptop was open upon it, its glow mixing with the tabletop lamp to illuminate the embattled features of his face. He didn't look tired; she knew him well enough to know it was stress. He sat back in the chair, casual in a Red Sox tee and athletic shorts, save for the deep crease in his forehead, and stared ahead with the oddest look of resolve on his face. He seemed a million miles away.

She tapped on the door.

He looked up, and as if she were a dose of warm water, the ice cracked in his features and he smiled to greet her.

"I'm sorry. Did I wake you?"

She shook her head. "No. I've been tossing and turning for a while now."

Sera padded across the rug and sat on the edge of the desk.

"I can't sleep either." He slid an arm around her waist.

"Then maybe we're both awake because we need to talk about all this."

"Talk about what?"

"About why you're in this office every night instead of getting some much needed sleep."

She looked at him, eyes wide open, wondering if it was the

right time to tell him. He was going to be a father and even more so now than before, they had to find answers.

"Will—" She stopped short when he cut into her thoughts.

"It feels like a mistake."

She paused, noting the poignancy in his eyes. "What feels like a mistake?"

"You going to London on your own."

Sera shook her head. "I'm not. Penny is going with me. There's nothing to worry about."

"You know I can't go with you. They won't let me leave the country right now."

"I know."

"I've prayed about this, Sera. At length. In more words than I can say. I've poured my heart out to God, asking him to heal the past and free me from it. And I wish I could explain everything . . . to make you understand . . ."

She swallowed hard. "What do you need me to understand?"

Sera reached out and touched a cautious hand to his shoulder. His muscle tensed under her fingertips, but he didn't answer her question. Instead, his eyes met hers in a debilitating plea.

"I'm asking you not to go. Please. Just leave it alone."

"Will, I know your father left your family at a very vulnerable time. He broke your sister's heart by not coming home for her wedding. And I'm not sure whether you would have even wanted him at ours," Sera said, and slid her hand down the length of his arm until her hand held his. She leaned into his side. "But I hate to watch you go through this. And if there's something I can do about it, I have to."

Sera wasn't an expert at being a wife, but the one thing she knew was they couldn't make it through the legal battle ahead unless they were united. They had to be able to trust one another. To lean on each other through their pain and uncertainty—to lean on Christ together. But to watch William now, to see the pain creased in the harsh lines of his face, Sera knew he was holding back. Something was gnawing at him and whatever it was had a forceful hold.

"Sera," he said on an exhale. "This is too much."

She sat back from him.

Of course she had no intention of sounding meek. Nevertheless, her voice hitched when she replied, "It's too much to talk to your wife?"

He shook his head. "That's not what I meant."

"Then help me understand what you did mean."

"You don't know my father, Sera. You don't know our history. There's pain left over from things that happened before you came into the picture. You'll be ripping the bandage off this family's mortal wound."

"You mean the inheritance? The problems with your grandfather's will."

"That's some of it, though not all."

"What is it that this family refuses to tell me, Will? Forgive me, but I'm wrestling with feeling nobody really thinks I'm a Hanover. Not if you all walk on eggshells around me. Why is everyone keeping me in the dark?"

He shook his head. "They don't know."

"They don't know what?" Sera stood. "Why your father left?"

"Sera, you can't do this. There's got to be a way to move forward without bringing my father into this. I'm determined to find it."

"Then can you tell me what your father did to make you have such hatred for him? Because I can see it in your face. You don't need to tell me any history because it's right here. Whatever happened, it's still holding you. And it's not who you are."

He paused, then in a gruff whisper, asked, "And what if I'm not the man you think I am?"

Sera's heart began constricting in her chest. William, the man who had become closer to her than any person in her life. The dream of him threatened to drift away on words like that.

"Will, is there any reason I shouldn't have complete trust in you?"

"No." He shook his head almost immediately.

"Because if there's something you need to tell me, whatever it is—I'll listen."

He shook his head, offering the same weak smile he'd given her for weeks.

"Then why—"

"I'm just wrestling with all this, love."

Sera exhaled a soft breath, feeling that the moment had passed. Whatever he'd come close to opening had been locked up tight again.

He reached over and closed the laptop.

"It's late."

"Well then, how about breakfast?" She offered a smile, hoping he'd bite on the lightness of the idea. "It's the middle of the night, we're both awake, and I feel like cooking an omelet for my husband."

William looked up at her.

She raised an eyebrow. "Well?"

"You're beautiful."

A laugh escaped her lips. "I am?" she asked, soft as air.

"Yes. And your faith in me," he added, standing up before her. "I don't deserve it."

"If you're trying to flatter me, husband," she whispered, offering him a spontaneous smile that overpowered the pangs of worry pricking at her insides, "it's working."

"I know none of this is making things easy for you, but breakfast—something normal—sounds right now. I'd give just about anything to see that smile more often these days."

Sera could have kissed him in that second.

If you only knew . . .

William ran a hand along the side of her face, then buried it in the hair at the back of her neck. "I couldn't do this without you. You know that, don't you?"

"Then lucky you're not without me."

He sighed and pulled her close, then brushed his thumb over the skin beneath her eye.

"You look tired. I think you've been working too hard. Is all of this too much for you?"

Sera had been exhausted, that was true. And sick with nausea from morning to night. It took everything in her to hide it from him. But the circles that darkened the skin beneath her eyes didn't lie. And despite how exhausted she felt, the last thing she wanted to do was compound his worries.

She'd tell him in good time. When he'd see a baby as a blessing and not another reason to doubt their future. For now, the caress of his loving words was enough.

"I'm fine." She shook her head. When he looked like he didn't believe her, she pecked a kiss to his lips and added, "Really."

"And you fully intend on going to London no matter what I say, don't you?"

She breathed out a sigh.

"I think the stakes are higher if I don't go, Will. Someone has to get through to your father. I'm not afraid of putting myself in a place of discomfort if the result brings me back to you."

"And you're prepared for what this could do to everything we have." His eyes searched her face.

Sera nodded, hoping to show him confidence.

"If Sophie could be brave with everything she went through, then so can I."

CHAPTER FOURTEEN

June 24, 1942
The Daily Telegraph
Fleet Street, London

The tea cup Kája had been holding nearly took a tumble off the edge of the desk in her haste to set it down.

Beneath the block-print word CONFIDENTIAL stamped in a glaring red, the headline screamed, "Germans Murder 700,000 Jews in Poland."

The sheet of paper had been buried in the stack of articles she'd been given to copy-edit before the paper hit the newsstands the following day, so the words before her were the last thing she'd expect. She moved her index finger along the bottom of each line, scanning the article.

Nazis murdering Jews.

Was this true? No. It couldn't possibly be.

Trixie plopped down in the chair next to her desk.

"You look like you've just seen a ghost, sugar. What's the trouble?"

"Trixie, I'm a secretary—" she mumbled, then stopped short of adding, "so why is this on my desk?"

Kája tilted her chin down, knowing her face must have registered shock. Or numbness. In truth, she felt like she'd been smacked across the cheek.

"Too right, doll." Trixie smirked and taking a slow drag on her cigarette, surveyed the bustling office. She puffed a cloud of smoke out into the air around them. "I only managed to sneak away from the switchboard for a cig and I'll bet within thirty seconds, they're hunting for me." She sighed. "Good luck to the woman hoping to land any kind of promotion in this office full of stuffed-shirt men. We women may have jobs here now, but I'll wager they'll try to send us right back to the kitchens once this war is over and the boys come home."

"That's not what I mean." Kája placed her hand over the stack of papers on the desktop, her heart feeling the weight of the horrific words again.

"Really? You got a story to tell that's better than a housewife's stolen ration book?" Trixie leaned in close on a lazy sigh.

"I actually think I might have," Kája admitted, chewing her bottom lip, thinking things through.

"I can keep a secret," she twittered, and smiled with her usual red pout more suited to a party-goer on a Friday night. "Spill."

Kája looked up at Trixie, whose face held a wide-eyed expression of bemused wonder. Her eyebrows arched up to a dizzying degree and she stared back, eager.

"Where is Mr. Edmunton?"

Trixie made a *tsk* noise under her tongue and tilted her head toward the end of the newsroom. "Old Herbert? In his office." She crossed her arms over her chest before continuing. "With the door closed—the crabby buzzard. Why?"

Kája looked to the glass-walled office. She could see him sitting behind the oversized oak desk, with a phone handset up to his ear and a stone-faced expression carrying his gaze to a point fixed somewhere out the windows. He ran a hand over the receding hairline at his brow.

The scene sounded alarm bells in her ears.

Kája shook her head. "Something's wrong."

"No doubt. He hasn't stepped out of that office for hours. I haven't seen him this quiet since the Blitz." Trixie lowered her voice. Kája had to lean in to hear over the ringing phones and incessant punching of typewriter keys that kept up a steady hum in the background. "And the boys on the war beat have been gone so long that everyone's beginning to wonder. The switchboard girls are all waiting for someone to tell us to head down to the shelters, like it's 1940 all over again."

On instinct, Kája stole a quick glance over at the desk in the corner.

His desk.

It hadn't been occupied today. Or all month, for that matter. And remembering the Blitz bombings always sent her thoughts back to Liam. Kája tried her best not to picture the dashing reporter dodging bullets as he typed up stories from behind enemy lines. At least once a day, sometimes more, her eyes would drift to Liam Marshall's prized 1920s-era Remington, which sat untouched atop his desk. It made the corner of the floor seem so lonely, and her lonely with it.

"I know what you're thinking. We haven't seen the ace reporter in a while." Trixie leaned in, laying a supportive hand on Kája's arm. "The girls have been listening for him, I promise. But it seems we only get calls from Kemsley House now. While the men in the print shop are sequestered up there just to make sure the paper's still printing, we sit here surrounded by empty chairs for weeks on end. All the London boys are off chasing a story somewhere, aren't they, now that they've been called up? So here we sit, with Edmunton and the rest of the bores. I don't know what they call that in Prague, but here in London we call it a *jip*."

She stared at their editor's office.

"Edmunton has been shut in there all day, hasn't he?"

"You should know—you're his secretary," Trixie chirped, then noticing the seriousness Kája had allowed to seep over her face, clamped a hand around her elbow. "Wait a minute. You've got something real, haven't you? What is it?"

Kája shot up from her wooden swivel chair as if a spring had been built in the hammered leather cushion and with the article in hand, stepped over to his office. She rapped her knuckles on the glass door and opened it enough to poke her head inside.

"Sir, might I have a moment?"

"Not now, Miss Makovský." Edmunton slammed the phone down in its cradle and waved her back.

Kája ignored his brush-off and stepped into the office anyway.

She closed the door with an intentional *click* behind her and stood, leaning up against the doorframe, waiting for him to look up. He didn't. Instead, he began scribbling something on a note pad and heaved a heavy sigh.

Receiving no notice, Kája decided to force her hand. She took a step toward the desk and held the article out in front of him. She let the paper float down to the desktop.

"That was mixed in with my articles for the day."

He took one look and shot a glance up to meet hers, eyes nearly popping out of his head.

"How did you get this?" he barked, and snatched the paper up. He waved it out in front of her and looked around the newsroom, as if her accomplices could be expected to join them in his office at any moment. "Who else has seen it?"

Kája wasn't offended, nor was she scared. On this day she would overlook the man's ill-mannered constitution in order to get what she needed from him: the truth.

She slid into the chair opposite the desk and sat, arms folded and unyielding. Her heart was melting and her knees would be knocking had her legs been uncrossed. Even so, she set her back pin-straight and calmly waited for him to offer the details she so desperately needed.

"You've made your point." One of his eyebrows arched up and

he eyed her, with what she judged was a most accusatory glance. With a gruffness that sounded like he'd swallowed a mouth full of stones, he charged, "But you'll answer me, Miss Makovský. Where did you get this?" He looked past her to the row of empty desks lining the wall beyond his office. "Did Marshall have anything to do with this?"

"Mr. Marshall has nothing to do with this. He's not been back to the office for weeks. You know that," she said, noting that because of what she knew of the crosswords, Liam's activities were tied with hers whether she liked it or not. "I think it's an honest mistake that it ended up in my stack of copy for the war beat. What I'd like to know is whether or not it's true."

"And as your superior in this office, I am the one who will be asking the questions."

"No one has seen it to my knowledge. Yet." Kája notched her chin a little higher as she delivered the veiled threat.

The usually gruff man surprised her then and exhaled, a rather sad expression taking over his features. "Yes. If what we're receiving on the wire is true, and it looks like it is . . . they're being killed by the thousands."

"But how could this happen? If it were true, how could the Nazis possibly hide something like this?"

"Have you forgotten? The Polish government is exiled here in London. It stands to reason that they'd have heard about it first. And as you are aware, we make it our business to know what's happening with this war, both for His Majesty's government and for the people of Great Britain. I don't need to tell you that if there's a story to be had, our chaps out there will hunt it down."

Kája felt her throat close up.

"It appears they've even found a way of gassing them by the hundreds at a time, poor souls," he said with a huff. "What does it matter how? The point is, they're doing it and the world has to know. We're running it tomorrow."

Kája's eyes popped open. "On the front page?"

"That has not been decided yet." Edmunton took the paper and rolled it in his hands.

There was only one thing left to ask, though she worried he would see straight through her to the beating heart in her chest.

"Did Mr. Marshall write it?"

Edmunton paused and eyed her. "And why would you think to ask that question?"

She answered immediately, "Gut instinct."

"Well, if you don't mind, I'll thank you to tell your gut to keep quiet and mind your work, Miss Makovský—the work you've been *assigned* to."

Her thoughts poured out then, in an almost inaudible series of whispers.

"It just doesn't seem real. It couldn't be. It's too horrible . . ." She felt her chin quiver slightly and her hand flew up to cover the show of emotion.

Her editor must have seen the slight vulnerability, because he cleared his throat with a soft *hrrumph* and looked back down at the stack of papers littering his desk.

"Miss Makovský?"

Kája shook off her momentary stupor and looked up. She met the older man's gray eyes staring back at her.

"Yes, sir?"

"The last thing I need is a woman weeping in my office," he said, though the brash of his usually harsh tone had turned unmistakably kind. "Now, unless you would like to stay and heat the water for my tea, I suggest you get back to work. And do be smart about it."

He raised his eyebrows and tilted his chin toward the bustling newsroom beyond the glass.

"Off with you now. And keep this to yourself until it runs." He pointed his pencil at her and for good measure, added, "That's an order."

Kája jumped when the phone on his desk cried out with a shrill tone that set her ears to ringing. He picked it up and nearly shouted, "Telegraph. Edmunton." And she found herself dismissed.

Kája stood and walked out, gingerly closing the door behind her. She froze for a moment while the newsroom continued erupting with its usual activity. She scanned the floor, feeling numb to the hustle of reporters as their resonant laughter and the pounding of typewriter keys created a hum of energy all around her. The sounds were impersonal, the air agitating.

She felt panic taking over and heaven help her, if she didn't escape the office she feared she'd scream in front of the lot of them.

Kája's feet seemed to have a life of their own; they carried her through the office at a quickened pace. She stopped at her desk just long enough to fumble for her purse and whisper a passing "I have to go," to Trixie, who folded her arms across her chest and stared dumbfounded as Kája ducked into the nearest elevator.

She didn't stop. Not until the elevator chimed at the bottom floor and she'd passed through the lobby, almost running in her heels, and burst through the front doors to the bustle of the London streets beyond.

Just like she'd done all those months before, when the Blitz had wounded them all so grievously, Kája stared up at the sky. She wasn't afraid of planes or bombs now; that fear had long since become commonplace in every Londoner's life. Instead, she stared into the deep blue overhead, wondering if God was up there watching.

Did he see what was happening in their world—in *her* world? With the headline came confirmation that the entire world was on fire.

Heaven help me, she thought, fresh tears stinging at her eyes. *I have to get my parents out of Prague before they're killed too.*

CHAPTER FIFTEEN

June 30, 1942
Paddington Station
London

Rain pounded the windows of the cab.

The end of June had been sunny and pleasant up to this point. But now the sky seemed to let loose with reckless abandon. It poured down on the Londoners hurrying along the streets, some with umbrellas pulled low and others braving the onslaught without any protection at all. Their figures darted under awnings and ducked into alleyways as water fell in unforgiving sheets around the city.

Kája gazed out as the car drove by monstrous piles of battered brick and timber that had come crashing down in the Blitz years before. Gutted buildings lay on both sides of the street like giant brick beasts slumbering in the pelting summer rain, their images bleeding into a cascade of ruddy reds and browns by the lines of water trickling down the glass.

Squeaky brakes drew her attention, and the cab slowed to a stop in front of Paddington Station.

"We're here, miss," the driver said, cockney accent thick even behind the weight of his smelly cigar.

Kája retrieved money from her purse and dropped enough to cover the fare into his outstretched hand. But she hesitated before stepping out, her palm fused to the door handle.

He checked his watch. "You'll be gettin' out, then, miss?"

"Oh yes." She'd hesitated only a moment, trying to steel her resolve. "I'm sorry."

After relaxing the cigar on his bottom lip, the burly man softened his tone.

"The train." He pointed to the busy platform beyond the car windows. "It's that way, if you be wanting to catch yer ride."

She nodded. "Thank you, I'm sure."

Kája tugged her small suitcase from the seat and pulled her handbag strap up over her wrist until it rested in the crook of her elbow. She opened the door to a rush of misty rain that sprayed her cheeks. Rain trickled down the chocolate brown–piped collar of her pale-blue suit, making it feel soggy and cold.

He'll be here . . .

Kája thought about the journey ahead. About what she had to do. And as she stopped at the ticket office and deposited her luggage with the porter, she tried to reassure herself that Liam would show up. He'd always been there before and he'd surely not let her down now.

She ran to the shelter of the platform and stopped under a dark-green awning adorned with a Union Jack garland, shaking raindrops off the lengths of her sleeves.

"You're always early."

Kája whirled around at the sound of the voice.

"Liam?" She peeked out from under the brim of her rain-soaked hat, disbelieving for a moment that the man standing tall in his officer's hat and military-issue coat could be the same laid-back reporter she'd come to know.

It had only been months, but he seemed older. Taller even. Somehow more confident. She'd never seen him in uniform and it hushed her that he almost looked like a different man because of it now.

"I checked with the station master. The next train doesn't

depart for another half an hour." He tipped his head toward the clock by the ticket office. "Your most predictable traits," he said. "Kája Makovský—she's always proper. Always follows the rules. But most importantly, she's early to every party."

"Yes. That does sound like me," she breathed out, relieved to find him standing there making small talk about her mannerisms when she hadn't heard from him in weeks.

"I received your message." He offered her a forced smile. "I was at Bletchley, thankfully. An hour and a half drive from the Buckinghamshire countryside is a sight better than trying to fly in from overseas, so I'm glad you caught me in time."

"Is that where you've been? Across the Channel?"

"You had to have known I would get leave soon," he said, avoiding her question. "You couldn't wait to talk this out?"

She looked up cautiously, then turned to sorting the contents of her handbag, looking for her ticket. She didn't know he'd taken a step forward until his fingertips brushed her elbow.

Every part of her froze.

Liam reached out for the handbag and gingerly pulled it from her wrist. He set it down on the bench behind them and tossed his hat down beside it. She refused to look up at him.

"Kája," he said, just loud enough to be heard over the trickles of rain pattering the awning roof. Her eyes met the soft sky of his. "There's no need to act as though you're searching for your ticket when I'd wager you know exactly where it is."

Kája took a deep breath and fought to find words, but he continued.

"Perhaps we can move past pretenses, then. Forgive me if I sound put off, but no one in her right mind would think to go hop-scotching through the middle of a war."

"Liam, please. I called you here to help, not badger me."

He took another measured step toward her, enough so that she thought he might step on the tips of her toes.

"I'm serious, Kája. When you send me a cryptic telegram that you're headed for the heart of Nazi-occupied territory, how am I supposed to react? You've gone completely mad."

"You don't understand," she muttered, looking down at the ground for a moment. She decided it was cowardly though, and faced him. "My family is all I have."

"Not true." He shook his head on the flat denial. "And you forget—I do understand what it's like to worry about a parent."

"I know you do," she backtracked, thinking of the terror they'd all experienced during the worst of the Blitz raids. "And I didn't mean to hurt you. I've built a life here. But all the while—what I've left behind has been there, in the back of my mind, on the surface of my heart. And now, knowing what the Nazis are doing to Jews?"

Kája held up a newspaper in front of him, its folds of water-logged newsprint smearing ink across her gloved hand. She pointed to the screaming headline of the Nazis' latest assault on humanity and half begged, "Tell me. Did you write it?"

He remained stone-faced.

"This I can't ignore. You must *see* that." Kája searched his face and when she felt brave enough, whispered, "Do you remember what I told you that night after the club?"

Liam nodded.

"I remember," he said, and placed his hand over her gloved fingers to lower hers. He turned round, spotted the bench behind them, and tugged her back. "Let's sit."

The gesture was so tender and unexpected that she felt compelled to obey. They slid into the bench, both watching absently as travelers bustled through the rain showering the platform.

"I knew it had something to do with the article," he said, shaking his head. "I just didn't think you'd take it like this."

"You knew about it then? That Jews are being murdered?"

He nodded. "We had a tip on the story from a Polish freedom

fighter who'd been sent to one of the camps. Auschwitz it's called, a death camp. Apparently one of the worst. He managed to smuggle a radio into his cell block and has been sending wires to the Polish government exiled here in London. We decoded some transmissions."

"Where is the camp?"

"Near Krakow."

"That's not so far from Prague." She exhaled a breath. "And what did this man say?"

"He's been imprisoned for months, watching people die all around him. He's been feeding information to the governments here. And what he had to say, well . . . they didn't want to believe it was true. We had to do our fact-checking, what there could be done. But then again, after the Blitz, we could believe just about anything from Hitler's army—horrific atrocities and all."

"So you've known for a while?"

He countered easily, "I've been gone for a while."

"You didn't tell me."

"How could I, Kája? Knowing you as I do, I was fearful you'd end up here, waiting to catch a train to goodness knows where. Forgive me, but your stubbornness seems to have overshadowed your will to follow propriety. Or to use your common sense."

"Liam, I'm half Jewish." She whispered the words, almost afraid to admit the truth with others around.

"Don't say it like it's a dirty secret." He raked his fingers through his hair in acute frustration.

"Isn't it? We're hated everywhere." She scanned the crowds of people walking by and added, "We're hated even here in London, though some are just not as forthright about it."

"You're not hated everywhere, and certainly not by me." He shook his head emphatically. "You may be half Jewish, but you're a whole person. I won't let you think any part of you is a bad thing."

"But you know it's real. They're killing Jews! Rounding them up, sending them away where some are never heard from again. They'll take my father if they haven't already. And my mother will choose to go with him. You see? That leaves me no choice. It's not like hiding in our London shelters while random bombs rain down. This threat is targeted. It's alive and searching them out. And if there's anything I can do to stop them from being sent away, I must try."

"What can you possibly hope to do against the whole of Hitler's army? Tell me that."

"Whatever I have to."

Liam grabbed her up in his arms so quickly that the action startled her. His hands were gentle and his voice whisper soft as his breath warmed her ear.

"I meant what I said, Kája. That night at Bethnal Green? I want you in my life."

She looked away from the directness of his eyes. He'd left the year before and had been back only sporadically since. And though he couldn't tell her where he was going or just when he'd be back, he had opened his heart and shocked her by voicing the truth of his affections.

Kája offered a soft nod. "I know."

"I'm a flawed man, Kája. I know that full well. But things changed after that day when the bombs first rained down on us. When the whole city exploded and I thought you . . ." Liam shook his head, his voice catching on emotion. "The war has kept me away. And I may have to go back and fight. But I can't do that unless I can come home and know you're safe. Don't you see?"

She said nothing. Thought nothing. Could barely breathe as the thunder roared in the background.

Kája leaned into him, thinking of the look in his eyes when he came after her during the Blitz raids on London. They'd rarely spoken of the night she'd almost been killed, but she still knew. She'd seen the fear in his eyes that night.

"Dear God, Kája. Do you realize what you're attempting to do?"

She nodded, leaning in until the top of her head just bumped the underside of his chin.

"I was hoping you wouldn't try to talk me out of it. I'm scared already."

"Did you ever think," he said, "I might be scared too? I'm sorry if it sounds selfish to want you alive, but there it is. I can't accept the thought of you starving or worse in some Nazi death camp."

She edged back from him, enough that she could look him square in the face.

"That won't happen, Liam." She paused and wiped a tear from her eye with a gloved hand. "Trust me. I can do it."

"I'd never think to doubt you. That's not what this is about."

"You've known for a long time, since Columbia Road . . . when I woke at the hospital. I told you then and I'm telling you now—I *have* to do this. I always knew I'd be called home, I just didn't know when."

His hand met hers, cupping her cheek with ready warmth. He held it there for a brief moment, then leaned back from her and rested his elbows on his knees. The pragmatic side of his personality appeared to have taken over.

He arched an eyebrow and looked her straight in the eyes.

"What's your plan, then?"

Kája chanced a look up at him and cleared her throat over the emotion that was building there.

"My father is a physician, so I can only pray his services are needed by the Reich. That's what he's been doing up until now. I'd received a letter by way of my sister, who is still living in Palestine. It was dated more than five months ago and it had already been opened, but it found its way to me nonetheless. Maybe they kept him there to work in the city."

"If he's still there, they'll be watching him for sure."

"Yes. I expect so."

He nodded. "What do you plan to do?"

I have to make him believe I'm confident. If I make him believe it, then maybe I will too.

"With the travel papers I have, I can get to the coast." Despite her best efforts, Kája felt her chin quiver under his intense scrutiny. "From there, I'll find a way to cross the Channel."

"Where?"

"I know I can't go through Portsmouth or Calais so . . . maybe in the north."

"Not good enough." He shook his head. "You may reach the shore, but what then? You'll just march through the front lines of the German army with an expired visa? Kája, these governments are in a state of anarchy. It's not like London. We've been bombed flat but at least the city is pulling together to get through it. We've had bucket brigades putting out fires and a stream of trains to take children to the countryside. There is some order to it. But out there?" He glanced to some place far off in the direction of the fading train tracks. "It's war. There won't be hands outstretched to help you. There's no orderly rationing of goods; there are none to be had. You'll be running for your life."

She closed her eyes. "I've been trying not to think about it."

"You're being naïve then."

Kája yanked back out of his grasp and shot to her feet.

"Please, Liam. You said you cared about me once."

She wasn't given a breath of time to finish her sentence before he'd grabbed her up in his arms.

"I do."

"And after losing your father in the raids and both of us surviving that first day"—she said the words softly, sweetly—"I know you'll understand why I have to do this." She gently pushed back from his chest. "And if you truly care about me, then you must let me go."

Liam stared back at her then, even as they heard the screech of train brakes behind them. She turned slightly, enough that she could see a cloud of steam rising around them.

Time stopped.

It seemed that the rain and the people moving around them faded away and it was only the two of them, lost in their own world.

"The train is early."

She nodded, never taking her eyes from his. "Yes."

"Then we haven't much time." Liam leaned in and brushed his fingertip across the scar that bridged her left temple. "My beautiful Kája—I can't keep you, can I? You'd never forgive me if I didn't let you do this, no matter how completely mad you are for trying it."

She blinked, content to stare back at him for the last few moments they had together.

"Never is a terribly long time."

He nodded. "Yes. Too long," he said, and pulled several papers from the inside pocket of his jacket. He held them out to her.

"What's this?"

"There's enough time here to get in and then get out again—all of you."

She scanned the travel papers and immediately looked back at him. "You got me a position with the Red Cross?"

He nodded. "It was the best I could do. But you're going to have to temper your accent."

"Liam, I don't know anything about nursing," she whispered.

"The Red Cross does far more than nursing. And your father is a physician. Do you have any knowledge you might have picked up from him?"

"Some," she muttered, then shook her head. "But not enough to pass as a nurse. Not if I'm traveling under the auspice of medical service."

"Then you'll have to align yourself to some other duty and pray it won't be called into question. Those papers will get you in but your smarts are going to have to get you out. You'll have a day or so to gather up your things—don't wait too long—and catch a train south through Germany. The International Red Cross has been granted access to travel through to Switzerland. Those traveling papers will ensure you get there in one piece."

Kája folded the papers, then cradled them to her chest and leaned back so she could look up into his eyes. "But how did you know I'd need them? When I didn't say anything in the telegram?"

He shrugged. Almost as cocky as a boy in a schoolyard. "You're stubborn to a fault." She thought she saw something sparkle in his eyes as he continued, "I knew you'd go with or without my help, but I'd rather you go with it."

She nodded and returned a weak smile.

"Right then," he said, and pulled her along toward the train. "We should board."

Her head snapped up.

"What did you say?"

"The train's about to leave and I'm going with you." Liam pulled a ticket from his pocket. "I can escort you as far as Amsterdam. After that, you're in God's care."

CHAPTER SIXTEEN

July 1, 1942
Norwich Thorpe Station
Norwich

The train had lulled over the tracks with such a soft song, and leaning back on the cushions had felt so right. Kája had closed her eyes just for a moment, not even realizing she'd greeted the solace of sleep until Liam's hands were gently gripping her shoulders, nudging her awake.

"You've changed?"

It was the first thing she noticed when she'd opened her eyes and found Liam looking back at her. Gone was his smart uniform. It had been replaced by a pin-striped shirt tucked into black wool trousers and a scratchy-looking tweed jacket that was a touch worn at the seams.

"Yes. Can't go past Norwich in a uniform. Not now. Any good spy knows that." Liam cracked a slight smile and tossed a brown paper bag onto the seat cushion next to her. "Here. You'll need to put this on before we leave."

"What is it?"

Kája opened the bag to find a thick uniform of dark navy. She ran her fingers over the silvery circle patch sewn just beneath the jacket's shoulder seam, the stitched cross in the center an unmistakably bright red. There was a white collared blouse and black tie tucked in with the uniform jacket and skirt.

"A Red Cross uniform."

Yes, she supposed she'd need one to travel with the Red Cross. She looked down at her clothes. Liam didn't need to say anything to confirm that her blue travel suit would never do where she was going.

"There are shoes and a hat too." He must have read her thoughts because he noted, "Not that the blue you have on isn't fetching."

Kája smiled in spite of herself. How could he always manage to do that—make her heart lighter no matter the circumstances?

"Here," he said, and dropped a leather satchel on the seat cushion. "I'll get your luggage from the porter so you can put your necessities in this. It's far more practical than dragging a suitcase behind enemy lines."

Kája ran her fingers over the seam of the worn leather.

She recognized it; the satchel Liam always carried when he popped into the *Telegraph* offices. It was worn in all the right places; the leather of the handle was soft with the hundreds of times he'd taken it in hand. The hammered brass nail heads had kept the bottom from much wear. But still, she could tell—it was a cherished old friend and he was willingly offering it to her.

"But this is yours. You carry it everywhere," she argued softly, and shook her head. "I couldn't."

"Please. Take it." Liam didn't appear to be willing to negotiate, given the boorish look on his face. Despite the softness of the request, he looked unwilling to budge. "That suitcase is going to get really heavy after a while. This way you can slip it over your shoulder."

It made sense. She decided to give him the victory.

"I'll take it in care," she said, and rubbed a hand over the handle. "Gratefully."

"Good." He nodded once. "Then you'd best hurry."

Liam tilted his head to the station sign out the window.

"We're at Thorpe. The station services for ladies are right over there." He motioned to a pair of doors at the bottom of a stairwell and checked his wristwatch. "But watch your step. This station was hit again by the Luftwaffe just a few days ago. The city's been under the threat of bombs since being thrust into London's Blitz nightmare with the Baedeker raids in the spring. Some of the major repairs haven't been completed yet so the platforms could be a bit chewed up here and there. The train leaves in fifteen minutes and it could be rough going out of Norwich. We can't know what we'll find."

"Then why do we go? There must be someplace else."

"Because we can't hope to get you across the Channel anywhere in the south. Going from Portsmouth into occupied France is out of the question. And Calais is under constant threat." He looked at her point-blank and said, "Even if we tried that way now, we'd never make it out."

She nodded. "I understand."

"Catching a boat from Norwich to Amsterdam is possible if you accompany Red Cross rations. But once we're there, that will be it—no turning back."

"I thought there was no turning back in London?"

Liam shook his head. "I'm not going to stop trying to convince you to stay," he admitted.

"What kind of responsible intelligence officer would you be if you didn't?"

He tilted his chin and gave her a more serious glare. "The kind who couldn't get you into the British Red Cross without pulling every string behind the scenes that I could find."

"You could get in trouble for this?"

"Let me worry about that. Just prepare yourself. I expect I'll try to get you to reconsider at each stop between here and the German-occupied border. You may very well wish to be rid of me by the time we reach Amsterdam."

Kája imagined each stop carrying her farther and farther into the blackness of Germany and shuddered.

"Then since you're sticking your neck out for me, I'll try to overlook your nature for now."

"Good."

A second or two passed awkwardly as she waited for him to move from blocking the doorway.

"Are you hungry?"

Kája hadn't thought about it until that moment, but a swift rumble in her stomach reminded her that yes, hunger was there in the background. She nodded immediately and stood, clutching the bag under one arm.

"Yes, actually. I am."

"Here. You can take this." Liam pulled a folded package of waxed paper from his jacket pocket and placed it in her free hand. "Sorry. It's only a lentil and cheese pie. I expect it will be bland but it's all they had left. London ration books are no good up here so I had to pay through the nose to get us that. I did see some fried potatoes if you're so inclined. And the merchant had cream scones, but knowing there was no sugar in them made me think to pass altogether."

Liam's hands were buried in his pockets. And he'd flown through the explanation with an almost boyish air. Quite unlike the sure-footed and sharp-tongued Liam Marshall. What was it about those tiny glimpses of vulnerability that she longed to see in him, especially when he was trying so hard to seem strong and unaffected?

Kája smiled lightly, then bit her bottom lip, keeping the thought to herself.

"I can go back and get them if you want," he offered, and leaned toward the compartment door. "I'm sure they'll have a few left if I hurry."

"No," she said, shaking her head. "This is fine, Liam. I'll just go—" Kája moved to pass by him, noticing how he tried to move out of the way at the same time and faltered. He stepped on the tip of her shoe. "Excuse me."

"Right," he said, and moved quickly to the side. "Sorry."

Liam looked like he wanted to say something, like he was battling in a way. Kája waited, expecting something else. But whatever had been there was gone soon enough and he seemed unable to speak of it. He tilted his head to the platform instead of adding anything further.

"I'll just wait for you here, then."

"Yes. Thank you." She nodded and then ducked under the doorframe to the platform.

"Fifteen minutes, mind," he cautioned, looking up to the station clock out the window. "Or they'll leave without us."

Kája nodded and threaded her way into the crowd.

Something about knowing he was standing behind her, watching over her even from afar, bolstered her with renewed strength as she weaved in and out of the passersby crowding the busy platform.

There were officers in uniform and women on their arms, tearful as they let their men go to board the train. She saw pockets of children here and there, huddled together as older adults looked after them. Kája tried not to notice how tired the adults looked. How battle weary they appeared. The children seemed quiet for the most part, and sad perhaps? She saw that some of the young ones had papers pinned to their shirts, likely with the name and address to whom they belonged. It was sad here, too, that the war had changed so many things, even in the north.

The mood that clung to the air irritated her already knotted stomach. She hoped the food Liam had purchased for her wouldn't turn it further.

Kája proceeded to the ladies' room and changed quickly.

She folded her suit and placed it in the brown paper bag,

packing the waxed paper pie on top of it. There'd be no eating now, despite her growling stomach. Butterflies occupied the space where hunger had been. Maybe they would settle and she could eat something on the train.

The whistle sounded, giving warning that the steam engine would soon be flying over the tracks. Moving quickly, Kája stepped from one of the wooden stalls with hat in hand. Though she'd hadn't intended to do so, she came to a halt before the mirror.

The sight of her was a shock.

The uniform was stark and cold. It echoed the seriousness of what she was about to do. And though she hadn't noticed it before that very moment, the reflection she saw looked every bit as severe. A hint of gray painted half-moons on the skin beneath her eyes. Her hair was still pulled back in a taut chignon, but gentle wisps had freed themselves and now hung soft along her temple. They looked unkempt and wild, and framed a face so solemn that she wondered just who was staring back at her.

Lord, she prayed, allowing the uniform hat and bag to drop to the floor at her feet. *Liam's here now and I'm grateful. So grateful. But what happens next?*

Tears burned her eyes then and she wiped at the coolness of them trickling down her cheeks.

I don't think I can do this alone . . . Kája ran her hand over her hair until it brushed over the rise of the thick chignon at her nape. She felt the cold metal of a hairpin and pulled it free. She found another and another, pulling each free until the fiery softness of her hair tumbled about her shoulders. She managed to breathe softly, almost automatically, and looked back at the frightened stranger before her.

Kája shuddered, feeling the full weight of what she was about to do.

She tilted her face, exposing light to the scar at her left temple. She'd tried to cover it with powder but the surface of it still

glistened slightly. She brushed the raise of skin with her fingertips. And she ran her hand down the span of the uniform coat
that covered her left arm. She could feel scars burning her skin
there, too, reminding her that bombs were real. The threat she
was walking into was real. Death was real. And the fact that she
was walking toward it alone—the truth of it echoed in her mind.

I don't have the strength to do this, she prayed, feeling terrified
and oh so altered from who she'd been before the war.

She hung her head, feeling only weakness left in her.

*Have not I commanded thee? Be strong and of a good courage; be
not afraid, neither be thou dismayed: for the* LORD *thy God is with thee
whithersoever thou goest.*

Kája was reminded of the promise in the book of Joshua. It
was a comfort. And truth. And letting her fear be replaced by a
strength she'd never known. She spoke aloud, praying that God
could find her in a little bathroom in Norwich, when she was
scared and alone and at her weakest point, when he could have
showed himself to anyone in the world.

The words flooded her heart and slipped out, whispered so
softly, falling from her tear-stained lips:

"Just please don't leave me. No matter what happens—just
don't leave me."

She placed her hands on either side of the porcelain sink,
using it for stability as she cried through the prayer.

The creak of the restroom door signaled the presence of
patrons who had just stepped through the portal. Kája wiped at
her eyes and quickly gathered her things.

She marched out to the platform again, toward the car she'd
share with Liam. The train whistle blew a second warning and she
quickened her pace, weaving through the current of fast-moving
crowds.

It wasn't until she came to the car and saw Liam through
the window, sitting with his attention affixed to her, that Kája

finally exhaled. She fused her hand to the rail, climbed up the steps, and met him in the train compartment's doorway.

Liam didn't say anything right away. Kája knew her eyes were red from crying and her hair was unkempt, tumbling about her shoulders in a torrential wave. She told herself that he'd badger her, just as he'd promised to do. He'd find the harshness of her appearance an abhorrence, given the fact that he'd been to war and fought bravely while she was crumbling before she'd even come close to it. Surely he'd see the fear, the evidence of shed tears, and would insist they turn around immediately.

Liam would see her weakness and pounce upon it.

Kája prepared herself as she stood in the doorway, waiting for him to comment on her disheveled appearance. But Liam stood and looked over the wildness of her hair, slowly surveying the emotion that was splayed across her face and without an ounce of condemnation, asked in a rough whisper, "Are you all right?"

Kája nodded and hugged the paper bag to her chest.

"Yes," she answered truthfully, and allowed him to latch the door behind them. "I am now."

CHAPTER SEVENTEEN

South Kensington
London

Their car came to a stop in front of a classic Georgian town-home in Onslow Square.

The white brick, all four stories of it, was pristine and popped against the blue of the sky. The double front doors were a sleek black and stood positioned in the center of large topiaries and an elegantly arched window flanking each side. A second-story balcony overlooked a charming garden across the way and a grove of shade trees blanketed the street with overhead shade.

Penny stepped out of the car and waved a hand for her to follow.

Sera inhaled a calming breath and stepped out, noting that even the air was perfumed with the scent of late summertime flowers. It was picturesque. Refined. Nearly perfect, she had to admit; this was the best London had to offer a weary traveler. So the fact that she felt positively sick to her stomach about going in made her wish she was anywhere else but standing in the lovely street.

A low whistle escaped Penny's lips. Her eyes traced the lines leading up four floors of the home's grandeur. Sera stood shoulder to shoulder with her, battling for a brave smile.

"Well—this is it. Our temporary home sweet home," she whispered.

"You seem disappointed." Penny nudged her in the side, no doubt hoping to lighten the moment. "I don't think it's any less grand than the big pile of Hanover bricks in California. You should be used to this by now, right?"

"I'm not sure I'll ever get used to this." Sera hooked an arm through her elbow. "I think that's what makes me most nervous about it. Will should be here with us. It just doesn't feel right without him."

"He'd be here if he could. You know that." Penny winked at her when the driver began pulling their bags from the trunk. "In any case, it was kind of your father-in-law to send a car to the airport. I can't remember the last time I've been treated like such a lady."

"I hope it's a good sign that we can expect a welcome," Sera replied, following the driver as he carried their bags to the front door.

Sera took a deep breath and touched a finger to the bell on the brick wall. It chimed loudly. They heard footsteps echo through the inside.

"Remind me to praise Paul later," Penny whispered as the footsteps neared. "I asked him to call ahead and he's managed to get something right for a change. Looks like your dear brother-in-law may be turning over a new leaf in favor of becoming a responsible guy."

The door opened and they were greeted by a silver-haired woman with sparkling lilac eyes smiling at them.

"Welcome, ladies. I am Mrs. Clark, Mr. Hanover's manager. And which of you would be our William's Sera?"

Sera raised her hand and found that she had a mere second to catch her breath before the woman bundled her up in a warm embrace. Sera returned the hug with a genuine smile and, her former agitation temporarily at bay, introduced Penny.

"Please come in," Mrs. Clark chimed, and led them into the entry. "I'll inform Mr. Hanover that you're here."

Sera nodded and looked around. The interior of the home was just as grand as the outside.

A spiral staircase took up an impressive span of the far wall, snaking its way up to a second-story landing of espresso oak with brushed wrought-iron spindles and a gleaming, polished rail. The entryway ceiling was two stories in height, the walls a crisp, classic white to offset the dramatic black-and-white check of the floor. A sitting room adjoined overlooking the street. Its walls were a warm robin's egg blue, with furnishings in white and shades of slate gray. The bright pop of orange flowers created a blazing focal point from a vase on the coffee table in the center of the trellis rug.

Sera peeked through to the hall ahead of them and saw another oversized sitting room, teeming with windows and the natural light of outdoor gardens beyond. She saw the edge of a granite counter and white stools, and guessed a modern kitchen flanked the far side of the house.

"Oh yes." Penny leaned in to whisper close to her ear. "I could get used to this."

"Shh," Sera tossed back, then straightened when Mrs. Clark appeared around the corner again and smiled in their direction.

"He's in the office just now. But please do come in," she said, leading them into an adjoining sitting room. "He'll be right with you."

He stood behind a set of glass doors, a tall man with dark, smoke-tinged hair and a trimmed mustache. He had a headset on his ear and a file folder in his hand. Sera had seen him in photographs, of course. But that's not how she recognized him now. It was almost as if they'd met before; he possessed the same set to his jaw as her husband. He even stood the same, with his shoulders back and his eyes fixed on a point off in the distance, focused completely on the task at hand. Even through the glass door of the office, Sera could see that he was in the middle of something business related.

He looked up at the sound of Sera's shoes clipping the floor. Upon connecting eyes with them, he froze.

They stood there for what felt like the longest of moments, until he slowly closed the file folder and dropped it down on the top of an oversized cherry desk. He said something inaudible into the phone, then clicked a button on it and discarded the headset atop the folder.

"You're Sera," he said as he opened the glass door. "I've seen the wedding photos. You are just as lovely in person as I'd expected you to be." He brightened with a smile.

Sera swallowed hard, feeling the weight of the moment bearing down on her.

She wanted so badly to make a good first impression on her new father-in-law. Trouble was, she had no idea how to balance it with the view she'd expected of him. William's apprehension had created visions in her mind of who the elder Hanover would be. Cold, uncaring. Disinterested in his family. Maybe breathing fire? Those were her expectations, but to have them dashed with a single smile—she'd not been prepared for that.

Sera took the outstretched hands he offered and returned what she hoped would be a sweet, neutral smile as he drew her into a light embrace. He stood back almost immediately and acknowledged Penny, who was standing just steps behind, surveying the scene.

"And you would be Miss Penelope Norton?"

Penny audibly choked a bit, but covered quickly and answered, "Penny. Yes, umm—Penny is fine," shaking his hand. "Thank you for the welcome."

"Yes, Mr. Hanover, thank you for having us. I know it was probably a surprise to hear that we wanted to come and see you. I'm just sorry Will couldn't be here . . . ," Sera offered, completely unsure of what to say next. It was awkward to be the guest of a stranger when the connection you're supposed to have is so much deeper.

"Well, my doors are always open to family and their friends," he said, and tipped his head in return. If she could judge his character in that instant, Sera would have to admit that this man had her perplexed. He seemed perfectly normal. Charming, even? The combination was the last thing she'd expected. "Please don't bother with 'Mr. Hanover.' You may call me Thomas if you'd like," he said, and slid his hands into the pockets of his suit pants. "My middle name. I'm afraid I'm like your husband in that I prefer to be known by something other than my father's name."

"Oh, yes." She nodded, feeling more awkward now that he'd mentioned William.

"Well, I expect you'd like to get settled in. The guest quarters are at the top of the stairs, second door. There is a bath adjoining your bedrooms and you should find everything in it. If not, Mrs. Clark pretty much runs things around here. Please do ask if you need anything."

When Sera reached down to pick up her suitcases, Thomas added, "No, you're guests. I'll have them carried up. And I'll see that you're brought a tray of tea. We can visit later if you'd like, when you've had time to freshen up."

Sera stole a quick look over at Penny. She didn't seem to have noticed the same inconsistency that Sera had. In fact, she was two steps toward the stairs and it looked like she wasn't inclined to slow up a bit.

"Thank you, Thomas." Sera hurried to catch up and nodded, adding, "That's very kind."

Sera trailed behind Penny as she took the stairs with fervor.

"*That twerp.* I swear I'll kill him." Penny dragged out the words on a harsh whisper, her tone dumbfounded as her sneakers stomped up the stairs. "Paul did that on purpose."

"Did what?"

"No one's called me Penelope since my grandmother at my high school graduation. He *knows* I hate it. The only reason he'd call ahead to his father and give him my full name is to get right under my skin."

"They why did you share that kind of information? You know Paul. He's going to use anything you give him." Sera laughed through trying to answer her friend.

She opened the door to the guest quarters and stepped into a simple but spacious sitting room.

It was fresh and clean, a welcome respite after a long plane ride and weight-bearing introduction to the family's London home. Eggshell white walls and a lofty ceiling soared overhead, with an intricately carved medallion holding a twinkling chandelier in the center of the room. Floor-to-ceiling windows at the back washed the room in a bevy of afternoon sunlight.

Penny dropped her bags on the hardwood floor and fell into one of the butter-yellow claw-foot wingback chairs by the fireplace. She pulled a cell phone from her pocket and began clicking away.

Sera sighed.

Leave it to her brother-in-law to shift the mood from a few thousand miles away.

She dropped into the chair across from Penny and stretched her legs out in front of her. Her hand rested on her belly, almost automatically. She patted gentle fingers against it, looking at their surroundings.

It was about what she'd expected; the oversized rooms boasted luxury through and through. The flat was gorgeous, as was the welcome. And so, with her mind running faster than Penny's angry typing fingers, Sera set out to make the connection between the Thomas Hanover her husband had presented and the genteel Londoner who'd shown nothing but kindness downstairs.

CHAPTER EIGHTEEN

Even in the midst of war, the Dutch city gave the appearance of possessing a certain measure of peace.

This Kája hadn't expected.

Everywhere else they'd traveled had been cloaked in a layer of darkness. Tired shells of buildings stood in ruins and solemn faces passed by everywhere, belonging to townsfolk who merely pressed on rather than thrived. The sight of a weary landscape had been their constant companion north of London, through the countryside up to Norwich. They'd been delayed there more than two days, waiting for a shipment of Red Cross trucks bearing food parcels they were to escort to the coast. It finally arrived, more than a week late. With rations in tow, they'd landed passage on a boat that had taken them into the heart of Nazi-occupied Amsterdam.

Kája had expected this, too, to be a dark welcome.

It was surprising to find that the train platform was brightened by summer sun and that many faces were not cemented in frowns. In fact, the Nazi-occupied city was not all grim. The city looked clean, almost as if it were lightly touched by war, save for the Nazi flags adorning buildings and the barbed wire and wood fencing that separated areas restricted for any Jews who might have been left in the city.

Liam led her through the crowds of people, keeping a keen eye on their surroundings. The pragmatic side of him had taken over and he repeated the instructions he'd given her on the boat to Amsterdam, running through them with a focused, business-like formality.

Kája faced him on the platform, trying to listen. But instead, she had to focus on steadying her sensibilities to think of boarding the next train on her own.

"You will accompany the civilian food parcels by train into Rotterdam. There a Mrs. Margot Sørensen will be waiting."

"Yes. I understand. She's my contact with the Red Cross."

Kája looked around as they spoke, distracted by the dark presence of German soldiers marching about the platform. They guarded throngs of people with suitcases and wrapped blanket bundles in their arms, standing around in lines that didn't appear to be moving. They all bore the yellow Star of David sewn on the front of their clothes.

Kája knew in her heart that she witnessed a transport of some kind.

"Don't look at that," Liam cautioned, drawing her attention back to him. "Look at me."

She exhaled low and nodded, connecting with his eyes once again.

"Yes, of course. Mrs. Sørensen."

"Good. She's Danish. And no-nonsense. All I can say is that she can be trusted implicitly. Listen to her. Do what she says without question."

"And how will I know her?"

"Mrs. Sørensen is an older woman with a stiff upper lip. Don't worry," he whispered, resolute. "She'll find you. Expect her at the station when the train comes in. She'll accompany you across the border into Dusseldorf and from there, farther into Germany. You'll be working to distribute aid to POWs and civilians there and through to Prague. Keep a low profile. Make an effort to speak very little. Understand?"

Kája nodded.

She watched as SS officers marched around the platform. She hated the look of them, so cold with the guns in their hands. She turned back to Liam, scared that they could see past her uniform and eye her as a Jew on sight.

"Remember what I told you. Meet me in Zurich at the train platform two weeks from today. I'll be waiting." Liam extended his arm, offering her the satchel. She reached out to take it and in doing so, felt his hand cover hers for the briefest of seconds. It was an action hidden at her side, but comforting nonetheless. "You're quite sure you want to do this?"

Kája swallowed hard and took the satchel from him. She nodded as she swung the bag across her body. "Yes. I have to."

"And if you don't meet me two weeks from now—"

"I will."

"But if you don't," he said, and leaned in to stare her directly in the eyes. The lines in his face tensed on a serious whisper. "The whole of the German army won't be able to hold me back. So help me, Kája, I'll come in after you."

She downturned her head, the intimacy of his words making her heart leap.

"It's like you said—I'm stubborn to a fault. If I set my mind to have us out in two weeks, I'll do it."

"Promise me."

"Liam, I must go," she said, not looking up until the train whistle blew.

"Two weeks," he said, eyes meeting hers. "You'll meet me in Switzerland in two weeks exactly. I want to hear you say it, Kája."

She hated to make a pledge.

What if something went wrong? Kája couldn't look back in those eyes and lie. Still, her heart tugged and she found herself agreeing. In the softest of whispers, she vowed, "Two weeks. I promise, Liam."

They stood fixed for a moment, holding on to her promise as the rush of people passed by. The train whistle blew again and Kája turned to it, feeling the call to go.

"Here," he said, and offered her a folded handkerchief.

"What is it?"

Kája unfolded the parcel to reveal an elegant cross on a dainty gold chain. It sparkled in the light.

"It's not much, but it's gold. You could sell it or barter for something you might need on the way," he started, then stopped just as quickly. He stared back at her and softly entreated, "It was my mother's. It's all I have that's worth anything at all."

Kája looked back at him.

The emotion was there in his words, painted across his face. She knew the necklace was important to him. And he'd given it to her. That made its worth invaluable.

"Thank you, Liam. I'll take good care of it." She folded the delicate linen back into a square and tucked the kerchief in her pocket. Kája looked away, noticing the small faction of other Red Cross workers quickly boarding the train. The squeeze of his hand to hers brought her attention back.

She offered him a faint smile and whispered, "I'll be okay, Liam. I promise."

"I never should have left."

"But you went to fight. You had to go."

He shook his head. "Not after Bethnal Green. I meant before that, at the Columbia Road shelter two years ago."

Was he feeling renewed guilt for that? Now?

"But I told you—it wasn't your fault. You did everything you could. You got me to the hospital. If anything, I owe you my life."

"That's not what I mean," Liam said, and shook his head. He looked away for a split second and cleared his throat before continuing. "I don't want you to feel like you *owe* me your life; I want you to *want* to give it. I never should have left you at that shelter and by God, I never should have wasted this much time. I wanted you to stay, from that very first day on the job. I'd give anything to have those moments back, to be sitting in the archive library with you right now instead of standing here in the middle of hell, leaving you to go into God knows what all alone. After all this time, I don't how to do this . . . I mean, I've never—"

"You don't have to feel guilty about letting me go, not if it's what I want." She eyed the crowd that was thinning and instinctively edged toward the train. "Liam, I need to board."

"Oh, blast it all. I'm such a fool." He sighed and blurted out, "I've never come close to asking a woman to marry me before. I don't know how to do it."

Kája stared back at him, blankly she was sure, unable to process what he'd just said.

"Look—I know I should have said I love you long before now. God help me." He glanced around, nervous. "I've nothing spectacular to offer you but a string of misadventures from this war and an old necklace . . . but I gave it to you because it's dear to me. *You* are dear to me. And I can't help but feel like I'm failing you somehow by letting you go."

"No," she whispered, blinking back tears. "You are a good man, Liam Marshall." She cupped a hand to his cheek. "And full of the courage I lack. You're the reason I know I can do this."

The train whistle blew its final call and knowing she had to run to meet it, Kája reached up and on a rush of unencumbered joy, pressed a kiss to his lips.

"I promise I'll meet you in two weeks." She leaned in and tipped up on her toes to whisper in his ear. "And I'll give you my yes then."

Her bursting heart carried her with courage the rest of the way to the train.

CHAPTER NINETEEN

*P*enny stuck a pen in the knot of waves at the back of her head.

She'd tossed a throw pillow on the sitting room floor and had for the last hour and a half proceeded to dive into research from her makeshift desk on the coffee table. She stretched her arms up high over her head and then drank down the last of the tea in her cup. It clinked against the saucer when she set it down.

"Well, that's it. I've gone through the entire list of buyers for the art, contacted them all." Penny held up sheets of paper, clearly triumphant in the momentary victory. "And you were right—none of the transactions were completed in person so no one could claim that they actually saw William do any of this. That's good news, right?"

Sera sat across from her on a cushy white chaise, gazing out the window to the garden beyond. It was lovely, blooming with a rainbow of vibrant hues as dusk began to fall. She'd been watching people walk through the iron gate at the entrance, wondering where their steps would take them. Wishing she had answers that would free her enough to take a casual stroll through a garden with carefree smiles like theirs.

"Sera, did you hear me?"

"Yes, I did. I'm sorry. I was just—" Sera turned her attention back to the room and her animated friend within it. "Anyway. That's very good news."

Penny gave her a speculative glare. "But you already knew that's what we'd find, didn't you?"

"I told you he didn't do it," she chided, teasing her with a confident smile. "Don't sound so surprised when you find evidence to back that up."

"I'm not surprised. You've managed to turn me into a champion for my honorary little niece or nephew's father, but I've still got to dot all the i's and cross all the t's. You know that."

"Of course. And I do too. I've been over those files a hundred times on my own. I can't find anything but my husband's signature staring me back in the face every time I look at them." Sera wound her hair round her hand and tossed it behind her shoulder so she could lean forward without it falling over her face. "And I don't mean to be distracted. I'm sorry. But I just keep thinking— Will's father is down on the first floor and we're up here. You and I are shut up in his guest rooms, continuing research that we could have done in California. I'm wondering if I just shouldn't bite the bullet and ask what I came to ask."

Penny winced as though she'd just been kicked by a mule.

"Are you sure? I mean, you did just meet him." She glanced around the room. "And we did just unpack."

"You think he'll make us leave if I point-blank ask him what he knows that could save his son?"

"Maybe . . ." Penny drew out the word, pausing to pout her bottom lip. She pulled her hands up to her chest in pleading fashion. "So why chance it? Please? The room is so pretty."

Sera tossed a throw pillow to wipe the satirical look from her friend's face. Penny laughed and began putting paper back in file folders. Now that her battle was won, she pushed the stack over to the end of the coffee table, seemingly giving up on research in favor of settling in for the night.

"I know it's pretty," Sera sighed. "That's the problem. All of this is too pretty. It's near perfect, right? It makes me think it's all a mirage."

"Right." Penny gave a supportive nod and leaned back against the chaise. She reached for the remote and raised the volume on the flat screen above the fireplace. "And that's why it would be a shame to have to leave it after only a few hours. Who walks away from paradise?"

"Right. Who does that?"

Sera picked up a few folders from the stack and began thumbing through them.

She'd seen everything before. If she was going to confront the Hanover figurehead in the morning instead of tonight, then at least her nervous fingers had something to keep occupied. Besides, Penny seemed enthralled in the old black-and-white movie on the television, so it appeared as though any further research was off the table for that night.

"This is the best movie," Penny whispered, and leaned forward as an airplane crashed down out of the clouds and an explosion ripped through a tree, lighting up the film's night sky. "I can't believe I've never seen it before."

"What are you watching?" Sera glanced up, her interest piqued. With her love of vintage, she was always game for a classic film. This one looked intriguing in the thirty seconds she'd seen of it.

"*Mrs. Miniver*, with Greer Garson and Walter Pidgeon. Have you heard of it?"

"Oh yeah—Sophie mentioned it in one of her letters to me. It's been a long time but from what I remember, it was a powerful film. I think it won several Academy Awards."

"It swept the Academy Awards in 1942. Can you believe that? I just looked it up. And here," she said, pointing to the screen on her open laptop. "This website says, 'Even Winston Churchill noted that it was more powerful to the war effort than the combined work of six military divisions.' I wonder if the Blitz was really like what's in this movie?"

Gunfire erupted across the film's quiet English countryside as a fire raged in the background. The scene was heart-wrenching. Sera was about to comment that she hoped the film was more fictional than factual, but she hadn't time. Her eyes had become affixed to a photograph in a file folder, and it stole her thoughts away.

"Penn?" She slapped the sheet of paper against Penny's shoulder, snapping her attention back from the movie.

"What's wrong?" She must have seen the shock all over Sera's face.

"What is this?" she asked, pointing to the photo of a plain gold chain with a tiny, diamond-studded cross charm. "It wasn't in with the others. I've never seen this before."

"That's right. I found it in the family file. The assets that weren't sold? Those are the ones the family still owns. I never included it with the others because it was given away instead of sold. It was only worth about $400."

"But Will's signature is on this one too."

"His signature's on all of them."

Sera pointed to the tiny block print at the bottom, with the recipient's name. "Yeah, but this one went to a K. E. Hanover."

While Sera thought she needed to go downstairs to confront William's father, the start of a new lead may have been right there in her hand all along.

"Penny. There's no K. E. Hanover that I've ever heard of."

CHAPTER TWENTY

July 5, 1928
Old Town Square
Prague

"What is it, Father?"

Ten-year-old Kája clutched her father's hand to steady her balance as she looked up.

"You've seen it before; it is a clock. A very *big* one."

The medieval clock tower was a stunning sight, the cornerstone of history in Prague's Old Town Square. Kája's father would take her for long walks on the nicest days of the summer. They'd stroll over the Charles Bridge, past the winding Vltava River, and stop to look at the masterfully rendered piece of architecture in the heart of the city.

The old clock was majestic and mysterious, and she loved it.

It was tall—three stories high at least—with ornate carvings and gold-gilded astrological figures of the moon and stars that turned in perfect precision with the schedule of the heavenly bodies above. It loomed up over the crowded square, having kept watch over Prague for centuries with its ancient stone wall and gothic figures peeking out from crevices in the front.

There were two little windows set high on the tower. Kája always liked to step up on her tiptoes, hoping to see inside their leaded glass. She wondered what dark secrets they kept.

They'd time their walks so they'd stand before the clock as it chimed at the top of the hour, sending the animated figures into movements around the face of the clock. Gilded figures of the apostles shook their heads back and forth as a skeleton looked on, appearing as a dark overlord to the scene.

"But the figures—they move!"

"They do," her father said, chuckling under his breath. "Especially that one. See the skeleton? What do you make of him?"

Kája wrinkled her nose. "I don't like him. He looks mean."

"Yes, yes. I see how you'd find him menacing," he said, and knelt at her side until his cheek was level with hers. He pointed up to the clock's face. "What else do you see?"

"It is a clock. To tell time."

"Of course. But it's more than that. Our clock is art, no?"

She thought about it for a moment and tilted her head to the side. "It does have colors on it. And statues. Does that make it art?"

"What do you think?"

She gave a confident nod. "I would say yes."

"Look. Just there." He motioned toward the astrological symbols of the sun and the moon and stars. "You see that all of time—even God's time—is set to a clock. All moves at his will." He took her hand and pointed her index finger, tracing the edge of the clock on air. "The golden hand over the ring on the outer circle shows the old time, beginning at dawn. This is our past. The golden hand that runs over the Roman numerals shows our time, here in Prague. This is our present. And the sun—do you see it over the curved golden lines?"

She nodded.

"What does it show?"

"Is it God's time?" she asked.

He turned to her and smiled.

"How clever you are. It shows us the Talmudic hour—the

Sha'a Zemanit. It is part of the law for the Jewish people showing the passage of our time from sunrise to sunset. It measures
the will of God for us to see another day. This is our future.
The sun will rise, the sun will set. And God will turn the hands
round the clock for his people to wake from sleep and worship
in another day. The idea of God marking time for us is art in
and of itself."

"But if it's God's clock, why is it here and not in heaven?"

"Well, he left the clock here for us, as a gift. He wanted everyone who passes by—even little girls—to be able to follow time by
the clock. It tells us when our work is done."

"And he calls us to be with him. Is that why the skeleton
moves when the hour chimes? We're called to the afterlife when
our work on earth is done?"

"Such a question, Kája. A big question for such a little girl."

Kája slid her black buckle shoes together until the polished
tips just touched. She stood a little straighter. "I am not little anymore," she said, chin high. "I am grown up now."

He seemed to doubt her assertion and raised an eyebrow.
"Are you? And at ten years old?"

"Yes, Father."

"And will you paint this too? Or will you write one of your
stories about God's clock?"

She pointed up to the tiny windows peeking out from atop
the clock's gilded face. "I want to write a story about the windows,"
she said, having cupped her hand to whisper. "I think there are
mysterious creatures that live there. We can't see them, but they
turn the clock's insides. They make the skeleton move."

"You think this is true?" He tilted his chin, as if considering
the matter. "What kind of creatures?"

"Not scary creatures—good ones. Those who are stronger
than the skeleton. They are masters over death. Angels, perhaps.
Or sparrows, with golden wings like the hands of the clock."

"Sparrows are stronger than the skeleton?" He chuckled at the thought. "But how can that be?"

"Sparrows soar on high; they are light and agile. They fly through the clouds unafraid and travel where the skeleton could never go. That is strength on little wings. And they fly about inside the tower, waiting for the sun to go down so they can open the windows and escape out into the night sky."

"And what do they do when they come out?"

"They rain tiny blessings down on the Jews of Prague while we all are asleep. They shine light in the darkness."

He smiled, a soft look that just stirred the laugh lines around the corners of his eyes.

"They sound like our Jeshua, perhaps? He shines light in the darkness too. He does so for all of his people. Do these little sparrows follow his command?"

"Oh, Father." Kája shook her head and raised a finger to her lips. "Shh. I cannot tell you. That would ruin their secret. I have to paint the story first."

He nodded quietly, as was his way. He patted her shoulder and smiled, almost as if proud of something.

"Soon you will grow up, little Kája. But not yet." He stood and clutched her hand. "That, too, shall happen in his timing."

July 6, 1942
Prague

The sky bled ink over the horizon as night folded in.

Its depth was unyielding, and the darkness frightened her like it had when she'd stared up at the clock as a child. The nature of the greeting made Prague seem foreign somehow, as if night hung over the old city with more than just the setting of the sun.

And the warm memories of trips to the clock made her wish her childhood stories were true. How she longed for the sight of little sparrows flying about with their sprinkling of blessings.

It all seemed so fanciful, and so foolish now.

Kája sat high up in a passenger seat of the large merchant truck, nervous as the driver lumbered along behind the vehicle Mrs. Sørensen led in the Red Cross convoy. They'd been charged with transporting truckloads of ration boxes containing tea, tobacco, barley and biscuits, small servings of fish and canned meat, processed cheese, and rudimentary medical supplies such as Band-Aids and peroxide.

The driver had assured they'd have a safe ride north to the Charles Bridge. From there, they'd move through the Nazi checkpoint to the heart of the city. She watched as the spattering of rain peppered the truck window, blurring images as the city flew by.

It had been only three years since she'd left but an awakening stirred within her: only a shadow of her beautiful Prague now remained.

The old buildings were still there, the architecture immaculate and laden with the memory of lost time. But shop windows were boarded and some painted black, their glass broken and the doors bolted tight. Homes appeared dark, some possessing the look of having been abandoned and others so ill-kept they might fall down altogether.

The truck slowed and her attention was drawn away.

Her heart nearly stopped when their convoy slowed to meet a swarm of German soldiers lining the street. They watched as the trucks motored by.

"Nebojte se," the driver whispered, telling her not to worry with a tone that was even and controlled.

He was an older gentleman from Prague who'd been working with the Red Cross for more than a year. Kája had to admit to herself that it brought a small measure of comfort to have a fellow countryman accompanying her into the city. But with her being half Jewish and not knowing his loyalties beyond that of a Red Cross uniform, she opted to converse in as few words as possible.

"They'll not stop us," he reiterated. "They know we're Red Cross."

He kept a keen eye trained on the large crowd of soldiers with his peripheral vision, but kept his chin inclined to the front windshield.

She swallowed hard.

"Where do we meet the German authorities to arrange for these provisions to be distributed to POWs and civilians in the city?"

"That's ahead in the city center, up by the river. The high-ranking Reich have taken over those homes. We should expect high security. You'll have to go through them if we want to distribute these rations."

Kája closed her eyes tight, knowing that her family home would be amongst them.

"Will they stop us?"

"Perhaps. There are no prisoners of war for the Red Cross to help. Not in Prague at least," the man stated matter-of-factly. "Unless you refer to the Russians. But the Germans will not allow any provisions to be given to them. Russia has not signed the agreement."

She knew what he referred to. "The Geneva Convention?"

"Yes." He looked her in the eye for the briefest of seconds, then observed, "Received a lot of schooling, have you?"

"Some." She turned and looked out at the brick buildings flashing by the window. She was lost for a moment, looking into the blackness of alleys and ghostly buildings lining the streets.

"It has a different look, yes? Prague?"

"*Jen troche.*"

"Just a little" was hardly the phrase for it. The city was darker than she'd ever imagined. "And what about the Jews of the city? Can we distribute the rations to them?"

He looked at her with a rather curious bent to his features and said, "There are few left. Nearly all have been transported."

Kája's heart sank.

"Transported?" She tried to seem innocent with her interest.

"Yes. You have not heard of Heydrich's assassination but a month past?"

Kája had read about the bombing that had mortally wounded the high-ranking Nazi official.

"Yes. I'm aware of what happened to him."

"The Germans wasted no time in their repartitions of the Jews after it. Heydrich died 4 June and they had a funeral but three days after. Filled up all the streets. It was a grand affair, with a processional the likes few have ever seen. And though most of the Jews had already been transported a year back, they rounded up most of the last of them weeks ago."

"Rounded them up? But couldn't the Jewish Council do something to prevent it?"

"Excuse me, miss, but have you been living under a rock? You don't sound as if you know much about this war to be in it as you are." He shook his head. "The Jewish Council hasn't a voice. Thousands were arrested. And word is the Nazis cleared Lidice as reprisal."

"What do you mean, *cleared?*"

"Flattened. Gone. Ležáky too. Burned and bulldozed to the ground for hiding the assassins. Whomever wasn't killed was deported with the rest. No way to tell if it's true though, not here."

God . . . please let my parents be safe . . . Let me find them.

The truck lumbered about, jostling them so Kája felt the

aggressive bumps along the ruts in every street. She held on to the doorframe for support.

"Where were the deportations?"

"Trade Fair Grounds." He waved his hand toward the outside of the truck. "Other side of the city. Near Stromovka Park."

Kája gripped the side of the truck until her knuckles burned.

What if I've come all this way—all this way, Lord—and they're no longer here?

Their convoy of trucks continued the trek through the city until they reached a checkpoint of German soldiers positioned on both sides of the road. All of the vehicles were stopped and from behind, she could tell their contents were being searched.

With shaking hands, Kája grabbed Liam's cross necklace from under her collar and kissed it. She needed the reminder that she was never alone, even in the menacing blackness of the war-torn city she'd once so affectionately loved.

She took a deep breath as the Nazi soldiers approached their vehicle.

———

The house smelled just as Kája remembered it, like nutmeg and sage from her mother's cooking, mixed with the citrus scent of lemon oil from the furniture polish. It was a welcome aroma, greeting her in a warm contrast to the rest of the city. But in looking around, Kája doubted the scents were real. It was far more likely that they were figments of her childhood imagination, forcing their way to the surface.

She looked around, pained to find that like the rest of the world, war had changed everything in the home of her youth. The front door had been locked, but she'd slipped her old key in the lock and it turned with ease. She'd come in and set the Red Cross ration box on the floor.

Kája took off her shoes at the door, as was customary in Prague. She noticed the polished *botník* was gone, the long box in which she and her sister had always left their shoes. Kája pushed her uniform shoes up against the wall and turned back to the entry.

In the hint of darkness shrouding the hall, she looked around.

The entry hall's lovely antique furniture that had been preserved and passed down for generations was still there, though it all looked buried in dust. Marble floors stretched out naked before her, having been shorn of their beautiful ornamental rugs. Paintings were missing from the hall, the telltale signs of their absence outlined against the faded wallpaper like square shadows. The crystal chandelier still hung in the entry, but it looked tired, greeting her with only a feeble shimmer of light.

Kája dropped the leather satchel from her shoulder to the marble floor and looked up the length of the curved staircase. She remembered the times she and her sister would slide down the polished banister as girls, much to their mother's chagrin, and would plop down in their father's waiting arms. She pictured it, the memory of that royal staircase, making her feel like a princess in a castle of her own world.

The sounds of joyous laughter and the vision of being twirled around in their father's arms—they, too, faded away into the fallen shades of dusk creeping about the hall.

"Hello?" Kája breathed out a hesitant whisper toward the landing on the second floor.

No answer.

Kája turned her attention to the back of the house and the most-used rooms: the kitchen, the dining hall, and her father's beloved study. She began taking steps forward, making sure that her footfalls were silent against the hard floor.

Each room she passed was uncharacteristically dark. They felt cold. Haunted almost.

She called out again, "Hello?" and continued taking measured, cautious steps through the first floor of the house. "*Matka?*"

The endearment was whispered and floated from Kája's lips out into the stillness that led to the dining hall. Its large doors were open wide, and one clung to an errant hinge as if it had been the recipient of some sort of aggression and fought to keep from crashing down to the floor. The oversized sideboard was still there on the back wall, though its top was bare; there was no grand cascade of food to welcome partygoers now. All that remained was a glass hurricane around a nearly finished candle. The long table that had once played host to dozens of guests was gone. Some chairs were left, stacked in the far corner in a jumbled heap and partially covered with a sheet that had long since lost its bright-white hue.

Kája scanned the hall, taking in the few broken windows in the back of the grand room and the spiderwebs that dotted every corner.

Oh Lord . . . what has happened here? Kája shook her head on the prayer, words bleeding from her heart. *Is everything I've ever known now a memory?*

"No."

Kája whirled around at the sound of the thick voice.

"Father!" she said, darting forward. "It's me—Kája."

"*No!* I prayed to God," her father cried out as one of his knotted hands came up to form a fist in the air, "you'd not come back! You must not come back here."

"But it is me." Kája rushed to his side. "I am well. See? I came for you."

She placed a hand over his waving fist, gingerly encasing it with the sincerity of a light touch. He looked around, almost as if he expected a convoy of people to have followed her into the house.

"How did you get here?"

"I'm traveling with the Red Cross," she said, and took her hat from her head, handing it to him. "See?"

"You've joined the Red Cross?" He muttered something further under his breath and shooed the hat away.

Kája lowered her voice to a soothing whisper and asked, "Am I not welcome here, even when I've come back to you, Father? I'm here to save you."

"No." He shook his head, emphatic. "We need no saving. There *is* no saving from this war."

"Yes, there is," she said, and pulled travel papers from the inside pocket of her uniform jacket. "See?" She held them out to him. "I have travel papers. These will get us out!"

He swiped them from her hand, rushed over to the sideboard, and struck a match upon its surface. He stood then, washed in the tiny glow of the match light, surveying the papers.

Kája felt like crying over what she saw.

The man before her was not the revered gentleman doctor she'd always known. He'd seemed tall, so dignified and robust in her memories. Now he appeared hunched as he stood over the sideboard, as if his bones were permanently curved to one side. His skin was gray and sunken in, and he'd lost weight. In fact, his belt and waistcoat were pulled tight over his middle, yet his trousers sagged noticeably and he looked to be swimming in his shirt. The once-tailored wool now looked like it dressed a withered scarecrow, not the society doctor whom she'd always pictured in a smart suit, with gold-rimmed glasses just tipping the edge of his nose. He'd possessed a white, toothy smile that seemed to linger upon his face.

He didn't smile now. Or have those beautiful glasses tipped upon his nose. He grumbled and scanned the paper with an odd, wide-eyed fascination from behind simple wire-rimmed spectacles that looked older than he.

"Father?" she whispered into the vacant room. The tiny word seemed to echo off the ceiling.

"How did you get these?"

"A friend—" Kája stopped short, finding her voice hitched ever so slightly at the mention of Liam. "He helped me."

Her father's shoulders sagged, defeat evident, and he slid into a chair against the wall.

"You never should have come here." He took the paper and folded it, very carefully, and shook his head. The folded paper drifted from his fingertips to his lap. "I prayed over and over that if God kept you safe, I'd live another day for him. I'd tend to the German soldiers. I'd care for them as their doctor, no matter how many people they sent away on trucks . . . no matter how many of us they killed. If you'd only be kept away."

Kája rushed over to him and fell to kneel at his feet. She looked up into his eyes.

"Were there soldiers here? Is that what happened to the house?"

"It was a hospital for some time," he said, looking around the vast room. "They were short of doctors, you see. The Reich took the houses from Jews in the city. This house is too exposed to air attacks, though—they won't have a general in a house along the river. But for the wounded, it was good enough. For a time, at least."

"And the furnishings? The paintings in the hall?"

He shrugged. "They took some. We sold others. Nearly all of your mother's jewels are gone, save for the pearl earrings handed down from your grandmother." His voice sounded mechanical and far away, drifting off. "Your grandmother would not have wished to live through the war, not to see this."

She cleared her throat, finding emotion had taken root and caused her voice to falter.

"But I'm here now. Try not to think about it."

"You are well?" He looked over her face, his eyes touching the angles of her cheekbones and her brows, accounting for the features he remembered.

"Yes." Kája nodded. She smoothed the wavy locks away from her brow and tilted her chin to the light, not knowing she'd exposed the scar along her temple.

"What is this?" He ran his finger along the scar.

Kája thought about the scar that spanned six inches of skin from shoulder to elbow on her left arm and softened the truth. "All healed. Just a scratch."

He held her chin in his hand and looked over the scar, his fingertips running along the small jagged line, surveying the wound as a doctor would.

"See? It's not so very bad," she offered, and turned her attention to the quiet shadows around them.

The house was too hushed to be in an occupied city. It was almost ghostlike in the way that there was no sound, save for the echo of their voices in the empty room.

"*Matka*. Where is she?"

"Your mother has not been well these many months." He patted the side of her hair before dropping his hands to his lap again. "Just tired, you see. She is sleeping."

"Shall I wake her? To let her know I've come home."

He shook his head. "When she can sleep, we must let her. Her heart will be broken soon enough when she wakes."

Hearing his agitated words felt like a reproach, and it cut straight to her heart.

"I had to come," Kája cried, tears cooling her cheeks without reservation now. "I read what the Nazis are doing to the Jews. Terrible things—"

"And I believe they are all true. Which is why our daughters were to stay far away from here."

His voice was so soft, so weak, that she couldn't help but cry for the anguish that was locked up inside. The tragedy of what he must have witnessed at the hands of the Nazis . . . Kája pushed it away. She'd not let her mind linger on such darkness.

"Please. Let me help you," Kája began, and wiped her cheeks with the back of her hand. "I have a friend. He's made it possible for us to travel to Switzerland with the Red Cross. They'll assure us safe passage."

Kája was stopped short by the muffled sound of her father's laughter.

"What? What is it?"

"There is no safe passage. Not anywhere."

"Yes, there is. I made it in, didn't I? And we'll be given transport out of Prague," she said, trying to convince him that there was hope. She squeezed the travel papers in her hand. "We have enough time to get out."

"Don't you understand? There is no time here."

She shook her head. "Whatever do you mean? You don't even want to try?"

"Always sweet," he said, and patted her cheek with a light caress. "It's like the times we used to go visit your clock. Remember? In the Old Town Square?"

"Yes," she said. "I remember."

"There was time then. And God kept your sparrows aloft in the sky." His hand dropped to his lap and he downturned his eyes. "But that is no more."

"But it still can be. Don't you see? We have to try. I've come all this way just so we could."

"Memories," he breathed out, and looked around the hushed silence of the great hall. "They whisper in this room. Do you hear them? *Listen*. People, friends, Jews—dancing away at the music of your mother's parties. The tinkling of crystal. The joy of laughter. Do you hear it, little Kája?"

"Yes, Father." She sniffed over tears. "I hear it."

"It is a ghost world."

Kája reached out for his hand. She took it in her own and gently kissed his fingers to her lips.

"I'm blessed that you're here. Did you know that, Father? Though your prayers to keep me away were not answered, the prayers I said to find you *were*. God is with us. He is still in Prague and he still holds our time in his hands."

He shook his head. "The devil is here now. He wears a swastika."

"Then we will take *Matka* and we will escape."

"No." His voice faltered ever so slightly, trembling on the next words. "I'd hoped you would stay away, write your stories far from here."

"And so I will," she whispered, nodding. "Yes. We'll do it together. You can come stay with me in London."

He shook his head and looked down to the worn leather shoes on his feet. "Not this time, Kája. We are on a transport list."

"What?" The words hit her like a splash of ice water to the face. "When?"

"We report in two days' time."

"Two days?"

Kája looked up at the wall.

The large grandfather clock that had always been there, ringing through the days with deep-chested chimes at the top of each hour, had been replaced by a hollow space. It was gone . . . time was gone, just like her father said. Even the old city clock seemed lifeless. There was nothing left to tick the precious moments by, nothing to gauge a future, or mark a past.

Kája lifted her chin and looked directly at her father.

"If you're to report in two days' time"—she grabbed hold of his hand and squeezed—"then we shall sneak out of Prague in one."

CHAPTER TWENTY-ONE

*M*ay I sit down?"

Sera tore her eyes from the backdrop of the charming public garden and turned to find her father-in-law standing on the paved path before her.

"Yes, Mr. Hanover," she started, then backtracked. "I mean, Thomas. Of course." She scooted over to the side, giving him room on the bench.

"Mrs. Clark said that you'd stepped out to the garden square," he noted. "And where is Penelope?"

Sera bit her tongue to keep from laughing. If Penny heard that again she was sure to board the next plane and smack Paul in person, rather than just over e-mail. She hoped to find a way to correct him gently, before the slip-up drew her friend's wrath.

"Penny's out sightseeing, making the most of her visit, I'd say. She's a bit of a history buff. Well, we both are. But I thought a walk in the garden might do me more good."

He sat and looked over the lovely garden surroundings with her.

"I see it stopped raining."

"A little while ago, yes. I came out when it had stopped."

"The aftermath of a quick thunderstorm in the last days of summer. Makes it nice for a walk."

It did that. Sera allowed her gaze to float around.

The garden was tucked away behind the row of houses, with thick brick walls, glistening ropes of ivy twisted in the spokes of wrought-iron gates, and lofty trees that greeted them with the dewy softness of a rainy summer evening. Dusk had fallen in hazy shades of blue and birds danced from branch to branch overhead as if painting trails across the sky.

"I can see how this garden would be a treasured place. I could see it from the window."

"It is beautiful, isn't it? I've visited here since I was a boy."

"You have?"

"Yes. Right over there." He pointed out a patch of green grass beneath a grove of trees where children played in the evening air while their parents looked on. "My father—William's grandfather, that is—used to take walks with me and my sister. Just there, over the hill. There's an old stone footbridge spanning a pond across the way."

"There is?" Sera inclined her head, looking over the edge of the hill, wondering what other magic could be found there.

"And a beautiful old church, Holy Trinity Brompton, is on the other end of Onslow Square. You might enjoy it as well."

"I'll have to take a walk down there to see it."

"It's nice to find peace in such a bustling city. I forget this is here sometimes." He smiled and turned to look at her. "But you seem to have found it on your very first day. That's luck, I'd say."

For how well Sera knew the looks on her husband's face, it struck her to notice how much William's smile favored his father's. She tried to picture what William would look like at that age, with fine laugh lines etched into the recesses of his eyes and mouth, the indication that a thousand smiles had been a guest there on his face. She wondered what their future would bring. Would his temples be touched with gray? Would he, too, have reason to smile?

"Well, I'm a New Yorker. We're used to exploring."

"That's right. William mentioned you are from New York. But you've moved to the West Coast?"

"Yes. Right after the wedding." She felt the need to add something to the statement. After all, she was living in his former home, with his family all around. It almost felt as if she'd moved into his life. "It's beautiful there, too, just a different kind."

Thomas sighed, and without warning stated, "We're not fooling anyone here."

"I don't understand." Sera began looking up the path, nervous, wishing William would come walking up over the hill and save her from the awkwardness of the moment. The last thing she needed was a confrontation with a man she'd only just met, even if they were now joined as family.

She had anticipated how difficult the trip would be without William by her side. She wished her fingers were laced with his at the moment instead of knotting in her lap.

"I owe you an apology."

Sera turned to him. "Whatever for?"

"We haven't been properly introduced, Sera," he said, inclining his head in what looked like genuine regret. "And that would have occurred had I been in attendance at your wedding. I apologize that I wasn't there."

"Thank you. But we understood. Or—at least Will does. I'm not sure I understand the inner workings of the family. I'm still new." She offered a polite smile.

"Yes." The sigh of frustration was unmistakable. "My son is quite a forgiving person when he makes his mind up to be."

"He is with me," she answered. "And I am with him. That's why I'm here. I'm sure Paul gave you the reasons for my trip when he asked if we could come and stay with you. You must have known that they were about Will."

"I can see that you love him."

"I do." She nodded. The acknowledgment felt like praise. "A great deal."

He paused again, looking out over the twinkle of London's lights through the trees.

"And the rest of the family? How are they getting on?"

"With all this? Not well, I'm afraid. But Macie and Eric are living close to his family in Seattle. They're busy, like any young couple, I'd say, but they did manage to come down for the wedding. And Paul is still playing music, living in Boston."

Thomas smiled, the laugh lines peeking out from the corner of his eye.

"And still in his leather jackets, I assume?"

Sera liked how each member of the family had their own character about them—Paul no exception. He was as undisciplined as anyone she'd ever met, but he seemed to like it that way. Playing music and touring in leather jackets—it fit his personality.

"Of course." She nodded. "And badgering our Penny every chance he gets."

"Yes," Thomas agreed easily. "Paul has always been Paul, and that's saying something."

He paused for a moment, looking over the garden. She noticed that his profile was strong, like Will's, and if she could judge anything in the stillness of this moment, the circumstances of his life had him feeling just as embattled.

"And Marian," he breathed out, almost whispering his former wife's name. "How is she?"

"Fine, I think. Staying busy. Worried about her son, of course, but still kind as always. She keeps everyone together as much as possible, especially through all this."

"Hmm." He nodded. "Yes, Marian always did have a kind heart. And a forgiving one. It's one of the things that I always found genuinely lovely about her. I never had it, that ability to see the good over the bad. William seems to have inherited that trait from me, I'm afraid. And I think that's what he holds against me about what happened."

Oh God . . . he thinks I know.

Whatever happened, he thinks Will told me.

Sera took a deep breath. She felt the guilt pulling at her for not correcting him. But if she was poised to find something to fill in the broken pieces of the past . . .

"I don't think it's in Will's nature to hold something against anyone."

"But he does. I could see the last time we were in the same room together. It was written all over his face. He won't forgive, and he certainly won't forget." Thomas cleared his throat. The truth—whatever it was—was clearly not easy for him to confront. "That was more than three years ago. And the only reason you're here now is because I refrain from going back to California."

"And why is that?"

He turned to look at her, a curious look on his face. "Because I promised to leave and never come back."

"Why?"

Thomas didn't hide the addition of genuine surprise to his features and added, "He told me to."

"Will told you to leave . . ." Sera turned away, the truth having stung. "And why would he have done that?"

He looked out over the green grass of the garden, his gaze transfixed on a point out in front of them. "Then he hasn't told you."

"No. He hasn't. He keeps whatever happened very close. But, Thomas, I have to tell you that I'm here to clear Will's name. I'll do anything to keep him from going to prison. Even ask for answers you might not be prepared to give." She looked up then, searching his face. "I know what happened between you two is a great source of pain and regret for my husband. And I've come all this way because I need to know if you can tell me anything that might change that."

"You want to know if he's really guilty."

"No," she answered with an emphatic shake of her head. "I already know he's not guilty. I just need the evidence to prove it."

"He guards his heart well."

"And I'm here to ask you to help open it."

When he hesitated and then quieted completely, Sera knew that he'd closed himself off from her. Whatever he'd come close to revealing had bobbed just beneath the surface, but was buried again before she could reach out for it.

Instinct told her he knew something more than he was ready to concede.

She took a sheet of paper from her jacket pocket and unfolded it before him.

"I wondered if you could tell me—have you seen this before?"

The tears that formed in Thomas's eyes were unmistakable. He ran a fingertip over the image of the cross, as if it were the delicate gold charm itself in his hand. He nodded, closing his eyes for the briefest of seconds.

"Yes. It was a gift."

"For K. E.?" Sera asked, holding her breath.

He refolded the paper and handed it to her, as if the sight of it pained him.

"Yes, it was for Katie Elizabeth. William must have told you he agreed to it."

Sera's heart sank.

With those words the first pangs of doubt pricked at her chest. William knew who K. E. was, and she wasn't some distant relative. Whatever this transaction was, it mattered to Thomas. Will had been a part of it—and he'd kept it from her.

"Well." Thomas slapped his hands to his legs and stood up. "It's growing darker out here by the moment. I think my son would have words with me if I left his wife to fend for herself in a public garden, no matter how charming it is. May I walk you back?"

Sera stood alongside him and as he offered it, took his arm. "Yes. Thank you."

They walked along the path, following the soft glow of street-lamps all the way to the house. And with each step, she tried not to allow fresh tears to squeeze from the corner of her eyes. They walked in silence, Thomas not knowing that Sera carried his first grandchild and a breaking heart with them.

CHAPTER TWENTY-TWO

July 7, 1942
Prague

Kája awoke to the sound of china shattering.

It traveled up the stairs and through the heavy oak of the chamber door, jarring her.

She'd fallen asleep in her uniform, meaning only to close her eyes for a few moments on top of the coverlet, resting until she could plan what to do. But after she'd removed her stockings, hat, and jacket and draped them over a chair in the corner of the room, sleep had been quick to overtake her.

She bolted upright, her heart beating wildly, the rest of her body frozen. She listened. Fearing. Praying there were no SS officers threatening to drag them away to the train depot.

She heard no shouts or, heaven help them, gunfire.

It was when she heard her mother wailing that Kája jumped from the bed and darted down the hall to the stairs, and took them as quickly as she could. She crossed the entry, its marble floors searing her bare feet like sheets of ice. She hurried through the study to the kitchen where the house staff had always prepared the meals, following both the light and the sound of her mother's cries.

The door was slightly ajar and she peered through to see her mother on the floor, slumped against the cupboard. She'd buried her face in her hands and was weeping mournfully. A tea cup lay broken at her feet.

Kája rushed into the kitchen and knelt down at her side.

"*Matka*," she started, hoping her mother would recognize her. "It's me, your little Kája."

Izabel Makovský peered up at her daughter with a curious look upon her face.

"Kateřina?"

"Yes." She smiled and blinked a few times, the dry air burning with the moistness that was gathering in her eyes. "It's me. I'm here. I'm so sorry I didn't tell you before now, but Father made me promise not to wake you."

Izabel shook her head. "Haven't you school to attend today?" She made a *tsk-tsk* sound. "Headmaster will be cross again at your tardiness."

"What?" Kája's heart began racing. *No, Lord.* She began again, gently. "But, *Matka*, I haven't any lessons today. I've been away. I've finished school and have been working in London all this time. Don't you remember? You and Father sent us away at the depot."

Izabel muttered, "Oh yes. That's right. I'd forgotten . . ." and looked back with vacant eyes. She turned and surveyed the room, as if she expected to see the evidence of their old life strewn about the countertops.

Save for the popping of the fire on the hearth, the room was dark and empty.

There was no gleaming brass fireplace gate or galvanized tub loaded with wood; there was nothing to the room now. Though it had been pleasant once, Kája looked at it now with acute sorrow. She remembered sitting on a stool by the hearth on snowy mornings, eating baked apple *koláče* and listening as their nanny spun fairy tales for her and Hannah, animating stories of dashing princes who rode on white steeds. The cupboards had been full then, overflowing, the shelves laden with porcelain and crystal that kissed at the light like they'd been washed in diamonds.

The room now was lonely and mournfully bare.

There were no more serving platters and pitchers, no crystal or fine china to line the shelves. One of the cabinet doors hung open on its hinge, an ominous sign that someone had gutted its luxurious insides some time ago, and had done so quite forcefully. The windows were dusty, the long work island empty.

"*Matka*," Kája began as gently as possible. She slid her hand into the pocket of her uniform skirt and retrieved the string of pearls her mother had given her at the depot. She pressed them into her mother's hand. "I brought them back for you. Remember? You said we would meet again. And so we have."

Izabel touched them, grazing them with her fingertips at first. And then as if memories had come flooding back, she grasped them tight with such emotion that her bony hands shook.

"The pearls."

Kája wiped at the tears that had formed under her mother's eyes.

"Why don't you let me help you? We're going on a trip. We'll need to pack your things today."

"A trip?"

Kája set about picking up the broken pieces of porcelain from the floor while she talked.

"Just a short one. So we'll need the lightest suitcase you have. And we'll pack some of your more comfortable things. A traveling suit, perhaps?"

"No." Izabel shook her head. "I shall need my best things. Your father has already ordered us to pack. Furs and dresses. Even our jewels—what little we have left that we can sell." She ran her fingertips over the pearls. "These as well."

Kája could have cried. Her mother was so feeble, nearly

broken. She'd have no chance of survival in a work camp if all she brought to wear was a silk evening gown and fur to graze her gaunt shoulders.

She gathered the larger shards of porcelain and placed them on the edge of the wooden butler's cupboard behind them. Adding a cheery tone to her voice, she offered, "Well now. We'll just see if we can't find you something practical for the trip, hmm? You can still bring the other things with you in your suitcase."

"But they are watching us." Izabel looked up into Kája's face and whispered, "Outside the windows. Everywhere."

The firelight danced across her face. She looked wild because of it, the lines deep around eyes that darted about, wide and afraid.

Kája knew they had to leave. Now.

"Where is Father?"

Izabel shook her head. "They came for him early again. The Nazis ordered him out this morning."

Kája's breath froze in her lungs. "Took him where?"

"To work for them."

Please, Lord, she prayed. *Please let them bring him back.*

"I cannot take a trip today. They'll be watching us."

"They won't be able to watch everything." Though no one could possibly overhear their conversation, Kája lowered her voice. Something about the vastness of the rooms and their eerie, echoing walls made her think that even they had ears. "*Matka,* I saw an advertisement at the train depot. There is a Hitler Youth Parade in Wenceslas Square today—in the shadow of the clock. We will pass by them. You'll see."

Izabel Makovský looked up, dazed it seemed, until she recognized Kája. Her eyes finally focused. "Kateřina, dear. What is this costume you're wearing? You're not suitably dressed."

Kája looked down at her wrinkled blouse and uniform skirt. No—she wasn't dressed in the finery that her mother's propriety had always demanded. But then, that was before the war. Everything was different now. Didn't she realize that?

"I know. I'll tidy up straightaway. But first," she said, reaching out to offer her arm. "May I help you up?"

Izabel kept hold of the pearls in one hand and braced against Kája's arm with the other.

She noticed the broken tea cup when she stood and stopped to touch a gentle fingertip to the pieces that remained.

"A cup," she noted, turning them over in her fingertips. "I've broken the last one. I thought we were to have tea today but I couldn't find the other set."

Kája swallowed hard, trying to understand. "Tea?"

"Yes. The ladies were to pay a call. I wouldn't want us to look shabby. We'll bake our best batch of *loupáks*. Or perhaps a cherry *koláče*? The fruit pastry is always appropriate." She waved a pointed finger at Kája. "And I know it is your favorite."

Favorite or not, Kája doubted there was a cherry *koláče* left in the world. Fruit filling, yeast, sugar . . . who could find such things now but in dreams? She was ever so hungry and until that moment, hadn't acknowledged the intense grumbling in her stomach. She put it and the talk of baked delicacies out of her mind and nodded, letting the matter go.

"And we must fix your hair." Izabel took one of Kája's deep fiery locks in her fingertips. "Pinned up, perhaps? And the pearls. Make sure you wear them today."

Kája angled her mother around the remains of the shattered porcelain at their feet and walked with her toward the hallway.

"It won't be a grand dinner party like in the old days." Izabel peered outside to the empty, rain-covered terrace. "But a ladies' tea nonetheless. And we must be ready for it."

Kája had no idea what to think.

She felt the heart breaking in her chest to admit that her mother was slipping away. She was frail in body and even more so in mind. Her own world was alive, but extended not a day beyond the parties of the early 1930s. To enjoy tea in the parlor with pearls and delicately pinned hair . . . it was difficult to imagine that had been their world.

Soft moonlight pressed in from the back windows. It danced upon them as they continued walking through the dark hall. And without warning, without a split second to ready her mind, Prague became the nightmare Kája had feared.

They stopped, limbs frozen and breathing shallow. Something was very wrong.

Truck engines roared and brakes screeched outside in the street. Izabel dug her nails into Kája's palm. They both stared at the shadows of men, soldiers with guns, their menacing forms outlined as they ran past the wall of drapes covering the windows.

The shouting came closer, so near it rattled the windows in their panes.

Kája knew she had but a moment to react.

Quickly, she deposited her mother in a chair behind the dining room door, hoping that if the front doors were broken in, they might not see the slight woman in the shadows. Kája ran up the stairs to her room, stopping to retrieve her uniform hat and jacket. She shoved her shoes in Liam's bag and having already hidden the travel papers in a loose board in her window seat, thundered back downstairs.

She ran through the foyer, almost slipped in her bare feet on her way back into the kitchen. With no more than seconds to make a decision, Kája stared at the roaring flames on the hearth and whispered, "Liam, I'm sorry . . ." before tossing her uniform jacket and hat to be devoured by the licking of hungry flames.

With the sounds of glass breaking in the street and murderous voices shouting loud, Kája turned from the burning uniform and hurried back to her mother's side. She held Izabel's hand, frail and ghostly as it was, and tried to whisper words of reassurance in the dark.

"Surely they know that Father is a doctor. They will not take us away, not when they need his services." Izabel's hand trembled to the point of convulsion. Kája brought it to her lips and kissed her palm, salty tears dripping down. "We are in God's care. We are his. They will not harm us. We must be strong and courageous."

Kája repeated the promises in Joshua 1:9 over and over, believing the words though the shouting continued outside. Izabel bit her bottom lip over the sound of agonizing screams as gunfire erupted.

It wasn't until they heard the splintering wood and shattering glass in their own entryway that Kája was forced to acknowledge the truth. She was sorry—so very sorry—for she'd have to break her promise to Liam.

CHAPTER TWENTY-THREE

July 10, 1942

Theresienstadt Concentration Camp

Terezin

*I*n a place called Terezin, Kája's beloved clock would have no time. This was certain.

They'd traveled for days. With no hour. No recognizable time save for the darkening of the sky as the sun hid away and night bled back onto the horizon. Kája was keenly aware of the lack of it, thinking on God's timing instead, willing her heart to stay strong as evil unfolded around them.

The train lumbered on its tracks, loud with forgotten souls in tow, and pulled into the station just as evening was falling. They were greeted again with shouting, harsh voices that crept up Kája's spine as a menacing chill. They exited the train and were force-marched into a line extending down the length of the platform. The old, the young, the feeble and wounded in spirit; they lumbered along, hauling their suitcases more than three kilometers through dust and dirt to the city called Terezin.

Her father had described it as a town.

He was right. Kája found it curiously provincial. And though she'd read about the Nazis' death camps, it seemed she hadn't landed in one, exactly. This was more of a halfway point, a

216

holding pen for Jews. She'd heard it called a ghetto. And she'd heard there were constantly transports out from the ghettos to the death camps.

At first glance the little town with its grove of trees and tired old buildings didn't appear threatening like she would have imagined. There were wooden fences on the walk, blocking out something from view on the other side. And there were large barracks, shops even, and dirty streets all along the way.

Those interned in the little city were somber, their expressions vacant. The old and feeble perched on benches, sitting like lost birds without a tree. Others walked about as dirt-covered ghosts, haunting the streets, their expressions of despair the most vivid thing about them.

Kája swallowed hard and sheltered her mother with an arm around her shoulders.

They came to a courtyard with multistoried brick buildings that boasted an aged stucco-like finish and lines of cracks up the walls that looked like fishnets. Flaking paint and arched openings cut into the wall on each floor, in which laundry had been draped over ledges to dry in the sun. The earth in the courtyard was dark, black almost, and appeared wet as the prisoners' tired feet kept marching on.

Soldiers shouted, causing Izabel to jump in Kája's arms. The rough barking of the SS predicated the formation of lines and the great mass of frightened, wide-eyed prisoners who looked around in shock at the ruggedness of their new home.

Nazi officials stood at the front of each line, reading over papers the Jews produced, then shouted and pointed in the direction in which they would go. It was quite systematic for a hoard of people who had no idea what was happening to them. Kája looked around, confounded at the proficiency with which the SS accounted for each man, woman, and child of the houses they'd emptied in Prague. They were efficient in their brutality.

A particularly old man was struck down in the courtyard and beaten about the head for no apparent reason.

Izabel cried out then and Kája's attention was brought back.

She grasped her mother round the shoulders, turning her head from the horrific scene. Izabel looked very much like a wounded bird as she fumbled to step in line, trying to cover her ears with her fists over the agony of the man's cries.

"*Matka*," she whispered against her ear. "You must look away. Do you hear me? Don't watch. Try not to listen."

Izabel sobbed into her hand, a silent escape of emotion that was deadened by her palm.

"I'll stay with you," Kája said, though her voice faltered just a bit and she cleared her throat before continuing with a sturdier voice. "We must be strong and courageous. God will sustain us."

"But God is not here." Izabel shuddered and lowered her head, feeble as a mouse. "Surely he is not."

"We'll just follow this line and do what they say. Yes?" she added, even as her voice continued teetering on the waves of fear. "We will show them that we are strong. We can work. We'll work and survive this."

Kája gripped her mother's shoulders and ushered her to the line in which she'd been pushed. She scanned the crowd, noticing that the women were being separated from the men and boys. She finally found her father across the way, engaged in conversation with one of the SS officials. He looked to be explaining something as he nervously shifted from foot to foot and glanced back in their direction every few seconds. Izabel shuddered again, and Kája diverted her attention back down to her mother's crumpling form.

She patted her shoulder and murmured, "Hush now, *Matka*. God will watch over us."

It had begun to rain then, a sorrowful crying from the sky. And a pang struck her in the moment, with the weight of what she faced now achingly clear. She pictured Liam, waiting at a train station, wondering where she was, standing tall through a steady rain like the one that dampened them now. He couldn't know it, but she'd keep him waiting, never to show.

She brushed the thought away as her father approached, the line pushing forward. His hair was wet, his glasses speckled with tiny drops of water.

"Father," Kája whispered, even as thunder created a rumbling backdrop behind them. "What will happen to us? To all the people here?"

"We can help these people more by not interfering."

"What can you mean?" She pointed over to the end of a block of buildings where two bodies lay in the rain-swollen gutters. "Look at what they've done!"

"Shh!" He hushed her without pause. "They have orders to send the Jews who are strong enough to work. There are factories here."

"They want us to work?"

"Yes." He dropped his voice to a whisper. "And I have signed a contract—it is a Home Purchase Contract with the SS, through the Union Bank of Prague. It is a statement of our property, our assets. We sign it over to the SS and they will give us protection."

"What kind of protection?"

"Better food rations. The best lodgings. A safer place to work." He furrowed his brow, looking around as if every somber set of ears were listening to his whispered dreams. "They have allowed us to take more luggage. We can bring our valuables with us. To sell. To keep heirlooms . . . They do not afford all this privilege, so you must remain quiet about this. But all is accounted for. I have made arrangements for when we reach the front of the line. Do you understand?"

Kája nodded, though it was with half effort and little hope.

With what she knew in the back of her mind, of Jews dying

systematically in camps in the east, she couldn't believe such compassion would exist in the SS. But still she agreed, without words, and followed her father's fanciful dreaming.

Her father nodded reassurance when they were careened off from the men, and she nodded back. They'd be privileged, he'd said. They'd be taken care of. Their wares would be safe. And what they witnessed before them surely would not be their lot to pass.

But contracts with the SS looked to mean nothing here.

The contents of Izabel's suitcase—furs and jewelry, evening gowns of silk and chiffon, even her grandmother's pearl necklace and earrings—they were all confiscated. Kája wondered if her father's suitcase was also taken, though there was no way to tell for sure. The line for the men was moving much faster than theirs.

Kája was grateful she'd taken Liam's necklace from her neck and hidden it deep in the seam of the worn leather satchel she'd carried. It was the only way she could think to keep it from being confiscated. It was a risk, she knew, even as the satchel was taken and inspected. All the while she held her breath, as deft hands searched the pockets and ran fingertips along the seams, feeling for bumps. Stacks of confiscated suitcases were tossed into great piles on wagons posted on both sides, but luckily the satchel was in poor condition, and it was returned to her without incident. Some were allowed to keep their wares, and she considered herself among the lucky for it.

They were given used clothes that reeked of some cleansing agent, which she bundled into the leather satchel on the walk to their assigned barracks. Kája kept one arm tight around her mother's shoulders and the other deftly holding on to the satchel and roll of blankets that had been tossed at them.

Kája had no sooner deposited her mother in the overcrowded barracks than she heard her name shouted out by a woman standing in the crowded building with a clipboard and a star on her dress. Kája responded immediately, looking up to see the woman's scowl, and replied, "I am here."

She approached and the woman looked her over, then marked a sheet on her clipboard.

"You are Kateřina Makovský from Prague?"

She stood before the woman, nervous but head held high. If Liam was right and she was inordinately stubborn, Kája had an inkling it would be a necessary component to her survival in this place. She notched her chin and answered, "Yes. I am."

The woman handed over a sheet of paper, a small rectangle, then answered, "You are to report to the ration line, then to the Jewish Council for medical inspection and work assignment. Memorize this number," she cautioned, though her voice was staunch and formulaic. "You must know this number. It is how you will be referred to from this point on. Do you understand?"

Kája nodded. "Yes."

"If you are asked, you must give this number immediately. At all times. There will be no opportunity for remembering."

"I understand. And my mother, Izabel Makovský? Will she be given a number as well?"

The woman looked over the sheets of paper affixed to the clipboard, rustling the papers slightly as her eyes scanned the names.

"She is not on my list." She waved Kája off and called another name, dismissing her to follow the orders that had been given.

Kája checked on her mother, who was cramped into a bunk with three other elderly women. She kissed her forehead and whispered, "I will return in a few moments. You just rest here a while, okay? I'm going to get us some food."

She strode out of the barracks and was greeted by a surprisingly cool rush of evening air.

It was July, but northern Czechoslovakia wasn't as warm

as London could be. The fortress at Terezin seemed to house its own layer of cold, packed in with the coolness of earth and some shade trees amongst the towering buildings all around.

Kája had felt this coldness when they'd walked the long road from the depot. She felt it now, and saw it in the lines of poor souls trailing out of a ramshackle building that looked like a stiff wind would tear the lot of it down. People appeared woeful as they waited for their food rations, whatever it turned out to be, standing about like tatter-clothed ghosts without a corner to haunt.

"Kája." He father's whisper drew her to an alley on the way to the courtyard.

She looked about and, relieved, ducked in to meet him.

"How is *Matka*?"

"She's fine for now," Kája whispered, shoulders hunched in toward him. "I left her to rest on a bunk. That's all they have here—wooden plank beds three high, with thin blankets, and that's if you're lucky enough to find an open one. I had to steal a bunk when others weren't looking, and three other women climbed right in with her."

If he was shocked at her admission, he let it pass. "That's the way of it here, I'm afraid. Until I arrange for our new lodgings. We'll have to manage a few nights."

"But there are women sleeping in stacks on a concrete floor. There's not nearly enough room for all the people here. And I've seen only one lavatory for what looks like hundreds of people in our barrack. One toilet and wash basin! Why, the line to use it was extending out the door. What are the SS thinking with conditions like this? You're a doctor. Surely you must know how quickly disease will spread."

He nodded sorrowfully and pulled her in closer by the sleeve of her blouse.

"I have made arrangements. It may take some time, but I promise I will do what I can to get us out of the barracks."

"Is that where you are, in barracks?"

He nodded. "Yes. It's the same for the men where I will sleep."

"And how long will it be before you can get us out?"

"I don't know."

"They gave me a number." She held out the paper to him, hand trembling slightly. Kája prayed it wasn't indicative of being placed on a transport list to somewhere even more horrible. "What does that mean?"

He scanned the document, then handed it back.

"This is your Passage Permit," he answered, his voice laden with caution. "You must have it at all times. Hide it in your shoe if you must, for it is like gold here. It allows you passage outside of the barracks so you may go to work."

"Work?" She shook her head. "What do they want me to do?"

"I have met with Jacob Edelstein. He is the head of the Jewish Council, and because of my standing as a decorated soldier in the Great War, he has made arrangements for all of us. I will work as a doctor at the hospital. And they will allow you and your mother to work as well."

"Doing what?" she whispered.

"Your mother was a seamstress before we married. She can work in the factory sewing repairs for uniforms and wares for the SS."

"*Matka* was a dressmaker for hobby, and even then it was decades ago. She sewed fashionable things, not clothes for soldiers. She's never sewn a uniform in her life!"

"Then she must learn quickly." He shook his head. "It is either work or go to the trains. Transports come in and transports go out. If one does not appear useful, the next day they are gone. This way she can sit. Her eyes are good, her fingers strong. She can sew."

Kája looked around at the movement of emaciated prisoners walking past the alley and shuddered. Were they workers too?

They were obviously starving by the looks of them. What was the distinction between the privileged, the worker, and the dying in this place?

"And what work do they want me to do?"

"There are hundreds of children and more coming on the trains each day. The Jewish Council wants them to attend school."

"School?" She looked at the inhumane conditions around them and shook her head in disbelief. "What kind of school could be here when there aren't even enough beds for people to sleep in? What does school matter in this place when the ration lines are ten thick and extending all the way out the courtyard?"

"The SS will not allow school at all, not in the way we think of it. The older children must work with the men laying pipe for the new water lines or weeding the vegetable gardens on the outskirts of the city walls. The older ones we cannot help. They will be at the mercy of the guards. But the young ones—the Jewish Council wants the young ones to be taught—secretly—and you can be a part of this. We even have a room set aside for the school. You can work with the young ones, Kája."

"Young ones. Work? What could they possibly do?"

"Some are just a few years old. They will stay with the elderly. But the children of five, six, and older—any child can come to you who is under fourteen years of age, or if they're small, fifteen. We can't fit them all, but you'll do your best. Assign them whatever you can. Cleaning. Painting for the theater. They can work as stage hands. You will be teaching them. And protecting them."

"Stage hands? They have a stage—a theater—here."

He nodded. "There is an arts community here. They have music, lectures, productions. The arts are important to the SS. I don't know why exactly, but the hope that the educated may be kept from the transports longer is more than enough explanation for me."

Dumbfounded, she surveyed the scene around her. It was

maniacal. To have a culture of the arts in such a hellish place . . .
and a school for children . . . what sense could it make?

Kája immediately shook her head. "I'm not a teacher."

"You must be now."

"But, Father, these children will be wounded. They're suffering starvation and disease—any fool can look around us here
and see that. How could I possibly help them? How could I teach
them one day, only to know that they'll be sent out on a transport the next? I know what happens in the east! I know what the
Nazis will do to them, and I cannot bear to think of it."

"No." The one-word rebuke was fierce. "You'll not speak of
what happens when the transports leave—not to anyone. Do you
understand me?"

"But I know!" she cried, unable to keep the horrors from
spilling from her heart and out her mouth. "*The Daily Telegraph*
printed stories about it weeks ago. The camps in the east are killing centers! Don't you see? They murder them with bullets, and
with gas—women, children—just because they're Jews."

Her father's hands—the ones that had so gently lifted her up
to see the clock as a girl, the ones that healed the sick with careful, knotted fingers and a sincere touch—they blistered her arms
now. He grabbed her, digging his nails into her skin, and barked
in a rough whisper, "You will not speak of it! Do you hear me?
It will cause a panic among the people. What is best for them
now—to know nothing of what will happen, or to incite panic
before their death? At least this way they shall have some measure of peace."

"That is false peace."

"And it is the way the Council must have it. The SS have
gallows here, in the courtyard by the prison. They will hang prisoners just for thinking such thoughts. You, daughter, will forget
who you were before this camp. Do you understand me? You
will forget everything and everyone who came before this very

moment in time. Your job now is to teach. And when you teach, you survive. I will not lose you. I will not watch my own flesh and blood die by their hands!"

Kája bit her bottom lip to keep from sobbing over his words.

Never had he spoken with such conviction. Never before had he raised his voice to her. But now, with death floating about on air, choosing victims indiscriminately, he'd succumbed to the same fear that gripped them all.

"What . . . ," she mumbled, trying to form words on her quivering lips. "What do I teach them?"

His fingers eased their hold one by one until they were once again hands that merely rested on her shoulders.

"Teach them to hope."

She shook her head.

"No. Surely, after what you've just said, I can only teach them fear. I'm not strong. I can't forget everything and—" Her voice hitched on a sob, thinking of Liam and the last moments they'd shared on the train platform in Amsterdam. She shook her head. "I know I can't forget everyone who came before this moment. I can't."

Kája's hand grazed for the necklace she'd worn, the ghost of it still there under her collar. She clamped her eyes shut, willing her mind to stop picturing Liam, her love, standing at a train depot in Switzerland. Waiting for her. Watching for a dream that would never come.

"I won't. Those memories are the only thing that can keep me alive. I know it."

"You must live here now." He patted her shoulder, urging her on. "You will use whatever is at your disposal to tell them stories. Give them hope, even if you know in your heart that there is none to be had."

"But how?" she cried, finally collapsing in his arms. "What do I say?"

"You tell them about our clock. Hmm?" he whispered. "Help them weave tales about the sparrows, the ones who fly free and strong and soar far away from here. The ones God watches over. Yes? Tell them stories and have them paint their own. Give them a pen, a brush, a task—any task. Use your gifts. And whatever that heart of yours is holding on to right now: keep it hidden. Keep your own hope hidden while you work, and you will survive."

CHAPTER TWENTY-FOUR

Sera's mind was playing tricks on her.

She was pacing back and forth in her London bedroom, marching through the early-morning light that just peeked in to greet her through the white gauze curtains. She was waiting for William's call and had practically worn a hole through the dark espresso wood flooring.

She'd been awake for hours, searching through the files again and again, finding nothing else but that one mention of K. E. Hanover. And now that her heart knew something was hidden there, she'd been considering every possible scenario that tracked through her mind.

Who is Katie?

Was she a relative of Thomas's? A cousin, perhaps? Or was she someone else completely?

The phone vibrated in Sera's hand and she nearly dropped it for how it startled her. She saw William's number and answered with a hushed, "Hello?"

"You're awake. I thought it might be too early."

Sera glanced at the alarm clock by the bed. "It's almost six. The sun's barely up."

"How was your flight?"

"It was fine. Long." Sera drifted down to the side of her bed, the inconsequential talk making her head ache. She pinched the bridge of her nose and closed her eyes, hating the fact that because of what she now knew, or suspected rather, the sound of his voice was hurting her. "Your father sent us a car. He, umm . . . he welcomed us here. I hadn't expected that."

"That's good. I'm glad he's treating you well."

"We had a conversation last night, Will. In the garden, he and I. And after it I walked away more confused than ever. You see, the man I expected to meet isn't here. Your father is not who I thought he'd be. Actually, he's not all that different from you. At least not in the way I've seen. The way he talked about his family . . . it wasn't with indifference. There was regret there—so doesn't that mean there's feeling there too?"

"Sera, please."

"No—I showed him something yesterday. A photograph Penny and I found. It wasn't with the rest of the artwork so it must have been overlooked. It was a cross necklace."

"A necklace?"

"Yes. It looked old and wasn't valuable. Not like everything else. But when he held it in his hands and looked at it, I almost thought I was seeing you. It's the way you've looked at me before. With such love. You have his eyes, Will. And whatever I saw in him, I couldn't ignore it."

"Then he's trying to fool you, Sera."

"Why would he? He told me you knew about the necklace and that you knew who received it. So, Will . . ." She breathed out his name, fighting so that he'd not hear the tears in her voice. "Who is Katie? And why did you let me come here? You knew I'd dig for answers. And that I'd eventually find them."

He paused and the line was loud with silence.

"I knew if I didn't let you go, you'd never forgive me."

"And do I need to forgive you for something? Because for the life of me, I'm feeling more than a few thousand miles away from you right now."

He sighed. It was heavy. Long. Tormented, even. He cleared his throat before asking, "Do you have a pen?"

Sera shook her head on instinct, forgetting for a moment that he'd not see it.

"What do I need a pen for?"

"So you can write down an address."

Sera walked over to the nightstand and grabbed a pen, then tore a piece of paper from the files she'd kept by the bed.

"All right. I'm ready."

"Katie Hanover lives in Primrose Hill. Number 7 Wadham Gardens."

She scrawled the address and stared back at it, the ink fairly burning a hole through the paper. "Why are you telling me this now?"

William paused and as if sitting right there in the room next her, whispered very softly, "Because I love you, Sera. And you'll never be able to love me back unless you know who I am."

CHAPTER TWENTY-FIVE

September 4, 1942

Terezin

*M*en stood up to their knees in earth.

The digging of trenches and the laying of pipe for the new water system looked to be grueling work. Kája walked by the faction of men lining the street, swinging their picks and shovels while SS officers shouted, looking on with guns all too easy to see shining in the holsters at their waist. She kept her head down, hoping to continue unnoticed as she made her way to the school building.

Kája wore a dress of gray blue that shone pale in the morning sun. It might have been lovely once, with its dainty flower pattern. But wear had faded the fabric so that each defined bud looked like nothing more than a hazy dot of white. It hung on her thinning frame generously, as clothes would on a line, lilting in the breeze for the lack of form beneath. A yellow star was sewn over her left collarbone. Save for her crown that shone glints of red in the sunlight, it was the only color about her. She kept her hair tucked back under a drab kerchief as she moved about the streets, hoping to be inconspicuous.

She darted past wooden carts of wares—old suitcases and such—probably from a transport coming or going. There were the Jewish guards on street corners, barking orders for women and wide-eyed children to form lines away from men. SS guards looked on, managing the scene from afar.

Kája turned her eyes from it and kept walking.

She noticed people going into the Magdeburg barracks, which held the Council of Elders and the Jewish administration for the camp. Her father went there often, as he'd been appointed a member of the council. He never took her of course, but she knew where the building was.

"Keep nothing about you that shall be remembered," her father had cautioned.

And so she walked along, basket clutched in hand each day, weaving her way from their block to the building that housed the tiny school. She never drew attention. Never spoke to anyone in Terezin unless she had to.

It was so otherworldly of a place in comparison to the life she'd lived in London mere weeks before.

Her thoughts drifted to Liam, to the life she'd had and the new one she'd so wanted to live with him. Would he have recognized her now, with her pale skin and woeful spirit? She'd been there mere weeks and already she feared she'd become irrevocably changed. If the war ever ended, and she could see him again . . . would he still want her, knowing the things she'd seen couldn't be sponged from her heart?

"You there!"

Kája's heart flip-flopped, but still she hurried along.

Lord, don't let them stop me!

"Passage paper!"

A commotion started, the clamoring of shouts and stomping boots growing somewhere off behind her. Kája quickened her pace, feigning innocence in the event they were trying to stop her. It was probably someone else, an unfortunate behind her.

Keep walking, she told herself, and quickened her pace along the line of workers laying pipe. She thought to cross to the other side, but there were too many carts, too many people lined up.

Speed up, Kája. Go by them.

Without notice, her path was cut short. An old man fell down to the ground, his aged hands barely able to catch his weight, and crumbled on all fours upon the cobblestones at her feet.

Kája gasped and stepped back, dropping her basket. It spilled the contents of paper and pencils on the ground around them.

The man rolled over and collapsed on his back, coughing and sputtering in the bright sun.

Her first instinct was to attempt to pick him up, and so she stooped without thinking. She knelt and with shaking hands, labored under his dead weight. She slipped an arm under his shoulders and attempted to tug him up with her free hand. If she could summon more strength, perhaps she could lift him enough to set him upright?

Kája turned to look over her shoulder and shuddered when she saw a line of Jews still wielding their picks and shovels, swinging away at the dirt as if nothing at all had happened. They turned away, fearful to engage, when SS officers started marching in her direction. They were far off, but they'd caught the activity in their sights and wouldn't take long to be at her side.

"Sir?" She patted the man's cheek frantically, pleading with him to wake. He was alive—mumbling and asking for water—but she couldn't stir him enough to respond. "Please! You must wake up. The guards will hasten our way."

"Water," he breathed out.

"I haven't any," she said, and tugged at him again, trying to will him into cooperation. He couldn't or wouldn't be budged. "Please get up."

Mere seconds passed, though it felt like agonizing minutes. Too many of them. Enough that the guards would surely punish

them both for the infraction. A loss of food ration, perhaps. Or—
God help them—worse.

In her restless efforts to force him awake, the kerchief gave
way from the back of Kája's neck and she felt her hair fall loose
about her shoulders. A wavy tendril swung down over her face,
obstructing her view. She turned back, enough to notice the
glint of the sun shining off an SS officer's unholstered gun as he
walked in their direction.

The sight took her breath away.

There was no time; she had to wake him or leave. That was it.
The man was part of the work detail, and if he couldn't perform the
duties at hand, there would surely be the harshest of reprisals—
and she, for interfering, could be just as culpable.

"We're going to sit up now, all right?" She tugged until the
man was in a sitting position. Still he mumbled, saying words
she couldn't understand, and exhausted, he fell back against her.

"Here. Give him to me." A man appeared at her side, kneeling,
and lifted the old man from her arms. She noticed the stitching
on the forearms of his jacket and drew in a shuddered breath.

He was clad in a Nazi uniform.

Kája released her hands and eased back, fingers trembling.
She kept her head down, staring at the lines of dirt between the
ancient stones of the street.

What should she do? Pretend she hadn't heard the SS officer?
Stand up and run?

"Pardon, sir. He—" Kája could barely speak from fear. She
swallowed hard and willed her voice to work, for however weak
and trembling it might be. "He fell and . . . asked for water . . ."

"It is all right." Though German in accent, the man's voice
was surprisingly human, not cold or laced with malice. "I'll take
him," he whispered.

Take him where? she wanted to ask.

There were no secrets in this place. If one couldn't work, they were sent to the death camps. If one faltered in their labor, there was a bullet to the head or a tightly knotted noose that would be waiting. And if they were sick, or exhausted, or even just a little old, as this man clearly was, there wasn't the tiniest shred of hope. Transport trains would seal their fate.

"I'll help him," he clarified, seemingly reading her thoughts.

Kája kept her head down but was so struck that she glanced up, eyes only, responding to the unbelievable blink of compassion she'd just witnessed. The officer wasn't wielding a gun. He was strong and intentional, taking the old Jewish man in his arms to raise him up to a sitting position. He knelt on one knee and stabilized the man's back.

"There's water. Just there—" He inclined his head to an old metal bucket at the end of the row. "Go and get it."

Kája connected with the light hazel of his eyes, as they were so much softer than she'd have ever expected, and nodded. "Yes."

"Bring it to me," he stated matter-of-factly.

She obeyed and rushed over to retrieve the bucket. It was only half full, and not as taxing to move as she'd have thought by its size. Kája moved quickly, taking short steps, and brought the bucket over to the officer. He raised the metal ladle to the man's cracked lips and poured water over them.

Kája's eyes teared almost on their own.

The sight of the man revived from the water, skin wrinkled and eyes glazed with exhaustion—it was too much. He grabbed the cup of the ladle and lapped at the water like a parched animal, uncaring that the cool liquid was dripping from his chin and wetting a trail down the front of his shirt. He was ravenous for it, and without dignity in how he begged for more like a lapping puppy.

The young officer dipped the cup in again and offered a second ladle to the man.

The other SS officers shouted then, tossing out orders to the old Jew. "Jude! Jude—back to work!"

They'd marched up not far from the pair, but had stopped short where they now stood, laughing in the bright summer sun. They teased, slapping their knees as they ridiculed the young officer for his actions, taunting that he apparently desired a hug from a dying Jew. They admonished him to drag the old fool into the alley and free up the spot in the work detail for another.

"Give him to me—I've an extra bullet," one shouted.

"Perhaps that girl could pick up the shovel in his stead! She looks as sturdy as any Jew I've ever laid eyes on."

They roared with laughter, just as a shiver took over the length of Kája's spine. She remained kneeling, frozen, unable to do anything but breathe in and out and wonder if any of them would make it out of the moment alive.

God . . .

She could scarcely form a prayer in her mind, save to plead his name through the intense fear.

One of the guards sighed in frustration and stomped up behind them. He grabbed the old man's shirt collar.

"No." The officer shoved him off, even as he stared into Kája's eyes. "This man is fine. Just tripped on a stone. He will work. I'll have him back up and in line," he shouted, and tossed the nearest stone he could find. It clinked against the street near the eager SS officer's boots. "And you see to it that the young boys remove these stones from now on, so it doesn't happen again. It's interfering with my workers!"

The other SS guard stared back with eyes narrowed to slits. He didn't look like he enjoyed being tossed at, though said nothing. Whether he was outranked or outmatched by the officer with the kind eyes, Kája didn't know. He stomped back to the crown of officers and turned his back on the scene thereafter.

The officer pulled the old Jew to his feet, roughly it seemed, though Kája noticed his hands were steadying as the man wavered to find his balance. The officer knelt and picked up the man's shovel.

"Back to work," he issued, and handed it back to the man.

Kája knelt on the ground, still frozen.

After the old man pushed the shovel blade down into the pile of dirt at his feet, the officer turned his attention back to her.

"You have your Passage Permit?"

Kája nodded and reached to take it out of her shoe.

"I don't want to see it. Just be sure you keep it with you. Though you can travel the ghetto, you ought to go straight to your destination."

"Yes."

"Gather your things and go," he admonished her. The words were barked in a rough whisper as he tilted his head up the street. "Now."

Kája broke the connection with his eyes, immediately looking down to the spilled wares around her. She wasted no time. Uncaring as to what was retrieved and how it was shoved down in the basket, Kája picked up the paper and as many pencils she could find—even the ones that had broken against the stones during the fall and had been soiled by the water spilled from the man's drinking.

She moved to leave as quickly as she could. It wasn't until Kája was a step or two away that she felt the curtain of hair at her nape get caught up in the light breeze and blow about her shoulders. Her hand flew up to it, remembering that the kerchief was the only one she owned. She turned then, thinking it must have fallen to the ground, and met him, blocking her path.

He stood there, quiet, with a set jaw and unmistakably kind eyes as he held out the kerchief to her. She stepped forward and with a cautious hand, brushed fingers with his to take it back.

"Don't ever come back by here," he ordered, and without

---

another word, turned his back to her as the work detail continued the endless swinging of tools through the air.

The cadence of shovels and picks in the dirt became a deafening death song as the Jews labored on in the sun.

Kája took the kerchief and stuffed it down in her basket, then almost faltered on the uneven stones of the street in her haste to get away. She hurried along, not even breathing until she'd rounded the corner and was clearly out of sight.

It was she that fell to her knees this time, sobbing against the nearest brick wall. With shoulders shaking and heart pounding, she slid down to sit on the ground and buried her face in her hands.

Be strong and courageous?

She shook her head.

It didn't seem possible. Not there. Not when death was constant and searching. Not when evil was so hungry. It could find anyone, even as they walked down the street.

God? she sobbed. *Where are you?*

238

CHAPTER TWENTY-SIX

December 19, 1942

Terezin

Kája entered the back door of the school building and quickly closed it behind her.

Walking past the guards each day had become her daily ritual in summoning fresh courage. After the confrontation with the Nazi SS guards in the street weeks before and the near-miss that could have ended her life, Kája's main focus each morning was to remain unnoticed before them and reach the safety of the supply room in which she now stood.

She remained there for mere seconds before she was startled by an unexpected voice from the hall.

"Miss Makovský? Is that you?"

After trying to shed any trace of shakiness from her voice, Kája called out, "Yes. I'm here."

She shrugged out of her coat just as a stout woman appeared before her with broad shoulders and ruddy brown hair dotted with sparks of gray. The woman stopped and surveyed her with an expressionless face.

"You are the art teacher," the woman declared rather than asked. Her Danish accent was thick.

"Yes. The Jewish Council has asked that I employ some of the camp children with jobs in the arts community, if that's what you're here to inquire after," Kája answered. She hung up her coat and patted her hair back slightly, trying to calm the tendrils that had come loose and fallen down to tip her shoulders.

"I was told to come and see the art teacher, so I'm here."

"If you're looking for supplies, I'm sorry to disappoint you. We haven't any food here. And as for the rest, I'm afraid we're rather thin at the moment. The paint's long since dried up and without any more brushes I just don't know . . ."

"Yes, well." The woman stood poker straight and with an unmistakably serious bent to her features, added, "I am not here for supplies."

"Oh." Kája was used to somber faces and hushed whispers. They spoke of news. Bad news. The kind of news that everyone became used to in the camp. She took a deep breath and cleared her throat, her attention now fully piqued. "Very well. How may I help you?"

"The Jewish Council sent me to notify you that a transport arrived this morning."

Kája nodded.

Another transport.

Terezin was bursting at the seams as it was. She suppressed a shudder, thinking of the people who would have to be shipped out to make room for new prisoners. It was a vicious cycle of death trains.

Kája looked back at the woman and saw the same fear in her eyes.

"Where is it from?"

"This one is from a ghetto in Poland." The woman dropped her voice to a whisper. "It was cleared, you understand. But there are more children. Twelve hundred and sixty of them. Most from Poland, though some are from Germany and Austria. All without parents, you see."

Kája exhaled and closed her eyes on the horror. She nodded, understanding the weight of the woman's message.

"Will any of them be coming to work here, then?"

"Yes. I expect so. If they are healthy enough—and young enough to avoid the work detail." The woman turned and looked farther down the hall. She inclined her head and ordered, "Come here, child."

It was the first time Kája realized they weren't alone.

She tilted her head to the side and looked past the woman to see a young girl standing behind, pale as a ghost with soft brown hair that just grazed her chin and wide owl eyes that stared straight ahead. Her shoulders were turned inward and she walked slowly, almost shuffling her feet as she came into view. She wore a polka-dot dress in a deep navy blue.

The sight of the girl caused a pang to register in Kája's chest and she placed a hand over her heart on instinct. She took a step forward and knelt down in front of the girl, who couldn't have been more than eight or nine years old, and asked, "What's your name, dear?"

The girl whispered a name Kája couldn't quite hear. She stared ahead as if entrancing pictures danced on the wall opposite her.

Kája looked at the woman. "Her name is Sophie," the woman said.

"Sophie?" She smiled and reached for the girl's hand, though the little fingers fell limp and lifeless in her palm. "Why, that is a lovely name."

The woman leaned in, then whispered, "She is from Austria. Her parents were killed by the Gestapo before she arrived there. Her brother too. She has no family left to speak of."

"I see." Kája took a deep breath against the hitch of emotion that formed in her throat. She turned her attention back to the girl.

"*Těší mne*—it's nice to meet you, Sophie. We have a lot of activities here. We have stage plays and music and even art shows. I've been asked to paint the sets for a children's play. I'm certain we can find something for you to do."

The woman cut in, "I've been sent to bring her to you, but not for work."

Kája shook her head. "I don't understand. The children are always brought here under the auspice of work." She lowered her voice and added, "It's how things are done."

"Not in this case." The woman leaned forward. "The SS has appointed you as her guardian."

Izabel did not stir when they entered the attic.

She lay on a plank bed, back turned to the door, her breathing even with the cadence of sleep.

Kája noticed Agnes, one of their roommates, sitting on the floor by the window. The setting sun bled in at choppy angles across the room, lighting bits of her brown hair and the wooden brace arches adorning the ceiling. The broken glass of the window behind her fractured what little light there was, creating odd shapes on the wall.

Agnes looked up from the book in her hands.

"How is my *matka*?" Kája asked.

"She's been this way since we came back from our shift," she whispered, her German accent pronounced. "She was so tired that she went right to sleep."

"Thank you," Kája replied. "I'm so sorry to be late after school. I would have come to walk her back from the factory today, but we have a new roommate who has joined us and I had to ensure we had everything squared away." She held up a rolled blanket from under her arm.

"*Ja?*" Agnes stood and laid her book on the window sill. "Then I am relieved it wasn't for what we'd feared. I made excuses with your mother, and it concerned both of us when you didn't show right away. I'm so relieved you're here."

"Me too." Kája inclined her head in an appreciative nod, adding, "And I'm very grateful to you."

Kája beckoned behind her, leading Sophie from the shadows into the dimly lit attic space.

"Sophie, this is Agnes. Along with my mother—who is asleep in the bed—and two other ladies whom you will meet later, she lives here with us in our room." She rested gentle hands upon Sophie's shoulders in presentation. "Agnes, this is Sophie. She comes to us from Austria and she's going to stay here for a while. She and I are going to look out for one another."

Agnes locked eyes with her over Sophie's head.

The questions were there.

Where are her parents? What has she survived up to this point? And why has a child been assigned to us?

Kája could read them and shook her head, having no way to answer.

Within a month of entering Terezin, Kája and her mother had been moved from the overcrowded barracks to a tiny attic in an old Terezin shop building. Though there were not hundreds in their barrack room any longer, the location was less desirable. They were far from the hospital in which her father worked. What was more, the conditions were no less miserable on one side of the camp than the other. They may have been in one of the buildings in town, but it was also in wretched disrepair.

Agnes and two other women, much older sisters from Austria, had been pressed into the same space, sharing three plank beds between them, with lice-infested blankets and a communal bucket that stayed in the corner farthest from where Agnes had sat. They took turns emptying it in the alley behind the building each morning.

"*Guten Abend*, Sophie." Agnes seemed broken from her

momentary stupor and spread a thin coverlet on the floor under the window. "Perhaps you'd like to sit by the light?"

Sophie didn't move right away.

Agnes met Kája's eyes. She whispered, "Would she like a book?" then added quickly, "Can she read?"

Kája mouthed back, "I don't know."

"Sophie? Would you like to look at a book?" Agnes walked a few steps to the other side of the room and laid her hand on a stack of old books on the wall's low shelf.

She made no move to retrieve a book.

"Well," Kája said lightly. "Perhaps later, then. Why don't you sit down and rest?"

It wasn't until Kája nudged Sophie in the direction of the window that her limbs began working and she crossed the room to the coverlet. She sat and pulled her knees up to her chest. She wore long, gray socks that tipped the bottom hem of her coat and scuffed black buckle shoes so old they no longer reflected when light was cast upon them. She sat with her back up against the wall beneath the window sill, looking up at them from across the room.

Kája swallowed hard.

The challenge of caring for a child who gave the appearance of a wounded animal was a far cry from fumbling through teaching a group of children in a classroom. Besides offering food and what little water they had, she wasn't sure what to do with the child. Sophie had haunted a corner of the classroom all day, sitting upon a stool without uttering the slightest sound.

She looked prepared to do the same through the night.

Kája took a few steps and knelt down before her. She slid a picture book from the shelf.

"Sophie? Lucky we are that this one has some beautiful pictures in it," she offered, and set the book down on the floor beside her. "I'd like to step out in the hall with Agnes for a moment. Would that be all right?"

Sophie didn't nod acknowledgment, though her eyes moved from Kája's face to the door and back again. She figured it was enough of a reply that she'd be all right if they stepped out for a moment.

Kája gave her the strongest smile of solidarity she could and with Agnes at her heels, ducked out into the hall.

"Kája, what is she doing here?"

She shook her head in the dim light of the third-floor stairwell.

"I haven't the slightest idea. A woman came to the school this morning and said that the Jewish Council had requested I be her guardian."

"But what does that mean?"

"I don't know, exactly. But she hasn't any parents. No family. A transport of children just arrived today, and all I know is that she's from Austria and she's alone. Beyond that, I haven't a clue."

Agnes peered into the attic room, the shades of dusk now taking over as the minutes ticked by. Little Sophie was shrouded in a haze of gray-blue light from the window, her tiny form popping against the faded red of the brick walls and the worn wood ceiling above her head. She looked like a tiny glowing angel in the midst of a drab cell.

"Has she said anything to you?"

Kája's heart was breaking. "Not a word."

"Are you sure we can care for her?"

"Well, I suppose they thought of me because I work with children all day. Or maybe my father said something to them. I can't say that I would have chosen myself, exactly. But she needs looking after. It's apparent she's severely hurt by whatever's happened to her. If she needs care, maybe that's why God brought her to us. We can be that for her."

"I worry how we'll all make it through winter without ventilation or heat. And no food? Think about what it's like up here.

Wouldn't she have a better chance in the barrack, with more children around her?"

Agnes's concerns were valid.

The attic was far worse than anything she'd seen in the barrack. Bed bugs and fleas crawled over them like armies marching drills through the night. No one was spared in sleep through their itching madness. There were no lavatory facilities to speak of. The roof leaked with each rain. Their little stove was broken, and their one window was cracked wide. What would they do? The worst days and nights of winter couldn't be far off.

Kája exhaled. "We could patch the window. I have some cardboard at the school. Maybe we could find something to attach it to the windowsill?"

"That might work for now, but what about when it rains? Or snows?"

"I don't know what the answer is, but we'll decide what to do later. Right now she needs care. That's all I can think. Even if it's in an attic with no water or heat. We'll have to fight for enough rations to keep everyone fed, but we can do that. She doesn't look like she'd eat much of what we'd offer anyway."

Agnes sighed.

"One more thing. I hesitate to bring this up now, but I don't know if this is a good idea because of your mother. Kája, she has me very concerned."

Kája's heart sank like a stone. "What? Why?"

"She's . . . confused."

"What do you mean, confused?"

It was the kind of comment Kája had prepared herself for. With her mother's bewilderment in Prague and her steady decline in the months since they'd entered Terezin, she knew it was inevitable.

"Izabel doesn't seem to know where she is much of the time. I try to remind her when I can, but she doesn't believe me. She's gotten up and tried to leave the factory more than once. And she can't keep up with the work, so much so that the guards are beginning to notice. I still make sure to sit by her each day, but I'm having trouble getting my work and hers done too. I've handed some of it off to the other girls near us, but I think they are resentful of it. I'm not sure how long she can keep up the sewing, and I don't know who we can trust if she doesn't. "

The only thing left to do was nod. Kája did so, blankly.

Her mother was slipping further and further away. She appeared a frail old shell, sleeping her hours away as if lost in a dream world. In the hours she was awake, Kája could only see glimpses of the woman who had borne her.

"She called me Hannah today."

Kája's tears boiled over at the mention of her sister. Her hand flew to her mouth seemingly on its own and she cried, biting at the side of her finger to keep the emotion hemmed in. She said a quick prayer thanking God that her sister and brother-in-law were still safe in Palestine, as far as she knew, and that it was very far away from the hellish attic in which they fought to live now.

Arms came around her then, the thin, bony arms of a young German woman who'd been in Terezin longer than she. They cried together, shedding the anguish that had been walled up inside their hearts for so long.

"I tried." Kája's voice came out in a muddle of tears. "I tried to get the Jewish Council to move me to the factory so I could be by her side. But they wouldn't relent. They're keeping me where I am."

"I didn't want to upset you, but I knew you'd want to know. And don't worry," Agnes whispered in her ear. "I'll be Hannah every day if I have to."

She welcomed Agnes's embrace, nodding, feeling the weight of the world bearing down on them both. They stayed in the hall for long moments, Kája wondering where hope had gone. Murmuring words of prayer up at the ceiling.

She thought of Liam and how he had worried over the safety of his father. Liam would understand how she felt right now. But for the first time, she was glad he wasn't with her. Glad he would never see her like this. All she could do was pray that like Hannah, he, too, was alive and safe.

Kája could hear people on the floor below them, women returning to their makeshift rooms and guards marching up the stairs for the nightly counts. Agnes pulled back and they both wiped at the tears under their eyes.

It wasn't until they'd stepped back into the room that Kája saw the sweet glimmer of hope. There on the bed next to her mother was a little girl in a navy polka-dot dress and gray knee socks, curled up and precious in sleep, hugging a picture book to her chest.

CHAPTER TWENTY-SEVEN

7 Wadham Gardens
Primrose Hill, London

Sera stepped out from the cab and into the quiet neighborhood of Primrose Hill.

The street boasted impressive, multistoried brick homes with manicured yards and gated iron and wood fences. They each had their own front garden and cottage feel, with trees lining the expanse of the sidewalk along the street and the sweet smell of honeysuckle perfuming the afternoon air.

Number 7 was on the far end of a high brick fence and a bower of tall trees.

Sera approached it, passing through the gate. And though her feet were heavier with each step, she walked up the cobblestone path to the front door and rang the bell.

She tried not to shift her feet while she waited. And as she heard a bustling noise from inside, the door was cracked wide and a young woman of perhaps twenty appeared before her, standing tall with dark hair and light-blue eyes.

"Hello?" She stood before Sera and with a curious bent, asked, "Can I help you?"

"Are you Katie?"

"Yes."

"Katie Elizabeth Hanover?"

She shifted her stance, giving a more reluctant, "Yes."

Sera nodded. "Then, umm, may I speak with you for a moment?"

Katie folded her arms across her chest and squinted into the sunlight. She looked back into the shadow of the house for a moment, then seemed to decide. She came out on the porch and closed the door with a soft *click* behind her.

"Look. If you're a lawyer, I'll tell you what I told the rest of them. We don't want any money. We don't want the Hanover name. We just want to be left alone."

"I'm not a lawyer." Sera shook her head. "And I'm not here to offer you any money. I just need some information, if you have it."

"Information about what?"

The girl was beautiful. She flipped dark waves over her shoulder, and Sera could tell she was making every attempt at appearing indifferent. But the expressive blue of her eyes gave her away. Sera could see—she was more interested than she was willing to admit.

"I'm wondering if you know a William Hanover?"

Katie answered immediately. "What does he want now?"

"Nothing. I—" Sera had thought to introduce herself as William's wife but based on the cool reception of the name, she was quick to think better of it. She took the folded paper photograph from her pocket and held it out in front of her. "I just need to know if you can help me identify something. It's a piece of jewelry in the family estate, and I have reason to believe it might be in your possession. I'm not asking for the jewelry back or anything. I just need to know if you've seen it."

Katie eyed it with a skeptical glare.

"Who are you?" she asked, and slid her hand back onto the doorknob.

"I'm Sera. And I'm not here to cause trouble," she replied.

"Please. I'm just hoping you can tell me if you've ever seen it before. That's all I ask."

Katie looked back at her, decision evident on her face. She sighed lightly, then nodded and took the paper in hand. It wasn't a second after she'd unfolded it that she handed the paper right back.

"Yeah, I've seen it. It's an old cross necklace that I received as a gift a few years back. But it's broken. The clasp doesn't work."

"It's broken," Sera said, looking up at her. "Wait, you mean you have it? Here?"

Katie nodded. "All I know is that it was sent to me from some grandfather in America whom I've never met. I received that necklace in the mail and then I heard that he died sometime after."

Sera's world felt like it was tumbling down on that quaint Primrose porch. She swallowed hard and with every ounce of restraint, asked, "I'm sorry. Did you say *grandfather*?"

"Yes. Why?"

"Would you mind if I come inside for a minute?" she breathed out, shock not yet settling in. "My name is Sera Hanover and I think I might be your sister-in-law."

———

The news that Thomas Hanover had another daughter was about the last thing Sera had expected to learn that day.

Even so, she'd managed to hold her composure enough to accept an invitation into the front room of Katie Hanover's home and proceeded to spend the next half hour with the half-sister William had never told her about.

Back at the Hanover townhome, she went straight up to the guest suite, praying to avoid both Thomas and Mrs. Clark in her desperation to talk to Penny. She ducked into the sitting room and finding it as empty, she slid into the chair by the fireplace and dropped her head in her hands.

"Sera."

William stood in the doorway to her bedroom, with a rather shifty-footed Penny nearby. She was wringing her hands like a good friend should, darting her eyes back and forth from husband to wife while doing her best to give Sera a supportive look.

"I think I'll just step out to the garden for a few minutes so you two can talk," she tossed out lightly, though the tension in the room could have set the entire house ablaze despite her attempt to cool it. She sent Sera a broken but encouraging half smile and headed for the door.

Sera waited until she heard the door close before moving. And though quite sure he knew exactly what she was going to say, Sera stood, looked him point-blank in the face, and said, "I'm leaving."

CHAPTER TWENTY-EIGHT

February 26, 1943
Terezin

There had been no transports to leave so far that February.
And then the trains began again.

It was early still, the sky barely cracked with the light of dawn, and a transport train had already come through the fog with scores of prisoners in tow. There walked the elderly, their hands barely able to hold their suitcase handles in the bitter cold. Several coughing children followed along. Kája wondered how many would show up at their schoolhouse door, and how many would be missing the day after that. The little ones walked along, heads down, holding the hands of adults with the same hunched shoulders. Parents, teachers, merchants, musicians . . . who had they been before Terezin? The guards had come out to keep watch, their unconcern evident in the way they enjoyed a casual smoke on the street corners.

The transport ambled by, a ghost army bound to haunt Terezin's city streets.

The lost were there too. The forgotten souls whose train had come in any day before this one. Mostly elderly, all starving; they wandered through the streets, looking for food when there was none, peeking into shop windows when there was nothing to buy. Kája had seen them on her walk from the train on her first day, too, the lost birds out in the cold. Though they had new faces now, their haunting presence remained. They took up benches, doorways, the corners of buildings even, dotting the streets like mournful markers on the route to the school building.

"She was here yesterday," Sophie remarked, the quiet shudder of her voice drawing Kája's attention.

A woman, clad in tatters with a curious purple silk scarf round her head, sat motionless on a bench ahead of them. Her feet were stretched out, warning that she'd trip anyone who walked by too closely.

Kája drew in a steadying breath when she saw the woman's face. It was not gray like the rest of the slowly starving. Her skin was pale as flour, frozen against the icy morning air. She'd slumped to the side sometime the day before and no one had noticed. Kája would probably not have noticed had Sophie not spoken. And how long would she sit here today? Tomorrow?

"Come along, Sophie." Kája tried to sound unconcerned and quickly turned them away from the bench to cross the street. "We'll walk along the other side of the street today."

She kept them going, heads down and hoping to go unnoticed.

The school was in an old dressmaker's shop past Neuegasse Street.

Shops had opened along it, curious oddities with street-facing windows and large signs, but no patrons who went inside. These were shops where no one made purchases. There was money in Terezin, official notes printed and handed out to prisoners for their purchasing needs. But what good did it do? There was no food. No medicine or clean water one could buy. Even the secondhand clothing shop boasted goods one would never need in such a place. Opera gloves and furs, silk dresses and jewels, all confiscated from the very suitcases that were being carried along the streets now. And who'd have need of them?

Kája glanced in the shop windows on that morning, never

expecting to stop. Never wishing to give the pain of seeing Jewish wares for sale any stronghold in her heart. But she paused now, still in mid stride with hand tightly fused to Sophie's, drawn by a wink of blue in one of the windows.

Her feet seemed to stop on their own, her breath freezing against the weathered glass before them. Sophie stood with her, squeezing her hand in confusion, trying to pull her along. Kája felt for a moment as dead as the woman they'd passed by on the bench. What did it all matter now? A purple scarf? Suitcases being carried and schoolhouses being readied for the day? She couldn't know, not when there in the front window, as if to torture her, was a string of pearls and their mates, unique little studs with tiny settings of emerald blue, for sale to no one.

———

They hadn't any desks, but instead used the large rectangular work table in the center of the shop as their work space. Stacked crates and large wooden spools served as chairs. An easel had been positioned at one end, which Kája used as her instruction space, and at the other, a small box stove that was fed with used paper and wood chips that the children collected on their way to the school each day.

Collages dotted the room, hung on the wall with old tacks or pinned to lengths of twine draped along the back wall. Theirs was art fashioned from life in Terezin, the children's expressions made from old newsprint and label paper from old cans. They used what they had. Stretched where they could. And all the while, Kája tried to believe that she wasn't feeding them false hope.

The pearls forced from her thoughts, Kája went about her duties for the morning, setting out what paper they had left and filling small jars with rain water they'd collected from one of the run-off gutter spouts behind the building.

"Your jars are ready," she said, and set them on the end of the work table for Sophie to distribute.

Sophie had become her silent partner of sorts, not saying much but bringing wares to the work table: old cans of pencils and boxes with broken crayons rolling around in the bottom. She worked quietly in her polka-dot dress, settling into the corner like a silent worker bee.

"Sophie, what we saw this morning . . . ," Kája began to explain, wanting to find some way to connect with the little girl, but was interrupted by a tiny knock at the door. She sighed and stood.

Kája dried her hands on a towel and walked over to open the back door, knowing the conversation would have to wait now that the children were arriving.

Little Adina, the younger of two sisters from Poland, stood in the cold. She blew air into her hands and whispered, "*Dobré ráno*, Miss Makovský."

"Good morning to you, too, Adina." She opened the door wide, having been unable to return the greeting with anything but a hard-fought half smile. "It is cold out, yes? Do come in and warm yourself by the stove."

Adina agreed with an enthusiastic nod and stepped inside. "The walk was cold."

Adina closed the door and proceeded to take off her winter wrappings. Kája looked around, alarm bells going off in her head.

Where is Ingrid?

When camp inhabitants did not show up when expected, that was never a good thing. She stood with hands on her hips and asked, "Your sister, Adina. Where is she today?"

Sophie looked up from the work table.

The little girl stopped in motion before hanging her coat on the hook by the wall. She kept her back to Kája, shoulders squared, and slowly shook her head. She hung her coat and without turning whispered, "Ingrid has a cough."

"A cough? But she was here yesterday and didn't seem ill." Kája knelt down before the little girl, taking her tiny hand in her own. "Tell me—how bad is it?"

"I don't know. She coughed through the night and woke with a fever. Mother thought it best she stay hidden in the barracks today."

"And has she seen a doctor?"

Adina shook her head, her lopsided braids tossing about her shoulders with the movement. "No. Mother was afraid they would think our barracks have illness and come to take us away. She refused to call a doctor. She made Ingrid promise to sleep under her bunk today and stay out of sight."

Kája exhaled, wishing there was something else she could do. If Ingrid was sick, the risk of accepting her at school with the rest of the children was great. Disease spread like wildfire once it found a victim. But leaving her to sleep on the freezing barrack floor was a greater risk. There would be no hope for the little girl if something wasn't done.

"Adina, I can go for a doctor. Do you think your sister has enough strength to walk here today if I went to go get her?"

"Yes. I think so." Her reluctant nodding left certainty far out of the equation.

"You must be sure."

It would do no good to bring Ingrid out in the cold if she couldn't walk. Carrying her in front of the guards was out of the question. But the thought of Ingrid alone in the barracks, with transport trains running again . . . they couldn't risk leaving her behind.

"I'll go with you."

Kája turned at the sound of Sophie's voice, so clear and strong in offering to help. She hadn't said much beyond small utterances since arriving in Terezin. But this? Sophie's declaration was so loud that it fairly echoed off the walls. She crossed the room and immediately began pulling on her coat.

"Sophie . . . I don't know. It will be faster if I go alone."

Sophie shook her head, wide-eyed and beautiful, with strength that astonished Kája. Where it came from, she hadn't a clue.

"I know where to hide from the guards," she vowed, voice firm. "I could sneak into the barracks and hold her up while we walk."

"Where?"

"There is a brick wall by the gardens. I saw it that first day I came here. We can pass by there without being seen."

"You're certain of this?"

Sophie nodded.

Kája exhaled, then walked over to the work table and took a scrap of paper and pencil in hand. She scrawled a note, folded it, and kneeling before Sophie, she slipped it in the girl's pocket.

"Leave this note behind when you take Ingrid out. Make sure it's under the bed. Understand?"

Sophie nodded again.

Kája buttoned the top of Sophie's coat and tied the green scarf over her ears like a kerchief, trying not to cry over the fact that Sophie had said more in the past minute than she'd uttered in the past few months.

"I suppose we are partners, then." She stood and looked to Adina. "You'll have to stay here and be our teacher when the other children come in. Just until I come back. Can you do that for me?"

The little girl nodded, face animated with the opportunity. Kája took off her apron and laid it across the work table, then reached for her own coat from the hook. She shrugged it up over her shoulders and quickly buttoned the front.

"But what do I tell them, Miss Makovský?"

"Ask them to paint a new world for me," she whispered, and tapped a finger to the end of Adina's pert nose. "You tell them I want to see butterflies and songbirds in every color of the rainbow. We'll write a story about them when I return. And mind that the boys don't use up all of your favorites colors, hmm?"

With an arm tucked round Sophie's shoulders, they stepped back out into the icy cold air.

They avoided the bench with the woman in her purple scarf. They passed by the ghosts as they hurried along toward the other side of the camp. She prayed with each step through the streets that they'd have something bright to hope for in the midst of the dark morning. A cough and a fever were never a good thing, not anywhere, and certainly not in Terezin. She'd seen the same thing over and over in the past months. A cough, fitful sleeping, and fever were the precursors to death.

Dear God, please don't let any more of the children die.

CHAPTER TWENTY-NINE

"Well?" Kája whispered from the foot of the bed they'd made up in the supply room, keeping her voice low so the other children wouldn't overhear them.

She chewed on her thumbnail, then turned to peek over her shoulder.

The children were seated around the long work table in the front room, all focused on their painting project for the day. Sophie and Adina, though, had their eyes keenly fixed on the room in which they stood. Kája gave them a smile, fake though the effort was, and turned back to Ingrid.

Kája toyed with the cross necklace between her index finger and her thumb. She made sure to keep it hidden beneath the collar of her dress, always out of sight. But still, it offered comfort, serving as a reminder of the moments they'd shared in a nursery car once, looking after children while the world fell down around them.

She absentmindedly ran her thumb over the tiny lump in the fabric as her father assessed little Ingrid. After several minutes of listening to her breathing and checking her pulse, he finally eased the stethoscope from his ears.

She lowered her voice to a barely audible whisper. "What is it?"

He shook his head, still kneeling by the side of the cot. He ran a hand over Ingrid's brow with a lovingly soft hand. "I'm sorry."

His body seemed to groan over weak, tired limbs as he pushed up to stand.

"This little girl has typhus."

Kája closed her eyes and downturned her head. "No."

He, too, lowered his voice. "She has a high fever. Cough. A rash on her trunk. All classic symptoms. And with all the vermin in this place, we can't know how quickly it will spread. People are coughing everywhere. The winter has been harsh."

"But she can't go back to the barracks. She'd never survive."

The weight of sending her back, walking through the streets— it wasn't humane. Ingrid had barely been able to stand when she'd arrived at the door. It wasn't likely that she'd have enough energy to get back to the barracks, let alone survive through the night.

"Yes," he agreed, and began packing wares into his medical bag. "I think you're right. I'll have to take her to the hospital with me."

Kája shook her head immediately. "No. Please. She'd never make it there either. The conditions are worse there than in the barracks." She stood tall against the idea. There was only one option. "She'll have to stay with us. I'll nurse her."

"And you don't think they'd notice her absence in the barracks?"

"I don't. I gave Sophie a note to leave for her mother. And the guards have long since stopped strict nightly counts with so many people packed in here. I think this is her chance and I'm willing to try."

Kája knew her father might have questioned her once.

He'd been unwavering in his overprotectiveness when they'd first arrived. He'd never have allowed her to walk past someone who sneezed from hay fever, let alone nurse a child sick from the typhus epidemic. But life in Terezin had melted into something different than it was before. There was no protection from death. No compassion either, unless one of the prisoners saw fit to extend it to another.

She judged him able to recognize that because he nodded, just once, and began packing up his bag.

"You understand the risks?"

"Yes." She nodded and knelt down at Ingrid's side. She brushed a gentle hand over her cheek. "I don't want her time to be over yet. I believe she has more to live for. They all do."

He looked past her to the group of children seated around the work table as they painted in silence and nodded.

"I've never thought to question you, my Kája. Not even when you came back to Prague. I was angry at God to see you there, but somewhere deep inside I knew you would walk through our door again. There is a light that guides you through this life, my daughter," he whispered, eyes glazing with tears. "It is Christ-like in its beauty. And because of that, I'll not question you now. Your strength will carry these children through the days ahead. I believe it is your calling now. This has been your journey."

Kája bit her bottom lip over the emotion his words generated. She'd hoped her calling was to pass through life at Liam's side as his wife. And as her father looked at her now, she couldn't speak of it. Not when he'd offered such praise. She rested her hand over the necklace at her collar, burying the remembrance that she'd been engaged once, and considered that God's path for her might have shifted in the way her father had said.

"And how is *Matka*?" he whispered into the room, his voice weighty. "I could not see her yesterday. There are too many sick at the hospital and I feared bringing illness in her weakened state."

"She is sleeping more."

"Is she? And what does she say when she's awake?"

"I remind her of the way things used to be. She listens to my stories. 'Remember the parties?' I say. 'The dancing on the portico over the river?' She likes those memories, though I doubt she truly remembers any of them. Maybe just hearing a voice beside her brings comfort, even if she no longer knows the face it comes from."

"Her heart is still there, despite the mind."

Her father placed a hand on her shoulder and paused on a tight squeeze. She covered his aged fingers with her palm. He sniffed loudly as he walked past, giving away his emotion in the moment.

"I'll return tomorrow. Make sure you work to keep the fever down. Bathe her in water, or ice if you can gather any from outside. And ensure she receives extra nourishment if she'll take it."

"I haven't much to give her," Kája answered, thinking of the rail-thin children in the front room and ration lines that never seemed to end. "Handfuls of old potatoes boiled in stale water."

"I know. But give it to her if she'll take it. And pray with her," he offered, having reached for his coat and put his hat on his head. "Pray with her and with *Matka*. Surely your voice will chase the shadows away."

———

Kája thought about Ingrid as the funeral wagon drove by.

The young girl had fought hard and survived the fever when so many others perished. But not long after, her number was called for transport and both she and her sister were lost to a camp in the east. She wondered now what had become of them as the horse-drawn carriage lumbered on the dirt road to the back of the prison complex. It was stacked some twenty coffins high and came to a stop where the graves had been dug.

She and Sophie kept their heads down with the others who walked along.

SS officers were there to watch over how the Jewish guards controlled the marched procession. They allowed it to proceed, standing back with mild interest. But oddly enough, one officer stuck out from the rest. She noticed that he'd removed his hat and stood, with what looked like a measure of respect, as the mourners ambled past.

It was so unexpected an action that she stared, unable to ignore it.

The unmistakable light green of his eyes reminded her of an incident that had occurred months before. She'd not seen him since, but Kája recognized him as the officer who had risked his life to pick up a fallen Jew. When the wagon passed by, only then did he replace his hat.

Kája watched, stunned by the silent action.

It didn't help ease the pain. It didn't eliminate the transport of children to the east. And it did nothing to comfort the line of tear-stained faces that ambled along with her. But for a moment, Kája was certain that the sun had come out. The officer's gesture brought light breaking through the clouds and for once, she didn't feel entirely alone.

God . . . , she breathed out, grateful for the fleeting glimpse of something humane. *Surely you are here.*

CHAPTER THIRTY

Sera rolled up her clothes and uncaringly shoved them down into her suitcase.

William opened the door and came into the bedroom. She looked up after his shadow cast lines across the floor. She could see the concerned look in his eyes even in the dimness of the lamp-lit room.

"What are you doing?" He closed the door with a soft *click* behind him, as though dealing with a jittery, caged animal. "Sera?"

"What does it look like I'm doing?" She tossed a pair of jeans in the suitcase and moved over to the bureau. She began dropping the jewelry she'd discarded there into a tissue she pulled from the box nearby. "I'm leaving."

"You're leaving tonight?" he asked, and took several steps in her direction. "I just got here. You can guess I was already on my way when we spoke this morning."

"I thought you couldn't come to London."

"I couldn't," he answered, still standing just far enough away that she could collect her thoughts. "Until our lawyers argued that I needed to come here to aid in my defense. The prosecutor relented."

"Well, I'm out of here. After all, I'd hate for your father to have to give me the news that my husband has in fact lied to me."

She bypassed him and dropped the tissues in the suitcase,

then stormed over to the closet. She pulled several garments from wooden hangers, jumbling the fabric in her arms. The hangers clanged together and swung there for a moment, making the only sound in the room until she marched over to the bed and began stuffing her suitcase again.

She zipped several pockets closed while he watched, dumbfounded.

"Did you—"

"Find Katie? Talk to her? Of course I did."

He exhaled and ran his hand through his hair. "I'm sorry."

"Well, there's not much we can do about that now."

"Sera, you can't leave this way. Please—"

"Why, Will? You obviously don't need me here. I'm not even sure why I came all this way except to be hurt all over again."

"What do you mean by that?" he asked, the ache evident in his voice, and reached out to grasp her elbow.

She yanked it from his fingertips and stood, chest heaving with pent-up breaths storming in and out. "I believed in you! I trusted you no matter what the charges. I even defended you to Penny when she questioned your innocence." She shook her head, knowing that the pain in her heart had shifted to a look of disgust on her face. "Now I can't even look at you."

"Sera, please." William edged closer to her and chanced reaching out, with arm in slow motion, and grazed her shoulder with his fingertips. "Let me explain. I can't lose you too."

"Oh—all of a sudden you want to talk?"

"I've wanted to talk about it since we met. I just didn't know how."

"You've had two years to do it. And I think I've been a patient wife. I haven't demanded that you tell me what's in your past, why you hate the thought of your father so much that you'd lie to cover it up."

William's features melted some. She guessed it was shame.

Or guilt. He was caught, and the proof of it was showing all over his face.

"I shouldn't have to pick up the pieces of who my husband is from fragmented conversations with his long-lost father and sister. We have to walk into that courtroom in less than a month and now I don't know whether you're innocent or not. You tell me you are. And I blindly believed you. But, Will—" Sera stared back at him, head shaking and eyes wide, battling tears, and whispered with emotion raw, "After all of this, I don't know. *Who are you?*"

"It's not what you think," he pleaded, eyes studying her face as she looked up at him.

"Oh good, because there are about a thousand theories floating around in my mind right now. Thank goodness it's none of those."

"When I met you I swore I'd turn my life around. I didn't want to go back. I'd never go back to who I was. And then we got on this road of looking for a painting and I didn't care about the inheritance anymore. I didn't want that life because all I could see was a life with you."

He placed a hand over hers, freezing it to the suitcase.

"Please don't go. Not like this."

"You may have changed, Will. You may even profess that God has changed you." She paused to pull her hand free. She zipped the side of her suitcase without daring to look back at him. She pulled the suitcase from the bed and it plopped down on the floor at her feet. "But as your wife, I think you owe me the truth. All of it. And unless you can give it to me right now, I'm walking out that door."

Silence had never been so painful.

Sera waited, standing before her husband with her heart bleeding. She stood there, hand fused to the grip of the suitcase handle, and prayed that whatever he had to tell her wouldn't rip it out completely.

William studied her for a moment.

"Please stay."

She turned from him, praying he wouldn't see the tears streaming down her face.

"I can't. And I don't know where I'll go just yet, but when you finally do come home from all of this, don't expect me or our baby to be there waiting."

CHAPTER THIRTY-ONE

William looked as though he'd been blasted with a splash of ice water to the face.

Sera closed her eyes on the harshness of the admission, instantly regretful that she'd told him about the baby in such a way. She stood, fused to the hardwood, waiting for him to reply.

"What did you say?"

She exhaled and opened her eyes. "I didn't mean to tell you like this." With the notch of her chin a little higher in the air, she confirmed, "I'm pregnant."

He started forward, as if on instinct.

Will's heart was a good one, she knew. She could see the joy in his face, the surprise and the pride that were all mixed into one embattled crease of the forehead as he crossed the room to her. It was so like him, tall and strong, to want to take her in his arms and protect whatever they had left. But for the pain of feeling forced into the admission when all she'd wanted from the beginning was honesty between them, Sera backed away.

She edged back, step by step, toward the door.

"Sera." He paused, shaking his head at the way she'd responded.

"No, Will. Not this time. I won't live with secrets anymore." She raised her hand out to form a gentle barrier between them. "We have more to think about than what we want, what we *feel*.

269

We're bringing a child into the world in a matter of months and so help me, I don't know how to do that if I'm alone."

"I won't let you go, not like this. We have so much to talk about. There's so much to say."

"I know." She nodded, feeling the heat of fresh tears stinging her eyes. "I know there is. And maybe, in time, we'll both be ready to. But not right now. You need to stay here, in London, with your father. You need to fix this—repair yourself before you come back and try to work on us. What you need to do is focus on the case. And I need to go."

"You can't think I'd just let you leave now, after this?" Will's shoulders sagged, as if pained by the very thought. He let out a deep exhale. "For a long time I was angry at a lot of things, but mostly at my father's absence. Always traveling, building wealth—his whole world was growing an empire out from under my grandfather's shadow. And I rebelled against his consuming need for business. I flunked out of three Ivy League colleges in two years. I eventually managed to slide by at a state school and barely earn a business degree. But by the time I woke up at twenty-five and realized I'd spent half of my adult years with a hangover, spending my family's money, my father was already ashamed of me."

"William." She hurt for him. Ached that he'd run for so long and that now, even at thirty-five, was still so wounded. She dropped the suitcase and walked over to his side. Her hands melted over his. "You could have told me this. I wouldn't have thought any worse of you. We all make mistakes."

"It was more than that," he said, and pulled back as if burned by her touch. "More than mistakes, Sera. He had to clean up our family name. He had to pay off my debt."

"What debt?"

"It was nothing the first time. A single-car accident in my

youth. He had the DUI charge wiped from my record. But the next time and the time after that? I should have gone to jail."

"How could you not have told me this? Will, everyone has a past."

He stared, eyes aching. "Yeah, but not everyone has their life paid for. He tossed money at lawyers. Judges. Whomever would cash a check. And I thought because of my sins, the way I shamed the family and he cleaned up after me, he owned me. I thought if I followed in my father's footsteps and did what he and my grandfather wanted, it would set things straight. They wanted a Hanover in the boardroom so that's what I would give them. I worked hard. Threw my life into it. I learned. I polished up in a CEO's suit and tie and by thirty years old, I'd become exactly what they wanted me to be."

"And that was?"

"Like them." He lowered his head. "I was loyal to family, yes, but loyal to money first. I was going to grow their name. And then *she* showed up at our door one day."

"Katie?"

He nodded. "She'd come to California, looking for the father she'd never known. I was the only one on the estate at the time and at first believed she was lying. Why wouldn't someone wanting money come along with a well-crafted story? But when I really looked at her, I knew. She had a birth certificate and a story with dates that lined up, but all I needed was that pair of Hanover eyes staring back at me."

"Your father's."

"Yes. Katie is about Macie's age. He'd had an affair and none of us knew we had a sister," William said, his voice racked with pain. He swallowed hard and continued, though she could see emotion clouding his eyes. "Everything I thought my father was—everything I'd tried to become for him—it was a lie."

"But none of this is your fault. Your father's the one who—"

"It is my fault, Sera. I confronted him about Katie, felt it was my duty as the oldest son to expose his shame. To protect my mother and siblings. I told him to choose," he admitted, shaking his head. "That we didn't want or need him anymore. I said I'd keep his secret, never tell Paul or Macie. They wouldn't have to know."

"Will—"

"And he left. Packed up his companies and walked out." He ran his hands through his hair.

"But how could you do that to your father? It wasn't your choice to make. Paul and Macie would have been shocked to know Katie existed, but if you'd have only given them time . . . and what about your mother? And Katie? I visited her today and she's hardened by all of this. She's grown up without a father. When she learned who she was and came to you looking for a family, you turned her away?"

"I came here, to London, after my father left. To confront him about the transaction to turn the artwork over to the company. Those signatures are mine but there was nothing illegal in it, not then, at least. We were going to use it as collateral to stave off the debt problems. But things started to turn around, and though the transaction to sign the assets over to the company was never supposed to go through, my father pushed it through anyway. Before he died, my grandfather told him he'd been cut out of the will, in part because of Katie. And by the time I'd found it buried in the company books, my father had already pocketed the money. I'd been liquidating the estate with property that was no longer mine to sell. I may have been a new CEO, but I wasn't stupid. The only error I made was trusting my own father. And he couldn't accept that the kingdom he wanted was about to be handed over to someone we'd never met. Someone who owned a painting of a Holocaust victim."

Sera felt her throat close up. "Sophie? Your father did all of this because the will had been changed."

William turned back to her, shoulders shaking.

"And he knew the decision of whether to keep the inheritance had been handed over to me."

CHAPTER THIRTY-TWO

————

April 13, 1943

Terezin

A hand came from behind so quickly that Kája hadn't time to react.

The palm covered her mouth so that any scream she might have let loose was lost, silenced by fingers pressed up hard against her lips. Another arm came across the front of her shoulders with lightning speed, pinning her against a man's chest.

She fought back, kicking about wildly. Her foot connected with a bucket nearby, sending it sailing with a crash across the floor.

"Hush! I'll not hurt you!" The fierce whisper came from a voice she thought she knew. A familiar tone, noted somewhere before. "Please! You must keep quiet if you want to live. Understand?"

She nodded her head under the weight of his hand.

"I'm going to remove this," he said, lightening the hard press of his hand upon her face. "But you must promise me that you'll not say a word. *Ja?*"

The accent was unmistakable. He was German. One look at the gold buttons on his sleeve and her heart sank—an officer.

Lord, help me!

Her breathing quickened. She tucked the load of bread in the folds of her skirt, praying that it had been too dark for him to see evidence of the theft.

"Can I trust you not to cry out?" he whispered close to her ear.

She nodded once more and immediately his hold on her relaxed.

"Keep your head down or they'll see you," he instructed, and with a firm but surprisingly gentle hand, pushed her head down below the top of the shop counter. "It's a death sentence if they do."

The beam of flashlights passed by outside, along with the bootfalls against pavement, and they were left alone.

Kája watched as he looked left to right, the flex in his jaw tight as his gaze methodically covered the span of the shop front. He looked out until all sound died away and they were once again alone with only the moonlight to pour in over them through the windows.

She finally caught her breath and bent over, nearly sick with how close she'd come to getting caught.

"Are you hurt?"

She managed to shake her head. "No. I'm all right." It had been fear that affected her most.

He sagged his back against the underside of the counter. It was then that she looked up, the moonlight casting a glow against his features. Her suspicions were confirmed—it was the officer from the street, the one who had helped the old man months before. The one who'd removed his hat at the passing of the cart full of the dead.

"You? I saw you that day . . . in the street."

He didn't acknowledge her comment. Instead, he flew into a series of questions.

"What are you doing here? Do you realize what could happen? That you could have been—" He stopped short, then continued in a rough whisper. "The guards are always monitoring the streets."

She knew it, yes. They marched around with guns drawn, that much she could see in their shadowed outline through the glass windows.

"Why are you out after curfew?" He was looking at her now and—curiously—seemed to have genuine worry painted upon his features.

Kája kept the bread hidden down in the fold of her skirt and with a barely there voice said, "My mother is weak with hunger."

"You're here for food."

She nodded. They were starving. Wouldn't anyone who snuck out after hours be scrounging for food? She couldn't let him know the whole truth, that her mother had taken ill with fever and desperately needed nourishment. If he knew, surely he'd send the guards to take her away.

"So you came here." He grasped her forearm lightly and pulled it forward. The bread was exposed to the light. He shook his head, jaw tighter than before when the SS were walking past the glass. "Do you have any idea what the penalty is for stealing? They'll send you to the Gestapo prison for this."

"I know." Kája kept her head down. She'd have felt a terrified weakling if he saw one tear form in her eyes.

"And any Jew sent to the prison is surely condemned to death."

She willed herself to speak, but could only nod through the abject fear of the Nazi officer standing before her.

"Then why take such a risk with your life?" He hooked a thumb under her chin and tipped her face up, his eyes finally meeting hers. "Your father is on the Jewish Council, *ja*?"

It was an authoritative question. One that she was sure he meant to use to intimidate her. He seemed to know who she was and that alone created a new feeling of panic.

Kája refused to answer. She merely kept her eyes down and fought with every breath to keep her whole body from shaking.

"You are afraid of me?"

He dropped his hand as if he'd been burned.

He turned then, found the hat that must have fallen from his head during the struggle, and yanked it up from the floor.

He raked his fingers through his hair and mumbled, "What did I expect," then slammed the hat back on his head. "What do you need?" he whispered, and offered his hand to help her up in the darkness. She climbed up from the floor with his assistance, but quickly dropped her hand from his as soon as she stood upright.

"Food . . ." She trailed off, still wondering if she could possibly trust him. Her voice was barely more than a whisper when she repeated, "We're desperate for food."

"How many are in your barrack?"

"Six." She shuddered, terrified she was sharing too much. "But we're not in the barracks. We are in an attic near the school."

"One small loaf of bread is not enough."

"It's all I could risk. I'd hoped for sausage or salted pork— some sort of meat. The butcher's block is so heavily guarded that I couldn't hope to get in and out without being noticed unless I came in at night."

He dusted off his uniform lightly. "Fortunate you are that you didn't try the butcher's. There isn't any meat there anyway."

"What? But why?"

"The shipment of meat won't be in until May, when the German Red Cross is expected." He shook his head. "That's what they say, at least."

"I've passed by all of the shops in town. Most of them sell wares taken from the transports in. Suitcases full of jewelry and fine clothing. What use would anyone have for it here? And they gave us money only good in the camp, some sort of currency. But who could use it? There's nothing to buy. I even saw my mother's own pearls in the window, the necklace and earrings given to her from my grandmother," she professed, trying to avoid the hitch of emotion from wavering her voice before him. "They mean nothing now, not when we're starving. I thought at least the butcher's shop would be a chance. They have meat casings hanging in the window and I hoped—"

"Painted plaster. They want it to look like there's an abundance of supplies." He exhaled and shook his head. "It is all for show."

He was the first German she'd ever heard that didn't identify with the rest of the SS. He hadn't said "we" but "they," as if he were separate from the SS in the camp. It was a small thing. So small, he probably hadn't noticed he'd said it. But she did. She looked back at him, wondering where the compassion had come from.

She judged it genuine.

"So meat. Bread," he noted, looking back at her.

Immediately self-conscious under the scrutiny of his gaze, she brushed back a lock of hair, wispy and soft, that had escaped the loose chignon at her nape. She thought of what she probably looked like to the officer, bony and thin, disheveled and dirty like the half Jew that she was. It forced her head down again.

He stood before her, quiet. Waiting. Then abating her fear with the softness of his voice.

"What else? What do you need for the children?"

"What?" she whispered, suddenly frightened that the guards would come back. It was too quiet. She could hear her own heart thumping through the shadows between them.

"The children," he whispered. "You work at the school. Surely you can use supplies."

She nodded, dumbfounded. "Yes—we can. But all I can think of is food. The children need nourishment to strengthen them. Something more than moldy bread and tepid soup."

"What else?"

"Umm . . . paper. We haven't any that's not already been used. I've been tearing cardboard and brown mailing paper from the ration boxes that arrive. The post office brings discarded letters here, the ones meant for inhabitants who have died or been transported out—"

"Paper. I believe I can find you some. Anything else?"

"Pencils—sketch pencils if you have them. Watercolors or pastels too. Anything with color, really. The children need it. And some means to create. I'll take anything beautiful for them. Tissue paper. Paste. Crayons."

Kája wasn't prepared to answer questions about the school, yet she found herself trusting the officer. She couldn't help asking for whatever one might dream of for the children.

"I don't know what supplies there are to be had, but what I can find, I'll bring."

"And books?" Kája's heart leapt with the request. "Any books you have. I know there is a library, but they won't allow the children to go there while they're working. Whatever you can find in German, Dutch, and Czech. We'll hide them—I promise. We'll even bury them if we have to. But they need to read. Books create the ability to escape into a different world, and the children are desperate for it."

He nodded and asked, "Where is your attic? What building?"

Her breath caught in her lungs for a moment.

Could she trust him?

"It's just two blocks away, but not there." She shook her head, thinking of the many people who shared their lodgings. "Bring them to the school. The doctor with the Jewish Council is my father, yes. He will know where to bring them."

"Good." He seemed to accept her idea and he asked nothing after that. "Come. You must go back."

She'd dropped the bread and bent down after it.

"The bread!"

He pulled her back sharply, so that she nearly lost her footing. He held her elbow in his hand, not harshly, and looked into her eyes.

"Please," she said. He tugged her by the hand toward the back of the shop.

"Can't you see? It's moldy. You'll only risk sickness. I promise you will have what you need by morning. But I don't want you getting caught with it now, not when it will do you no good to eat it."

He held on to her hand as they walked through the shop toward the back door, an action that both shocked and rained guilt down on her. Was she actually poised to trust him, to find something good in him, to allow a Nazi to touch her skin without coiling back in revulsion?

"You must listen to me," he said, pulling her with him until they came to the back alley. He poked his head out and looked left to right, then turned back to her. He pulled back just until they were both steeped in shadow. "I promise you'll have what you need. Go to the back door of the school at dawn. I will leave a box for you there, hidden behind a stack of crates."

Kája pulled her hand out of his grasp. "You know that I am a Jew. Why would you care? Why would you help any of us?"

He gave an embattled nod and took a last look down the street.

"I know you are a Jew," he said, and finally sprang forth into the alley. She followed close behind. "That's why I'm helping you."

"Your name, sir?" she asked as they crouched down by stacks of crates on the street corner.

He seemed surprised by her question. He wrinkled his brow slightly, then whispered, "Dane." He pulled her with him along the bricked wall behind the school building. "You can make it if you run the rest of the way. Stay out of the light."

Kája nodded, though her feet wouldn't move. She longed to understand why. Why would he help? And why still would he wear the uniform of death and help the Nazis in their gruesome activities? What kind of contradiction was he?

She lowered her eyes, hoping only to avoid those strikingly kind eyes of his.

"Thank you," she managed to say, and it was more than she'd ever imagined conceding to a Nazi.

"Go now. It's clear," he ordered in a stern whisper, and melted back in the shadows while she took steps away from him.

Then she turned, fear penetrating all points of her insides again, and ran as fast as she could. She didn't stop until she was inside the building that housed their little attic room and collapsed, heaving, her back against the inside of the door.

What had just happened? The officer had not turned her in. In fact, he had given her his name.

Dane.

He'd offered it. Freely. Without pause. And yet hadn't inquired or allowed her to give hers. She wondered, as she wiped the sweat from her brow and silently climbed the stairs—was it because he already knew?

She had her answer when she arrived at the school early the next morning, and she and Sophie found a crate of supplies left at the back of the schoolroom door.

There was food—more of it than they'd seen in months, a little banquet of bread and salted meat. Colored pencils. Watercolors in glorious blues and yellows. Kája could have kissed them she was so happy. Everything was a dream, right at the back door of their school. It was marked with a note, a single word written on it: her name. And with it, a box of paper. Dane had brought stacks and stacks of paper for the children to use.

Kája smiled for the first time in forever; they were up to their elbows in the useless currency of Terezin.

———

CHAPTER THIRTY-THREE

"So, you're at the airport. You're going home?"

Penny had concern in her voice. Why wouldn't she? Sera had just unloaded the entire messy business of William's past and now she sat in the busy terminal at Heathrow airport, alone, pondering her next steps. She had a ticket to San Francisco in her hand, but she still had no idea whether she'd actually use it.

"Maybe. I don't know."

"And he's staying here?"

"For now. Yes. I told him I was going home to think things through, but now I just don't know what to do." Sera slumped down in the chair, dotting at her eyes with a tissue as she spoke. "There was no shouting. No anger, even. I just told him that he needed to focus on the case and I—well, we—were going home so he could."

"So you told him about the baby?"

Sera pinched the bridge of her nose and closed her eyes, trying to relieve the tension there.

"Yeah. I did. In the worst way possible. I told him that when he finally did come home, we wouldn't be waiting."

Penny said nothing right away.

The ability to perfectly time when to react and when to remain silent; it was an admirable quality in a friend. And for what it was worth, as she sat, staring out into the throngs of travelers bustling by, Sera found herself grateful for Penny's mastery of it.

"Okay. And how'd he take it?"

"He asked me to stay, tried to reach for me as soon as I mentioned the baby. But I pulled away." She shrugged, though no one was there to notice it. "And he let me go."

"Sera." Penny's voice was sweet and whisper soft. "There is no way on God's green earth he really wanted you to go. I'm sure he thought he was only protecting you."

"He's got a funny way of showing it."

"Well, he's right," Penny scoffed. "For once. I'm inclined to agree with him."

Sera's jaw dropped. "About what?"

Not Penny. Sera couldn't believe that he'd even managed to win over the one person in the world who was supposed to be on her side without question.

"You need to go home, honey."

"That is why I'm here at the airport."

"No, I mean that you need to go *home*, and that home is with your husband—wherever he is. Home is not an estate house or a loft in the city. It's certainly not at his father's townhome, though I guarantee he won't stay in London a minute longer than it takes to hop on a plane and go after you now. The point is, you need to be at his side, and you need to be *on* his side."

"But he lied to me! How could he not tell me about a sister he'd turned away? And all this time he knew about the art. The money. Everything."

"I know. I'm not making excuses for the man." Penny sighed. "Believe me—I'll be all too glad to smack him as soon as I get off the phone. He's really botched this, that's true. But what I am saying is that you love him, past mistakes and all. Isn't that what you said when you pledged your heart to him? Did you tell me right after your wedding that you trust him, no matter what?"

"Trust is earned."

"And it's also a choice. I know you, Sera. You have a forgiving heart. And you made a covenant to love this man all the days of your life. Didn't you think there would be some in there where he would make mistakes?"

"Penn—"

"Okay. Big mistakes. Lots of mistakes here," she countered. "We're not arguing over the fact that these are some king-sized flubs. I know. But think about it. Where did all this come from? He's scared. Right? Just like you were when you met him."

"And he lectured me about living in the past back then."

"Maybe it was because he didn't want someone he cared about to have to live the way he was? Look. He's a stupid man from time to time—"

"How is this helping?"

"Not a cut, just an observation. William is like his brother. Those Hanover men need some looking after, I can tell you. But at least your William is smart enough to know what he has in you. And that, I'm sure, is what kept him from sharing any of this until now. If William thought he'd lose you, then I'd wager he was prepared to live in his guilt—even to go to prison for something he didn't do—because he felt like he should pay for past sins. Sera, that's not the mark of bad man."

Penny paused and was quiet on the line.

"I know it's not. He's a good man. But I don't know what the answers are. I'm so confused."

A final boarding call chimed over the loudspeaker.

Sera heard it over the bustle of the travelers hurrying by.

Paris.

A plane, somewhere, was boarding passengers for Paris. Her heart fluttered on the thought.

She looked at the clock on her cell phone.

"Penn, I have to go."

"Okay. So tell me what time your flight leaves. I'll come meet you and we'll work through this thing together."

Sera pulled her suitcase along behind her, threading her way through the crowd. "I'm going home."

"Good." Penny sighed into the phone. "You've come to your senses."

"I'm just taking a detour first."

—

"My dear, the fact that you are standing in my doorway should not come as a shock."

Sera stood in the hallway of Sophie Haurbech-Mason's apartment building with her suitcase and a small jewelry box in hand.

"I was so grateful you sent the pearls to me for my wedding. And I was going to ship them back, but seeing as I was so close to Paris . . ."

Sophie was a tiny sprite of a woman, with hair so gray it looked glazed with violet in the light and a congenial warmth that only a wise old friend could offer. She opened her door wide and accepted Sera, who was by then exhausted in body and all cried out from the plane ride to Paris.

"Come in, my dear. I've been expecting you and those pearls to find their way back to me again."

CHAPTER THIRTY-FOUR

December 7, 1943
Terezin

The moon shone high overhead, illuminating the alley in a swath of blue-silver light.

Kája stood in the shadows. She was huddled up against the stucco wall of the building that held their attic room, tugging the collar of her coat up around her neck to ward off the severe chill of the night.

"I brought food for the children," Dane whispered, and looked over his shoulder before handing over a paper-wrapped parcel. "The guards confiscated the Red Cross food rations that came into the post office. The parcels were mailed to the Danish prisoners and they actually made it here. I was forced to steal this when the others weren't looking. But there is canned meat and cheese. Black tea. There's even a box of biscuits—the children will be strengthened by this, I'm sure."

Kája nodded. She took the wares he offered, hugging them to her chest.

"What's wrong? I thought you'd be overjoyed. We haven't seen food in the camp this regularly in more than a year."

"Dane." Kája's voice was carried out on a winter breeze that blew around them, whistling slightly as it filtered in the alley. She kept her head down, unable to meet his gaze. The only action that could keep her from crying openly was to bite her bottom lip and she did so, even as she said, "My mother died today."

He studied her, standing near, having removed his hat to turn it over in his hands. He scanned back and forth between her withered form and the empty street behind her.

"Is there . . . is there anything I can do?" His breath froze on a fog.

"No. My father is incapable of accepting help right now. He's kept us strong, both of us. I wouldn't have been able to work unless he'd seen to it. And my mother wouldn't have survived a single night if not for his presence here with us. And now?" Kája shook her head, the weight of sorrow pulling her eyes down to the ground. "I'm afraid it will break what will he had left to survive in this place."

She turned away from him then, her tears too intimate a thing to share.

"I've never held someone's hand as they passed from this world, not until I came here. And now? I can't count all the hands that have clung to mine and then just slipped away. I've seen transports come in and ghosts of people go out. I remember every single face of the lost wandering around the town square." She looked around the empty alley, shaking her head and whispering out against the bitter cold, "When did it become commonplace to see such a thing? Bodies in the street. Discarded. Covered in snow. Burnt in ovens. And what of my children, painting pictures of guards with guns trained on them? Dreaming of food but receiving a transport order instead. It's too much. I don't want to live in a world like this. Even bombs raining down on London never felt this hopeless. When did we become animals?"

Dane was silent. The night made slight sounds around her— the whisper of the wind and drips of water greeted them as ghostly companions. And then she heard his boots scrape in the ice at their feet.

"I want to help you."

She opened her eyes. Yes, he'd taken a step toward her. She could feel him standing but a breath behind her. And a hand had reached out; she felt it, softly, barely warming her sleeve. It squeezed her shoulder from behind.

"I went to the shop, you know." She half turned, looking up at him. "I went back with some of the paper you left for the children—the money? I went to buy my mother's pearls. It was silly, but I thought if she could see them again, that the memory might trigger something in her mind. But she was already gone. And so I have her pearls. But her earrings? I passed them by. I had to forget them." Her voice choked out on a sob. "Because she'll never leave this place."

"Kája, I'm so sorry."

She turned to face him. "Are you? Are you really?"

"You know I am."

"But you're one of them, aren't you? You are a Nazi."

"Please don't say I'm one of them." His tone was ragged, teeming with regret.

"You're an engineer, I know. But you still do their bidding. You still walk by. You watch the people starve. They're worked to death before your eyes and yet you stay. You take orders, don't you? Tell me, have you ever killed anyone just because they told you to?"

He didn't answer. He stood still, stone-faced in the cold. And she couldn't determine if it was because he actually had taken a life and didn't want to tell her, or because he was shaken that she'd even had to ask.

"But what does it matter, right? Men can't change. We can hope, but it's dashed by apathy."

"And I can only pick the people up off the ground, one person at a time." His voice was a rough whisper—one with defiance and, unmistakably, heart—as he took a step closer. He looked down on her, a depth of feeling evident in the way he searched her face. "I may not be able to save every child, but if I can give you this parcel and save just one, then it's all been worth it."

Kája hugged the parcel tighter in her arms, it somehow feeling like a lifeline that might help save them all.

"Tell me what to do. Please—how can I help you?"

"My father is . . ." Kája paused, looking for the right words. "Disconnected. Umm—dazed, I would say. I sent for him as soon as she got worse, but this all happened so quickly. She had a fever that wouldn't break and the life just faded out of her eyes."

Kája shook her head, unable to continue.

"Do you need anything?" He sniffed over the cold, though his eyes registered sincere emotion. "I could have a nurse sent in to tend to you."

Kája shook her head. "No. I couldn't let anyone from the hospital be sent over when there are so many sick that need care. It wouldn't be right. And I don't want to give the impression that there is illness in the block here. They would—"

She couldn't continue. Her hand flew to her mouth, clamping down on a wail of emotion that fought to the surface. She shook with it, feeling the tears spill over until they formed hot trails that turned to frozen tracks down her cheeks.

Dane stepped forward, his hat discarded on the ground. Without the necessity of words, he wrapped his arms around her.

They stood, cloaked in darkness, neither one breaking the moment by looking over a shoulder to see if an SS guard lurked in the shadows nearby. She simply cried and for that single moment in time, he let her. Her fists balled up at his shoulders and she melted into him, her face buried in the scratchy wool of his lapel. His chin rested on the top of her head.

"You're right. They would clean out the block if they knew a nurse had been sent in. Typhus is running rampant everywhere."

"I know," she said, crying. "We lost one of the children last week. A young girl. Nine years old. Sweet as can be. And I was the only one with her at the school. I don't even know who her parents are to tell them their baby is gone." She sobbed against his coat.

His arms tightened their hold around her.

"What is this place?" She breathed in and out, icy air coating her lungs with each painful breath. "Is it hell on earth? Is it worse? When I worked at *The Telegraph*, we printed stories of death camps like this, but deep down, I couldn't believe it. I thought man incapable of such evil. And then I come here and find that misery is thriving. It's alive and well, smiling, pulling triggers at people's heads while dressed in Nazi green."

"Kája, I swear I didn't come to add injury to you, God knows." He paused, then continued with an iron resolve to his voice. "I had another reason for coming to find you tonight, other than to bring the food. But we don't need to talk about it now. Not after all this."

"No," she said, and rose up to look at him.

The openness in his eyes made her realize that he was still holding her. She abruptly took a step back and wiped at her eyes with the backs of her palms, thinking of Liam with a pang. Should she feel guilty for accepting the warmth of another's embrace in this terrible place, on such a terrible day?

"Good or bad—I'll not be afraid. I refuse to be shocked by any news now. I won't give them that power over me. Not after they've taken everything from us." Kája notched her chin in the air. "What is it?"

"I've been charged with the cleanup of the camp." When she tensed, he raised a hand in clarification. "No. Not *clearing* the camp. Cleaning. It's not like that. You are safe. All of you."

Kája exhaled. "Then what?"

"Beautification. SS Colonel Karl Rahm—you have heard of him?"

"Yes," she answered. Her father had mentioned the Nazi commander on occasion.

"He wants the camp to look its best. Wants to improve things for the prisoners here. Do you remember when you first arrived and we put in the water pipes?"

She nodded. To her knowledge, there had been no running water before their arrival. The wells that were on the property had been infected with disease and after the pipes had gone in, sanitation had improved some.

"It will be like that, only on a much larger scale. I've been given supplies, money even, to ensure civic improvements around the camp. Those improvements will benefit the people here. Health. Human services for cleanliness. Medical care."

"And food?"

"Yes. We are to make it a place where people will thrive while they work." He nodded. "Look." He held out a handful of small papers. "Tickets. I got them for you and the children."

She hesitated. "Tickets for what?"

"They are opening a café on Neuegasse Street—tomorrow, across from the square. These are tickets so you and the children can attend. They'll have food. Coffee. Desserts, even. And a musical show, just like the concerts and the stage plays we've seen in the camp. The SS has allowed the arts community to thrive here and now we have the chance to do even more."

"Dane. I'm sorry, but I don't understand any of this."

"What don't you understand? It's food. Take it."

"Do you remember that day when you picked up the man in the street? You were knee-deep in mud and you risked your life for him. The other SS ridiculed you for it. Then I saw you again, at a funeral for the prisoners here. And you've left rations at the school. I didn't understand then and I don't now. I asked my father why you were helping us. And do you know what he said?"

Dane shook his head and whispered, "No."

"My father said of the officer working alongside the people, 'There is a man of God.' Is that true? Is this why you've brought these tickets? Or is it for another reason?"

"I don't know if I'm a man of God or not. I'm not sure he exists." He turned to pick up his hat, then slammed it back on his head, as if the addition to his uniform might remind her that he was a Nazi and any measure of praise was therefore foreign. "I'm trying to figure out what's right and what to do about what I see in this place. Where's the difference between what I'm ordered to do and what I *hate* doing? There is a line thin as smoke between them. But all I know is that I'm determined to do good here. Whether it's from God or not, I haven't a clue."

"Why have you really come, Dane?"

He paused, flipping the tickets against his gloved hand. "I need your help."

"My help? What could you need me for?"

"Rahm intends to highlight the arts community here and I need your help to do that."

"But why me? Why now?" She looked about. "And why would they even care about musical performances and stage plays when people are dying all around?"

"The International Red Cross will be here. The Danish government's wish for their visit is finally being granted and we've been charged with preparation."

The Red Cross.

She hadn't thought of it in months, how she'd once worn their uniform herself. Memories of the train compartment in Norwich where Liam had given it to her flashed before her eyes.

"What?" He read whatever had splayed across her face.

"It's just that I once knew someone in the Red Cross."

"Who?"

"No one," she said, shaking her head. "We had a mutual friend in London, that's all."

"Well, we don't know who will arrive yet, but I hope it's your friend, for your sake."

"Whomever comes, what do they expect to find when they get here?" Her eyes sailed up to the broken attic window up above, wondering what her father would think as he sat by her mother's bed.

"A model camp. That's all I know. They expect me to make it happen by June. I need someone who can work with the people here. To organize the arts for the children. Will you help me?"

"Yes. I will."

"I hoped that's what you'd say." He swallowed hard and nodded. "And I know, even more now, what it means to hear you say it."

"I won't let them win. And I won't give anything else back. These children deserve it," Kája breathed out, the frozen air forgotten now that she had something new to hope for. "So we will help you. When do we begin?"

He extended the stack of tickets again and offered, "Is tomorrow soon enough?"

CHAPTER THIRTY-FIVE

$\mathcal{S}$era left her suitcase by the door and melted into one of the cushy chairs by the fireplace. Sophie eased her tired body into the chair opposite her.

The furnishings in Sophie's apartment were exactly as Sera remembered: quaint and Parisian, in floral shades of primrose and violet. The mantle still boasted the rows of antique frames sheltering black-and-white photos, so many that it looked like they might fall off the edge if one were touched. An old typewriter still sat atop a desk in the room's far corner.

She looked around, finding such warmth in her old friend's presence.

"I'm sorry to drop in like this," she said, and laid the box of pearls on the side table.

"When you called me after your wedding to let me know that William had some legalities to work through, well . . . I wondered if you'd eventually show up at my door again."

"It's different this time. I'm not hunting for a painting."

"No, you are not. You're running." Sera's head popped up and she met Sophie's eyes, which were curiously arched high above the outer rim of her glasses. "This is life talking, isn't it? Real life. Love is a messy business."

Sera nodded. "It is."

"And you are wondering about your William, hmm? Those

294

stuff-shirt lawyers are telling you stories, causing you to have doubts about him."

"I didn't have doubts, not at the beginning. I thought I knew him. I had more than a year to learn who he was. But as time has gone by, I realize he's been keeping things from me."

"Ah." Sophie settled into a chair. "So he hasn't been perfect. And you are now forced to believe in the William you know, not the William you thought you knew."

Sera felt a reluctant smile find its way to her lips.

It was endearing, how this woman could distill down all of her troubles, all of the hurts and misunderstandings into one, reliable truth.

"It's something like that."

"Sera, do you remember when you came to see me last? You were searching for the ending to a story. A painting, rather, and the meaning behind it."

"Of course I remember. Adele and Vladimir," she replied, and instinctively looked to the photo of the happy couple beaming out with smiles from the front of the mantle. "Theirs was a story of beauty. It was heartbreaking, but beautiful because they fought for each other, held nothing back. After everything that's happened now? I'm not sure I understand a love like that."

"I think you do, if you look deep enough."

"But, Sophie, I'm pregnant." She tipped her shoulders up in a soft shrug. "And I'm scared."

The old woman smiled and nodded. "Of course you are. Every mother-to-be is scared. That's what this is all about, whether you know it or not."

"You're not surprised, then."

"No. I am not." Sophie shook her head. "Couples have babies, Sera. I had two myself. There's nothing to be afraid of."

Sophie's response created the first smile Sera had managed in quite some time.

"Sera." Sophie held out a knotted hand to point at the mantle. "Do you see that photograph, the large one in the back?"

"The one of the bride?"

She nodded. "Yes. Go and get it. Bring it here to me."

Sera obeyed.

She was ever so careful as to not disturb the other photographs. But she retrieved it, taking the 11 x 13-size frame in hand, and walked back over to kneel at Sophie's side. She presented her with the portrait and only then realized she'd seen the face before.

"Is that—" Sera ran her finger down the edge of the frame. "That's the missing journalist, right? The one who became your teacher in Terezin. You sent me the newspaper article about her."

"Kája was her name." Sophie took the frame and with gentle, lovingly aged hands, ran fingertips over the bride's image. "She was beautiful, wasn't she?"

"She was, yes." Sera agreed, nodding.

"A remarkable woman. And not so unlike you, my dear. She, too, had a journey to endure. She had love, yes. But she also had strength—more than even she knew at the time. She was the woman who gave me my life back while in Terezin, but she also became the parent who took me into her life for the rest of it. She adopted me."

"And she saved you."

Sophie nodded. "Yes. She did."

"How?"

"It's not as you might think—she didn't wield weapons. She didn't fight off the German army. In fact, she befriended an officer with the SS. She found good in a Nazi. Would you believe that?"

"Not if you hadn't just told me."

"She saw the good that was deep down in him, when he couldn't even see it himself. For him and the children of Terezin," she was the teacher of hope. She refused to judge with the harshness of life around her. She had courage that to this day astounds even me."

"How?" Sera leaned forward, arching her neck so she, too, could look at the beauty in the portrait.

"She boarded a train to Auschwitz because she was willing to give her life for mine. I never had to walk that lonely road from the train tracks to the crematorium. I shudder to think of the children in my little Terezin schoolroom who did. They were Jews. They were the walking wounded with me. And I've wondered in years since: *Why did I survive and they did not?*"

"And what was your conclusion?"

"That God was not saving me"—she pointed to her chest—"but I survived because Adele and Kája allowed him to work through their lives. It is all about the choices we make. Do you know, my dear Sera, that if I had walked off that train in Auschwitz, Adele would have had to watch as her violin played me to my death. Remember that the Women's Orchestra of Auschwitz had to play for those walking to the gas chambers? I would have been there and she would have seen me. The girl she and Vladimir had given up everything for would have died anyway, only it would have been right before her eyes. Wouldn't that have crushed her spirit beyond repair?"

"Oh, Sophie." Sera's heart ached with the thought. "Thank God for both of you it didn't happen."

"So you see how many lives were changed by my adoptive mother? Kája allowed God to use her. And she saved me from the train because of it."

"How, Sophie? How did she save your life?"

With the faintest hint of a smile, Sophie turned the frame over in her hands and pulled the cardboard backing open. She pulled it free and with a soft smile, turned over a sheet of paper that had been concealed in the frame behind the portrait.

"Because she gave me this."

Sophie handed Sera a painting, obviously by a child's hand.

It was masterful in its simplicity. There was a clock, a tower of sorts, standing tall against a watercolor blue sky. And there were birds, tiny little winged birds that dotted the sky around it, weaving in and out of the renderings of fluffy white clouds.

"She gave you a painting?"

She chuckled under her breath. "No. She gave me a story. She told me about a clock—a very *big* one. And you know what it was that I painted because of it?"

"No."

"Look there—in the sky." She pointed at the tiny flecks of faded watercolor wings. "Do you see? She gave me hope. She gave me a story with wings so I could fly."

"A story? You think that's what I need to hear?"

"Mm-hmm. You're welcome to stay and visit, of course. But after you hear this, I'm not sure you'll want to be anywhere else but home."

CHAPTER THIRTY-SIX

December 21, 1943
Terezin

Kája heard the noise in the front schoolroom long after the children had left for the day. It was soft and barely discernable, but she instinctively knew what it was.

Crying.

She walked from the supply room down the length of the hall and pushed the door open just wide enough to peek in. She was thankful that the hinges were silent for once.

Sophie sat there alone with her tiny shoulders slumped, her back to the door. The length of her body shook with soft, heart-breaking sobs, one for each breath, as the tiny hands covering her face muffled her cries.

Kája's heart constricted at the pitiful sight.

She stepped through the door and closed it behind her. Sophie quickly dried her eyes on her sleeve. She tried to cover the show of emotion, as if it were shameful somehow to be discovered crying in their empty schoolroom. She moved to the edge of her stool, almost like a wounded animal ready to flee.

"I didn't mean to disturb you," Kája whispered. "I heard something and came in to see if someone needed help." She took another step closer. "Can I help you, Sophie?"

She shook her head, bobbing her short hair in a wave against her delicate chin.

For so many months, she'd not been able to crack the surface of a relationship with the girl. Kája had taken her into the attic room, clothed her and cared for her and fed her from the rations Dane brought to the school. She'd taught her with the other children, always hoping that little Sophie would show the tiniest spark of interest in the books or the paintings and drawings that the other children created. She was a dutiful helper, but always for the benefit of the other children at the school. Sophie had remained withdrawn.

Kája sat on the wooden bench next to her and folded her hands in her lap.

"How can I help you?" She leaned in low, whispering close to Sophie's profile. "Is there something you want?"

Sophie turned to her and with tear-stained cheeks nodded. She reached out and in tiny fingers clasped the cross necklace that had fallen down out of the collar of Kája's dress.

"I want to know about him."

Surprised, Kája asked, "You know what this is?"

Sophie nodded. "He loves children, doesn't he?"

Kája felt a smile burst forth on her face and nodded.

"Yes. I believe he does."

"And what does he say about children who die?"

Kája certainly couldn't have guessed that some of the first words Sophie spoke on her own would be about this, but she inclined her head and quietly asked, "You're thinking about your brother?"

"Yes."

She walked over to the art box on the shelf and took it down.

"I'd like to tell you a story. It's about a clock—a very *big* one." She smiled and began taking supplies—paper, paint, and brushes—and began laying them out on the table. "There is an old town square in Prague, where I lived as a girl. And in this square is a very old, very important clock."

"What does it do?"

"Well, it tells time. But more than that, it holds a secret. A wonderful story about God's people—the Jews, and Jesus, and how he cares for every child. Would you like to hear it?"

Sophie dried her tears with the back of her palm and nodded.

"Good. That's what I hoped you would say," she whispered, and patted her cheek. "But before I do, I wonder if you could do something for me? I'd love it if our class had a painting of yours to add to our collection. So as I tell this story, I wonder if you'd help me and paint what it makes you feel. Try to create what you imagine the clock looks like and what you'd see if you were standing with me beneath it."

Kája opened one of the jars of paint and reaching out, handed her a paintbrush.

"Do you think you can do that for me?"

Sophie took the brush in hand.

As Kája began her animated tales about the skeleton, the moving figures of the sun and moon, and how the little sparrows turned the insides of the tower, something changed in that schoolroom.

Sophie stopped crying and her hands came alive.

They moved with the dexterity of a master, as a painter who owned her canvas and gave herself up to the picture she was bringing to life. With tears still wet on her cheeks but resolve and strength somehow pouring out of the brush, she listened. And moved. And created with a passion that sparked and hope that caught fire.

"Can you tell me about him, about Jesus?" Sophie asked, still occupied with putting paint to canvas with her soft, intentional movements.

"What do you want to know?" Kája's tears were soft and battled their way from the corners of her eyes.

"What did he suffer?"

"Much. He suffered very much."

"Did he die for us?"

Kája nodded and bit her lip on emotion. "Yes, Sophie. He did."

"He was a Jew."

"He was, just like us. And if he were here right now," she noted, watching as Sophie painted a trail of light blue spanning the sky behind her clock tower, "he'd be suffering. He'd be crying for what we do to each other."

Sophie dotted the sky with tiny birds, soaring overhead.

"If he were here right now . . ." Sophie set the paintbrush aside and her voice trailed off.

Kája knelt down until her face was level with Sophie's and with gentle hands wiped the tears from her cheeks.

"Darling, he *is* here. He sees. He knows our pain. And for every single sparrow that has fallen in this place, he has cried too."

Sophie buried her face against Kája's chest and they held each other, crying in the silence of the room. And for a time, all was forgotten. The constant threat of transport trains melted away . . . the memory of walking to a graveyard faded . . . and the pain of loss was cleansed.

When Sophie's cries finally softened to tiny hiccups against her shoulder, Kája released her. She looked at the lovely painting with its large clock and wonderfully sunny sky. And with a stubborn notch to her chin that would have made Liam proud, Kája took it and crossed the room.

With a clothespin, she hung the painting on the twine next to the other children's art. They stood in reverent silence, looking at the beauty they'd created together.

Sophie reached out and clasped her hand.

Kája turned and, hopeful, asked, "Are you hungry?"

"Yes." A tiny, unexpected smile peeked out from the corners of her mouth. "I am so very hungry."

As she placed a small portion of bread in Sophie's hand and watched her so innocently eat, Kája made a vow. She had no way of knowing whether they'd make it out of Terezin alive. More than that, she wasn't sure of ever seeing her Liam again. If her life could mean anything now, she pledged to do whatever God asked of her in defense of the children of Terezin, even if it should take her own life to do it.

CHAPTER THIRTY-SEVEN

*S*era dropped her bags at the door and grabbed up the first thing she saw, which happened to be a spatula from the counter in the loft's kitchenette. She held it up in front of her and proceeded with quiet steps through to the back corner of her San Francisco loft.

The noise continued. A clanging first, and then a shout, followed by nondescript murmuring.

Sera had been walking slowly, cautious that someone had broken into the loft, until she heard William grumbling under his breath. She came around the corner to the bookshelf-lined reading nook in the back of the loft.

William was kneeling there with his back to her, crouched over a box of white wooden slats and parts that had been strewn about the floor. She smiled and bit her bottom lip over the instant hitch of emotion that caught in her chest.

Her husband was trying, and failing miserably, to put a crib together.

She set the spatula down on a side table and cleared her throat to get his attention. He turned, saw her, then leaned back on his heels and threw his hands up in mock defeat.

"Well. The truth is out. Never let me try to fix anything myself or it will be a total disaster."

"I can see that."

He stood and dusted off his hands on his jeans, walking toward her. "It was supposed to be a surprise."

Sera scanned the dimly lit loft that she'd been slowly but surely preparing to be an art gallery.

So that's what was different. She'd been so fixed on the noise that she hadn't even looked around. She and Penny had left for London in such haste that the loft had been in a state of chaos—boxes and crates stacked all around Sera's furniture purchases. It hadn't looked like much more than an oversized storage room. But now the sight fairly took her breath away.

In the days she'd stayed on with Sophie in Paris, William had made them a home.

She turned round, surveying the room with her hand over her heart.

A new table and chairs had been unpacked and set in the far corner, ready for family dinners. There was a sitting area off the kitchen, in which the couch and chairs now occupied space opposite the fireplace. There were two tall bookcases lined with her collection of art books and his of theology. She guessed that the back room could have been turned into a master bedroom for them.

And where they stood, the reading nook had been touched by a sweet sense of magic that only a new baby could bring.

There was a changing table boasting the glow of a tiny lamp in the corner. And opposite, a rocking chair with a blanket and stuffed bear, and a shelf with books nearby. The parts of a crib were strewn on the floor around the husband who was standing in the midst of it all, keenly watching her reaction to what he'd done.

"Do you like it?"

"Will . . . it's beautiful. Of course."

He raised his hands palm up, offering, "I wanted to have it all put together before you came home."

When she moved to ask, he read her thoughts.

"Penny told me you were on the way back." He tilted his head to the baby furniture. "I had no idea what to buy but thankfully she schooled your clueless husband in the art of outfitting a nursery. And apologies."

"I see." Sera nodded, then with caution said, "I thought you'd be at the estate house with the lawyers, getting ready for court."

"To be honest, so did I. Until I realized my future is here," he said, and directed his gaze at her middle for a split second, then reconnected with her eyes. "With the two of you."

"And what does that change, William?"

He stood in the center of the room, several steps away from her. But if she could judge him, Sera knew he wanted to cross the floor more than anything.

"It changes everything for me."

"It does?"

"Yes," he answered, his voice heavy with feeling.

"But why? Why couldn't you just share who you really are with me? I wouldn't have turned you away. I would have carried that burden with you."

He shoved his hands in his pockets in a boyish show of vulnerability and offered the softest of words: "I was scared."

He took another step forward.

"When I met you, my whole world changed. You made me want to be a better man. You gave me the courage I'd always lacked. But I didn't want to scare you away."

Sera's hand went to her middle. She gave an embattled nod, thinking of the story Sophie had told her.

Sophie was young once. She'd been innocent; a precious child, beautiful, wounded like all the rest in Terezin. And it was that story playing over and over again in her mind that urged her to take another step closer to William now.

"I don't need a reminder that I married a good man. Mine is

a husband with a heart once wounded, and who just like me, will never be perfect. He needs someone to support him. Through the storm. He needs someone who will promise to weather it with him, no matter what comes." She took another step, matching his, until they were no more than a foot apart. "I'm not afraid anymore."

"Me neither," he whispered, reaching out to brush a lock of hair behind her ear. "But I owe you an explanation. And an apology—a hundred of them."

"I owe you one first." She shook her head and taking a folded piece of paper from her pocket, offered it to him. "Remember this? The photo of the cross necklace? Your grandfather sent the necklace to Katie when he found out he had another granddaughter. It wasn't worth much by the world's standard, but I think he sent it to her because of how much it meant to him."

"I don't understand. Where did it come from?"

Sera let loose with a genuine smile. "The necklace belonged to Sophie's adoptive mother. Would you believe that? She said it was a promise on a chain. Sophie kept it after her mother passed away. And do you know that when your grandfather approached her about changing the course of his grandson's life by altering his will, she sent him that necklace as her promise to always help you should you need it. In his way, I think he was trying to say the same to Katie."

He held the paper in his hands, staring down at the image of the cross.

"Am I always going to be offered redemption with you?"

Sera thought how sorry she'd once been at the prospect of moving into the loft. But it didn't matter now. As she nodded a yes to his question, she found herself enveloped in the strength of William's arms. He kissed her. Whispered words of apology. Over and over.

William drew back then and shook his head slightly.

"What made you come back?"

"You know I went to see Sophie." She smiled. "Our old friend. And believe me, she thinks the world of you. She practically shoved me out the door when I realized I wasn't ready to give up on us."

"She did?"

Sera nodded.

"I'll have to thank her for that someday," he added, smiling for the first time in what felt like weeks. She leaned in close and he touched his forehead to hers, squeezing his eyes shut on the moment. "You always had me, you know. Despite all of this. Despite who I was and no longer wanted to be. You've always had that part of my heart."

"I know." The words were simple, but strong. "And I promise you, we'll walk into that courtroom together, William. We'll fight this and we'll win."

William looked up. He stared back in her eyes and with what looked like genuine relief painting his features, whispered, "Sera, I pray we won't have to."

CHAPTER THIRTY-EIGHT

May 14, 1944
Terezin

The beautification of Terezin had been astounding to watch. In the months following the order that the camp should be readied for the International Red Cross's visit, Kája found herself witness to nothing short of a miracle. The SS threw themselves into a fervor of civic improvements.

The streets were cleaned. Broken windows replaced. Buildings were painted and flower boxes were built on nearly every corner. With Dane's involvement, the Jewish Council oversaw the building of a community hall, the construction of theaters, and even a wooden music pavilion at the newly opened market square. The Jewish administration offices were renovated. The hospital was improved and a nursery school built. There were even real shops now, ones that stocked food and carts of vegetables and offered freshly baked bread doled out with rations. Even Kája's little schoolhouse helpers were soon employed in nearly round-the-clock practice for a play that would be performed for the Red Cross.

Kája was cleaning up the school for the night, long after the children had returned to their barracks. Sophie had fallen asleep on a bench near the stove and with only the last of the dirty paint water to dispose of, they were almost ready to go back to the attic room.

She picked up the bucket, laboring to carry it toward the back door.

"Kája."

She stumbled back at the sound of her name and gasped, almost dropping the bucket. She squinted in the dim moonlight that shone into the back room.

"Dane?" She took a few steps forward when she recognized him. "What are you doing here?"

"I had to see you."

"Why?" She took a quick glance around, making sure they were alone. "Is something wrong?"

He nodded, wasting no time.

"You're on the transport list for tomorrow, you and your father."

"What?"

Fear surged through her and she dropped the bucket to the ground. Water sloshed over the edge and ran down the side, creating a ring on the floor around it.

"That can't be. My father is part of the Jewish Council."

"It doesn't matter. You know that. Edelstein was a co-chair of the Council of Jewish Elders and they still deported him last December. Or have you forgotten?"

"What about the children?" she cried. "What will happen to them?"

"They will go as well."

"My children? All of them?" It was too horrible to believe. "But why now, when the SS has done so much for the people here?"

Dane grabbed her by the arms and shook her.

"Don't you see? It's all been a ruse. They put in new sinks and bath houses, but none have pipes or running water. There is still painted plaster hanging in shop windows, there's just more of it. And you've seen the camera crews, *ja*?"

It was true. She had seen a camera crew moving around,

shooting some sort of film about the camp. But she'd been too busy to think about why.

"They are making a film for propaganda. They chose children. Gave them bread and butter as a treat, dressed them up with new clothes and smiles, and filmed how well the Jews are being treated here. There is even a route marked in the streets where the Red Cross will walk. They'll see only what the SS wants them to see and nothing more! All the while, the camp is plagued with overcrowding. And as the Red Cross must see a model settlement, not a camp teeming with death and disease, thousands of Jews must go in order to make the lie believable."

Kája's legs felt weak. She fell out of his grip and melted down to sit on a nearby crate.

"And after all that we've done. We hung the children's artwork. And we built the theater. I even helped the children practice their lines for the play." She shook her head. "I can't believe it."

"You must." He looked over his shoulder, then knelt by her side. "And we don't have much time. I've come to get you out of here—tonight."

She turned to face him, her senses awakened by the fervency in his voice.

"But how? There are too many of us—near a hundred in total. How could you possibly get us all out?"

He shook his head and with sadness, she saw the light go out of his eyes with it.

"Kája."

Realization dawned.

He hadn't come to get *them* out; he'd come for her.

So that's why he'd come so late. That's why he was looking over his shoulder every few seconds, almost as if he expected guards to come charging down the alley. He was shaking, whether from fear or adrenaline she couldn't be sure. But the meaning of why he'd shown up that night was abundantly clear.

"You mean you've come for me alone."

"Yes." He nodded sorrowfully. "I can't let them take you. Not when I can do something about it."

"You realize what they'd do to you if you're caught."

"We won't get caught," he issued firmly.

It was brave for him to show up; she told herself this.

He wasn't audacious like Liam had always been, running toward danger all noble and brave. No, Dane had a quiet way about him. A solidness that for some reason drew him to her in this place. She longed for Liam. But had he forgotten about her? Was he even alive? She was plain and dirty, a ghost of a woman in a sea of yellow stars that flooded inside the walls of Terezin. Would he even have recognized her in this ocean?

"I don't understand."

"Don't you?" He studied her face and then cautiously lowered his hand to hers. "I've never met anyone like you, Kája Makovský. You are fine and beautiful and strong. You make me want to be a different man and in the midst of all this, that is remarkable."

"Dane . . ." She wouldn't let herself believe that his kindness was for her. Because he cared more than he should. She slid her hand out from under his. "I was promised to someone once."

He stared back at her, eyes raked by surprise.

"I suspected that might be the case, though we've never spoken of it."

"Who speaks of such things in a place like this?" She looked around the dark supply closet and the alley beyond, where shadows lurked in every corner. "Who remembers yesterday or dares to dream of tomorrow? I don't pretend to have a future. Not now."

"But you could, if you choose it."

She wished she could, but deep down, Kája couldn't forget the picture of Liam Marshall, standing upon a train platform in Switzerland, still waiting for her. The dream of him was engraved upon her heart. And though he was but a memory and a good man stood before her now, there was nothing she could do to make herself forget.

"Dane," she whispered, and reached up to touch his cheek. "You are a good man. Surely God has seen what you've done for me and my father, and for the children in this place. We owe you our lives. You will always have my heartfelt gratitude, but I cannot give you more than that. And I can't go with you, not when my children will have to go on alone." She shook her head. "I won't walk out on them."

He stepped back then, shaking his head. "Do you realize what you're saying? You'll be going to your death!"

"I know." Kája squeezed her eyes shut. Her hands trembled in her lap. "I'm trying not to think of it. But at least my children won't be alone. I may know what is happening to us when we get off that train, but they won't have to. Not until the end."

"You're saying no."

"I must say no." She nodded, just once, and opened her eyes again, adding, "But if you can take one person out, I beg of you to take someone and run, and never look back."

Dane backed away, shaken, and stood. "You'd give up your place for someone else?"

"God help me." Her entire body felt taken by tremors. "Yes."

"I see."

He studied her for another moment, then whispered, "They'll notice I'm gone."

He went to the door but stopped short of stepping out into the night.

"Dane?" She rushed up to him, whispering, "One more thing? Where does the transport go?"

He looked sick about it, standing in the shadows with his hand fused to the doorknob. "Auschwitz."

God. Not Auschwitz.

Not the place of my nightmares.

"And you know what you're doing, *ja*?"

"Yes, I do." She felt a cool breeze filter in and she turned her face to it, allowing it to caress her cheeks and lift the hair off her shoulders.

"Kája, I can't come back for you tomorrow. So you must be sure."

"I am. Take whomever you can and get them out of here."

After a last look between them, Dane turned and hurried off into the night. Kája stood in the alley with tears burning her eyes, watching until he disappeared into the shadows.

CHAPTER THIRTY-NINE

Christmas Day
Sausalito, California

William turned when Sera walked up behind him.

She handed him a mug of coffee and sat down next to him in the sand.

He took a drink. "It's good." He warmed his hands around the sides of the porcelain.

"Of course it is. It's hazelnut."

"Your favorite."

"I thought you could use it." Sera wrapped her Fair Isle sweater tight around her shoulders and shivered as a near icy wind blew in around them. It cut up from the choppy water, stirring the sand on a blast of air. "Especially since it's as cold as it looks out here. Brr. How can you stand it?"

"You should go in," he said, and brushed a hand over her growing belly. "Please. I won't be long."

Cold or not, William had been out on the beach for some time that morning.

Sera had watched him from the moment he'd stepped out the back door of the estate house kitchen. He'd been on the phone with his father that Christmas morning—surprise, surprise— and had paced back and forth across the terrace for the duration of the call. It wasn't until he'd walked off toward the beach and not returned that Sera had thought to go after him.

She knew where she'd find him.

"Everyone was getting worried."

He smiled. "Paul's giving you a hard time because he has to wait to open his presents? Classic Christmas morning with the Hanovers. He drives Macie nuts with it every year—always guesses what she's gotten him before he tears one piece of wrapping paper."

"I think our Penelope may be giving him a hard time this year."

Will arched an eyebrow. "Penny?"

Sera nodded, feeling a smile appear at the thought. "I've been watching those two, and they bicker more than any two people I've ever seen. I guarantee that sometime in the future, Penny's going to be a real aunt to our little one here—not just an honorary one."

"Really. Well, if you're right, I'll have the pleasure of watching Paul squirm under Penny's glare for the next forty or fifty Christmases." He returned her smile with a bit of boyish enthusiasm. "I'll never need another present again."

"Believe it or not, it wasn't the presents this time, or your younger brother that sent me after you. I think your mother was concerned." She leaned in to his side and dropped her head to his shoulder. "I could see it in her face when you didn't come back. She thought maybe you'd received bad news with the unexpected phone call."

William nodded and swung his free arm around her shoulder. "No bad news. Not this year, at least."

"I was really surprised that your father called this morning. What did he say?"

"Well, let's just say it was a Christmas gift I'd not expected to receive," he answered, and drew in a deep, steadying breath. "He wanted to wish you a happy Christmas. And he said his lawyers are trying to convince the prosecutors to drop all the charges against me."

Sera's head bumped his chin when she shot up, startled.

"What?" She gripped the front of his shirt, scarcely able to believe what he'd just said.

"I'm in a bit of shock myself. I knew they couldn't have any real evidence against me, but that doesn't mean someone didn't transfer the art over to the company. You and I both know my father took the investors' money and tried to filter it back through the company books. The lawyers are going to know that if it wasn't me, it had to be someone at the top. He's turning himself in to clear my name."

"Oh, Will. I don't know what to say."

He turned and stared out over the toiling water, the hair on his forehead brushing back and forth with the ebb and flow of the sea air.

"Are you all right?"

"I am now," he admitted, and ran a hand over the side of her face. "It's not over—not by a long shot. And I won't say my father is going as far as to admit his own guilt. He'll have his lawyers working on it, I'm sure. He'll do what he does best."

"But he would have let you go to prison for something you didn't do? That doesn't seem to be the man I met in London. He had love in his voice when he spoke about you and about Katie. About all of you."

Sera closed her eyes on the admission, feeling horrible.

"I know what you're thinking, love. You're wondering whether I hate him for what he's done."

Sera thought about arguing the point, then thought better of it. Instead, she glanced out at the storminess of the bay and leaned in closer to his side. She looked up, just enough to view his profile, and was rewarded with a smile that softened the corners of his mouth.

"Your thinking is so loud I can hear it over the wind."

"Is it? And what am I thinking?"

"You're thinking I'm a changed man. That God has changed me. And that regardless of the fact that my father has left so much damage in his wake, I shouldn't hate him for it. You're telling me to think to the future, to where God wants me. That I shouldn't hold bitterness against the father who left, even though I told him to go. And you hope that I can finally forgive him, which is something I've never quite been able to do."

"Goodness," Sera beamed back at him. "I thought all that? I'm much wiser than I give myself credit for."

William touched a hand to the apple of her cheek, then dropped a soft kiss to her lips.

"The truth is, I do forgive him, Sera. I have to. You were right before, when you said it hurts only me. And I can't hang on to it anymore."

"I'm glad. For your sake," she whispered, then ran her hand over her belly. "And for hers. She'll be much happier with a daddy who smiles."

"I plan to, for you both. And for what it's worth, I'm not ready to give in. I'll keep trying with Katie, whether or not she'll give her brother a second chance. And I'll keep working on the lines of communication with my father. It's a long shot, but—" He stopped short, kicking the sand at their feet.

"But what?"

"It hurts to admit, but I don't want to be like him." William shook his head. "I'd rather be flawed and ordinary by the world's standards than be wealthy and respected by his."

"You're far from flawed or ordinary."

"Nice of you to notice, wife."

Sera elbowed him in the side, with a little spring about it. "I'll have you know that I fell in love with you on this beach. And even now, sitting here in the same place, it almost feels like we've come full circle, doesn't it?"

"I think so."

"Me too. And that's worth a second cup of coffee on this lovely Christmas morning," she whispered, and tilted her head toward the house. She arched her eyebrows. "With your family?"

He stood and reached for her hand. He pulled her up carefully and brushed her long, loose braid over her shoulder.

"Come on—let's get you two inside."

CHAPTER FORTY

May 16, 1944
Poland

Their faces were blasted with fresh air when the boxcar doors flew open.

Several of the children shrieked and pushed back against Kája, packing as far as they could into the back of the car. All that could be seen was the reflection of the moon against the pitch black of the night sky and fields of tall grasses and the branches of far-off trees, creating an eerie backdrop all around.

Kája pushed the children behind her as best she could, fearing the worst. But instead of guns pointed from a cruel camp train platform, they saw nothing but night and heard only faint shouting in the distance.

It was not at all what she'd expected to find in a greeting at Auschwitz.

"Get out! Now!"

Several of the children cried out, startled at the shout.

Kája might have done the same, had she not been shocked to a stupor at the man who appeared at the side of the car. His hair was wind-swept and he wore plain traveling clothes instead of an officer's uniform, but the eyes looking back at her were the same.

Dane's gaze connected with hers only for a split second before he rushed into action.

"Everyone out, now!" he shouted, and began pulling children from the train. He set a little girl down on the ground and nudged her forward to a thick forest beyond the clearing of the tracks. "Now run. Go!"

"Dane? What—"

"We have no time. We have to get them off the train."

Kája grabbed hold of his arm as he lifted another child to the ground.

"Dane—what have you done?"

He looked toward the front of the train, his breaths labored as if he'd been running for miles, then looked back at her.

"Nothing that can be undone now." He smiled through the darkness and continued pulling another girl to the ground. He put an older girl's hand in the younger one's and nudged them off toward the trees. "There's a group of us. We have a plan."

"But they'll hang you for this!" Kája shouted into the night, terrified for what he'd done. "You'll never be able to turn back. It's not like bringing food to the school. You've stopped a train!"

"Ja. With a military-issued pistol. Pretty remarkable."

He grinned. *Grinned!* At a time like this.

Kája wished she could have smacked some sense into him. She would have, had she not been so happy to see him standing there, arms working like mad to lift children to the ground. Of all the things she'd expected to see when the doors slid open, his face staring back had been the last.

"You told me to get someone out. You're the someone I chose. It just so happens there are several hundred people in tow."

"You can tease at a time like this?"

"We're all dead anyway, Kája," he shouted back. "If we don't stand up and do something now, what's the point? The human race will never recover from what we've done to your people. I don't intend to stand before God and have to answer for a train full of children making its destination when I could have done something to stop it. If it's selfish to have a conscience, then I guess I'm guilty of it now."

Their heads both turned at the indiscriminate sounds of increased shouting somewhere down the tracks.

"Help me? Please?" His eyes appealed to her. Even in the dimness of night and the reflection of the moon outlining his shoulders, she could see their ardent plea.

Kája nodded and flew into action. She tossed her leather satchel behind her back and grabbed up the children one by one. She handed them to Dane, who repeated instructions for them to run to the trees.

"Run as fast as you can, *ja*?" A young boy nodded as Dane pushed him forward into the blackness of night. "And stay with the young ones. I'm trusting you. Now *go!*"

"Here," Kája said, reaching for Sophie. She shrunk back to the side of the boxcar, shaking her head. "Sophie, what's the matter? It's time to run."

"I don't think she'll go with me," Dane shouted, and caught a young boy who'd jumped down into his arms. He dropped him by the side of the tracks and the boy ran into the night. "She knows I'm one of them."

"What?" She pulled at the hem of the Sophie's dress but she recoiled sharply. "Sophie—come here this instant! We must get you off the train."

"Forget it," Dane said, wasting no time in moving on. "We'll get everyone else off first and take her with us last."

He moved on to assist other children that were ready to go. Several of the brave boys plopped down to the ground on their own and took off, melting into the summer night like freed birds from a cage.

"Where will we go?" she asked, lifting another child to his waiting arms.

"To the trees," he said, breathing hard through the effects of the quick lifting. "There's a village not far, that way. There's an abandoned wine cellar." He pointed to an indiscriminate spot out on the horizon, long past the forest, and helped the next child he could get his hands on.

"Run," he told a boy of possibly twelve or thirteen. "See the lights through the forest? Run to them and then keep going. Don't stop until morning."

Kája squinted through the blanket of night and saw the faint dotting of gold flickering through the trees.

"There's a village? Who would dare take everyone in?"

"Kája, I haven't been able to think that far ahead. All I know is, it was this or Auschwitz. Those were my options. The alternative of tramping through a forest was better."

They continued rushing children from the train. Kája took care to tighten up any shoe laces that she could and offered gentle whispers of encouragement as the children were passed from her hands to Dane's arms.

A telltale pop tore through the night and froze their frantic movements. Dane's eyes connected with hers and then a second pop was followed by a third. Then a fourth and more, all in rapid succession. Machine-gun fire.

God, no! Spare us this at least . . .

Kája stared back at him, quite sure that the terror that came with gunshots was evident on her face. "Hurry, children!" she yelled out, frantic. She'd have tried to soften the alarm in her voice, but it would have been no use. Her heart was thundering in her chest and her entire body was shaking, causing any gentleness in her voice to vanish.

Dane lifted the remaining few children to the ground before he reached for her. He clapped his hands together and held his arms wide.

"Sophie," he shouted. "You must come now."

She shrank away.

The thought, the only one that came to Kája's mind, was to give her something she could trust. And in that instant, the memory of a long-ago parting on a train platform came to mind. She remembered when her mother had taken a string of pearls and pressed them into her own hand, infusing her with courage.

Kája yanked the cross necklace from her neck and urged it into Sophie's tiny palm.

"Here," Kája whispered, kneeling down before her. "Hold on to this. It will get you through. And I am right behind you. I promise. We'll be together again soon."

"Sophie!" Dane shouted. "Now!"

Sophie looked wary, but obeyed and jumped into Dane's arms as the popping in the background came closer.

"Wait!" Kája halted and looked up the tracks, desperation having taken over. "My father! He's in one of the other cars!"

Dane shook his head with Sophie buried in his arms. "We've no time to go back. But I promise you he'll get out. We opened those cars first before I came back to this one."

Kája shook her head as tears burned her eyes. She could not leave her father alone. Not after losing her mother.

Dane entreated her, tugging at her elbow, pulling her toward the field grasses. "Kája, you must come with me now. It's the only way."

She looked into Sophie's doe eyes, so soft and innocent, and found that she couldn't leave her. She said a quick prayer that God would watch over her father until she could find him again and with a burst of energy tore off to the trees. They heard shouting behind them, and the terrifying barking of deep-chested dogs as each of their steps crunched down in the tall grasses bordering the tracks.

Kája could think of nothing but staying upright on her feet, though the night heat was unforgiving and the ground woefully uneven. Her feet nearly lost their footing a dozen times before they reached the cover of the birch forest, its dense grove of trees growing up out of the ground like skeletal appendages clawing for the sky.

She heard sticks breaking somewhere not far off, probably from the footfalls of the prisoners running free at different points all around them. And then shouting and horrific pops of gunfire followed them as they maneuvered through the thick underbrush.

Kája ran behind, keeping her eyes fixed on Dane's tall form. He was fast and strong, and jumped through the obstacles quite nimbly for a man with a child in tow. She, however, felt awkward and unsure as she trekked along with a growing stitch in her side that made it increasingly difficult to breathe.

They ran for what felt like hours, over inclines and back down the side of small hills. They wove in and out of trees.

"Almost there!" Dane shouted over his shoulder.

Thank you, God.

Kája wasn't sure how long she could continue on, for the pace was unyielding at best. She grabbed on to her side with her free hand and prayed that God would give all of them the strength to keep going, and then the provision to find someplace—anyplace to hide.

"In here," Dane shouted in a rough whisper, and stopped short of a sod-covered outbuilding hidden on the underside of a hill. He tore open the door and reached his hand out for her. She took it and found herself pulled inside.

He bolted the door from the inside and pulled them into the dark.

Kája tried her best to stand strong, though the intense run had left her weak and sputtering for breath. She tripped on something, a root or clump of earth, and felt herself tumbling down in the dark.

"Are you all right?"

Dane flicked a lighter on, washing his face in the glow.

"Yes," she breathed hard, doubled over from the pain in her side. "I fell and I just need . . . a minute . . . to catch my breath. Where are we?"

Dane leaned in and looked at her, then whispered something to Sophie and immediately put her down. She edged back against what appeared to be a tunnel wall, staring wide-eyed at them.

He returned and knelt down in the dirt.

"Don't worry about that right now. You're safe," he admonished, and eased in closer to Kája.

"I'm sorry." She shook her head, feeling the overpowering weight of weakness overtaking her. "I'm not as strong as you are. Leave me . . . behind if you have to. I'll catch up."

"I don't think you would," Dane said, and covered her hand with his, pressing down hard on her side. She gasped, feeling like the wind had been knocked out of her.

He pulled his hand away and turned it over, exposing his palm to the flicker of light.

"Kája, you're bleeding."

CHAPTER FORTY-ONE

*K*ája had fallen into an unrepentant sleep for what felt like days.

The fresh smell of earth filled her lungs.

She awoke with a start, expecting to find herself and Dane holed up in the abandoned tunnel with Sophie in tow. There was a single candle upon an upturned wine barrel near the bed in which she slept, though it had burned low amidst a small circle of wax in the rusty holder. It offered enough light to see that she'd been placed in a cellar room with dirt walls and a drafty-looking ceiling overhead. The silvery glow of moonlight peeked in through several cracks. Wooden racks and old barrels marched up the side of the back wall. Strange metal hooks hung empty from a leather strap in the corner, and what few wooden shelves she could see were bare.

She could only hope it was the one Dane had spoken of, and that they were safe for the moment.

Kája felt warmth beside her and glanced down. She saw that Sophie was curled up in the bed, nuzzled up on one side, the cadence of her breathing gentle in sleep. She ran a hand over Sophie's brow, brushing the hair back, and gently kissed her temple.

A sound drew her attention across the room.

Kája turned and realized in horror that someone was attempting to turn the knob on the room's only door. She sat up and moved with careful intention, edging off the bed. A sharp pain ripped her side, stealing away the air in her lungs. She fell to the floor, gripping her middle tight as she fought to breathe.

She reached down and felt a swath of bandages; they poked out from a hole torn in the side of her dress.

The door was poised to open and someone would come inside.

She couldn't stop it now. The only thing left to do was to reach for whatever she had. Her eyes darted to the ceiling and she flew into action. She untangled a hook and slipped the end off the strap, and after blowing out the candle, huddled behind the door. She gripped the makeshift weapon until her knuckles felt frozen to it and lay in wait.

With the screech of a rusty hinge, the door was pushed open and a trail of light washed across the center of the room.

A figure stopped in the portal.

There was little light, but with dread, Kája could discern one thing: the figure of a swastika shining out from the shoulder patch of a uniform.

Oh God!

Her insides tore at her, fear having taken over, causing her carefully controlled breathing to become choppy and unrestrained. The figure stepped inside and looked around. He turned and surveyed the sleeping girl in the bed, then shifted his focus.

There was just enough light, she knew, to illuminate a thin strip of her face. The figure turned, appeared to notice her. With painfully thin, worn-out arms, she held firm.

The Nazi-clad figure reacted slowly. He raised a hand up, seemingly meant to calm her.

"Kája. Please put that down."

Her insides rocked, her heart lurched, and the hook fell to the ground with a *thud*. Had her ears played tricks? The man in the Nazi uniform swung the door wide and they were both bathed in light.

With a breath of hope that she'd held for the last two years, she finally exhaled, just as Liam Marshall walked into the room.

"I said I'd come after you."

Kája shook her head, not believing this man could be real.

Relief covered her and she crumbled, unashamed to sob quietly in the safety of his arms. She clung to the lapels of his coat and kissed him with every ounce of stored-away longing she had.

He broke away after a moment, looking upon her as if he, too, needed to make sure she was real. He held her face in his hands and stared back, his own eyes glazing with tears as his fingers touched the warmth of her cheeks and ran over the side of her hair.

"You're alive," he managed, his voice laden with feeling. "You're a bit late, I'd say. But you came back to me."

She nodded, hiccupping over tears.

He suddenly released her and looked down at her side.

"You're all right? You're not in too much pain?"

"A little. Not much now," she said, shaking her head. "What happened?"

"Here I was, thinking to look in on my sweet Kája, who'd been grazed by a bullet in the side." His mouth tipped up at the corners in a proud smile. "But she doesn't need looking after, does she? She's stronger than even she knows. It's not the first time I've been privy to her incredible will."

She sobbed against him then, in a release of pent-up exhaustion.

"I just want to know that you're really here."

"I told you I would be. Didn't you believe me?" He tipped his thumb up under her chin. "I'm not an RAF pilot, I'm sorry to say, or I would have flown the first plane in here that I could get my hands on. As it was, British intelligence isn't as foolproof as one might think."

"You looked for me."

"I went into every office I could and yelled back at the men who told me you weren't a British citizen and there was nothing they could do. I'm surprised I didn't land in the brig for every superior I insulted." He sighed and hooked a stray lock of hair behind her ear. "But what do you think? That I would let you go without a fight? Edmunton helped me. We watched transmissions at Bletchley, read transcripts looking for your name. We found out that the Red Cross had gone into Prague, we just had no idea when you'd gone out. I got Edmunton to print an article on you, hoping it would bring any leads. It just took a little longer to find you than we expected, that's all."

She nodded. The months had muddled together, bleeding into years—and he'd looked for her, all that time?

"How did you find me?"

"Dane. We couldn't let you reach Auschwitz, knowing what would happen."

She stepped back, startled. "You mean it was you—all along? On the tracks. You were the one who helped him stop the train?"

Liam shook his head. "There was no other option. We made an explosive device out of an old Ford Rheinland and put it on the tracks. Between that and Dane's army-issue pistol, it bought us enough time to get all the boxcar doors open."

"But how did you know? I mean—how did you find him?"

"It was he who found us some months back. He sent letters out to the Danish Red Cross seeking a volunteer who may have once known a Kája Makovský from Prague. It took some doing, but he found Margot Sørensen. From there, after almost two years of searching for a woman who had vanished into thin air, we finally knew where you were. And when we had enough credible evidence that you were inside a Nazi ghetto and that you were alive, I was able to convince the higher-ups at Bletchley to let me try and get you out. We were in the midst of planning but before we could do anything, your name showed up on a transport list. And the plans went out the window."

Liam looked down at her. She hated to think of what he saw. She was wounded; so frail and battered by Terezin, so altered by the things she'd seen, never again to be the refined woman he'd once known. Who would they be now?

"Liam, we're still in Nazi-occupied territory. We have nowhere to go."

"We had no choice, Kája. Dane found this abandoned cellar near an old winery and we planned where to do it, SS trailing us or not." His voice was whisper soft. And kind. And endearing in a way she'd long since forgotten. "As for the children—we'll do everything we can to find them all. I promise you that."

"We'll all be hunted."

Liam nodded. "Only until the war ends."

"And you think it will soon?"

"We have every reason to hope so, and that it will end in Germany's defeat. There's no way to know yet." He ran a finger over the scar at her temple. "Even still, I would have done anything to find my fiancé and bring her back home."

"Is that really what I am, Liam? We said some things, so long ago—before all of this. We're different people. I'd never hold you to it now."

"Do you remember that night in the archive library, when you told me about the clock, about the time God's given us?"

"I didn't know you were really listening. I thought you were angry because I'd labeled you a spy."

"I kept thinking after that night, about what you said. And I told myself that if I found you, I'd never let you go again. I'd ask God to forgive me, to change me, to make me a man half worthy of you."

"I never wanted to change you, Liam. I only wanted you—as I'd come to love you—as the man I was privileged to know. The one who really knew me."

"I pictured you like this for so long," he said, touching his hand to the side of her hair. "Your hair was down about your shoulders when you got on that train in Norwich. Remember?"

"Yes. I'd been crying. I knew you could tell and still, you didn't comment on it."

"I don't think I could have spoken had I wanted to. I was trying to think of the words to say to ask you to marry me." He laughed, so softly she might have believed it was the caress of wind outside. "And every thought I ever had before that was gone. I'd never seen anything like you." He paused, blue eyes entreating hers. "And I swear I'll get you out of here if you still want to go with me."

"It's all I've wanted," she cried against him, feeling a rush of hope as long as his arms were securely around her.

"We can stay here as long as it's safe. Let you heal up a day or so. Get your strength back. Then we'll get you out. I wish I could say the plan was more definitive than that but well, we're making this thing up as we go along."

"What about my father? Did you see him?"

Liam shook his head. "Not yet. But I promise—we'll do whatever we must to find him."

"And Sophie?" She paused, so unsure of what his response would be. "She hasn't anyone."

He pressed his lips to her forehead. His breath warmed her skin.

"She goes with us. She's part of you now, isn't she? That makes her part of me too."

She wiped her eyes with the back of her palm and feeling safe now, turned in his arms and looked back into the room.

"And where's Dane?" she asked. "I have to thank him. We

wouldn't have made it from the train if he hadn't come back for us."

When Liam didn't respond as Kája expected, she leaned back to look him in the face.

"Dane?" she asked, a scared feeling growing in her midsection. "Where is he?"

"Kája . . . we don't have to talk about this now."

"We don't have to talk about what?" She paused, searching his face, her eyes pleading for an answer that was different from the one that was etched on his face now. "Tell me where he is."

With a soft tone and the unmistakable note of regret painting his features, he said, "We went out after the children, and Dane didn't come back."

CHAPTER FORTY-TWO

Spring
San Francisco

There's another one down here!"

William called up the stairs to her, indicating that they had yet another crate to unpack before the gallery opening.

"Can you unpack it for me? I don't think I can walk down those stairs again without falling the rest of the way down," Sera shouted back, and plopped down in the rocking chair in the nursery. "And maybe remind me next time I'm opening a gallery to time it more effectively around childbirth?"

They were mere weeks away from meeting their new little girl. Despite swollen ankles and feeling like she was the size of the entire loft space, Sera couldn't have been happier.

William was free. His father had been true to his word and eventually all charges against him were dropped. There were still wounds in the family as Thomas embarked on his own legal battles and the rest of the Hanovers tried to move on. But surprisingly, Sera found that she and William had a measure of peace in the midst of it.

Sera ran her hand over her belly, feeling the little bumps of errant kicking from her daughter, and smiled.

"You have the disposition of your father," she whispered,

talking aloud to her little girl as if she were already in the room. "And you are lucky for it, little one."

William's knuckles rapped on the doorframe.

"Sera?"

His tender gaze was the first thing she saw when she looked up. He held a small shipping crate in his arms and walked over with a smile that spread wide across his face. He knelt at her side and nudged the package up to her.

"What's this?"

"I think you're going to want to unpack this one yourself."

He handed her a screwdriver and quietly leaned back on his heels.

She gazed back, smiling.

"Will—what's going on? Is it some sort of baby gift? You shouldn't have. Look around you. There is enough stuff here to start a day-care center if we had a mind to."

"Just open it," he whispered, and nudged her on with a tilt of his chin.

Sera couldn't begin to think of what he was doing with the mysterious crate. But she took the look on his face as one of joy. It looked important to him, so she went to work. She pushed the screwdriver up under the top of the crate and tilted up the lid. It clanged down on the wood floor.

"Keep going," he whispered.

Sera felt a rush of adrenaline as she pulled out several handfuls of packing paper and tossed it on the floor. She found the edge of a black frame and with careful hands, pulled it free.

Her heart thumped, uncaged in her chest, and tears sprang to her eyes.

The beautifully rendered painting of a clock and a handful of soaring birds stared back at her from the confines of the large frame. With it, a note from Sophie.

A gift, from one of God's precious sparrows to another.

With love,

Sophie

"Will, look. It's the painting. The one I told you about? The one Sophie made in Terezin as a child."

He nodded, knowingly. "I had a feeling. Somehow I knew you'd want to open it yourself."

"It's beautiful. And it's exactly what I would have wished for our little Adele," she cried. "It'll be perfect in here. It feels like this is the way things should be, doesn't it? It's more than I ever hoped."

"And . . ." With a coy smile, he produced a hammer from behind his back and took a nail from the pocket of his plaid button-down shirt. "I think there's the perfect place for it, right over there."

William crossed the room and pounded the nail into the wall in the center of the floor-to-ceiling bookshelves. He took Sophie's painting in hand and hung it, then stepped back over to her side.

"Dance with me."

"William . . ."

He laughed, showering her with the praise of a light-hearted grin. "You are forever turning down my offers to dance. We'll have to do something about that one day, I think."

"Are you sure?" Sera pushed up against the back of the chair and with his help, stood up straight. "I'm not even sure you'll be able to get your arms around me."

He held them out wide.

"Lucky for you, I have an impressive wingspan."

Sera exhaled long and low, and with the giddiness of first love, nodded acceptance.

William wrapped her in the shelter of his arms and they danced, swaying to their own song, lilting in the shadow of the clock. Without the past to weigh them down, and despite the uncertainty of the future, Sera leaned in to him, thankful for the measure of peace she'd found in his arms.

"I never thought it could be like this."

"What?" William arched a brow at her. "Was my dancing that bad to begin with?"

"No." She laughed aloud. "I meant peace. That's what it feels like. God's peace showering down on us. And it's not because we haven't seen storms. I think it's because he gave us the strength to weather them—no matter what."

CHAPTER FORTY-THREE

The room had turned cold, like a blast of icy air had bled down the walls and frozen over every inch of the abandoned cellar. It caused Kája to shake uncontrollably, until she feared standing was no longer an option.

Liam wrapped a woolen coat around her shoulders, urging her out of the room and into a chair at the far end of the cellar. "Come. Sit."

He settled her down in a wooden spindle chair. Kája sat, numb and in a state of bemused shock, trying to process what she'd just heard.

"What do you mean, he didn't come back? Dane's still out there somewhere?"

Liam pulled a stool up before her and took her trembling hands in his. She tried to focus as he sat across from her, searching the contours of his face, the lightness of his eyes, the concern etched on his mouth—anything so that she'd not have to consider the reality of what she was about to be told.

The compassion in his eyes was what frightened her more than anything. She stared back at him, preparing her heart.

"A group of us came here to stop the train—two other agents are hidden away in the town nearby. But after we treated you and I knew you and Sophie would be safe, we went back after as many of the children as we could. Just knowing they wouldn't have a prayer out there alone . . ." His voice was strong and the hands that cradled hers so gentle, she could feel the emotion coursing through them into hers. His thumb brushed the underside of her palm. "I want you to know that Dane wouldn't give up. They had spotlights and dogs. We'd get one child to safety and he'd still go back out for another. And even when the SS caught up to him, Dane refused to turn us in. I need you to know that."

"What happened to him?"

Liam swallowed hard. "They executed him on sight. One shot."

Kája's heart lurched in her chest, making it difficult to breathe.

"And did you see it?"

She squeezed her eyes shut until she heard him answer with a heart-wrenching, "Yes."

"I didn't want to hurt you by telling you this way," Liam said, then reached down to the dirt floor and retrieved something that had been stashed against the wall. Aged brown leather, wet from the dew outside, was held out before her. "But he wanted you to have this."

"Your satchel," she said, tearing up as she drew her hands down upon it. "I've had it in the camp all this time. They let us take luggage on the train. Even though I knew what would happen to it when I reached Auschwitz, I wanted to take you with me. And my mother. She gave me her pearls once and they found their way back to me. I tucked them in the bottom of the bag, thinking they would give me courage on yet another train ride."

She ran her hands over the worn leather.

"Everything happened so fast. I didn't even realize I'd dropped it."

"You must have, running from the train. And whether it was by luck or by God, Dane found it out there. He made me promise to bring it back and put it into your hands. There's something in there he wanted you to see."

Kája looked back at him for a moment, the face of the man who had remained alive in her heart for so long. And he was there now, saving her all over again.

She opened the bag and as expected, the pearls slid out first. But on their wings, something else much lighter floated out. What fell into her lap was the one glimpse of beauty she'd found in Terezin.

"My children!" she cried, the softness of paper feeling like spun gold in her fingertips.

The children's artwork—paintings, watercolors and drawings, poetry even—Dane had taken them from the school when she'd been loaded on the transport train. He'd managed to hide them somehow, keeping the memory of her beloved sparrows alive. It was mercy she held in her shaking hands; he'd gone back and found it for her, in every color of the rainbow.

"Liam," she whispered, heart bleeding for what they'd been through.

Emotion caught in her throat and she swallowed hard, as tears rolled down her cheeks.

"I wish I could tell him what this means to me—to thank him for stopping that train, for saving my sparrows. For every one of the children who will survive because of what you and he have done, I will be forever grateful. And it's my wish that someday, when we are both very, very far away from this war-torn world, I might call him my friend openly. And we would no longer be Nazi and Jew. Or captor and prisoner. But friends. I pray the world would someday allow us to call him that." She placed her hand atop his and added, "When the time comes, will you help me?"

He used a finger to brush the tears away from her cheek.

"Of course."

Wednesday, October 19, 1949
Trials of War Criminals before the Nuremberg Military Tribunals
Nuremberg, Germany

"Your father is almost finished giving his deposition," Liam whispered, and squeezed Kája's shoulder to get her attention. "They said they'll be ready for us next."

Kája looked up, then tried to give a light roll of the eyes to indicate she'd brushed the cobwebs of memories away.

She'd been lost in them as she sat outside the U.S. military court at the Palace of Justice in Nuremburg, Germany. And for a few vivid moments, she'd been back on the transport train to Auschwitz instead of sitting where she was, in a tailored cream suit with her hair coiled soft at her nape and her husband seated at her side.

"Your mother would be glad to know you're wearing them today."

Her fingers had been toying with the pearls at her collar; she hadn't even realized it until he'd smiled and whispered next to her ear. She dropped her hand to her lap and looked up, admiring the strength of his profile.

"I hope she'd be proud of us. What we're trying to do for Dane? Something inside me says it's the right thing to do. I hope she understands."

"I believe she does, Kája. And we're here with your father. He's testifying for Dane too." His hand slid over hers. "Take comfort in that."

"But do you suppose if she were here now, she'd want us to go in? What will they think of us if we go to defend a Nazi? I mean, I never imagined we would be called to a place like this, to speak out in this way."

"You told me you wanted to. Remember? We don't want to miss our chance." He offered her an encouraging smile. "And I know you, Kája. I know what's in your heart. I can't share what you and Sophie endured in that camp. God knows, I wish I could take the bad memories and burn them away somehow. I don't want you to have to live in them. But you have a bond with Sophie, your mother, and with Dane, that other people could never understand. You have the ability to make this right for him."

The oak doors creaked open and a court clerk stepped out.

"Mr. and Mrs. Marshall?"

"Yes," Liam answered and reached out to take her elbow as she stood.

"Wait," he said, pulling her back ever so slightly. "I have something for you."

He pinned a brilliant red poppy to the lapel of her suit.

"It's for the remembrance of those who gave their lives for others." Liam smiled and with tenderness, ran a hand over her cheek. "And I know you're fond of them. They remind you of home."

She nodded, touched by the memory, thinking now that her memories of home would be wherever he was.

"Thank you."

"Let's go," Liam whispered, then nodded to the clerk. "We're ready."

Kája hugged the folder of the children's art to her chest as they walked.

She imagined a future so unlike the present.

One in which Jew and Nazi were not enemies. One where the little sparrows cared for each other and where there was no room for hate, because the hearts of men were too focused on love to let it grow. And one in which people, rather than paintings, and the red flowers of peace, rather than war, became the witnesses to a changed heart.

In your time, God, she whispered, and stepped through the door Liam held open for her.

We will be made whole.

AUTHOR'S NOTE

*O*n April 19, 1943, three Belgian resistance fighters placed a red paper-wrapped storm lantern on the tracks between the Mechelen transit camp and Leuven, Belgium. Armed with only one pistol and a pair of pliers, Georges Livschitz, Robert Maistriau, and Jean Franklemon succeeded in making the ruse appear as a warning signal and stopped the train en route to Auschwitz. The three men forced open cattle car doors from the outside, helping deportees escape.

Combined with prisoners' attempts to use hidden tools and pry open the cattle cars from the inside, it is estimated that these men helped some 231 prisoners to flee the train that night: 26 were found and killed by the pursuit of SS guards, 116 were eventually recaptured, and miraculously, the remaining 116 are thought to have avoided certain death in the gas chambers of Auschwitz by disappearing into the night.

In August 1943, the SS moved to liquidate the Bialystok ghetto, northeast of the Treblinka killing center in northern Poland. The only survivors, 1,260 children aged fourteen years and under, were deported to Theresienstadt (the German name for Terezin) on August 24. In order to prevent firsthand accounts of the liquidation from reaching the rest of the camp population, the children were sequestered in isolated barracks along with their 53 appointed guardians. Later, in October 1943, the

1,196 surviving children and their guardians were transported to Auschwitz.

None survived.

In this book, I wanted to focus on a lesser-known part of art history: the children's art of Terezin. Though fictional, Kája's journey in *A Sparrow in Terezin* recounts just two of the stories of brutality and heroism, of preciousness lost, as a result of the Holocaust. One of the books that most affected me during this research was *I Never Saw Another Butterfly: Children's Drawings and Poems from the Terezin Concentration Camp, 1942–1944*. In it, the children's cut paper collages, watercolor paintings, pencil sketches, and poetry become stunning and haunting storytellers, left behind by the little sparrows who are now and will forever be unnamed to history.

Of the 15,000 children who are believed to have passed through the walls of Terezin, fewer than 100 ultimately survived the Holocaust. I pray, with so many of you, that we would never forget. For every one of those little sparrows who fell, God's hands were open.

ADDITIONAL READING

—

I Never Saw Another Butterfly: Children's Drawings and Poems from the Terezin Concentration Camp, 1942–1944, 2nd edition (New YMC: Schocken, 1994).

United States Holocaust Memorial Museum, http://www.ushmm.org.

Terezin Memorial, http://www.pamatnik-terezin.cz/.

READING GROUP GUIDE

1. From the moment Kája fled Nazi-occupied Prague in March of 1939, she vowed to find a way back home to her parents. Despite almost losing her in the Blitz, Liam understood Kája's heart and used his connections to help in her quest. Would Kája still have gone to Prague without Liam's help? How would the outcome have been different if Liam wouldn't have continued his own quest to find her after she'd gone missing in Prague?

2. The walled garrison town of Terezin, known as Theresienstadt to the Germans, was a combined ghetto and concentration camp in which the arts community thrived. Prisoners were able to participate in stage shows, attend concerts and lectures—even borrow from the more than ten-thousand-volume Hebrew library on the grounds. How did Kája use her education and abilities in the arts to affect the lives of others? Did they aid in her own survival?

3. Between 1942–1944, more than fifteen thousand children passed through Terezin while awaiting transport to one of the Nazi killing centers. It was the care of in-camp guardians and teachers like Kája who would have infused these children with hope, despite the horrific conditions. How much of an impact did Kája have on Sophie's ability to heal, using art as the method? How would Terezin have looked from a child's point of view versus that of an adult?

4. Sera and William's life together began from the moment they said "I do," though their journey as husband and wife was hampered by William's past. His inability to overcome the fear of losing Sera prevented him from being open about the pain he'd been through, even though he continued to seek God in his life. How did William's mistakes affect the rest of the Hanover family? Would William and Sera have been able to forge a future together without the practice of Christ-like forgiveness in their marriage?

5. Sophie survived the war in part because of the willingness of Kája, Liam, and Dane to risk their own lives for the children of Terezin. Though Dane was a Nazi, Sophie remembered that God had changed his heart, and encouraged Sera to give William another chance for the sake of her own child. How did Sophie's attitude influence Sera's ability to forgive her husband? How did Dane's sacrifice affect Sophie's ability to see good in others, despite their mistakes?

ACKNOWLEDGMENTS

One of my dad's favorite verses was Joshua 1:9 (NIV), and from it came the faith element in this book:

"Have I not commanded you? Be strong and courageous. Do not be afraid; do not be discouraged, for the LORD *your God will be with you wherever you go."*

Much like Kája's journey, this book came to life on the hinges of a year of change for our family. After a brave battle with leukemia, my dad went home to be with the Lord on October 19, 2013. It's the village that surrounded us during this time that I now thank for the care and support in helping to bring this story to life, and to help our hearts heal.

To Becky Monds and Rachelle Gardner—you are the editors of every author's dreams! I am humbled by your unwavering faith in me, and am continually in awe of your brilliance in the story craft. Just knowing you're a text away makes all right with the world. To the wonderful team at HarperCollins Christian fiction: Daisy Hutton, Jodi Hughes, Amanda Bostic, Katie Bond, Elizabeth Hudson, Becky Philpott, Karli Jackson, the amazing sales and marketing teams who share our stories with so many, and the editors with whom I shared a meal in "Paris," you've made this year of firsts one of the best in my life. Thank you for inviting me into your family.

To Kristen Ingebretson—your cover designs make the waking moments better than my dreams.

In the 1940s, letters were a lifeline between friends separated by too many miles. To find that I can go to the mailbox now and receive encouragement from you, Sharon Tavera, is more than vintage wonderful—it's a blessing in pen and ink. And to Maggie Walker—there couldn't be many things I look forward to more than a cup of coffee and fellowship with you.

Sisters in the Lord are one of the greatest treasures a woman can have. Thank you, Joanna Politano, Cara Putman, Katie Ganshert, Sarah Ladd, Katherine Reay, Mary Weber, Beth Vogt, and Colleen Coble—you are all amazing women. You have invested in me, asking nothing in return, and I'm so grateful for your love and encouragement. And to Heather Kauffman and Maria Schaefer—the mark you make on the lives of others defines leadership at its most valuable level. You are beautiful women with generous hearts, and I am honored to know you.

To my dear friends, Bonnie Underwood and all of the members of the Cancer Care group at Northside Christian Church—words cannot express my gratitude for your love and support during the last year. I pray I could be a fraction of the blessing you are to so many others. And to the heroes—the cancer-fighting champions who are already home with our Savior: Eve Sparks, Jessica Schroen, Pete DuBois, and my dad, "Cowboy" Rick Wedge. The beauty of your legacy is lasting. We miss you every day.

My readers and friends: I've met so many of you over the past two years. How can you know how much this has meant to me? I've been blessed by your prayers and generous encouragement. I am so grateful to each of you. To our parents—Robin Buczek, Pat and Cindy Cambron, and Linda Wedge—thank you for your love and support. And to the best of me—Jeremy, Brady, Carson, and Colt. It is a blessed woman to have one godly man in her life; I'm honored to have four.

Whether old journeys or new ones, it's not a surprise that every step in life begins and ends with you, Jesus. My life would be nothing without you to guide it.

With Joy,

Kristy

Looking for more riveting historical fiction?
Check out *Snow on the Tulips* by Liz Tolsma.

A STRANGER'S LIFE HANGS IN THE BALANCE.
BUT TO SAVE HIM IS TO RISK EVERYTHING.

"In an adventurous tale that reads like a movie script, Liz Tolsma
weaves faith in seamlessly, moving the reader with her characters'
convictions to create a captivating debut novel."

—*BookPage*

Available in print and e-book

THOMAS NELSON
Since 1798

ABOUT THE AUTHOR

Photo by Danielle Mitchell Photography

Kristy Cambron has been fascinated with World War II since hearing her grandfather's stories. She holds an art history degree from Indiana University and has fifteen years industry experience as a corporate learning facilitator and communications consultant. Kristy writes World War II and Regency fiction and placed first in the 2013 NTRWA Great Expectations and 2012 FCRW Beacon contests. Her debut novel, *The Butterfly and the Violin*, was nominated for the RT Reviewers' Choice Awards' "Best Inspirational Novel" of 2014. Kristy makes her home in Indiana with her husband and three football-loving sons.

Visit her website: www.kristycambron.com
Twitter: @KCambronAuthor
Facebook: Kristy-Cambron